JUN — 2016

Oh, **KILLSTRIKE**™

MAX BEMIS • LOGAN FAERBER • JUAN MANUEL TUMBURÚS

BOOM!
STUDIOS™

ROSS RICHIE .... CEO & Founder
MATT GAGNON .... Editor-in-Chief
FILIP SABLIK .... President of Publishing & Marketing
STEPHEN CHRISTY .... President of Development
LANCE KREITER.................... VP of Licensing & Merchandising
PHIL BARBARO .... VP of Finance
BRYCE CARLSON.. Managing Editor
MEL CAYLO .... Marketing Manager
SCOTT NEWMAN .... Production Design Manager
IRENE BRADISH................................... Operations Manager
CHRISTINE DINH .... Brand Communications Manager
SIERRA HAHN... Senior Editor
DAFNA PLEBAN.. Editor
SHANNON WATTERS... Editor
ERIC HARBURN .... Editor
WHITNEY LEOPARD ....Associate Editor
JASMINE AMIRI..................................Associate Editor
CHRIS ROSA ....Associate Editor
ALEX GALER .... Assistant Editor
CAMERON CHITTOCK................................ Assistant Editor
MARY GUMPORT .... Assistant Editor
KELSEY DIETERICH.................................... Production Designer
JILLIAN CRAB .... Production Designer
KARA LEOPARD.. Production Designer
MICHELLE ANKLEY........................Production Design Assistant
AARON FERRARA................................Operations Coordinator
ELIZABETH LOUGHRIDGE..................... Accounting Coordinator
JOSÉ MEZA..Sales Assistant
JAMES ARRIOLA .... Mailroom Assistant
STEPHANIE HOCUTT ....Marketing Assistant
SAM KUSEK .... Direct Market Representative
HILLARY LEVI ....Executive Assistant
KATE ALBIN..Administrative Assistant

BOOM! STUDIOS

OH, KILLSTRIKE, March 2016. Published by BOOM! Studios, a division of Boom Entertainment, Inc. Oh, Killstrike is ™ & © 2016 Boom Entertainment, Inc. Originally published in single magazine form as OH, KILLSTRIKE No. 1-4. ™ & © 2015 Boom Entertainment, Inc. All rights reserved. BOOM! Studios™ and the BOOM! Studios logo are trademarks of Boom Entertainment, Inc., registered in various countries and categories. All characters, events, and institutions depicted herein are fictional. Any similarity between any of the names, characters, persons, events, and/or institutions in this publication to actual names, characters, and persons, whether living or dead, events, and/or institutions is unintended and purely coincidental. BOOM! Studios does not read or accept unsolicited submissions of ideas, stories, or artwork.

A catalog record of this book is available from OCLC and from the BOOM! Studios website, www.boom-studios.com, on the Librarians page.

BOOM! Studios, 5670 Wilshire Boulevard, Suite 450, Los Angeles, CA 90036-5679. Printed in China. First Printing.

ISBN: 978-1-60886-818-6, eISBN: 978161398-489-5

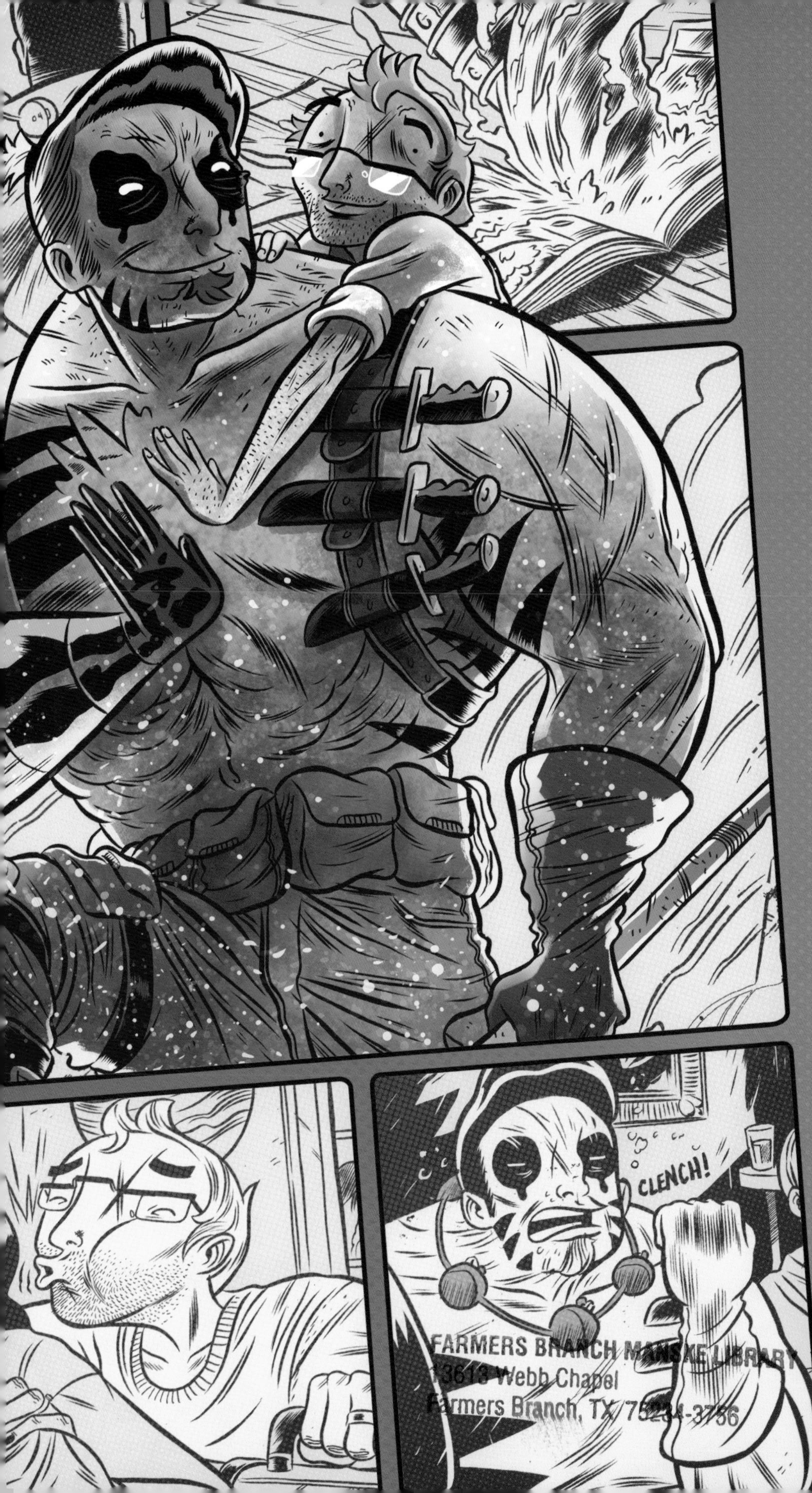
CLENCH!

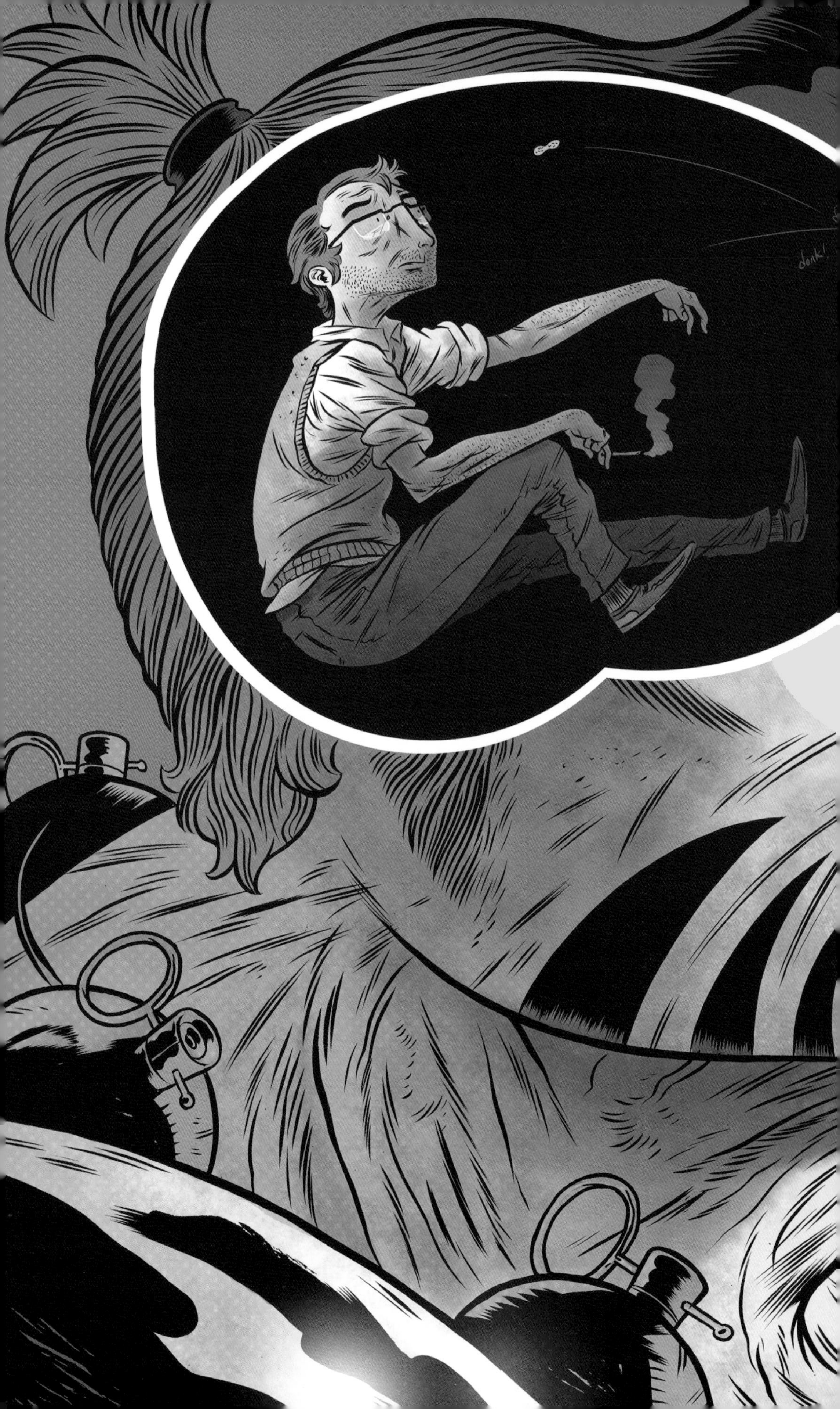
donk!

CREATED BY
MAX BEMIS & LOGAN FAERBER

WRITTEN BY
MAX BEMIS

ILLUSTRATED BY
LOGAN FAERBER

COLORS BY
JUAN MANUEL TUMBURÚS

LETTERS BY
JIM CAMPBELL

COVER BY
LOGAN FAERBER

DESIGNER
JILLIAN CRAB

ASSOCIATE EDITOR
JASMINE AMIRI

EDITOR
DAFNA PLEBAN

chapter
ONE

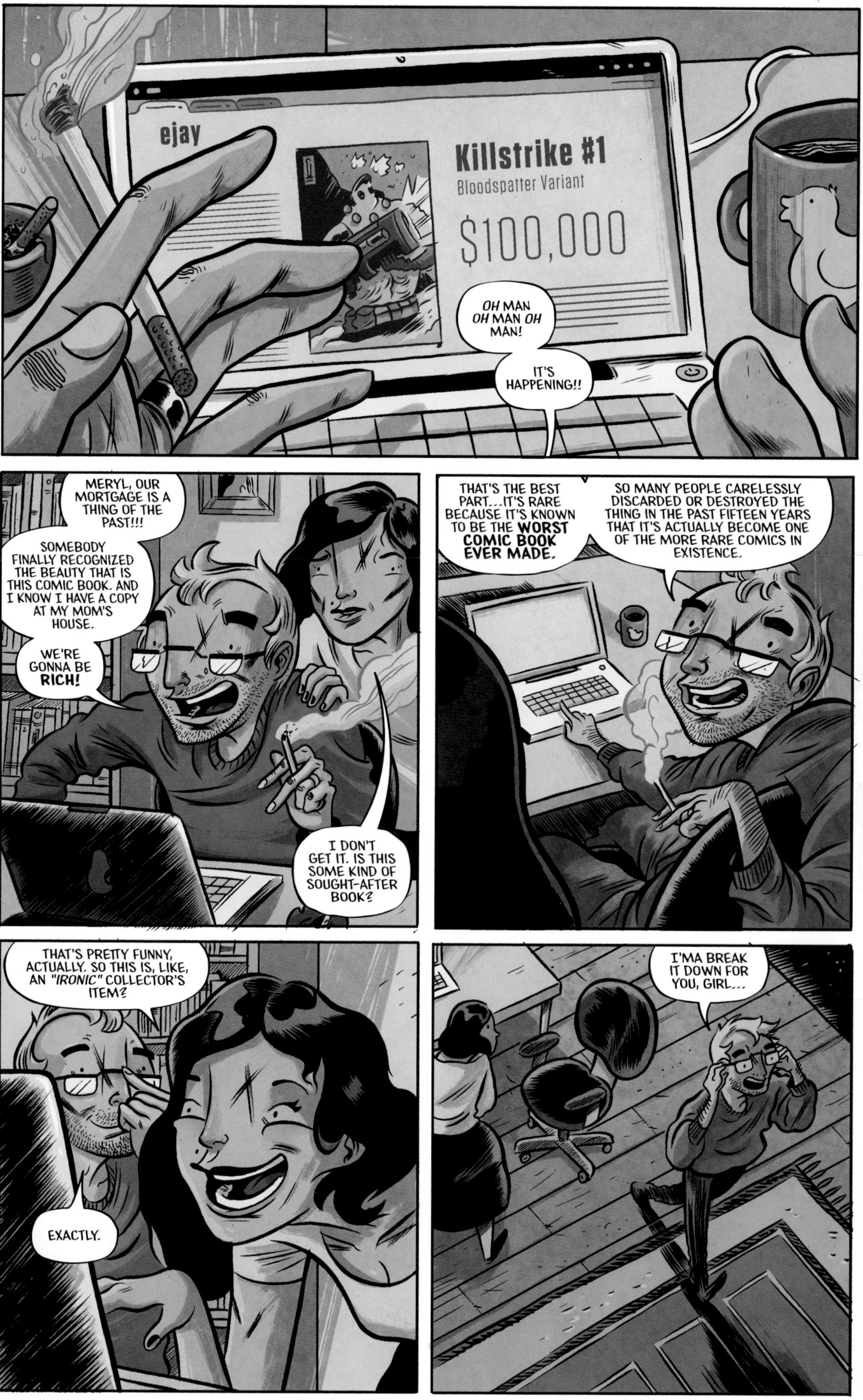
ejay
Killstrike #1
Bloodspatter Variant
$100,000
OH MAN OH MAN OH MAN!
IT'S HAPPENING!!
MERYL, OUR MORTGAGE IS A THING OF THE PAST!!!
SOMEBODY FINALLY RECOGNIZED THE BEAUTY THAT IS THIS COMIC BOOK. AND I KNOW I HAVE A COPY AT MY MOM'S HOUSE.
WE'RE GONNA BE RICH!
I DON'T GET IT. IS THIS SOME KIND OF SOUGHT-AFTER BOOK?
THAT'S THE BEST PART...IT'S RARE BECAUSE IT'S KNOWN TO BE THE WORST COMIC BOOK EVER MADE.
SO MANY PEOPLE CARELESSLY DISCARDED OR DESTROYED THE THING IN THE PAST FIFTEEN YEARS THAT IT'S ACTUALLY BECOME ONE OF THE MORE RARE COMICS IN EXISTENCE.
THAT'S PRETTY FUNNY, ACTUALLY. SO THIS IS, LIKE, AN "IRONIC" COLLECTOR'S ITEM?
EXACTLY.
I'MA BREAK IT DOWN FOR YOU, GIRL...

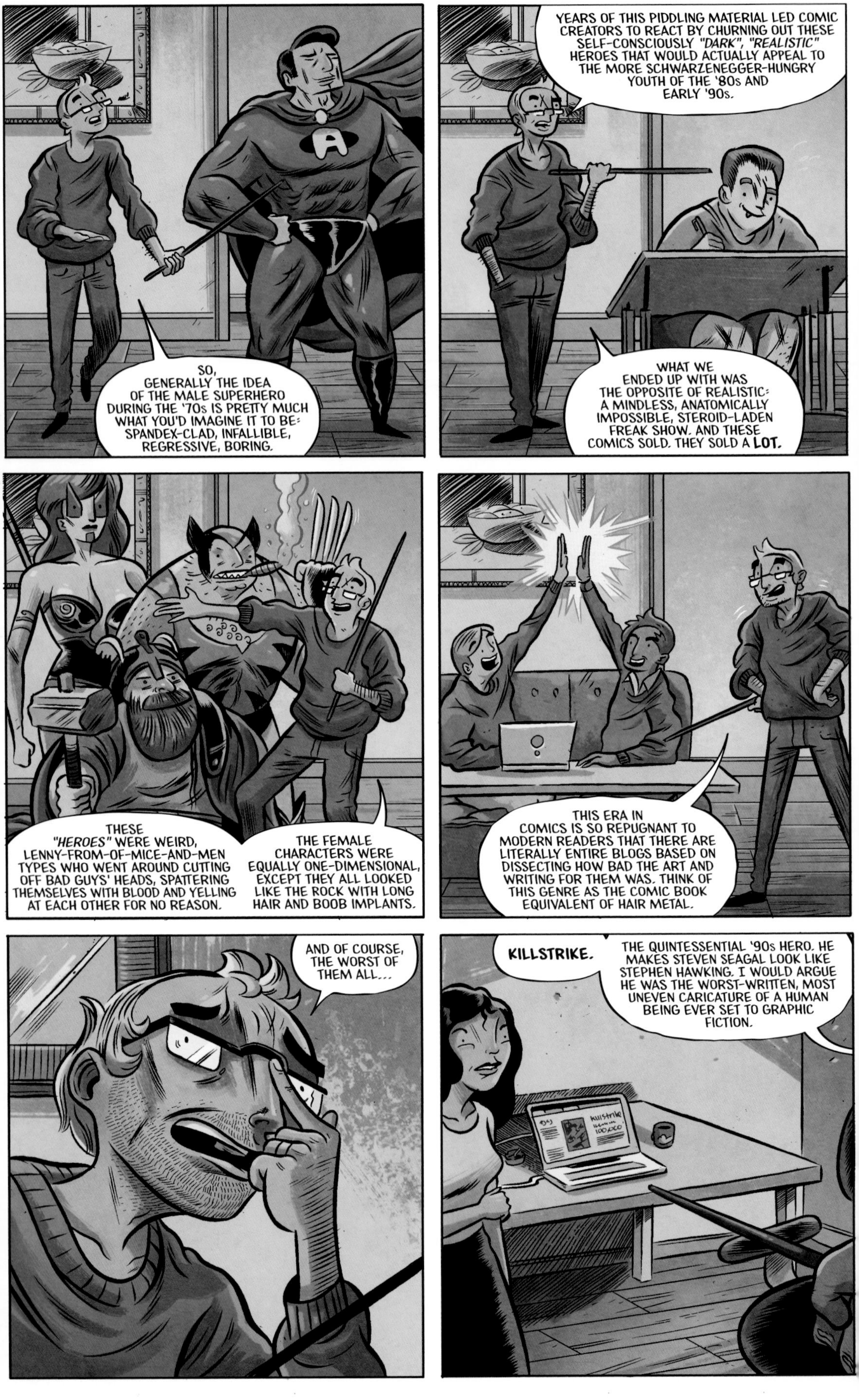
SO, GENERALLY THE IDEA OF THE MALE SUPERHERO DURING THE '70s IS PRETTY MUCH WHAT YOU'D IMAGINE IT TO BE: SPANDEX-CLAD, INFALLIBLE, REGRESSIVE, BORING.
YEARS OF THIS PIDDLING MATERIAL LED COMIC CREATORS TO REACT BY CHURNING OUT THESE SELF-CONSCIOUSLY "DARK", "REALISTIC" HEROES THAT WOULD ACTUALLY APPEAL TO THE MORE SCHWARZENEGGER-HUNGRY YOUTH OF THE '80s AND EARLY '90s.
WHAT WE ENDED UP WITH WAS THE OPPOSITE OF REALISTIC: A MINDLESS, ANATOMICALLY IMPOSSIBLE, STEROID-LADEN FREAK SHOW. AND THESE COMICS SOLD. THEY SOLD A LOT.
THESE "HEROES" WERE WEIRD, LENNY-FROM-OF-MICE-AND-MEN TYPES WHO WENT AROUND CUTTING OFF BAD GUYS' HEADS, SPATTERING THEMSELVES WITH BLOOD AND YELLING AT EACH OTHER FOR NO REASON.
THE FEMALE CHARACTERS WERE EQUALLY ONE-DIMENSIONAL, EXCEPT THEY ALL LOOKED LIKE THE ROCK WITH LONG HAIR AND BOOB IMPLANTS.
THIS ERA IN COMICS IS SO REPUGNANT TO MODERN READERS THAT THERE ARE LITERALLY ENTIRE BLOGS BASED ON DISSECTING HOW BAD THE ART AND WRITING FOR THEM WAS. THINK OF THIS GENRE AS THE COMIC BOOK EQUIVALENT OF HAIR METAL.
AND OF COURSE, THE WORST OF THEM ALL...
KILLSTRIKE.
THE QUINTESSENTIAL '90s HERO. HE MAKES STEVEN SEAGAL LOOK LIKE STEPHEN HAWKING. I WOULD ARGUE HE WAS THE WORST-WRITTEN, MOST UNEVEN CARICATURE OF A HUMAN BEING EVER SET TO GRAPHIC FICTION.

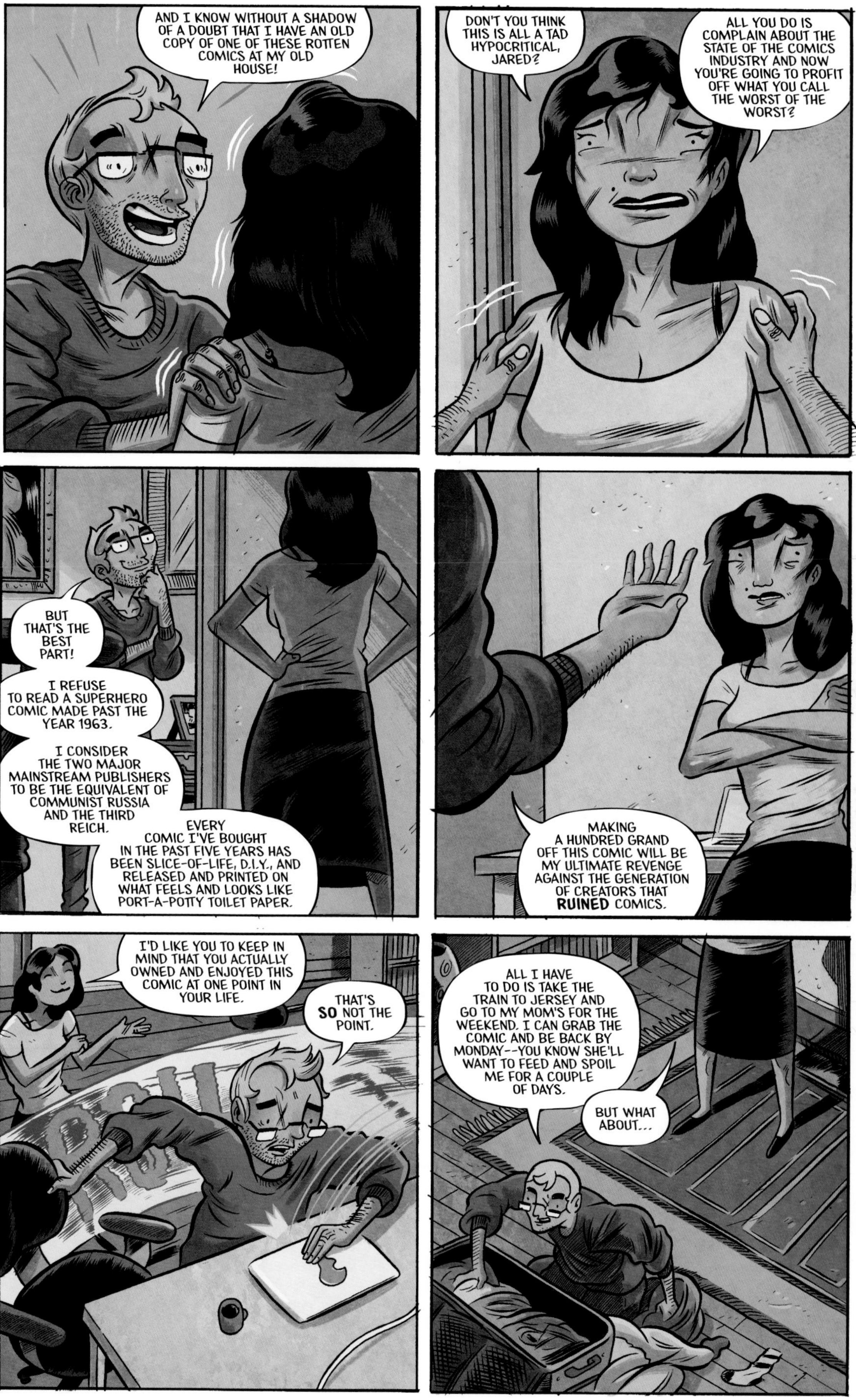
AND I KNOW WITHOUT A SHADOW OF A DOUBT THAT I HAVE AN OLD COPY OF ONE OF THESE ROTTEN COMICS AT MY OLD HOUSE!
DON'T YOU THINK THIS IS ALL A TAD HYPOCRITICAL, JARED?
ALL YOU DO IS COMPLAIN ABOUT THE STATE OF THE COMICS INDUSTRY AND NOW YOU'RE GOING TO PROFIT OFF WHAT YOU CALL THE WORST OF THE WORST?
BUT THAT'S THE BEST PART!
I REFUSE TO READ A SUPERHERO COMIC MADE PAST THE YEAR 1963.
I CONSIDER THE TWO MAJOR MAINSTREAM PUBLISHERS TO BE THE EQUIVALENT OF COMMUNIST RUSSIA AND THE THIRD REICH.
EVERY COMIC I'VE BOUGHT IN THE PAST FIVE YEARS HAS BEEN SLICE-OF-LIFE, D.I.Y., AND RELEASED AND PRINTED ON WHAT FEELS AND LOOKS LIKE PORT-A-POTTY TOILET PAPER.
MAKING A HUNDRED GRAND OFF THIS COMIC WILL BE MY ULTIMATE REVENGE AGAINST THE GENERATION OF CREATORS THAT RUINED COMICS.
I'D LIKE YOU TO KEEP IN MIND THAT YOU ACTUALLY OWNED AND ENJOYED THIS COMIC AT ONE POINT IN YOUR LIFE.
THAT'S SO NOT THE POINT.
ALL I HAVE TO DO IS TAKE THE TRAIN TO JERSEY AND GO TO MY MOM'S FOR THE WEEKEND. I CAN GRAB THE COMIC AND BE BACK BY MONDAY--YOU KNOW SHE'LL WANT TO FEED AND SPOIL ME FOR A COUPLE OF DAYS.
BUT WHAT ABOUT...

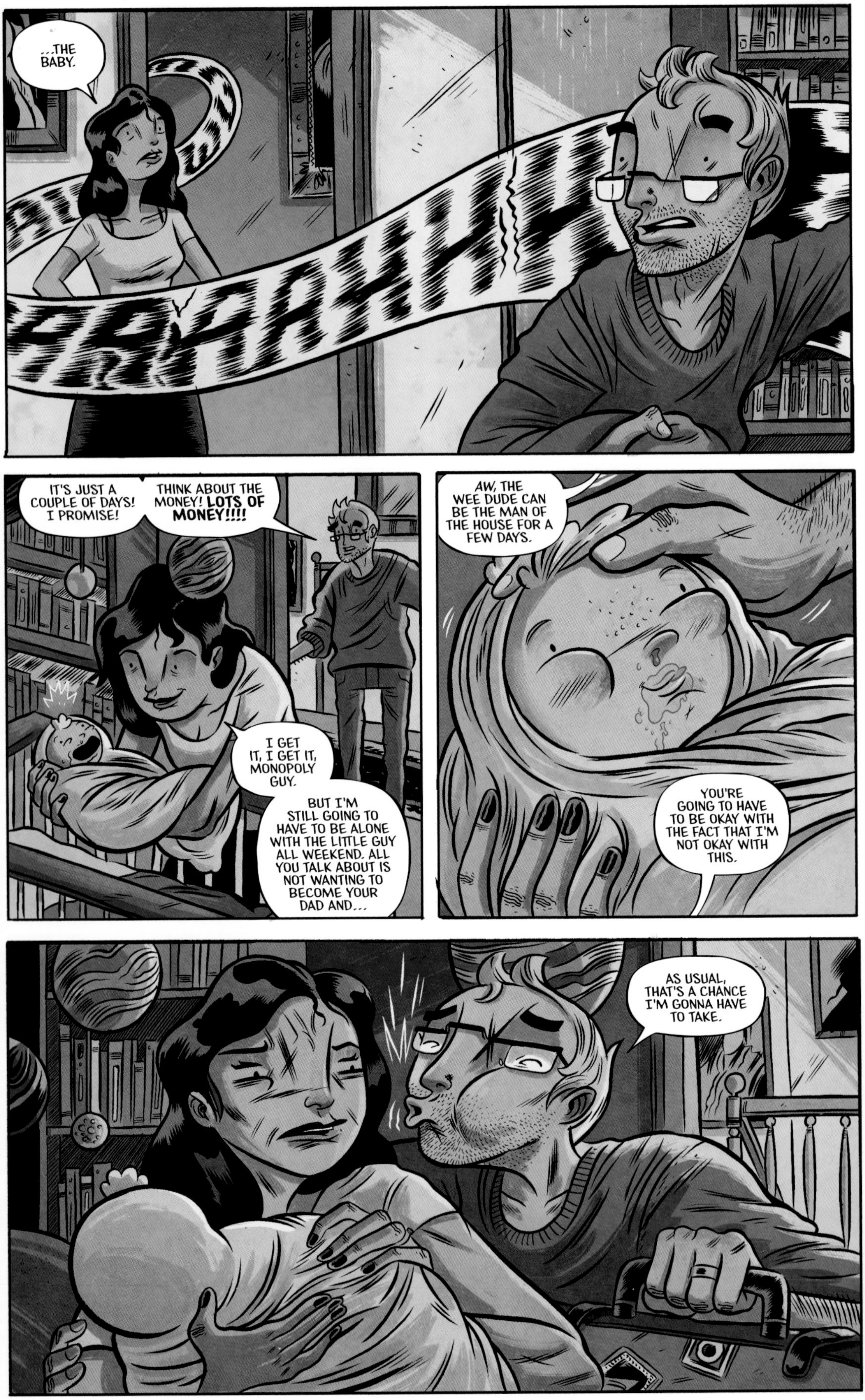
...THE BABY.
WAAAAHHHH
IT'S JUST A COUPLE OF DAYS! I PROMISE!
THINK ABOUT THE MONEY! LOTS OF MONEY!!!!
I GET IT, I GET IT, MONOPOLY GUY.
BUT I'M STILL GOING TO HAVE TO BE ALONE WITH THE LITTLE GUY ALL WEEKEND. ALL YOU TALK ABOUT IS NOT WANTING TO BECOME YOUR DAD AND...
AW, THE WEE DUDE CAN BE THE MAN OF THE HOUSE FOR A FEW DAYS.
YOU'RE GOING TO HAVE TO BE OKAY WITH THE FACT THAT I'M NOT OKAY WITH THIS.
AS USUAL, THAT'S A CHANCE I'M GONNA HAVE TO TAKE.

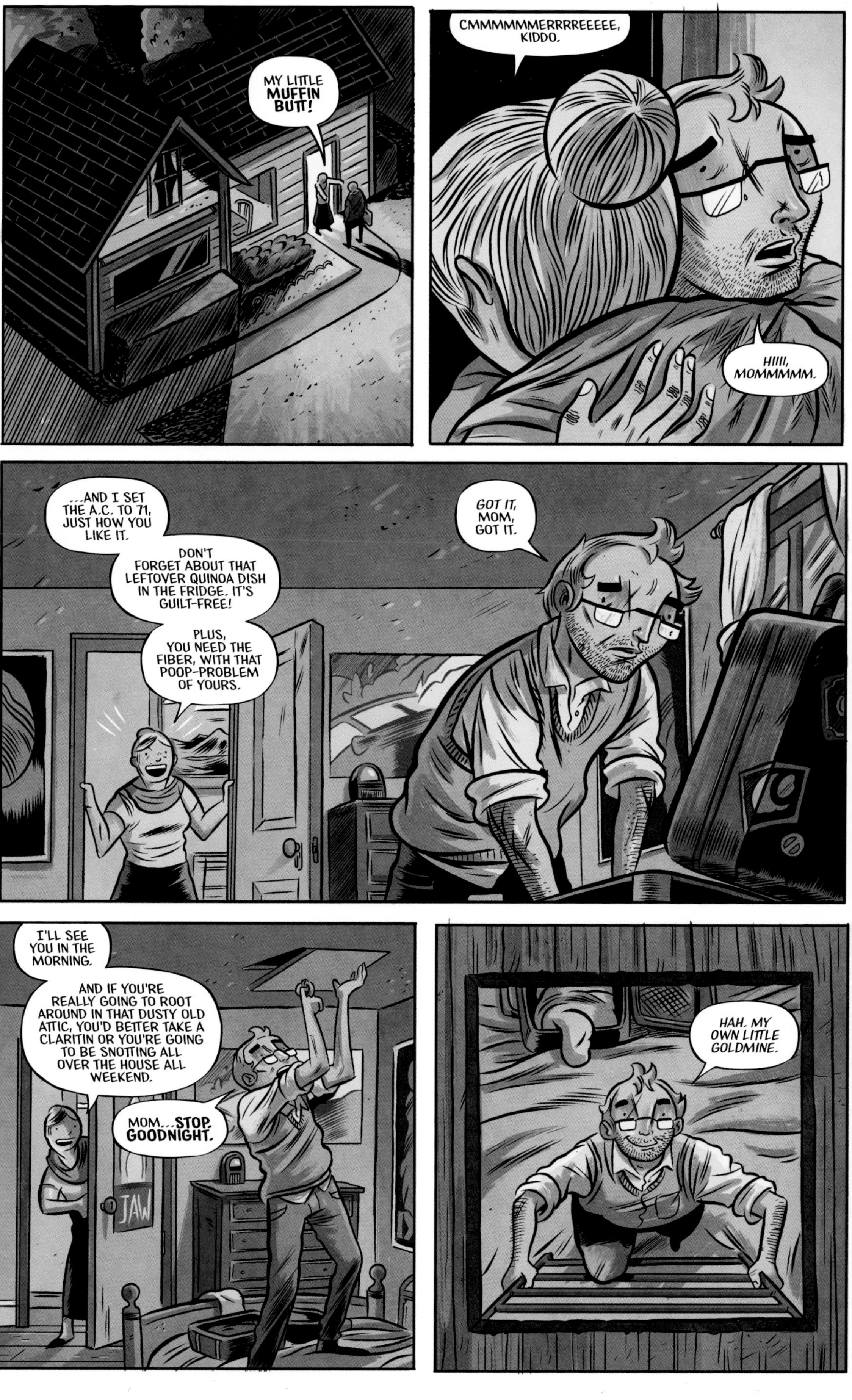
MY LITTLE MUFFIN BUTT!
CMMMMMMERRRREEEEE, KIDDO.
HIIII, MOMMMMM.
...AND I SET THE A.C. TO 71, JUST HOW YOU LIKE IT.
DON'T FORGET ABOUT THAT LEFTOVER QUINOA DISH IN THE FRIDGE. IT'S GUILT-FREE!
PLUS, YOU NEED THE FIBER, WITH THAT POOP-PROBLEM OF YOURS.
GOT IT, MOM, GOT IT.
I'LL SEE YOU IN THE MORNING.
AND IF YOU'RE REALLY GOING TO ROOT AROUND IN THAT DUSTY OLD ATTIC, YOU'D BETTER TAKE A CLARITIN OR YOU'RE GOING TO BE SNOTTING ALL OVER THE HOUSE ALL WEEKEND.
MOM...STOP. GOODNIGHT.
JAW
HAH. MY OWN LITTLE GOLDMINE.

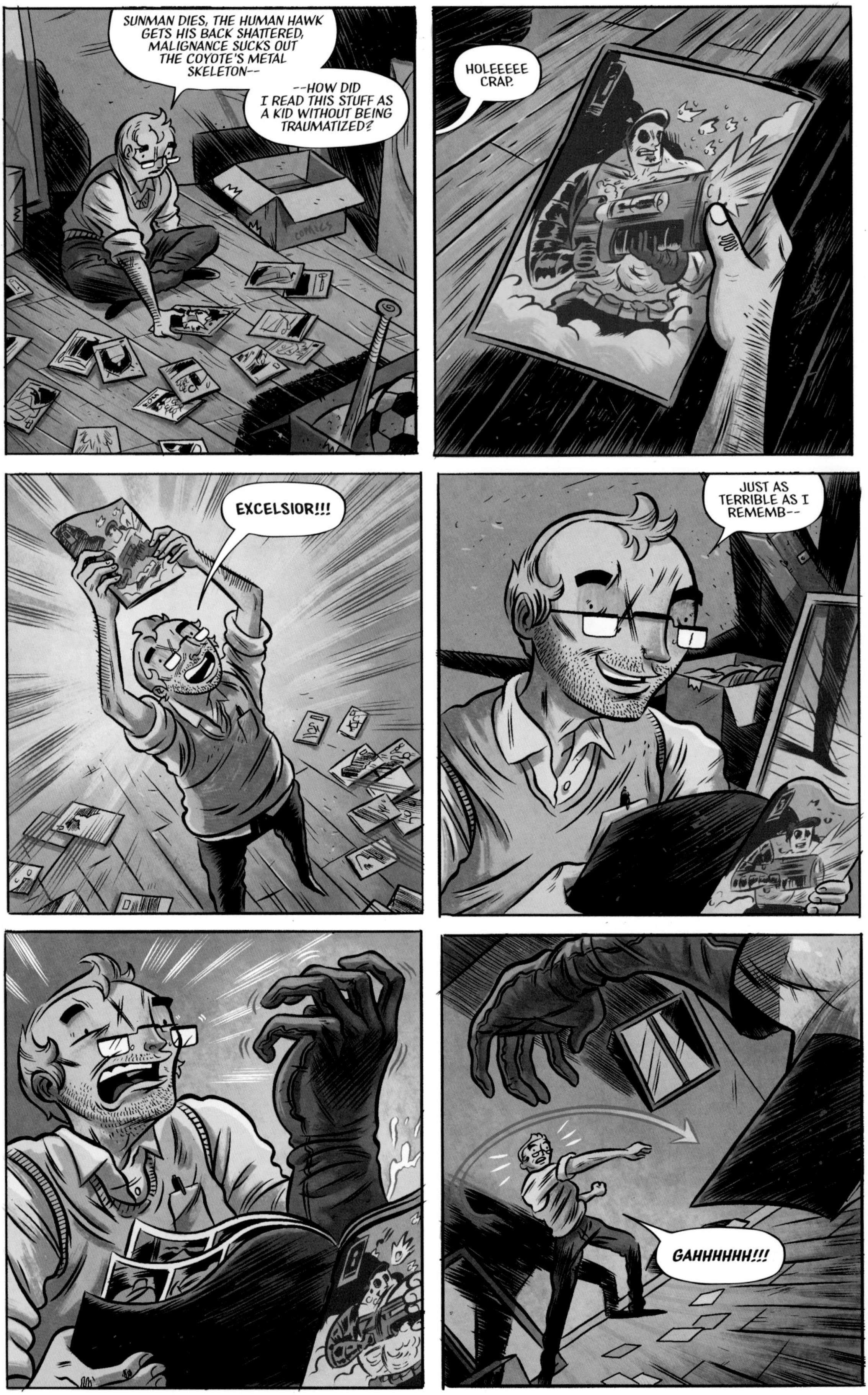
SUNMAN DIES, THE HUMAN HAWK GETS HIS BACK SHATTERED, MALIGNANCE SUCKS OUT THE COYOTE'S METAL SKELETON--
--HOW DID I READ THIS STUFF AS A KID WITHOUT BEING TRAUMATIZED?
COMICS
HOLEEEEE CRAP.
EXCELSIOR!!!
JUST AS TERRIBLE AS I REMEMB--
GAHHHHHH!!!

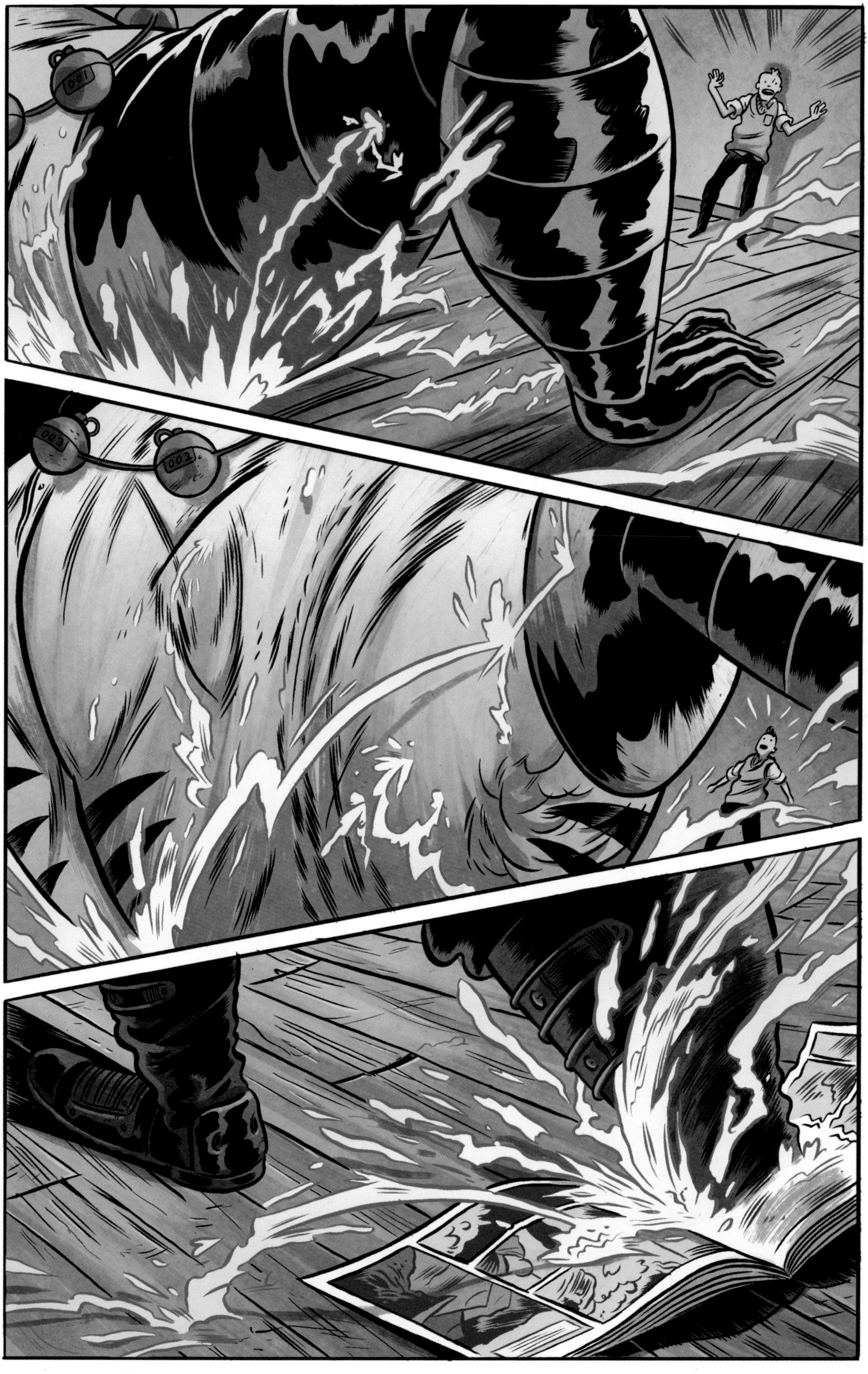

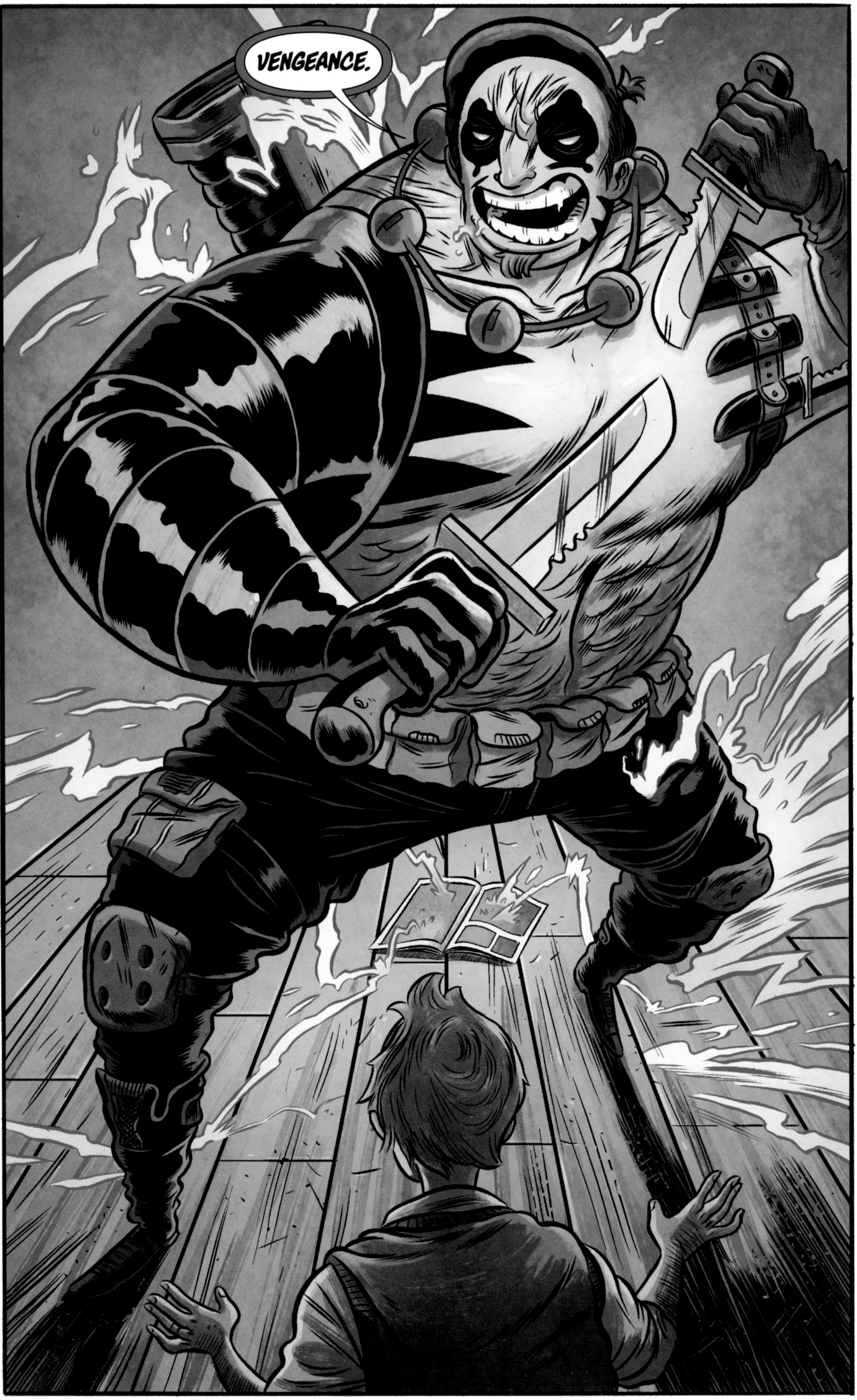
VENGEANCE.

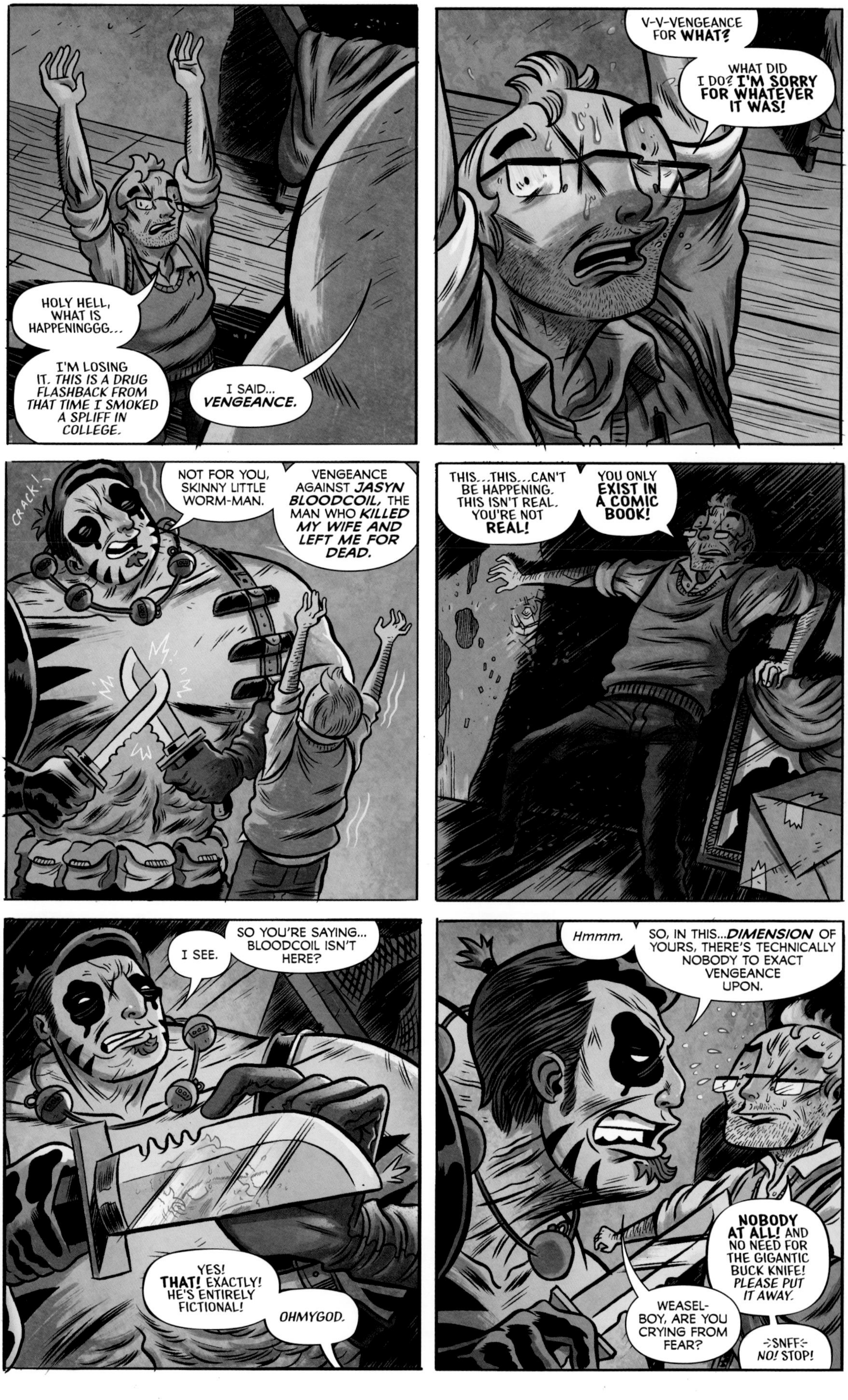

HOLY HELL, WHAT IS HAPPENINGGG...
I'M LOSING IT. THIS IS A DRUG FLASHBACK FROM THAT TIME I SMOKED A SPLIFF IN COLLEGE.
I SAID... VENGEANCE.
V-V-VENGEANCE FOR WHAT?
WHAT DID I DO? I'M SORRY FOR WHATEVER IT WAS!
CRACK!
NOT FOR YOU, SKINNY LITTLE WORM-MAN.
VENGEANCE AGAINST JASYN BLOODCOIL, THE MAN WHO KILLED MY WIFE AND LEFT ME FOR DEAD.
THIS...THIS...CAN'T BE HAPPENING. THIS ISN'T REAL. YOU'RE NOT REAL!
YOU ONLY EXIST IN A COMIC BOOK!
I SEE.
SO YOU'RE SAYING... BLOODCOIL ISN'T HERE?
YES! THAT! EXACTLY! HE'S ENTIRELY FICTIONAL!
OHMYGOD.
Hmmm.
SO, IN THIS...DIMENSION OF YOURS, THERE'S TECHNICALLY NOBODY TO EXACT VENGEANCE UPON.
NOBODY AT ALL! AND NO NEED FOR THE GIGANTIC BUCK KNIFE! PLEASE PUT IT AWAY.
WEASEL-BOY, ARE YOU CRYING FROM FEAR?
SNFF NO! STOP!

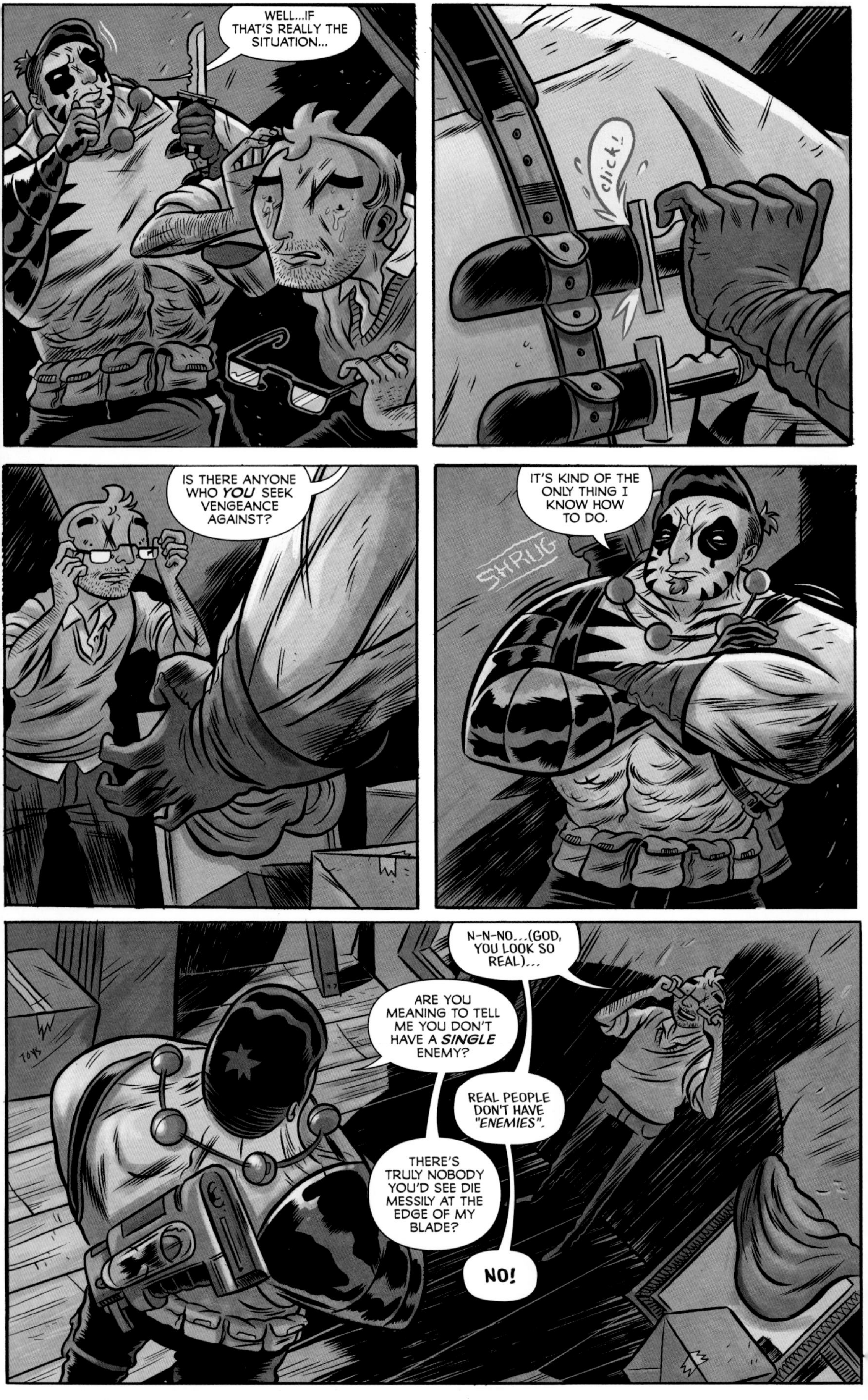
WELL...IF THAT'S REALLY THE SITUATION...
click!
IS THERE ANYONE WHO *YOU* SEEK VENGEANCE AGAINST?
IT'S KIND OF THE ONLY THING I KNOW HOW TO DO.
SHRUG
N-N-NO...(GOD, YOU LOOK SO REAL)...
ARE YOU MEANING TO TELL ME YOU DON'T HAVE A *SINGLE* ENEMY?
REAL PEOPLE DON'T HAVE *"ENEMIES"*.
THERE'S TRULY NOBODY YOU'D SEE DIE MESSILY AT THE EDGE OF MY BLADE?
NO!
TOYS

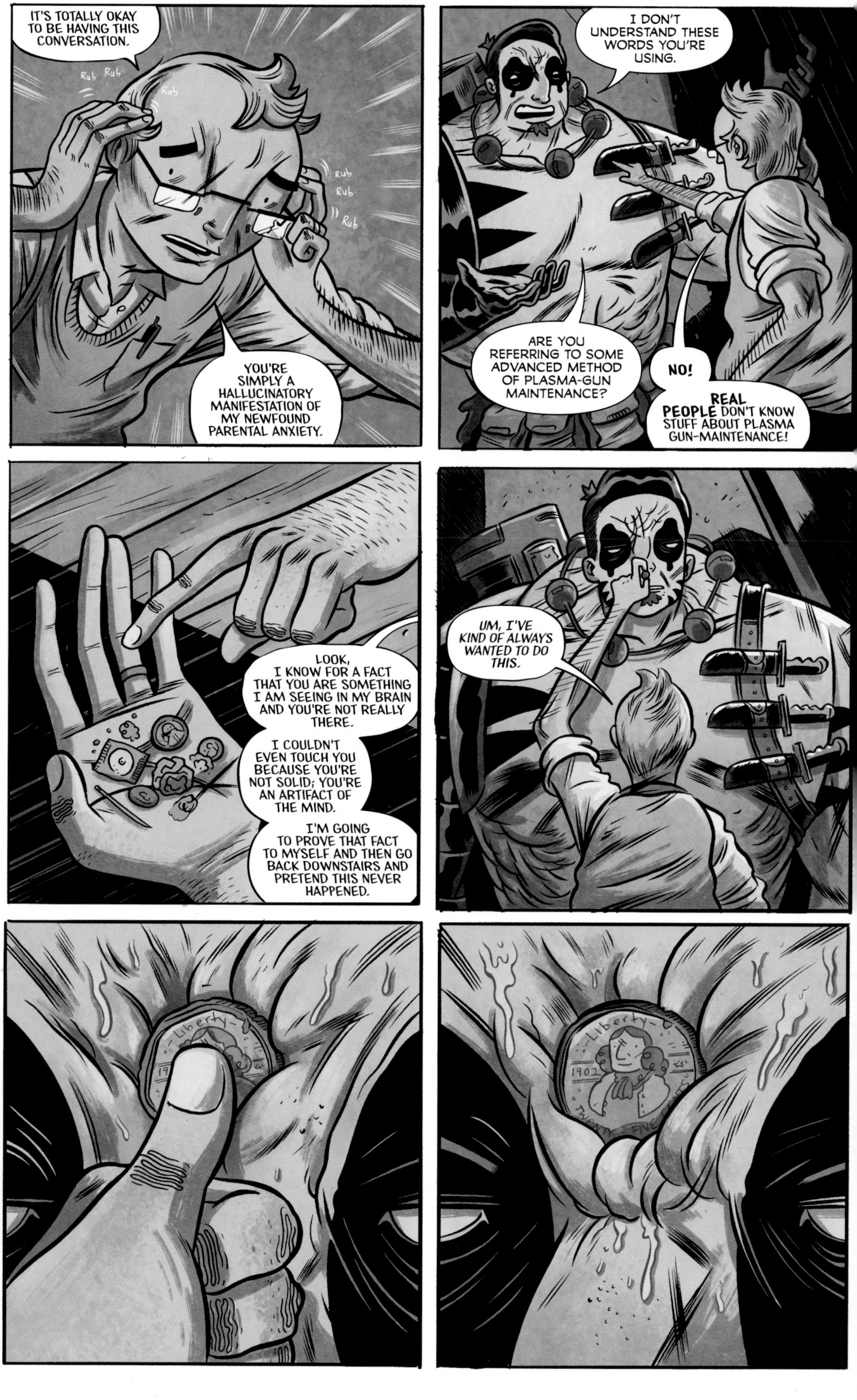
IT'S TOTALLY OKAY TO BE HAVING THIS CONVERSATION.
Rub Rub
Rub
Rub
Rub
Rub
YOU'RE SIMPLY A HALLUCINATORY MANIFESTATION OF MY NEWFOUND PARENTAL ANXIETY.
I DON'T UNDERSTAND THESE WORDS YOU'RE USING.
ARE YOU REFERRING TO SOME ADVANCED METHOD OF PLASMA-GUN MAINTENANCE?
NO!
REAL PEOPLE DON'T KNOW STUFF ABOUT PLASMA GUN-MAINTENANCE!
LOOK, I KNOW FOR A FACT THAT YOU ARE SOMETHING I AM SEEING IN MY BRAIN AND YOU'RE NOT REALLY THERE.
I COULDN'T EVEN TOUCH YOU BECAUSE YOU'RE NOT SOLID; YOU'RE AN ARTIFACT OF THE MIND.
I'M GOING TO PROVE THAT FACT TO MYSELF AND THEN GO BACK DOWNSTAIRS AND PRETEND THIS NEVER HAPPENED.
UM, I'VE KIND OF ALWAYS WANTED TO DO THIS.
Liberty
1902

AHHGADDD!
I TOLD YOU SO.
THAT'S IT. I'M LEAVING.
I'M A GROWN MAN AND I CANNOT CONTINUE INDULGING THIS MANIC EPISODE.
I WILL FIND YOU, PINT-SIZED MONKEY-MAN.
I CAN FIND ANYONE.
I'M NOT HEARING THIS.
I'M NOT HEARING THIS.
I'M NOT HEARING THIS.
I KNOW YOUR STENCH NOW, MOMMA'S BOY.
YOU'D BETTER--
SLAM!
HEF. HEF. HHHHH.

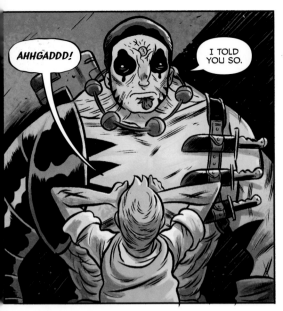

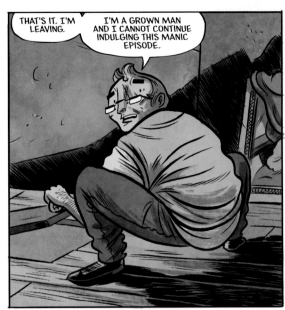

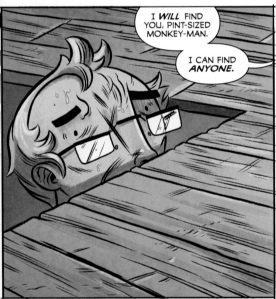

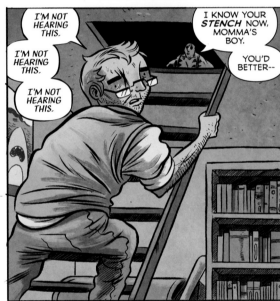

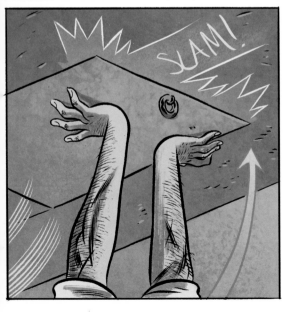

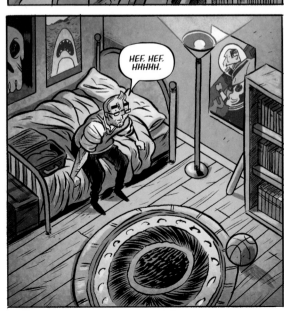

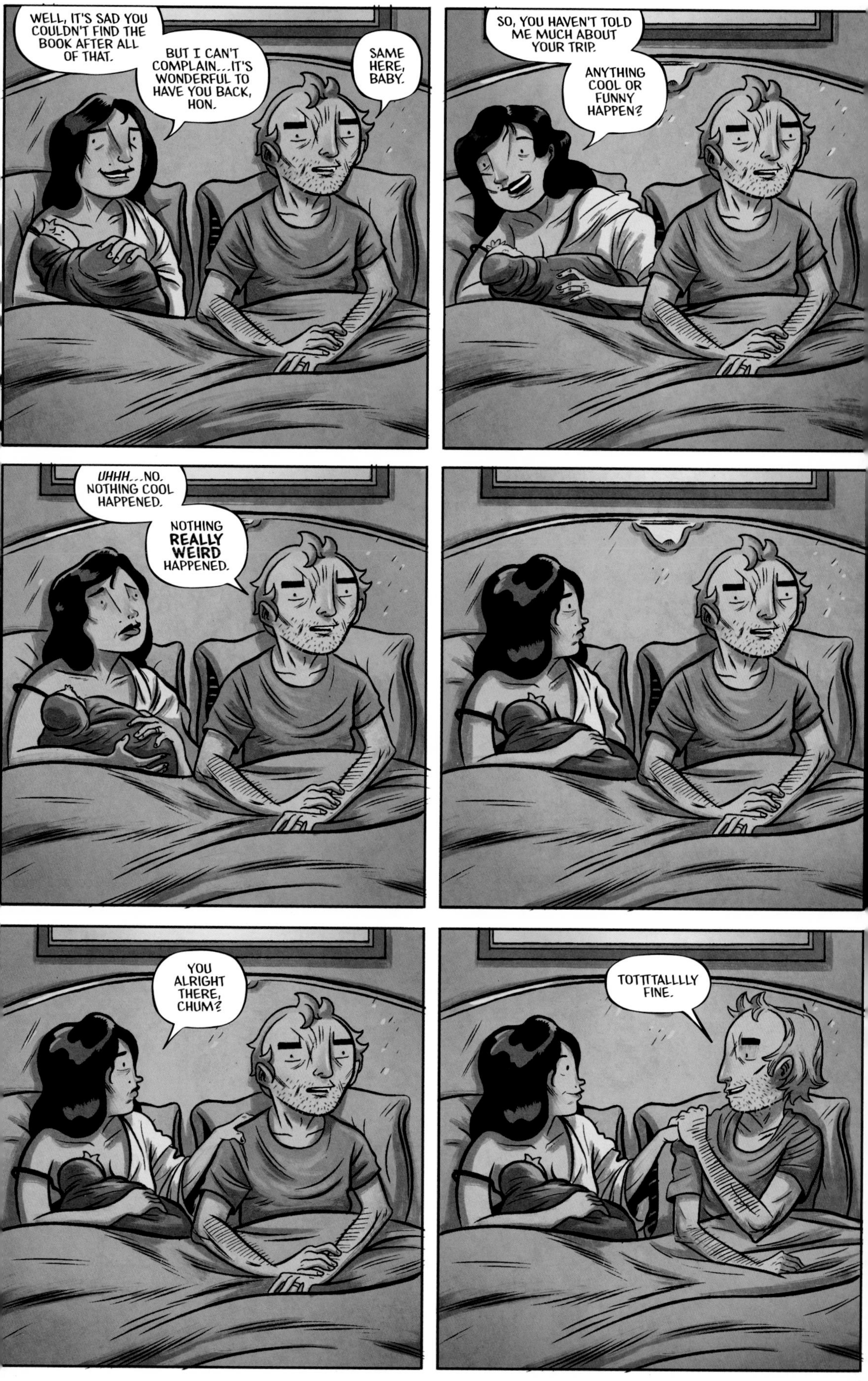

WELL, IT'S SAD YOU COULDN'T FIND THE BOOK AFTER ALL OF THAT.
BUT I CAN'T COMPLAIN... IT'S WONDERFUL TO HAVE YOU BACK, HON.
SAME HERE, BABY.
SO, YOU HAVEN'T TOLD ME MUCH ABOUT YOUR TRIP.
ANYTHING COOL OR FUNNY HAPPEN?
UHHH... NO. NOTHING COOL HAPPENED.
NOTHING REALLY WEIRD HAPPENED.
YOU ALRIGHT THERE, CHUM?
TOTTTTALLLLY FINE.

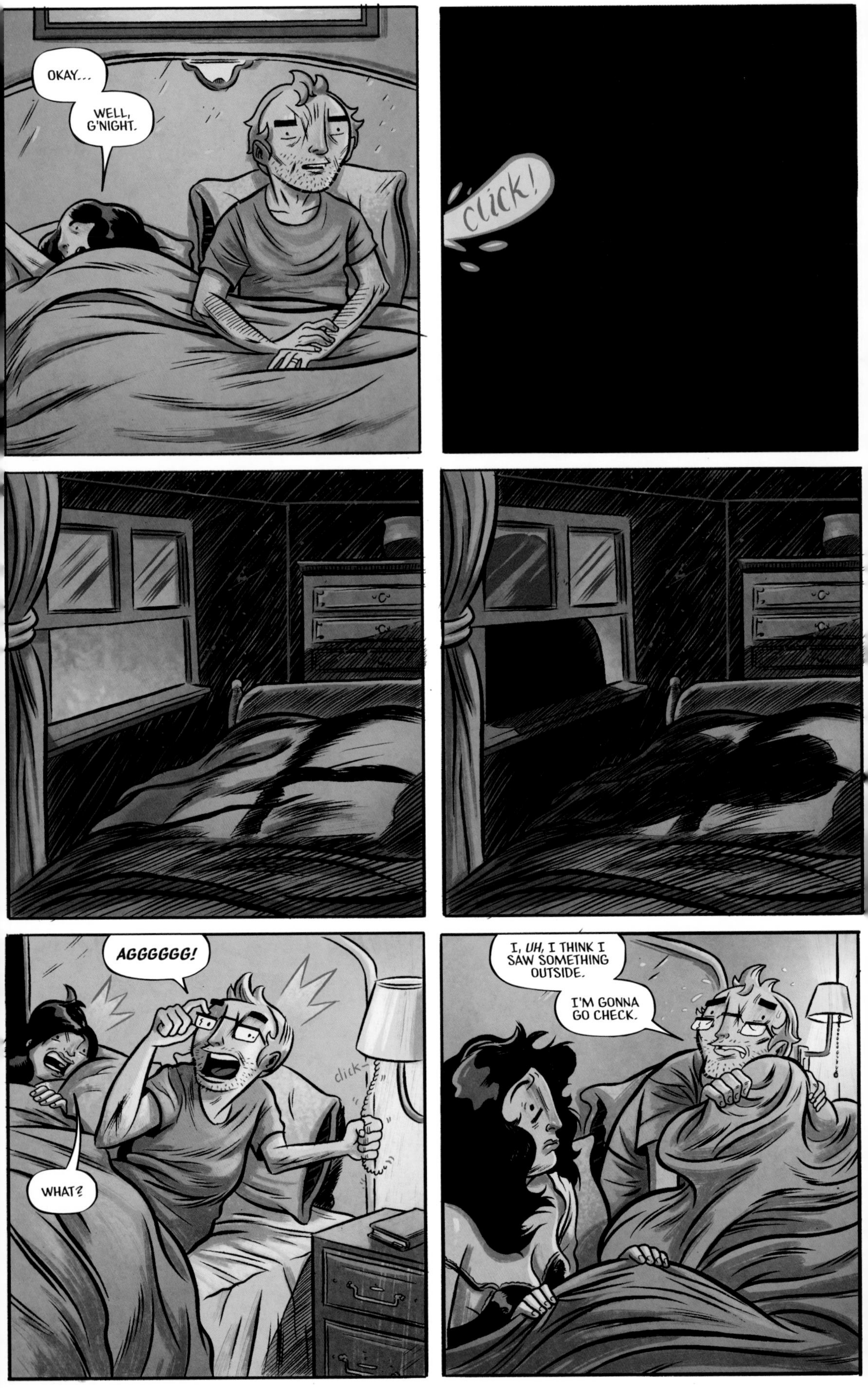
OKAY...
WELL, G'NIGHT.
CLICK!
AGGGGGG!
click-
WHAT?
I, UH, I THINK I SAW SOMETHING OUTSIDE.
I'M GONNA GO CHECK.

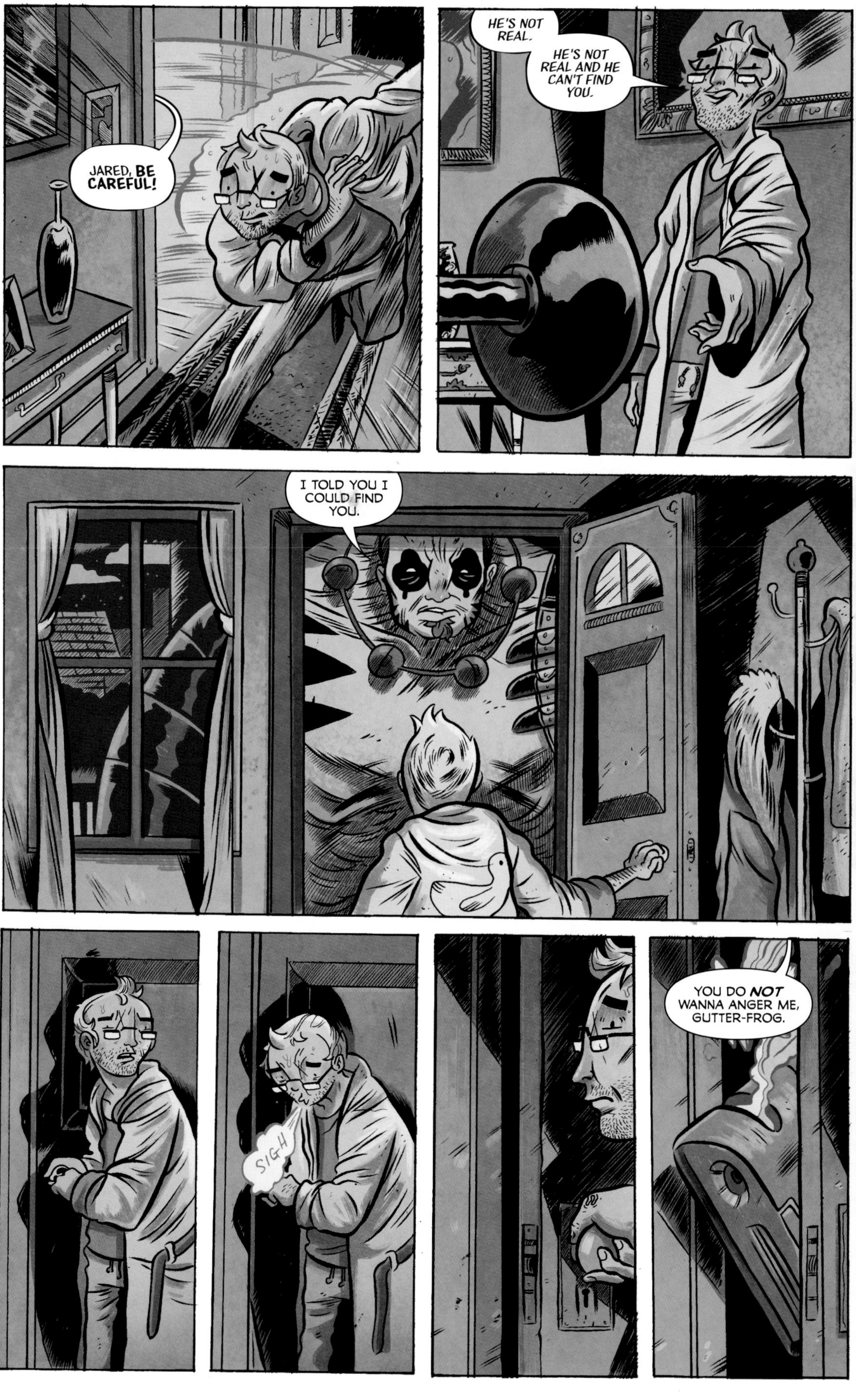
JARED, BE CAREFUL!
HE'S NOT REAL.
HE'S NOT REAL AND HE CAN'T FIND YOU.
I TOLD YOU I COULD FIND YOU.
SIGH
YOU DO NOT WANNA ANGER ME, GUTTER-FROG.

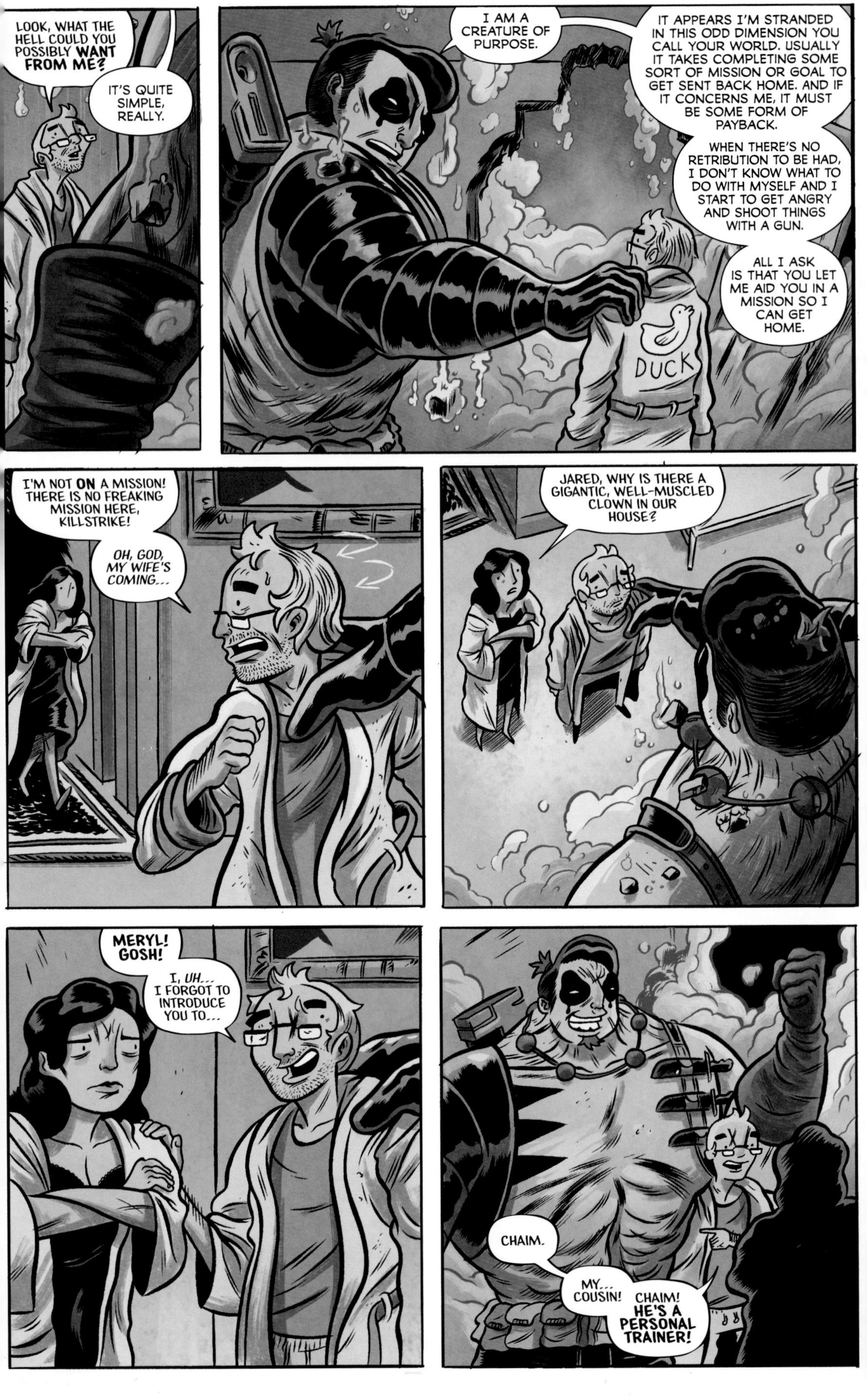
LOOK, WHAT THE HELL COULD YOU POSSIBLY **WANT FROM ME?**
IT'S QUITE SIMPLE, REALLY.
I AM A CREATURE OF PURPOSE.
IT APPEARS I'M STRANDED IN THIS ODD DIMENSION YOU CALL YOUR WORLD. USUALLY IT TAKES COMPLETING SOME SORT OF MISSION OR GOAL TO GET SENT BACK HOME. AND IF IT CONCERNS ME, IT MUST BE SOME FORM OF PAYBACK.
WHEN THERE'S NO RETRIBUTION TO BE HAD, I DON'T KNOW WHAT TO DO WITH MYSELF AND I START TO GET ANGRY AND SHOOT THINGS WITH A GUN.
ALL I ASK IS THAT YOU LET ME AID YOU IN A MISSION SO I CAN GET HOME.
DUCK
I'M NOT **ON** A MISSION! THERE IS NO FREAKING MISSION HERE, KILLSTRIKE!
OH, GOD, MY WIFE'S COMING...
JARED, WHY IS THERE A GIGANTIC, WELL-MUSCLED CLOWN IN OUR HOUSE?
MERYL! GOSH!
I, *UH...* I FORGOT TO INTRODUCE YOU TO...
CHAIM.
MY... COUSIN!
CHAIM! **HE'S A PERSONAL TRAINER!**

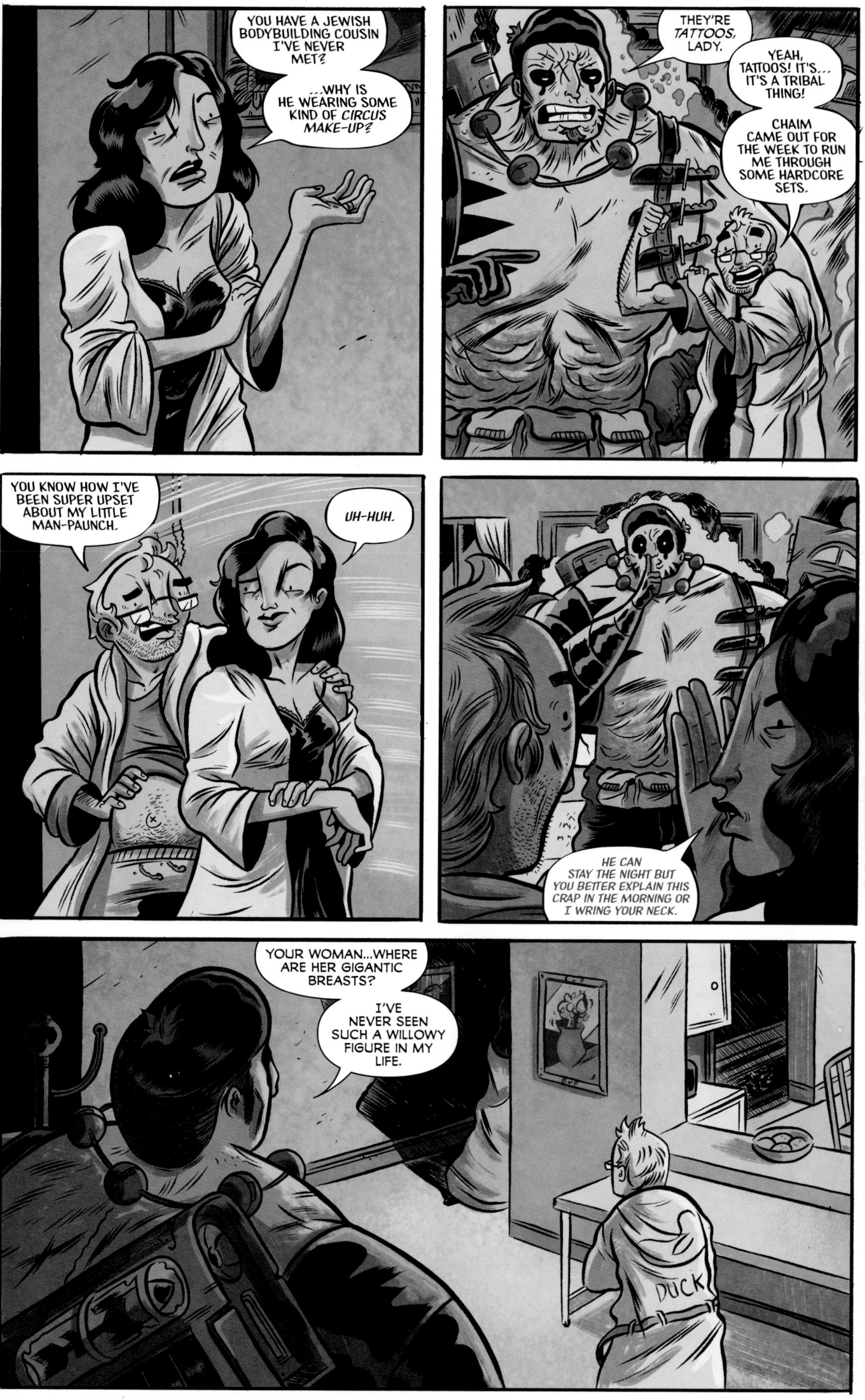
YOU HAVE A JEWISH BODYBUILDING COUSIN I'VE NEVER MET?
...WHY IS HE WEARING SOME KIND OF *CIRCUS MAKE-UP*?
THEY'RE *TATTOOS,* LADY.
YEAH, TATTOOS! IT'S... IT'S A TRIBAL THING!
CHAIM CAME OUT FOR THE WEEK TO RUN ME THROUGH SOME HARDCORE SETS.
YOU KNOW HOW I'VE BEEN SUPER UPSET ABOUT MY LITTLE MAN-PAUNCH.
UH-HUH.
HE CAN STAY THE NIGHT BUT YOU BETTER EXPLAIN THIS CRAP IN THE MORNING OR I WRING YOUR NECK.
YOUR WOMAN...WHERE ARE HER GIGANTIC BREASTS?
I'VE NEVER SEEN SUCH A WILLOWY FIGURE IN MY LIFE.
DUCK

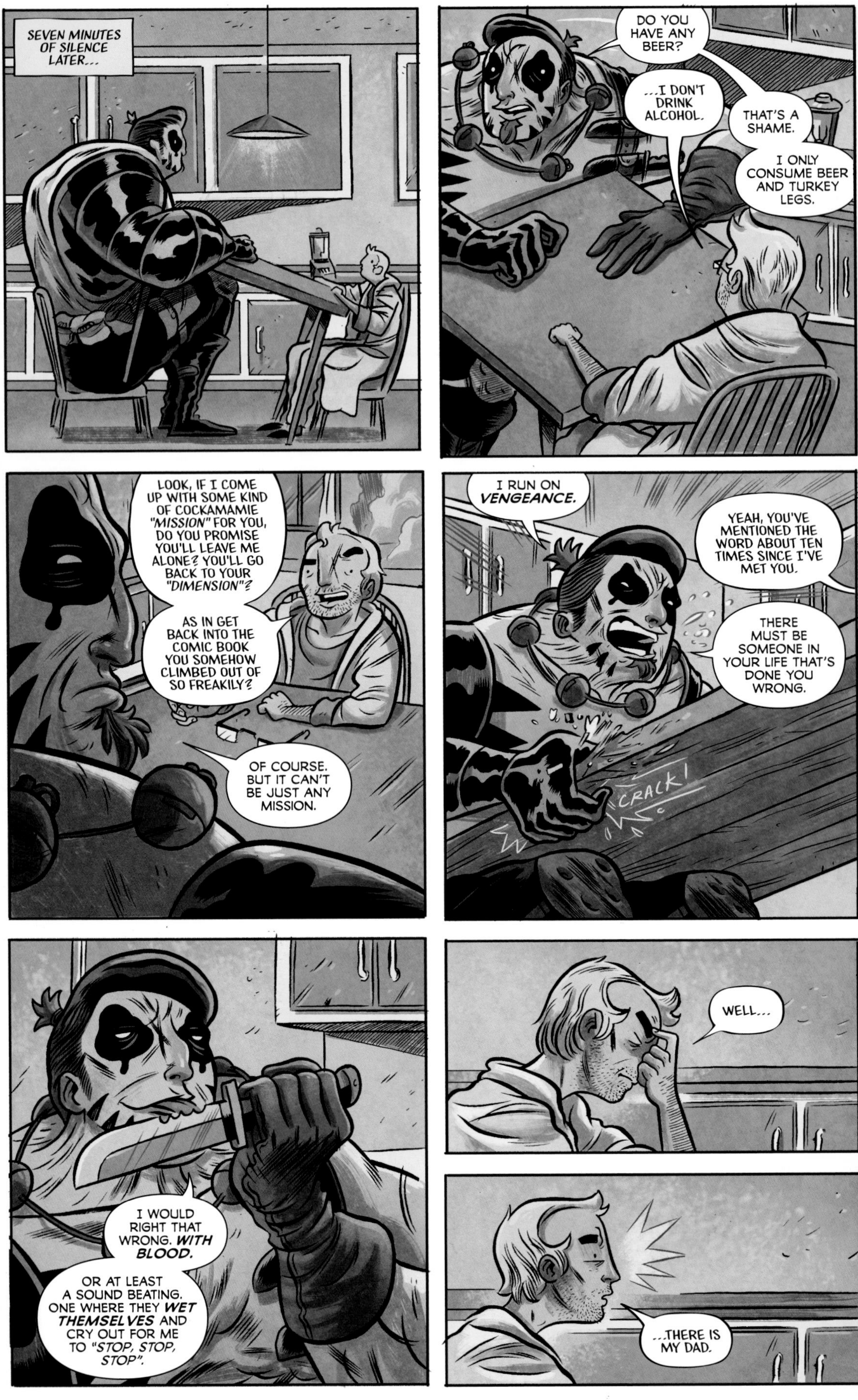
SEVEN MINUTES OF SILENCE LATER...
DO YOU HAVE ANY BEER?
...I DON'T DRINK ALCOHOL.
THAT'S A SHAME.
I ONLY CONSUME BEER AND TURKEY LEGS.
LOOK, IF I COME UP WITH SOME KIND OF COCKAMAMIE "MISSION" FOR YOU, DO YOU PROMISE YOU'LL LEAVE ME ALONE? YOU'LL GO BACK TO YOUR "DIMENSION"?
AS IN GET BACK INTO THE COMIC BOOK YOU SOMEHOW CLIMBED OUT OF SO FREAKILY?
OF COURSE. BUT IT CAN'T BE JUST ANY MISSION.
I RUN ON VENGEANCE.
YEAH, YOU'VE MENTIONED THE WORD ABOUT TEN TIMES SINCE I'VE MET YOU.
THERE MUST BE SOMEONE IN YOUR LIFE THAT'S DONE YOU WRONG.
CRACK!
I WOULD RIGHT THAT WRONG. WITH BLOOD.
OR AT LEAST A SOUND BEATING. ONE WHERE THEY WET THEMSELVES AND CRY OUT FOR ME TO "STOP, STOP, STOP".
WELL...
...THERE IS MY DAD.

YOUR OWN FATHER? **YES!**

HOW **GORGEOUSLY TWISTED** YOU ARE, BOY.

SHUNK!

WHAT DID HE DO TO YOU? *Huh?* **TELL ME EVERYTHING.**

DID HE ACCIDENTALLY KILL YOUR DAUGHTER?

RAT YOU OUT TO A COVERT TEAM OF GOVERNMENT CUTTHROATS?

IS HE AN ALIEN SHAPE SHIFTER?

KILLSTRIKE, I REALLY DON'T THINK YOU SHOULD GET INVOLVED.

YOU WILL TELL ME *EVERY DETAIL* OR I WILL INTERROGATE THAT SWEET OL' MAMA OF YOURS.

FINE!

HE ABANDONED MY MOTHER AND ME WHEN I WAS VERY SMALL. I HAVEN'T SEEN HIM IN OVER 25 YEARS. I DON'T EVEN KNOW WHERE HE IS.

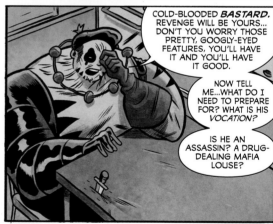

COLD-BLOODED **BASTARD.** REVENGE WILL BE YOURS... DON'T YOU WORRY THOSE PRETTY, GOOGLY-EYED FEATURES, YOU'LL HAVE IT AND YOU'LL HAVE IT GOOD.

NOW TELL ME...WHAT DO I NEED TO PREPARE FOR? WHAT IS HIS *VOCATION?*

IS HE AN ASSASSIN? A DRUG-DEALING MAFIA LOUSE?

ACTUALLY... HE WAS A COMIC BOOK WRITER.

Ah-hah! HOW *PREDICTABLE!*

SO THAT'S WHY YOU HAD SO MANY GIRL-FEELINGS ABOUT ME POPPING OUT OF ONE!

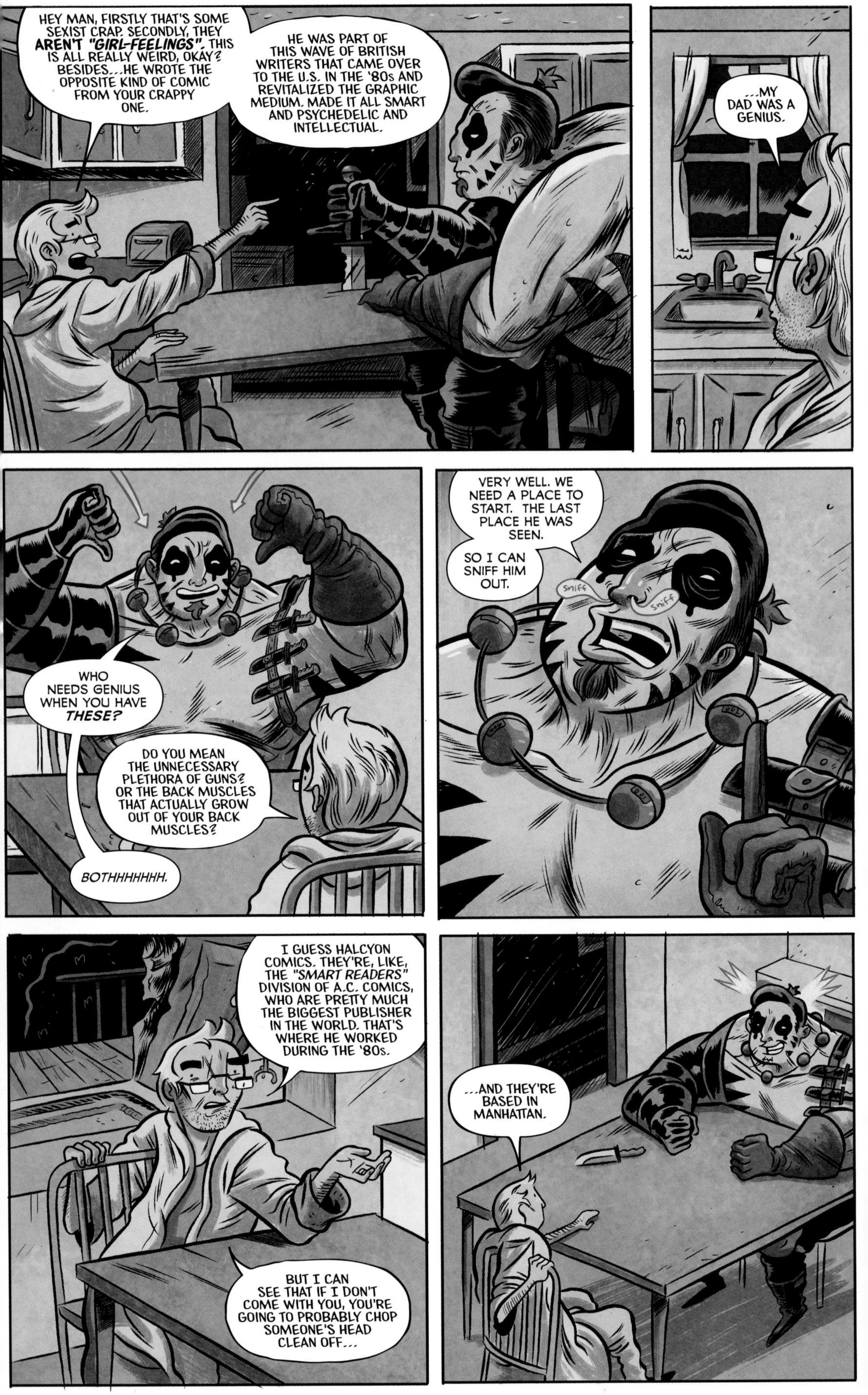
HEY MAN, FIRSTLY THAT'S SOME SEXIST CRAP. SECONDLY, THEY **AREN'T "GIRL-FEELINGS"**. THIS IS ALL REALLY WEIRD, OKAY? BESIDES... HE WROTE THE OPPOSITE KIND OF COMIC FROM YOUR CRAPPY ONE.
HE WAS PART OF THIS WAVE OF BRITISH WRITERS THAT CAME OVER TO THE U.S. IN THE '80s AND REVITALIZED THE GRAPHIC MEDIUM. MADE IT ALL SMART AND PSYCHEDELIC AND INTELLECTUAL.
...MY DAD WAS A GENIUS.
WHO NEEDS GENIUS WHEN YOU HAVE *THESE?*
DO YOU MEAN THE UNNECESSARY PLETHORA OF GUNS? OR THE BACK MUSCLES THAT ACTUALLY GROW OUT OF YOUR BACK MUSCLES?
BOTHHHHHHH.
VERY WELL. WE NEED A PLACE TO START. THE LAST PLACE HE WAS SEEN.
SO I CAN SNIFF HIM OUT.
sniff
sniff
I GUESS HALCYON COMICS. THEY'RE, LIKE, THE *"SMART READERS"* DIVISION OF A.C. COMICS, WHO ARE PRETTY MUCH THE BIGGEST PUBLISHER IN THE WORLD. THAT'S WHERE HE WORKED DURING THE '80s.
BUT I CAN SEE THAT IF I DON'T COME WITH YOU, YOU'RE GOING TO PROBABLY CHOP SOMEONE'S HEAD CLEAN OFF...
...AND THEY'RE BASED IN MANHATTAN.

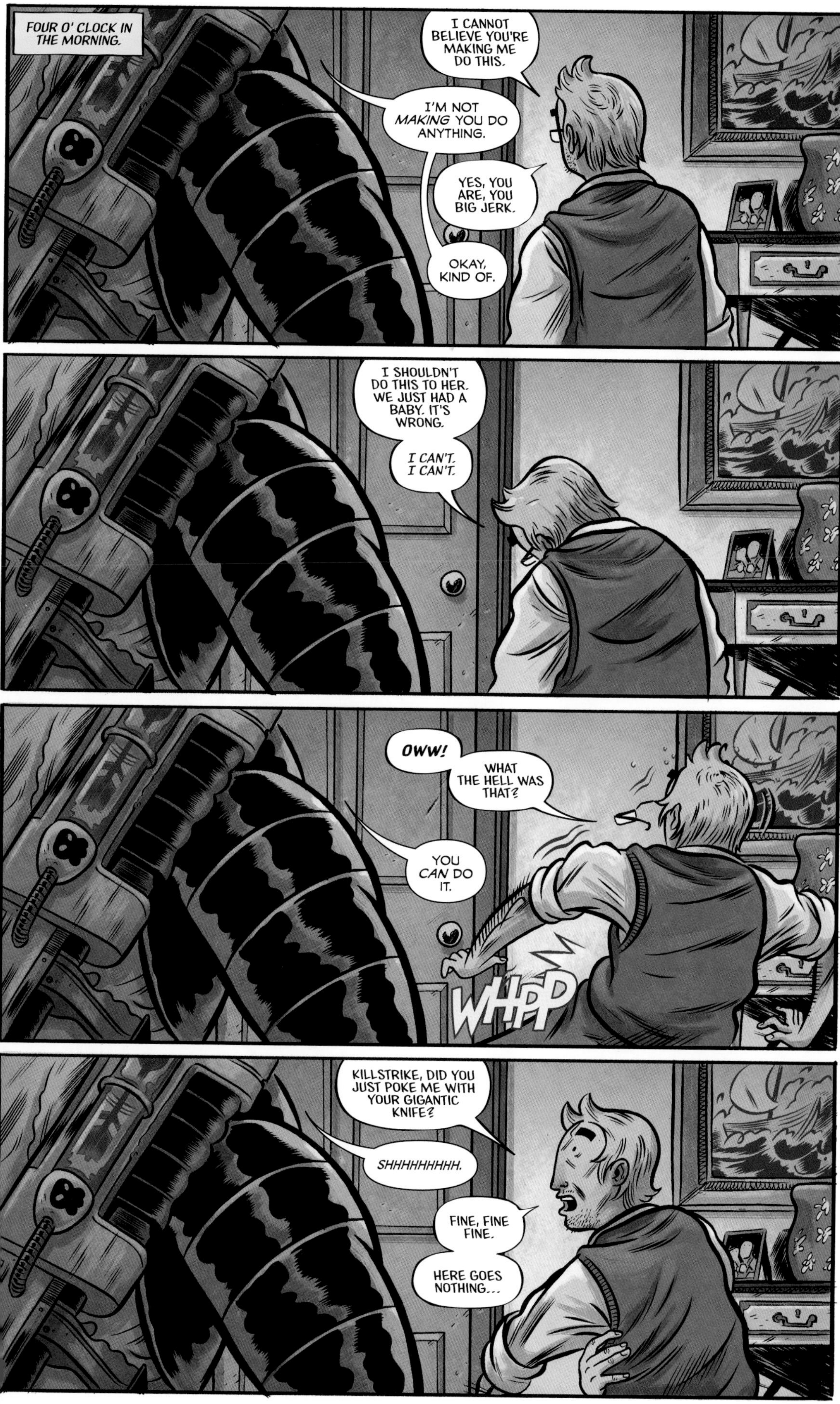
FOUR O' CLOCK IN THE MORNING.
I CANNOT BELIEVE YOU'RE MAKING ME DO THIS.
I'M NOT *MAKING* YOU DO ANYTHING.
YES, YOU ARE, YOU BIG JERK.
OKAY, KIND OF.
I SHOULDN'T DO THIS TO HER. WE JUST HAD A BABY. IT'S WRONG.
I CAN'T. I CAN'T.
OWW!
WHAT THE HELL WAS THAT?
YOU *CAN* DO IT.
WHPP
KILLSTRIKE, DID YOU JUST POKE ME WITH YOUR GIGANTIC KNIFE?
SHHHHHHHHH.
FINE, FINE FINE.
HERE GOES NOTHING...

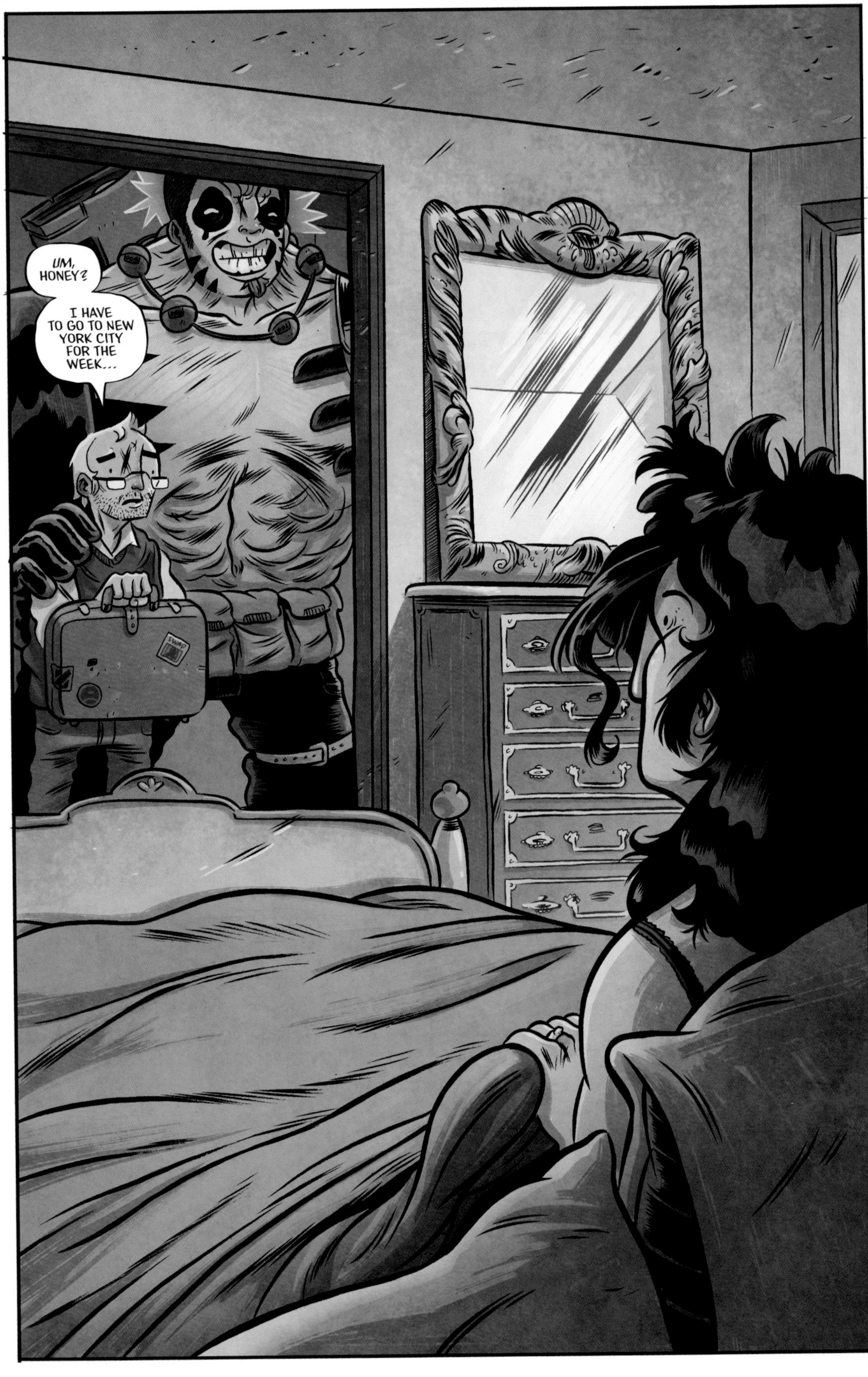
UM, HONEY?
I HAVE TO GO TO NEW YORK CITY FOR THE WEEK...

POW POW

chapter
TWO

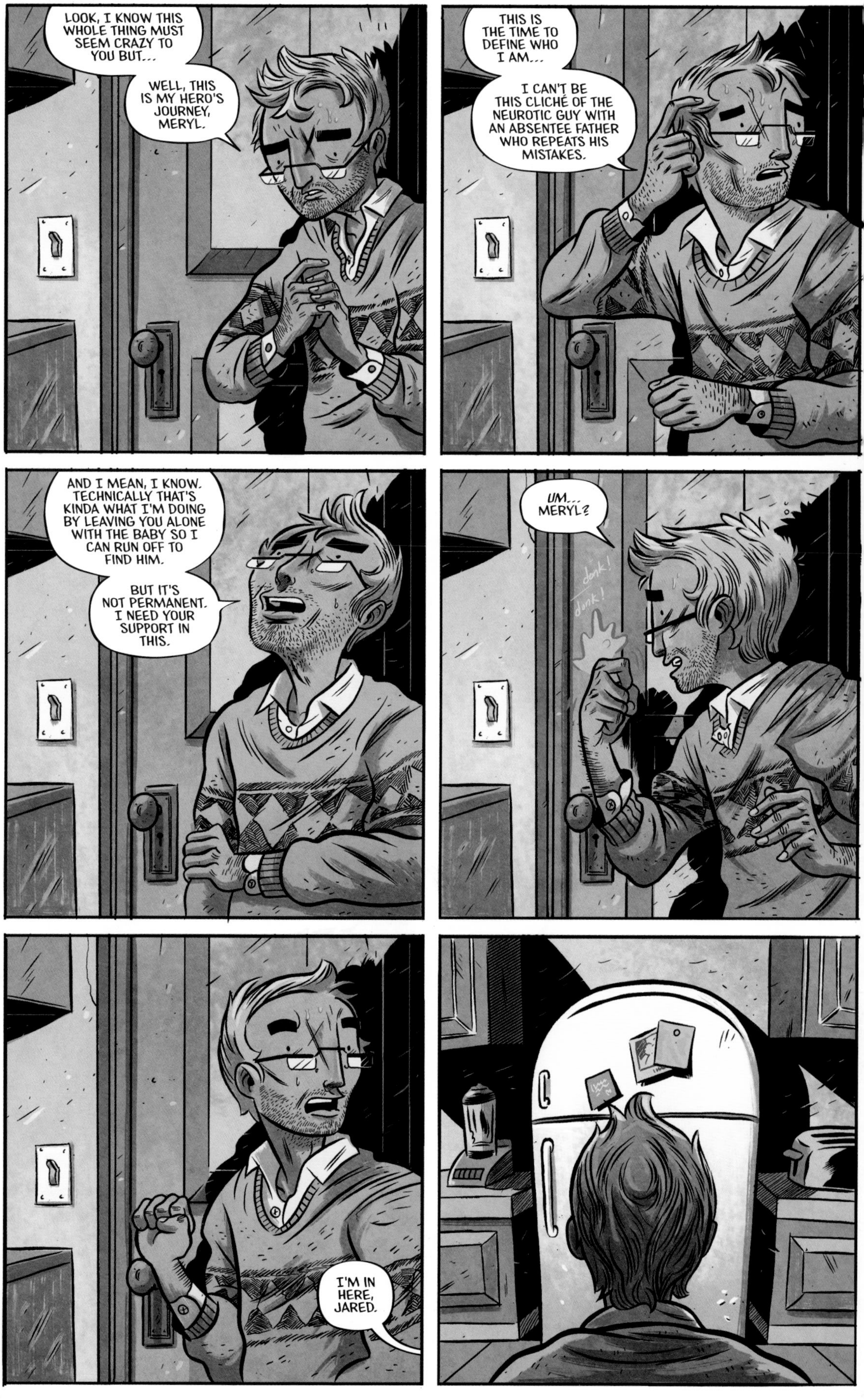
LOOK, I KNOW THIS WHOLE THING MUST SEEM CRAZY TO YOU BUT...
WELL, THIS IS MY HERO'S JOURNEY, MERYL.
THIS IS THE TIME TO DEFINE WHO I AM...
I CAN'T BE THIS CLICHÉ OF THE NEUROTIC GUY WITH AN ABSENTEE FATHER WHO REPEATS HIS MISTAKES.
AND I MEAN, I KNOW. TECHNICALLY THAT'S KINDA WHAT I'M DOING BY LEAVING YOU ALONE WITH THE BABY SO I CAN RUN OFF TO FIND HIM.
BUT IT'S NOT PERMANENT. I NEED YOUR SUPPORT IN THIS.
UM... MERYL?
donk! donk!
I'M IN HERE, JARED.

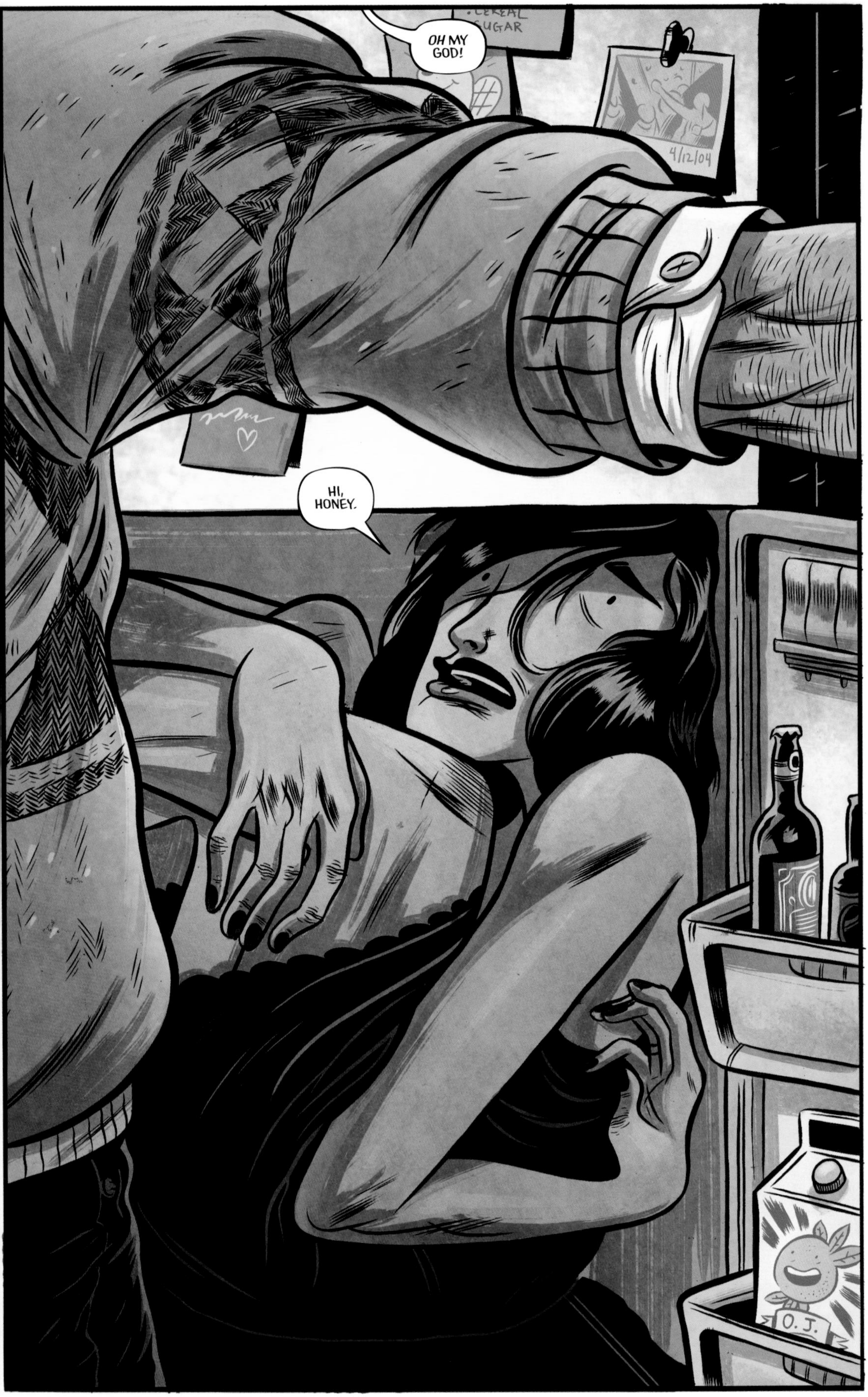
OH MY GOD!
HI, HONEY.
.CEREAL
SUGAR
4/12/04
O.J.

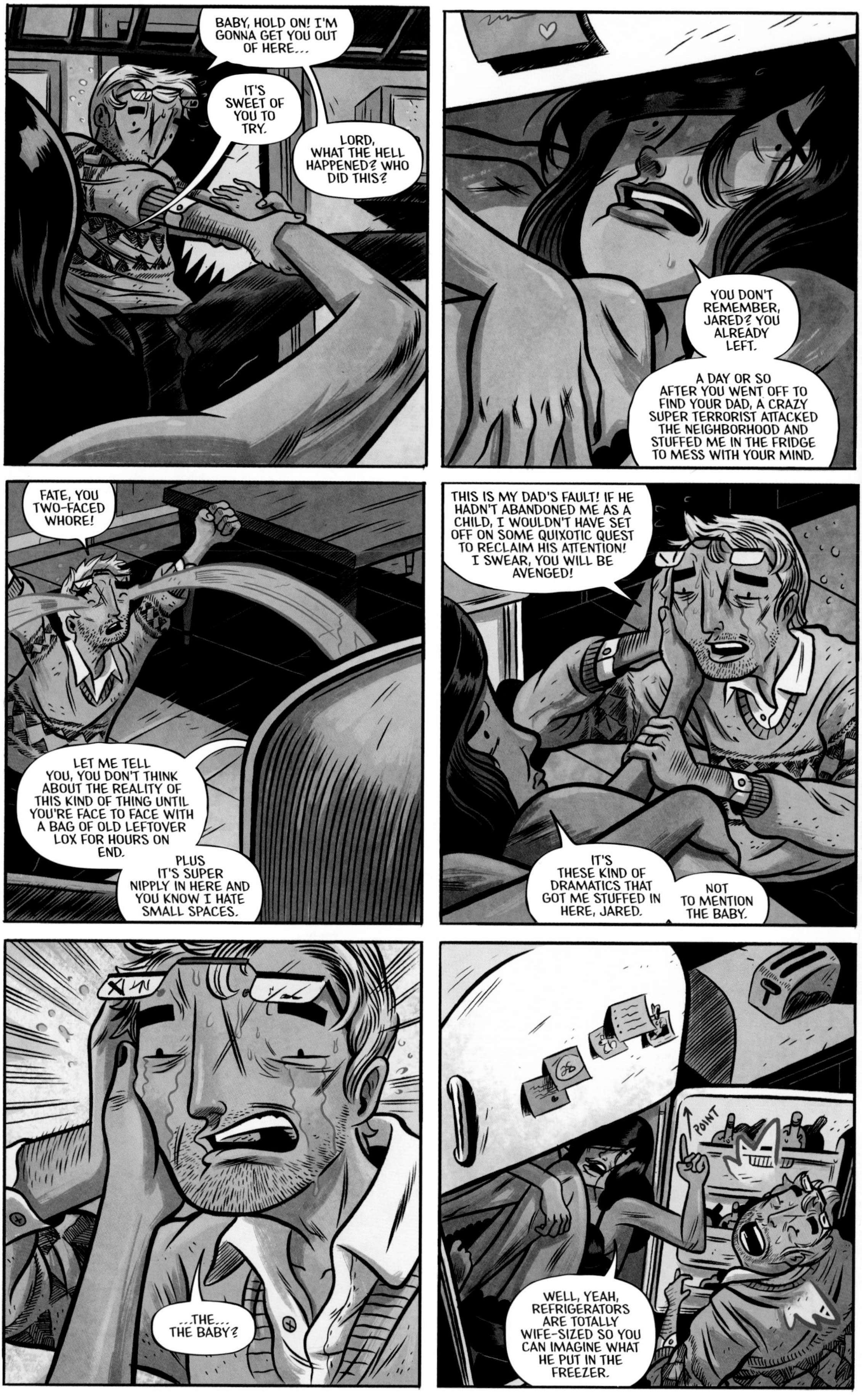
BABY, HOLD ON! I'M GONNA GET YOU OUT OF HERE...
IT'S SWEET OF YOU TO TRY.
LORD, WHAT THE HELL HAPPENED? WHO DID THIS?
YOU DON'T REMEMBER, JARED? YOU ALREADY LEFT.
A DAY OR SO AFTER YOU WENT OFF TO FIND YOUR DAD, A CRAZY SUPER TERRORIST ATTACKED THE NEIGHBORHOOD AND STUFFED ME IN THE FRIDGE TO MESS WITH YOUR MIND.
FATE, YOU TWO-FACED WHORE!
LET ME TELL YOU, YOU DON'T THINK ABOUT THE REALITY OF THIS KIND OF THING UNTIL YOU'RE FACE TO FACE WITH A BAG OF OLD LEFTOVER LOX FOR HOURS ON END.
PLUS IT'S SUPER NIPPLY IN HERE AND YOU KNOW I HATE SMALL SPACES.
THIS IS MY DAD'S FAULT! IF HE HADN'T ABANDONED ME AS A CHILD, I WOULDN'T HAVE SET OFF ON SOME QUIXOTIC QUEST TO RECLAIM HIS ATTENTION! I SWEAR, YOU WILL BE AVENGED!
IT'S THESE KIND OF DRAMATICS THAT GOT ME STUFFED IN HERE, JARED.
NOT TO MENTION THE BABY.
...THE... THE BABY?
POINT
WELL, YEAH, REFRIGERATORS ARE TOTALLY WIFE-SIZED SO YOU CAN IMAGINE WHAT HE PUT IN THE FREEZER.

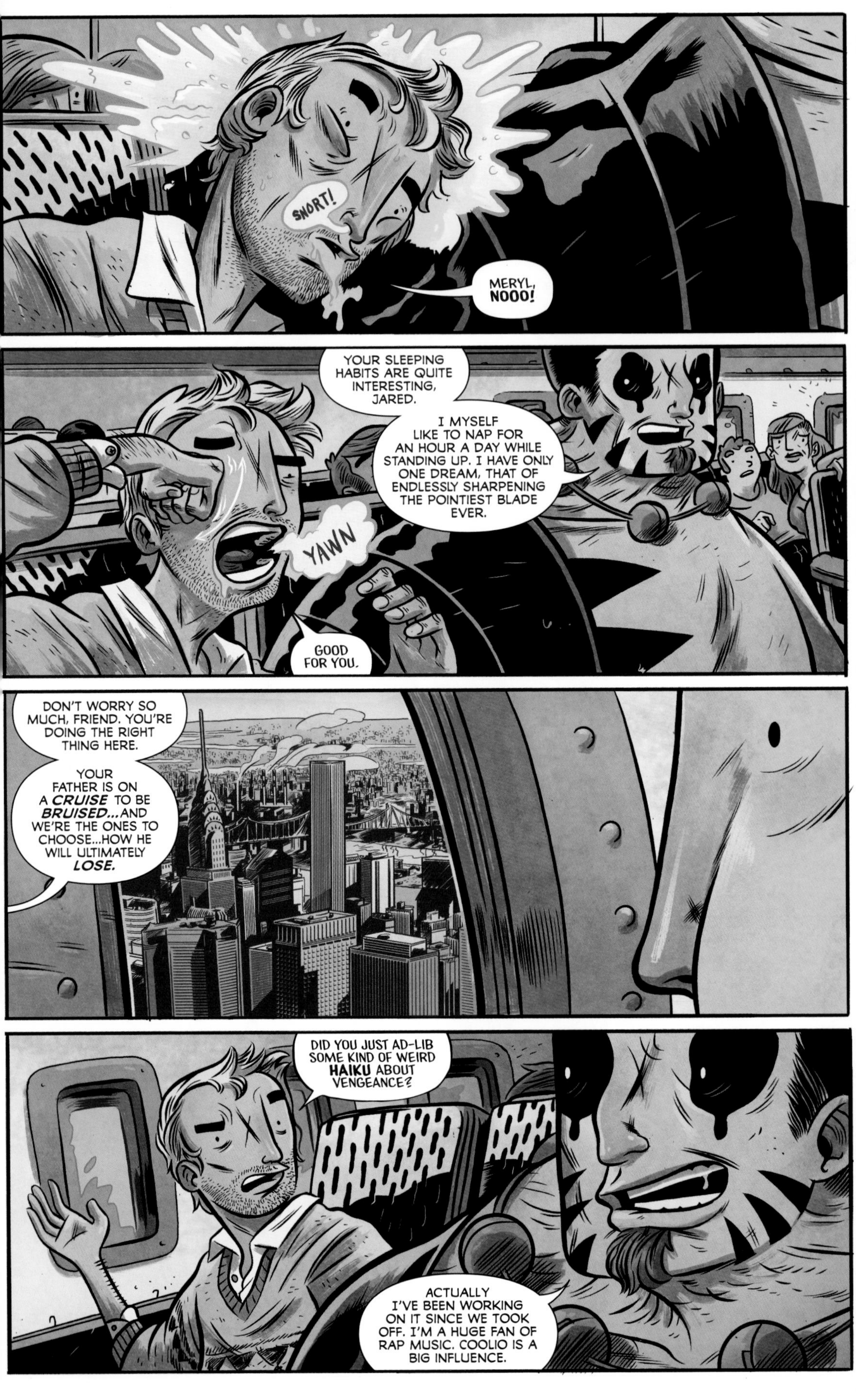
SNORT!
MERYL, NOOO!
YOUR SLEEPING HABITS ARE QUITE INTERESTING, JARED.
I MYSELF LIKE TO NAP FOR AN HOUR A DAY WHILE STANDING UP. I HAVE ONLY ONE DREAM, THAT OF ENDLESSLY SHARPENING THE POINTIEST BLADE EVER.
YAWN
GOOD FOR YOU.
DON'T WORRY SO MUCH, FRIEND. YOU'RE DOING THE RIGHT THING HERE.
YOUR FATHER IS ON A CRUISE TO BE BRUISED...AND WE'RE THE ONES TO CHOOSE...HOW HE WILL ULTIMATELY LOSE.
DID YOU JUST AD-LIB SOME KIND OF WEIRD HAIKU ABOUT VENGEANCE?
ACTUALLY I'VE BEEN WORKING ON IT SINCE WE TOOK OFF. I'M A HUGE FAN OF RAP MUSIC. COOLIO IS A BIG INFLUENCE.

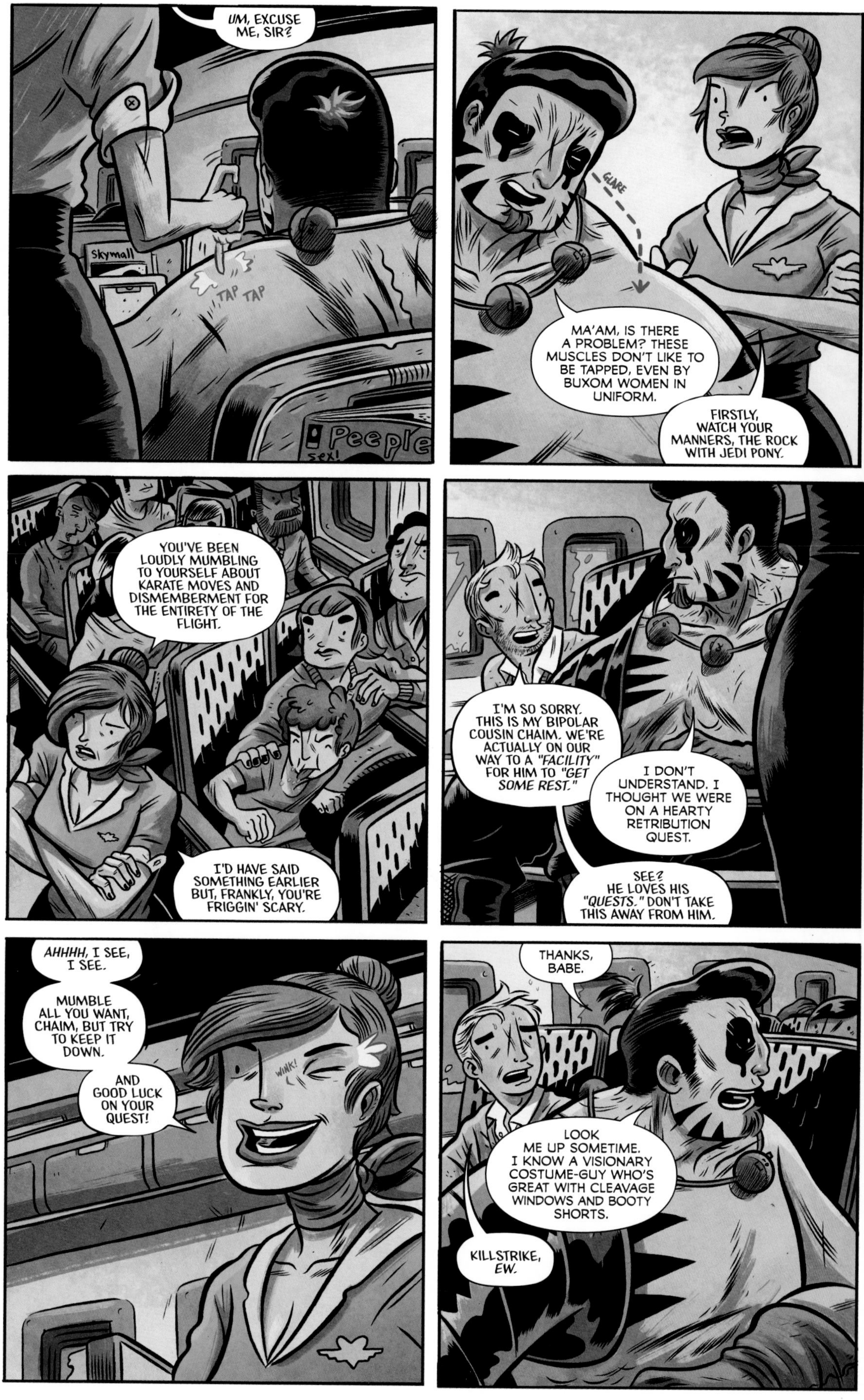
UM, EXCUSE ME, SIR?
Skymall
TAP TAP
Peeple
SEX!
GLARE
MA'AM, IS THERE A PROBLEM? THESE MUSCLES DON'T LIKE TO BE TAPPED, EVEN BY BUXOM WOMEN IN UNIFORM.
FIRSTLY, WATCH YOUR MANNERS, THE ROCK WITH JEDI PONY.
YOU'VE BEEN LOUDLY MUMBLING TO YOURSELF ABOUT KARATE MOVES AND DISMEMBERMENT FOR THE ENTIRETY OF THE FLIGHT.
I'D HAVE SAID SOMETHING EARLIER BUT, FRANKLY, YOU'RE FRIGGIN' SCARY.
I'M SO SORRY. THIS IS MY BIPOLAR COUSIN CHAIM. WE'RE ACTUALLY ON OUR WAY TO A "FACILITY" FOR HIM TO "GET SOME REST."
I DON'T UNDERSTAND. I THOUGHT WE WERE ON A HEARTY RETRIBUTION QUEST.
SEE? HE LOVES HIS "QUESTS." DON'T TAKE THIS AWAY FROM HIM.
AHHHH, I SEE, I SEE.
MUMBLE ALL YOU WANT, CHAIM, BUT TRY TO KEEP IT DOWN.
AND GOOD LUCK ON YOUR QUEST!
WINK!
THANKS, BABE.
LOOK ME UP SOMETIME. I KNOW A VISIONARY COSTUME-GUY WHO'S GREAT WITH CLEAVAGE WINDOWS AND BOOTY SHORTS.
KILLSTRIKE, EW.

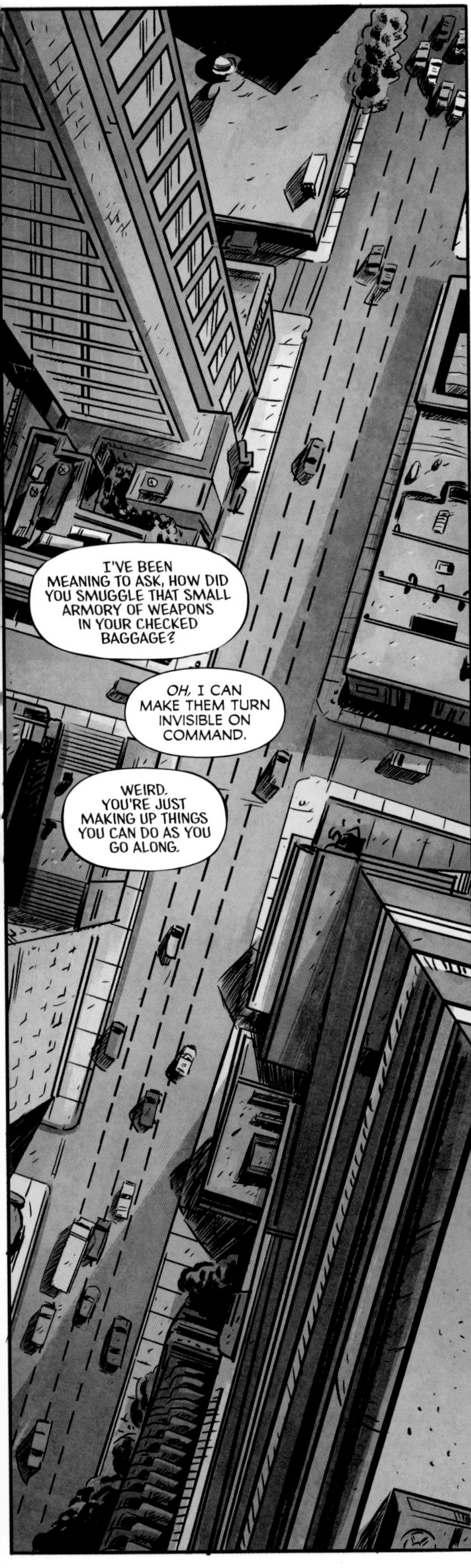
I'VE BEEN MEANING TO ASK, HOW DID YOU SMUGGLE THAT SMALL ARMORY OF WEAPONS IN YOUR CHECKED BAGGAGE?
OH, I CAN MAKE THEM TURN INVISIBLE ON COMMAND.
WEIRD. YOU'RE JUST MAKING UP THINGS YOU CAN DO AS YOU GO ALONG.

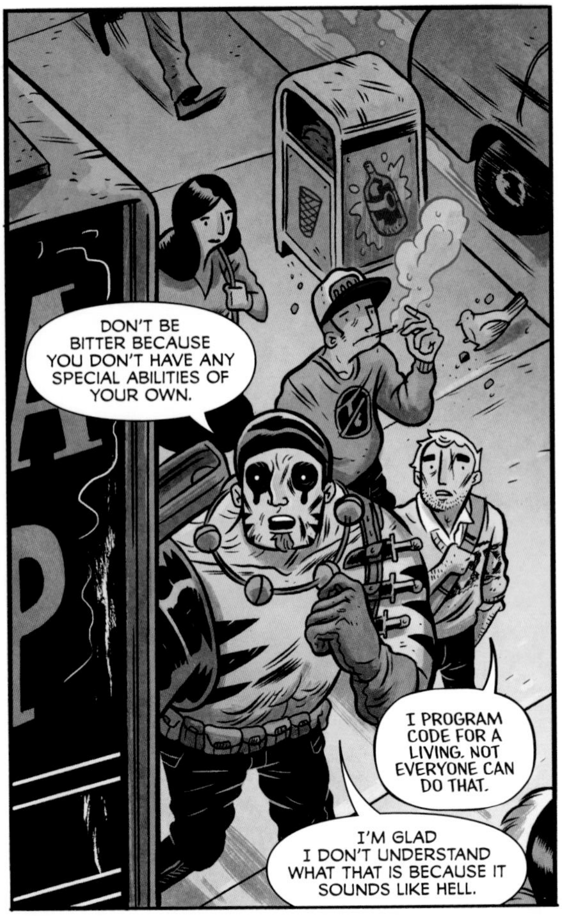
DON'T BE BITTER BECAUSE YOU DON'T HAVE ANY SPECIAL ABILITIES OF YOUR OWN.
I PROGRAM CODE FOR A LIVING. NOT EVERYONE CAN DO THAT.
I'M GLAD I DON'T UNDERSTAND WHAT THAT IS BECAUSE IT SOUNDS LIKE HELL.

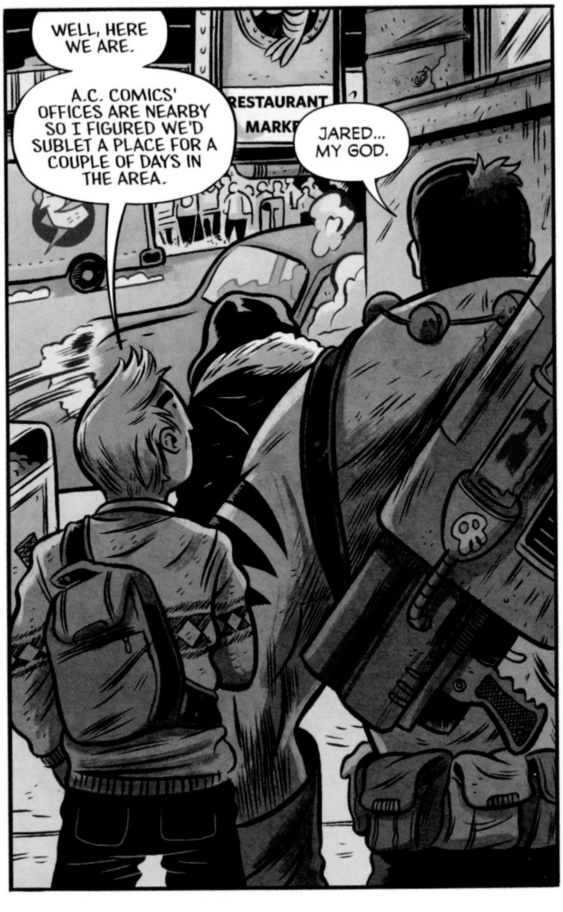
WELL, HERE WE ARE.
A.C. COMICS' OFFICES ARE NEARBY SO I FIGURED WE'D SUBLET A PLACE FOR A COUPLE OF DAYS IN THE AREA.
RESTAURANT
JARED... MY GOD.

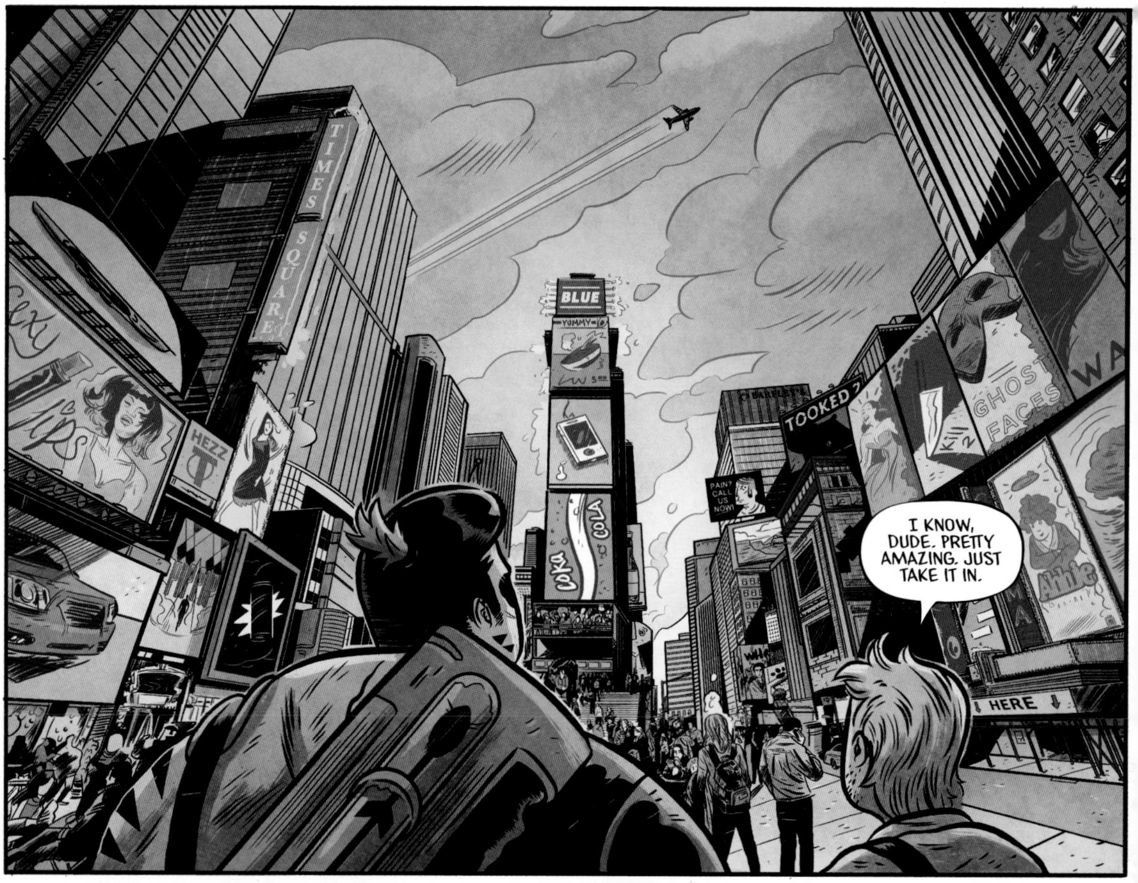
TIMES SQUARE
BLUE
YUMMY
COKA COLA
PAIN? CALL US NOW!
TOOKED 2
GHOST FACES
HEZZ
HERE
I KNOW, DUDE. PRETTY AMAZING. JUST TAKE IT IN.

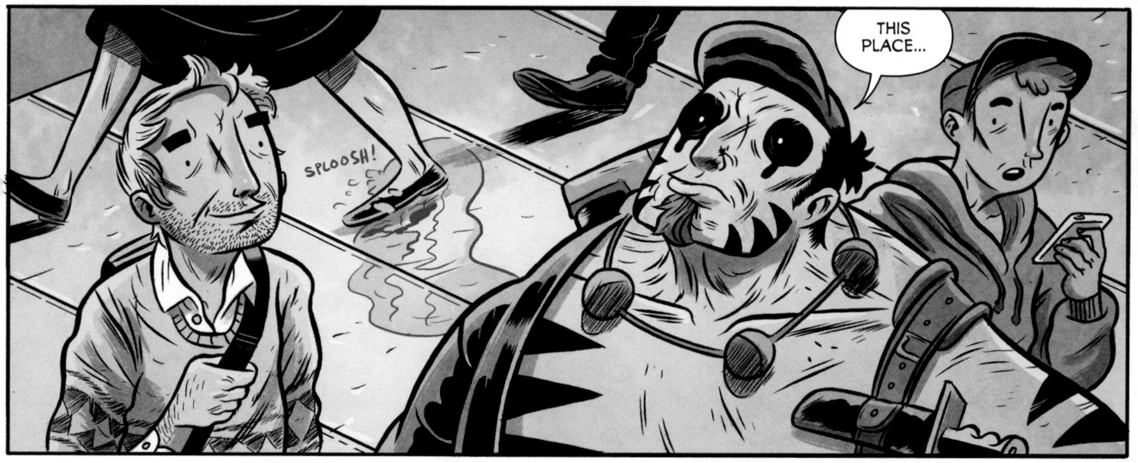
SPLOOSH!
THIS PLACE...

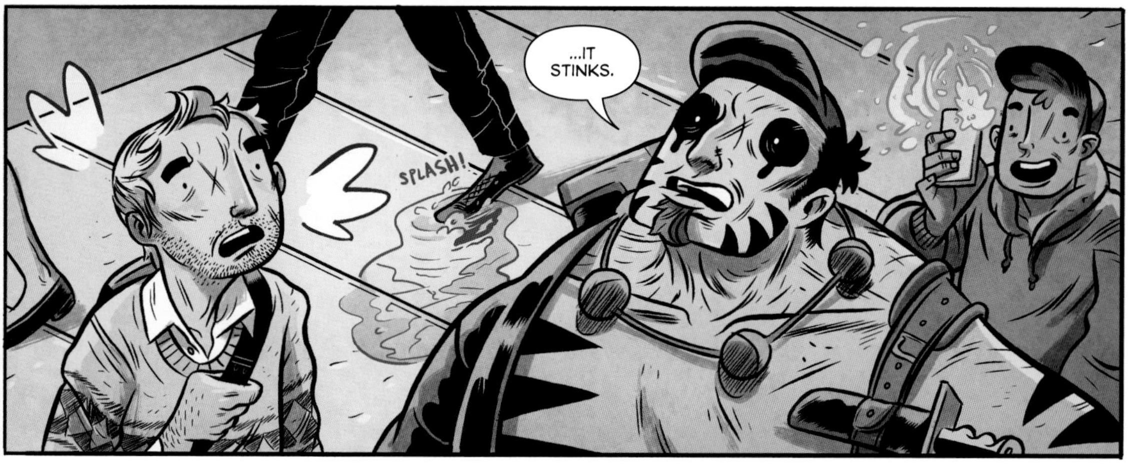
SPLASH!
...IT STINKS.

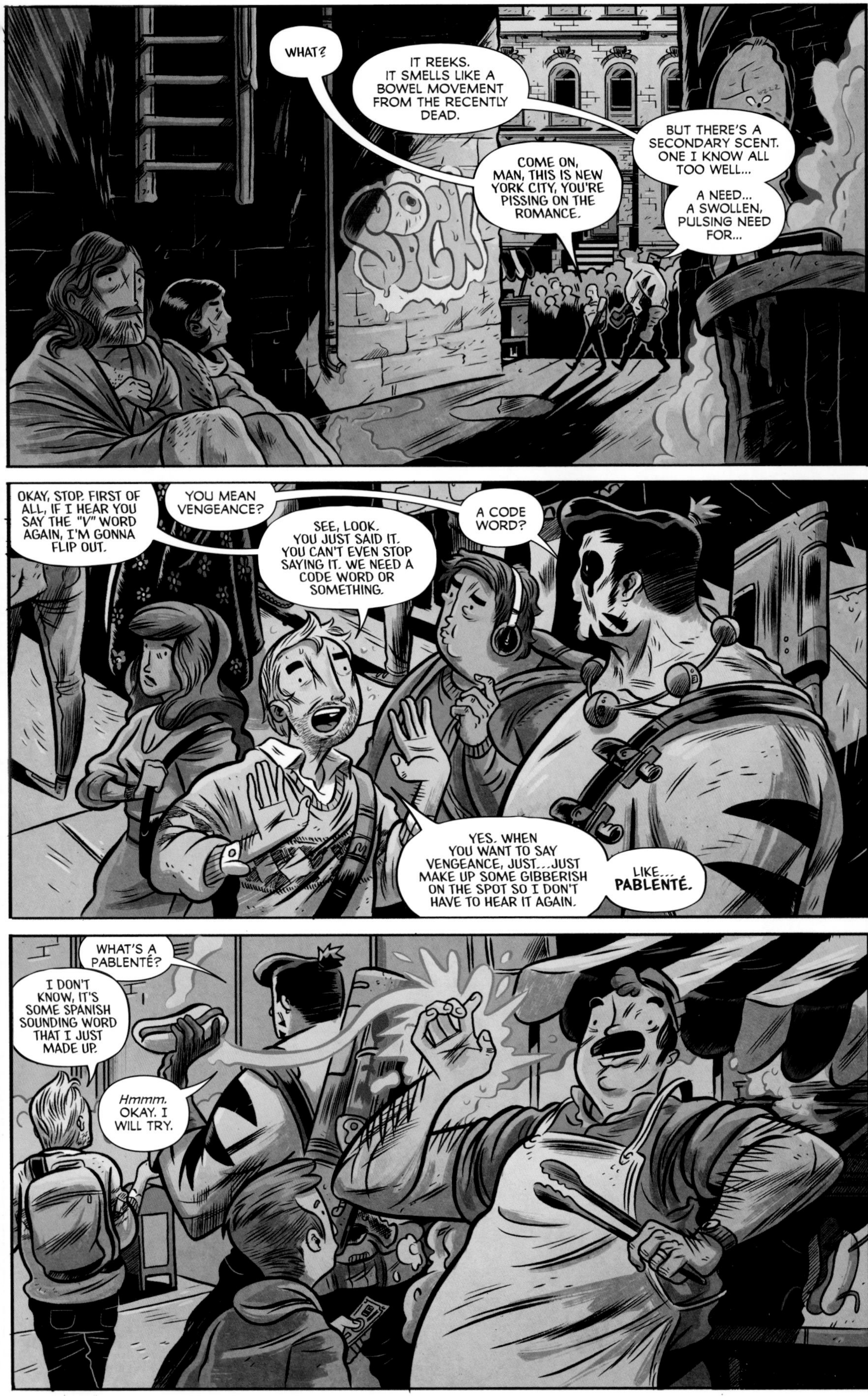
WHAT?
IT REEKS. IT SMELLS LIKE A BOWEL MOVEMENT FROM THE RECENTLY DEAD.
COME ON, MAN, THIS IS NEW YORK CITY, YOU'RE PISSING ON THE ROMANCE.
BUT THERE'S A SECONDARY SCENT. ONE I KNOW ALL TOO WELL...
A NEED... A SWOLLEN, PULSING NEED FOR...
OKAY, STOP. FIRST OF ALL, IF I HEAR YOU SAY THE "V" WORD AGAIN, I'M GONNA FLIP OUT.
YOU MEAN VENGEANCE?
SEE, LOOK. YOU JUST SAID IT. YOU CAN'T EVEN STOP SAYING IT. WE NEED A CODE WORD OR SOMETHING.
A CODE WORD?
YES. WHEN YOU WANT TO SAY VENGEANCE, JUST...JUST MAKE UP SOME GIBBERISH ON THE SPOT SO I DON'T HAVE TO HEAR IT AGAIN.
LIKE... **PABLENTÉ.**
WHAT'S A PABLENTÉ?
I DON'T KNOW, IT'S SOME SPANISH SOUNDING WORD THAT I JUST MADE UP.
Hmmm. OKAY. I WILL TRY.

OKAY, SO IF WE'RE GOING TO ACTUALLY DO THIS, WHICH I CAN'T BELIEVE WE ARE, WE NEED A PLAN.

GO IN. BEAT EVERYONE UP UNTIL THEY SING LIKE CANARIES.

NO. THAT WAS RHETORICAL, KILLSTRIKE, I ACTUALLY ALREADY HAVE A PLAN. THAT'S NOT CRAZY.

ATM

wimp soda

SWIPE!

HALCYON HAS BEEN GETTING A LOT OF FLACK FROM BLOGGERS IN THE PAST YEAR DUE TO REBOOTING ALL THEIR COMICS.

SOMETIMES A BLOGGER'S OPINION CAN MAKE OR BREAK SALES ON A BOOK.

THE THING IS...GENERALLY NOBODY KNOWS WHAT THEY LOOK LIKE.

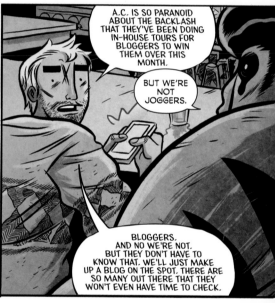

A.C. IS SO PARANOID ABOUT THE BACKLASH THAT THEY'VE BEEN DOING IN-HOUSE TOURS FOR BLOGGERS TO WIN THEM OVER THIS MONTH.

BUT WE'RE NOT JOGGERS.

BLOGGERS. AND NO WE'RE NOT. BUT THEY DON'T HAVE TO KNOW THAT. WE'LL JUST MAKE UP A BLOG ON THE SPOT. THERE ARE SO MANY OUT THERE THAT THEY WON'T EVEN HAVE TIME TO CHECK.

SO *THEN* WE BEAT THEM TO A PULP.

NO, KILLSTRIKE, WE DON'T EVER DO THAT.

CLENCH!

WE'LL JUST SNEAK INTO THE HALCYON EDITORIAL OFFICE AND TELL THEM THE TRUTH.

I'M SURE THEY'LL BE REASONABLE WHEN THEY HEAR I'M PHILLIP HOLLYWEATHER'S SON.

EXCELLENT!

TACTICAL BRILLIANCE, JARED.

UM, THANKS, 'STRIKE.

HA HA, GAY!

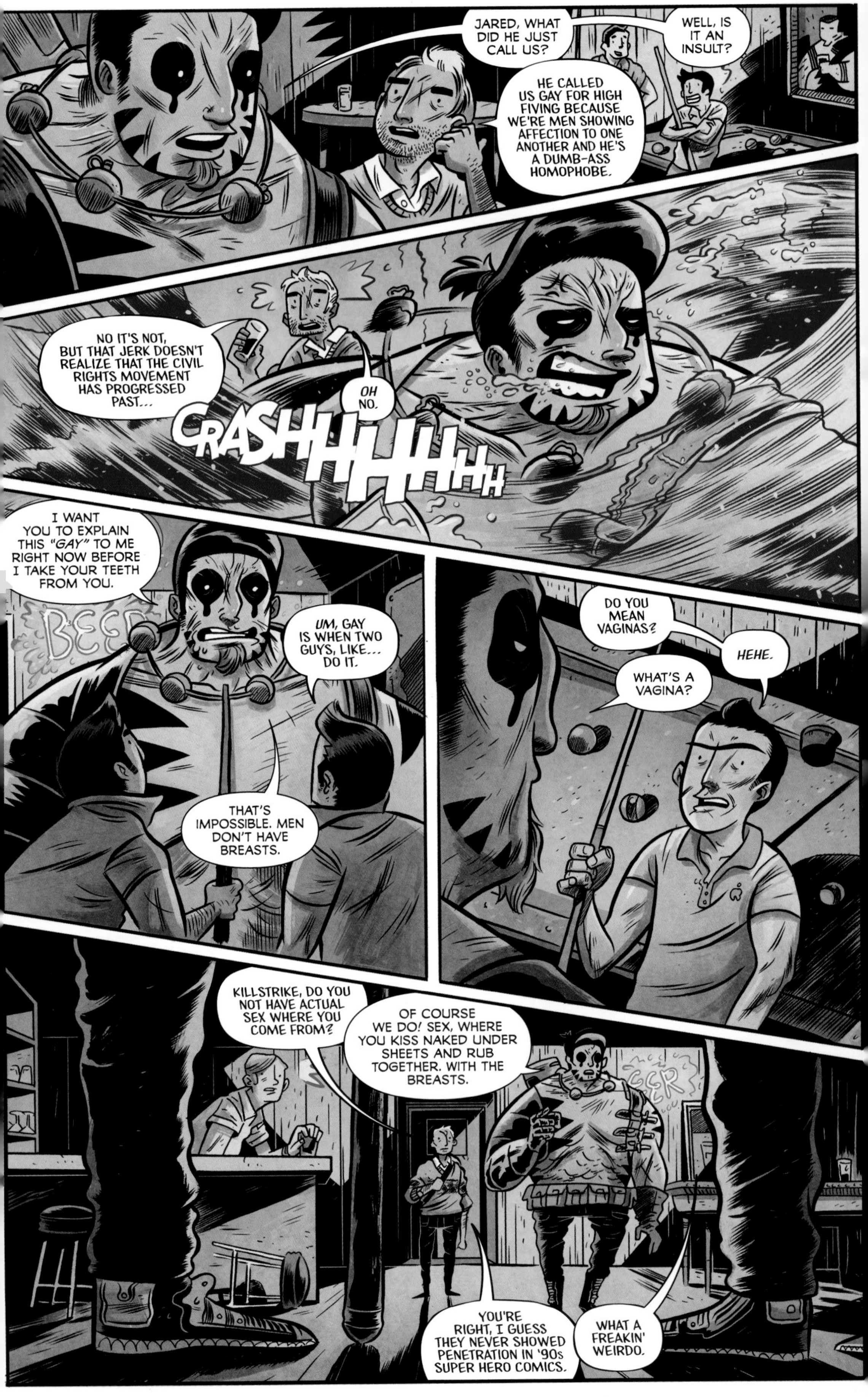
JARED, WHAT DID HE JUST CALL US?
WELL, IS IT AN INSULT?
HE CALLED US GAY FOR HIGH FIVING BECAUSE WE'RE MEN SHOWING AFFECTION TO ONE ANOTHER AND HE'S A DUMB-ASS HOMOPHOBE.
NO IT'S NOT, BUT THAT JERK DOESN'T REALIZE THAT THE CIVIL RIGHTS MOVEMENT HAS PROGRESSED PAST...
OH NO.
CRASHHHHHHHH
I WANT YOU TO EXPLAIN THIS "GAY" TO ME RIGHT NOW BEFORE I TAKE YOUR TEETH FROM YOU.
UM, GAY IS WHEN TWO GUYS, LIKE... DO IT.
THAT'S IMPOSSIBLE. MEN DON'T HAVE BREASTS.
DO YOU MEAN VAGINAS?
HEHE.
WHAT'S A VAGINA?
KILLSTRIKE, DO YOU NOT HAVE ACTUAL SEX WHERE YOU COME FROM?
OF COURSE WE DO! SEX, WHERE YOU KISS NAKED UNDER SHEETS AND RUB TOGETHER. WITH THE BREASTS.
YOU'RE RIGHT, I GUESS THEY NEVER SHOWED PENETRATION IN '90s SUPER HERO COMICS.
WHAT A FREAKIN' WEIRDO.

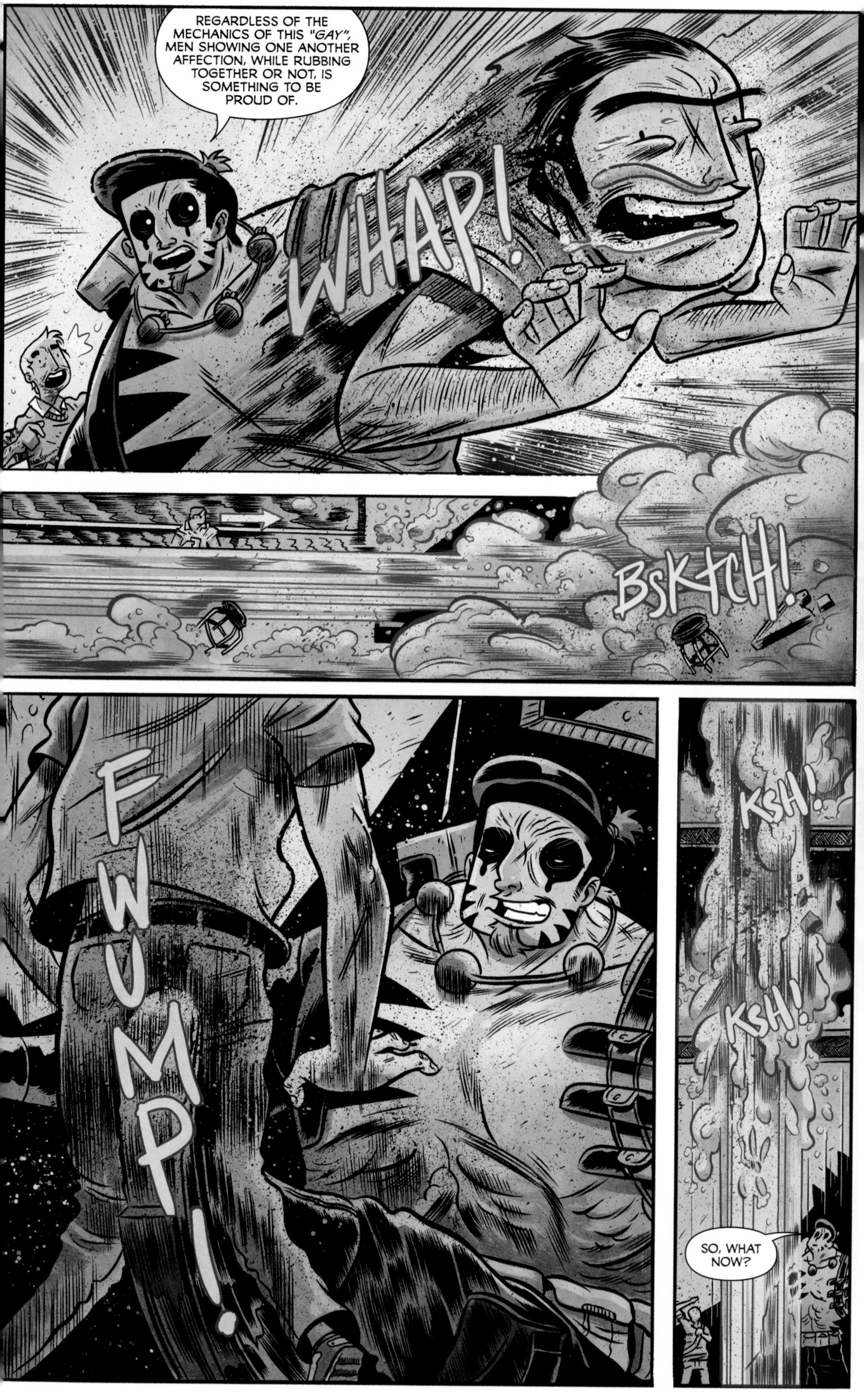
REGARDLESS OF THE MECHANICS OF THIS "GAY", MEN SHOWING ONE ANOTHER AFFECTION, WHILE RUBBING TOGETHER OR NOT, IS SOMETHING TO BE PROUD OF.
WHAP!
BSKTCH!
FWUMP!
KSH!
KSH!
SO, WHAT NOW?

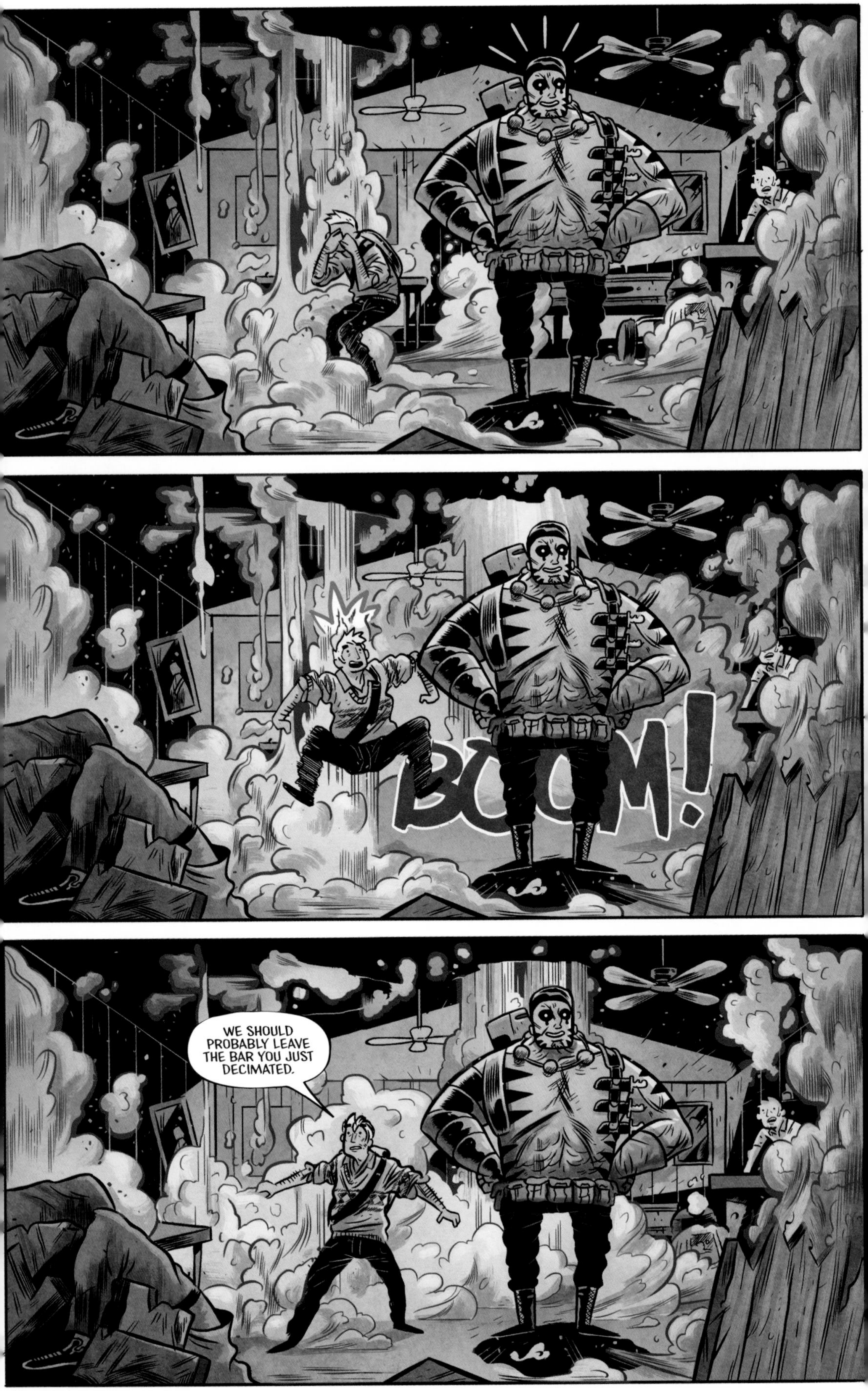
BOOM!
WE SHOULD PROBABLY LEAVE THE BAR YOU JUST DECIMATED.

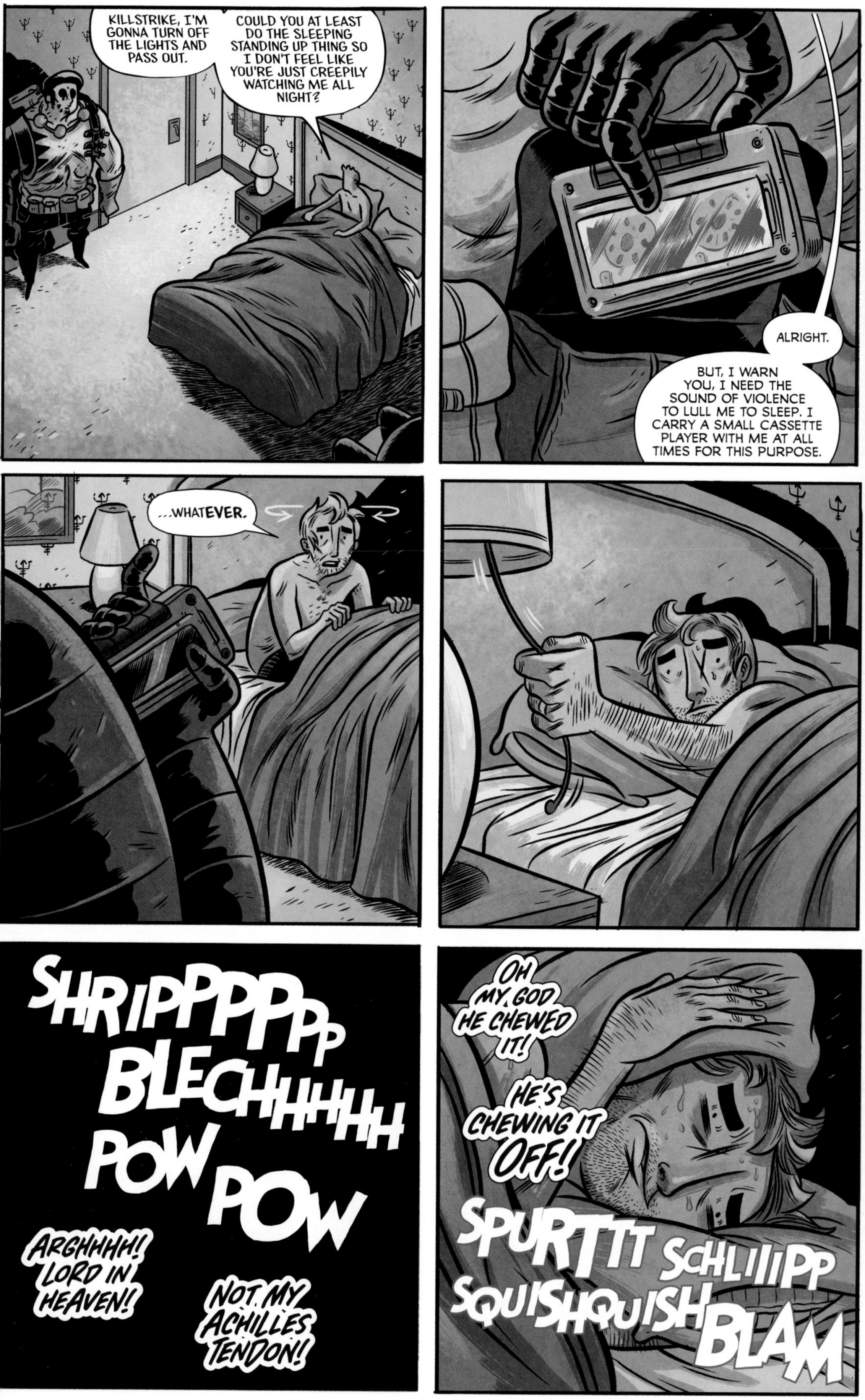

KILLSTRIKE, I'M GONNA TURN OFF THE LIGHTS AND PASS OUT.
COULD YOU AT LEAST DO THE SLEEPING STANDING UP THING SO I DON'T FEEL LIKE YOU'RE JUST CREEPILY WATCHING ME ALL NIGHT?
ALRIGHT.
BUT, I WARN YOU, I NEED THE SOUND OF VIOLENCE TO LULL ME TO SLEEP. I CARRY A SMALL CASSETTE PLAYER WITH ME AT ALL TIMES FOR THIS PURPOSE.
...WHATEVER.
SHRIPPPPPPP
BLECHHHHHHH
POW POW
ARGHHHH! LORD IN HEAVEN!
NOT MY ACHILLES TENDON!
OH MY GOD HE CHEWED IT!
HE'S CHEWING IT OFF!
SPURTTT SCHLIIIPP
SQUISHQUISH BLAM

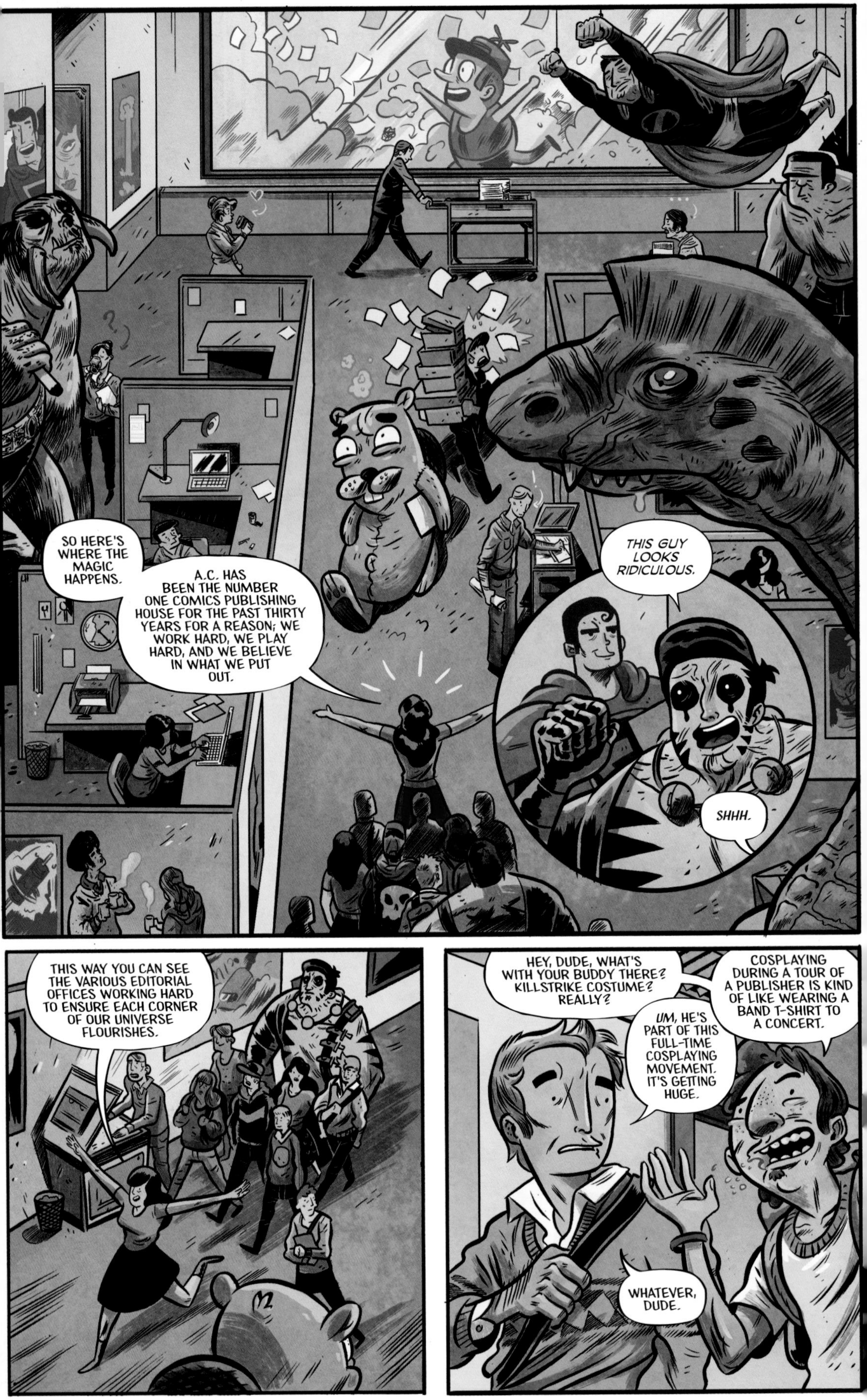
SO HERE'S WHERE THE MAGIC HAPPENS.
A.C. HAS BEEN THE NUMBER ONE COMICS PUBLISHING HOUSE FOR THE PAST THIRTY YEARS FOR A REASON; WE WORK HARD, WE PLAY HARD, AND WE BELIEVE IN WHAT WE PUT OUT.
THIS GUY LOOKS RIDICULOUS.
SHHH.
THIS WAY YOU CAN SEE THE VARIOUS EDITORIAL OFFICES WORKING HARD TO ENSURE EACH CORNER OF OUR UNIVERSE FLOURISHES.
HEY, DUDE, WHAT'S WITH YOUR BUDDY THERE? KILLSTRIKE COSTUME? REALLY?
UM, HE'S PART OF THIS FULL-TIME COSPLAYING MOVEMENT. IT'S GETTING HUGE.
COSPLAYING DURING A TOUR OF A PUBLISHER IS KIND OF LIKE WEARING A BAND T-SHIRT TO A CONCERT.
WHATEVER, DUDE.

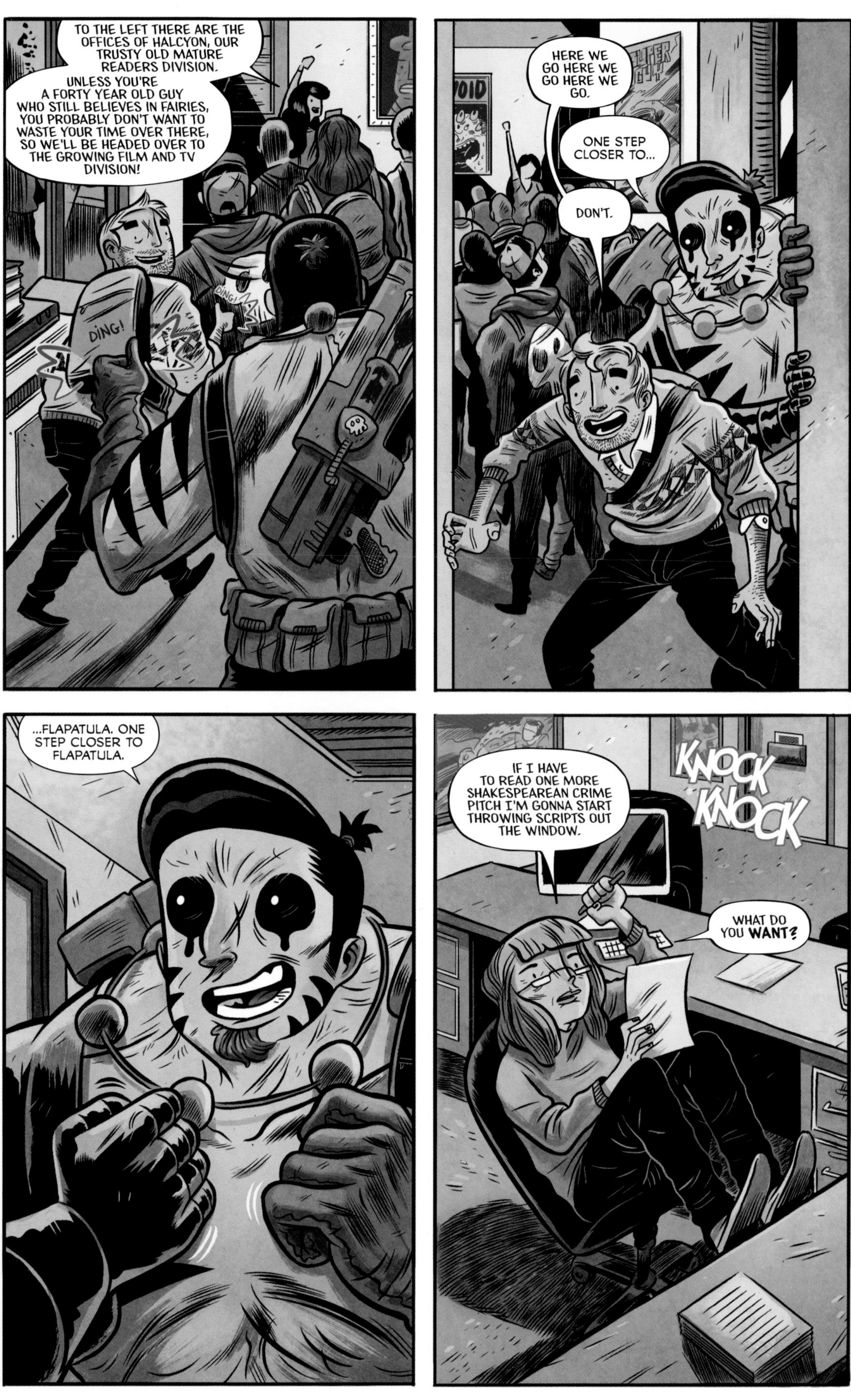
TO THE LEFT THERE ARE THE OFFICES OF HALCYON, OUR TRUSTY OLD MATURE READERS DIVISION.
UNLESS YOU'RE A FORTY YEAR OLD GUY WHO STILL BELIEVES IN FAIRIES, YOU PROBABLY DON'T WANT TO WASTE YOUR TIME OVER THERE, SO WE'LL BE HEADED OVER TO THE GROWING FILM AND TV DIVISION!
DING!
DING!
HERE WE GO HERE WE GO HERE WE GO.
ONE STEP CLOSER TO...
DON'T.
...FLAPATULA. ONE STEP CLOSER TO FLAPATULA.
IF I HAVE TO READ ONE MORE SHAKESPEAREAN CRIME PITCH I'M GONNA START THROWING SCRIPTS OUT THE WINDOW.
KNOCK KNOCK
WHAT DO YOU **WANT?**

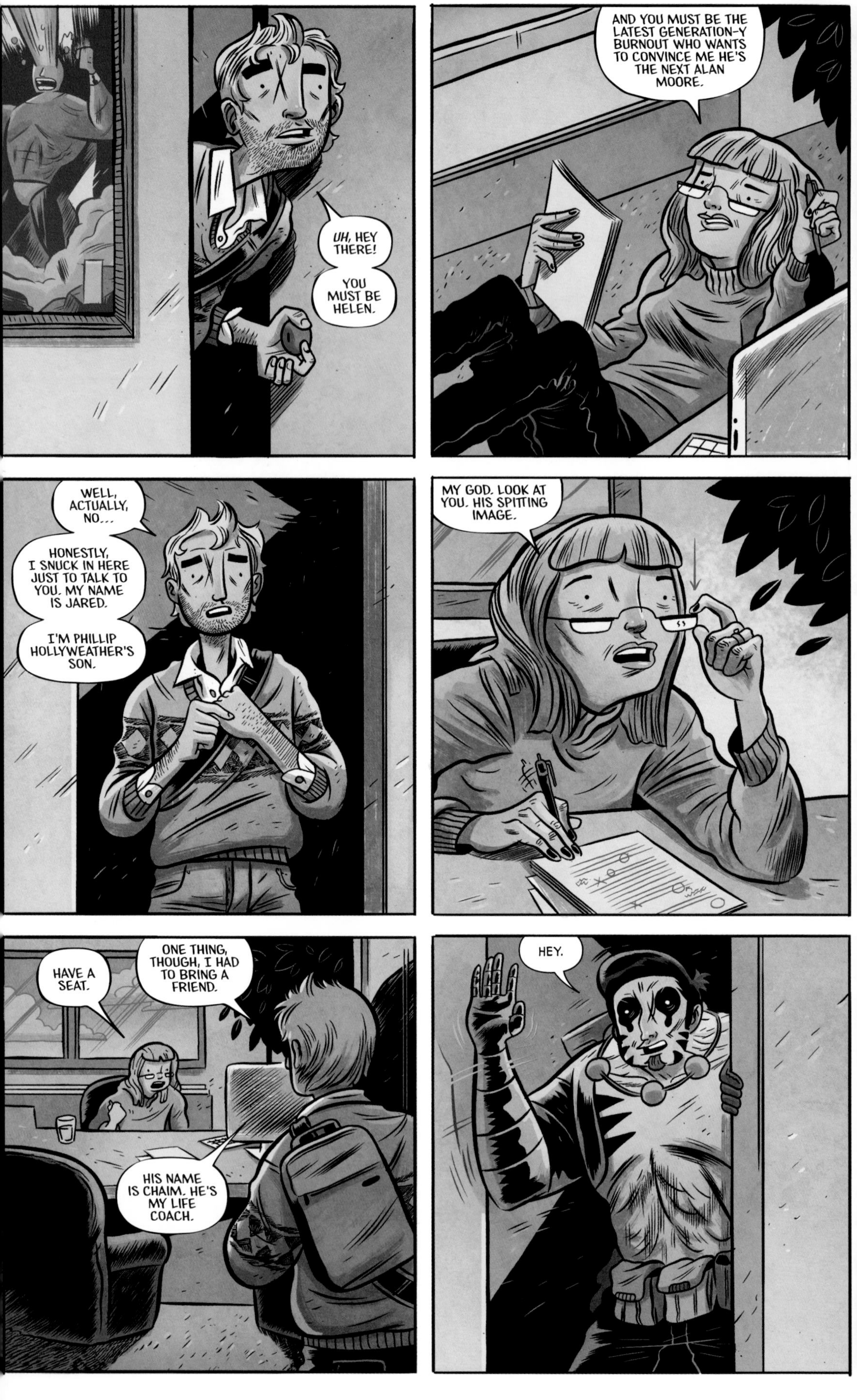
UH, HEY THERE!
YOU MUST BE HELEN.
AND YOU MUST BE THE LATEST GENERATION-Y BURNOUT WHO WANTS TO CONVINCE ME HE'S THE NEXT ALAN MOORE.
WELL, ACTUALLY, NO...
HONESTLY, I SNUCK IN HERE JUST TO TALK TO YOU. MY NAME IS JARED.
I'M PHILLIP HOLLYWEATHER'S SON.
MY GOD. LOOK AT YOU. HIS SPITTING IMAGE.
HAVE A SEAT.
ONE THING, THOUGH, I HAD TO BRING A FRIEND.
HIS NAME IS CHAIM. HE'S MY LIFE COACH.
HEY.

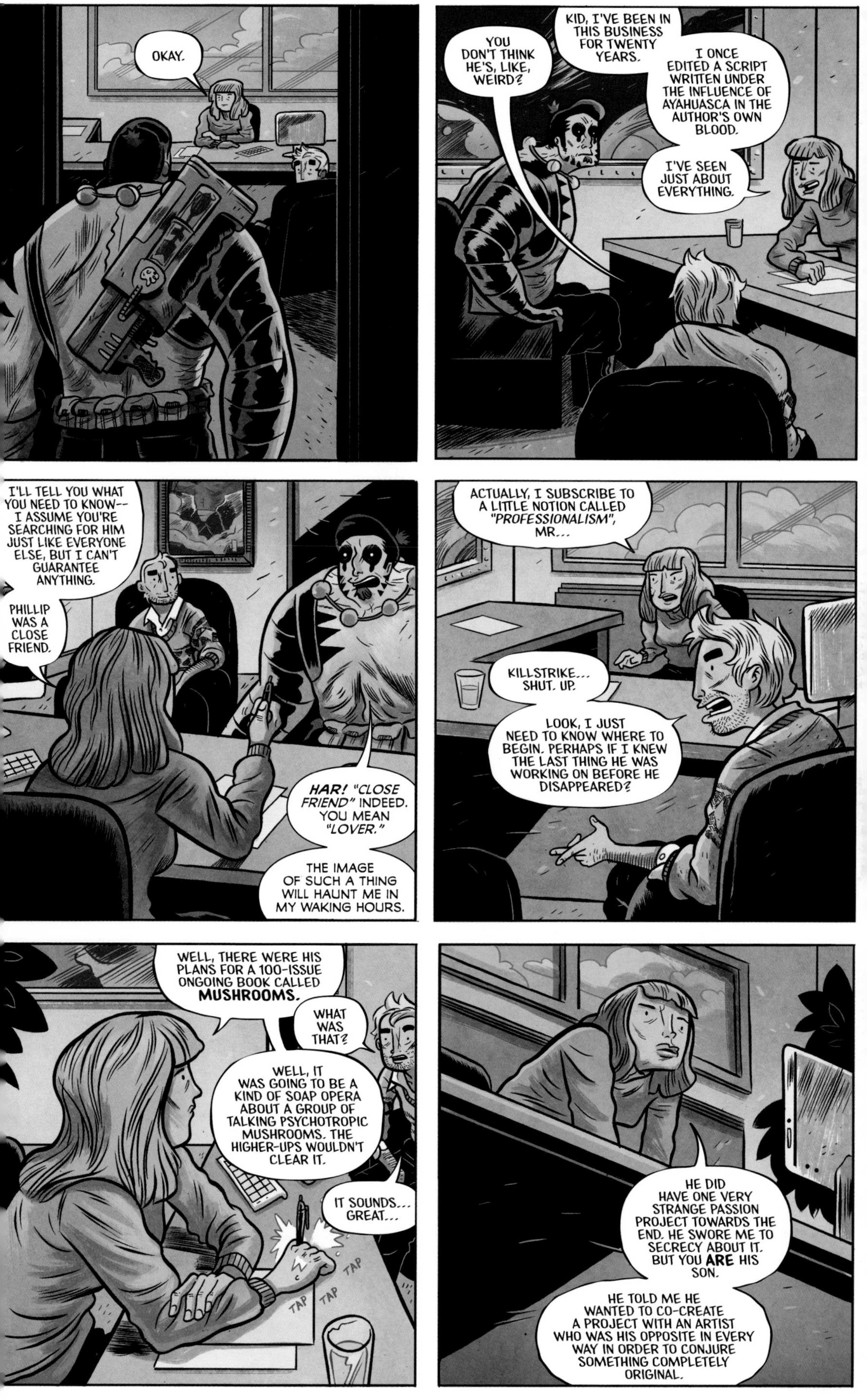
OKAY.
YOU DON'T THINK HE'S, LIKE, WEIRD?
KID, I'VE BEEN IN THIS BUSINESS FOR TWENTY YEARS.
I ONCE EDITED A SCRIPT WRITTEN UNDER THE INFLUENCE OF AYAHUASCA IN THE AUTHOR'S OWN BLOOD.
I'VE SEEN JUST ABOUT EVERYTHING.
I'LL TELL YOU WHAT YOU NEED TO KNOW-- I ASSUME YOU'RE SEARCHING FOR HIM JUST LIKE EVERYONE ELSE, BUT I CAN'T GUARANTEE ANYTHING.
PHILLIP WAS A CLOSE FRIEND.
HAR! "CLOSE FRIEND" INDEED. YOU MEAN "LOVER."
THE IMAGE OF SUCH A THING WILL HAUNT ME IN MY WAKING HOURS.
ACTUALLY, I SUBSCRIBE TO A LITTLE NOTION CALLED "PROFESSIONALISM", MR...
KILLSTRIKE... SHUT. UP.
LOOK, I JUST NEED TO KNOW WHERE TO BEGIN. PERHAPS IF I KNEW THE LAST THING HE WAS WORKING ON BEFORE HE DISAPPEARED?
WELL, THERE WERE HIS PLANS FOR A 100-ISSUE ONGOING BOOK CALLED MUSHROOMS.
WHAT WAS THAT?
WELL, IT WAS GOING TO BE A KIND OF SOAP OPERA ABOUT A GROUP OF TALKING PSYCHOTROPIC MUSHROOMS. THE HIGHER-UPS WOULDN'T CLEAR IT.
IT SOUNDS... GREAT...
TAP TAP TAP
HE DID HAVE ONE VERY STRANGE PASSION PROJECT TOWARDS THE END. HE SWORE ME TO SECRECY ABOUT IT. BUT YOU ARE HIS SON.
HE TOLD ME HE WANTED TO CO-CREATE A PROJECT WITH AN ARTIST WHO WAS HIS OPPOSITE IN EVERY WAY IN ORDER TO CONJURE SOMETHING COMPLETELY ORIGINAL.

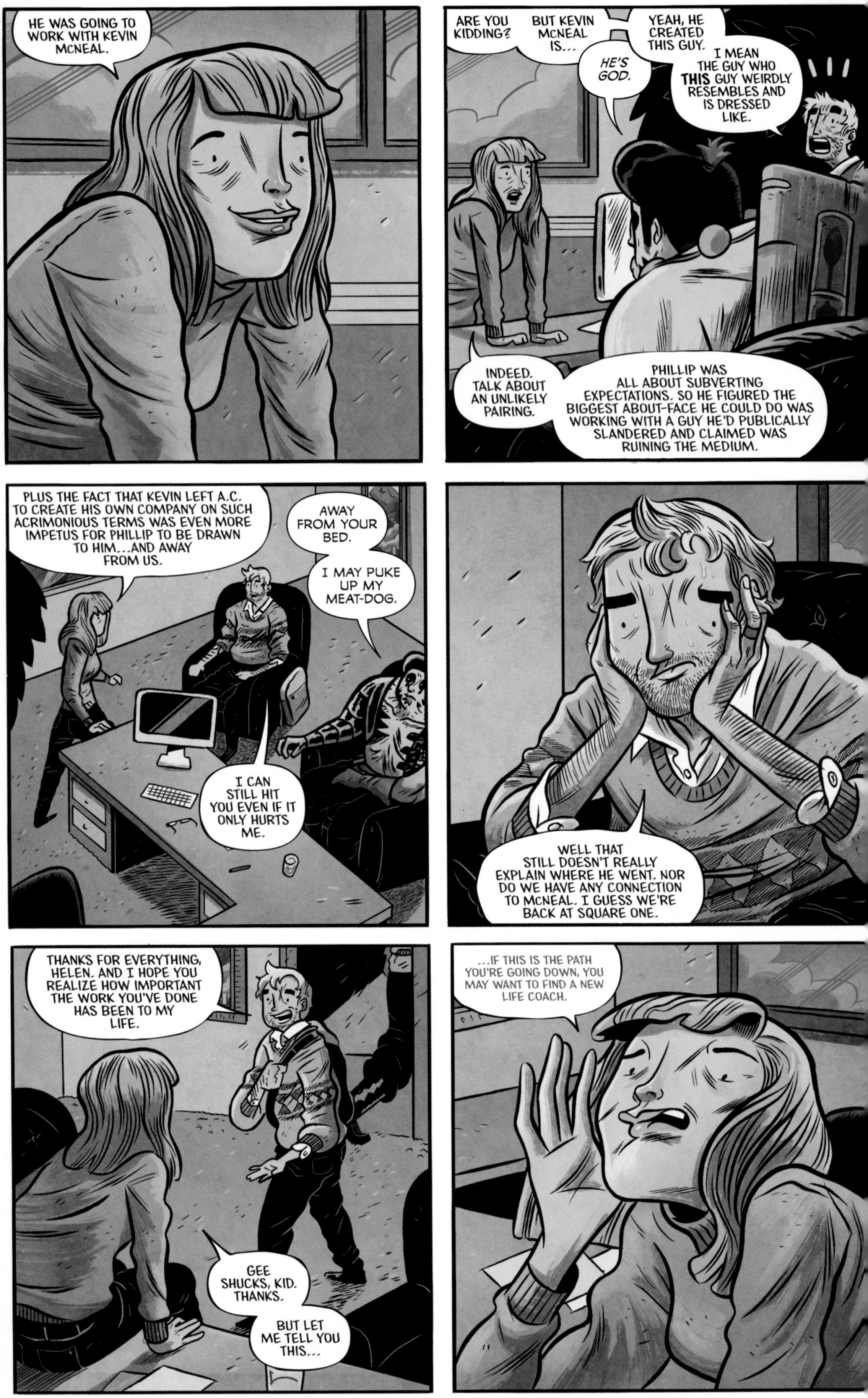
HE WAS GOING TO WORK WITH KEVIN McNEAL.
ARE YOU KIDDING?
BUT KEVIN McNEAL IS...
HE'S GOD.
YEAH, HE CREATED THIS GUY.
I MEAN THE GUY WHO THIS GUY WEIRDLY RESEMBLES AND IS DRESSED LIKE.
INDEED. TALK ABOUT AN UNLIKELY PAIRING.
PHILLIP WAS ALL ABOUT SUBVERTING EXPECTATIONS. SO HE FIGURED THE BIGGEST ABOUT-FACE HE COULD DO WAS WORKING WITH A GUY HE'D PUBLICALLY SLANDERED AND CLAIMED WAS RUINING THE MEDIUM.
PLUS THE FACT THAT KEVIN LEFT A.C. TO CREATE HIS OWN COMPANY ON SUCH ACRIMONIOUS TERMS WAS EVEN MORE IMPETUS FOR PHILLIP TO BE DRAWN TO HIM...AND AWAY FROM US.
AWAY FROM YOUR BED.
I MAY PUKE UP MY MEAT-DOG.
I CAN STILL HIT YOU EVEN IF IT ONLY HURTS ME.
WELL THAT STILL DOESN'T REALLY EXPLAIN WHERE HE WENT. NOR DO WE HAVE ANY CONNECTION TO McNEAL. I GUESS WE'RE BACK AT SQUARE ONE.
THANKS FOR EVERYTHING, HELEN. AND I HOPE YOU REALIZE HOW IMPORTANT THE WORK YOU'VE DONE HAS BEEN TO MY LIFE.
GEE SHUCKS, KID. THANKS.
BUT LET ME TELL YOU THIS...
...IF THIS IS THE PATH YOU'RE GOING DOWN, YOU MAY WANT TO FIND A NEW LIFE COACH.

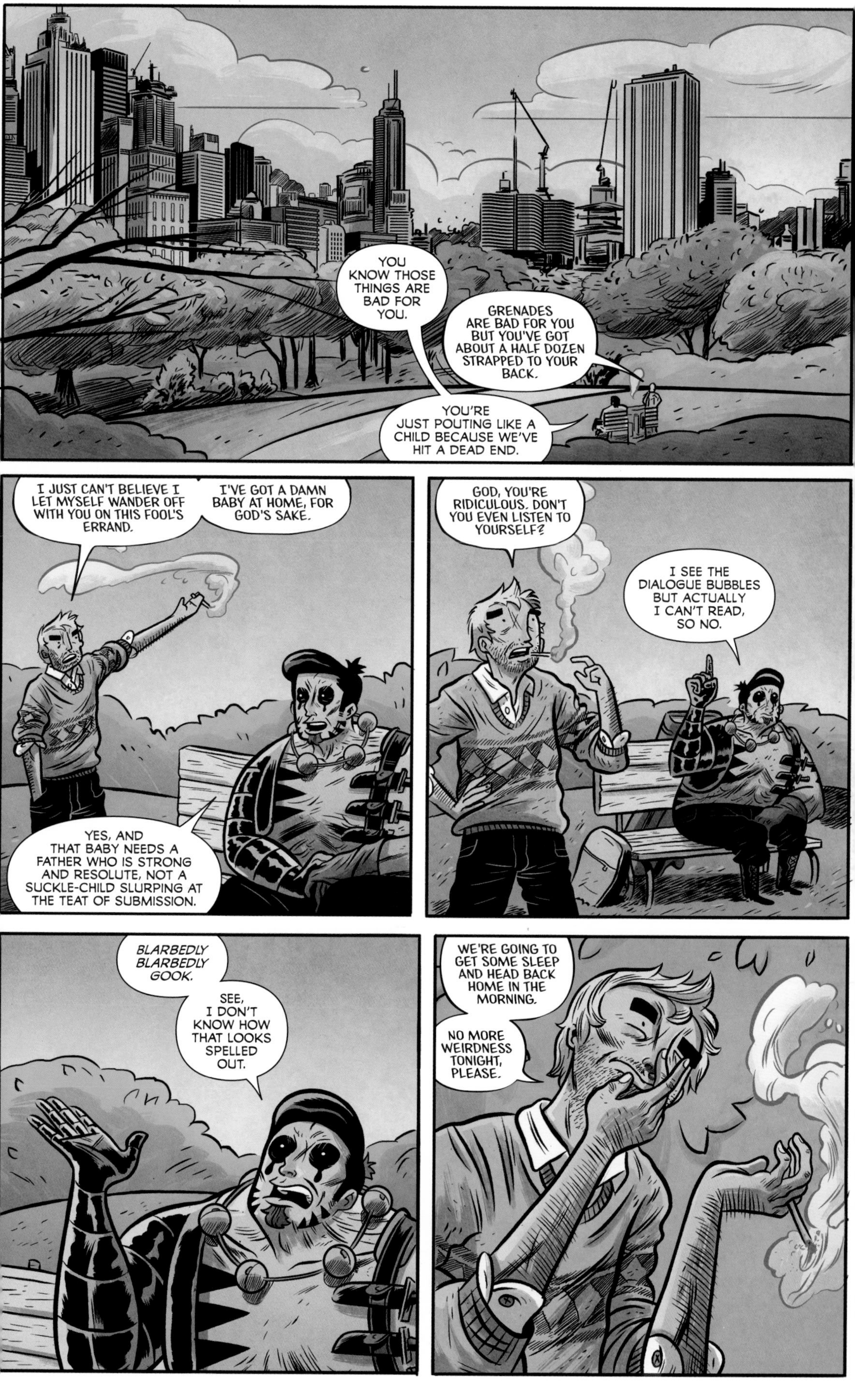
YOU KNOW THOSE THINGS ARE BAD FOR YOU.
GRENADES ARE BAD FOR YOU BUT YOU'VE GOT ABOUT A HALF DOZEN STRAPPED TO YOUR BACK.
YOU'RE JUST POUTING LIKE A CHILD BECAUSE WE'VE HIT A DEAD END.
I JUST CAN'T BELIEVE I LET MYSELF WANDER OFF WITH YOU ON THIS FOOL'S ERRAND.
I'VE GOT A DAMN BABY AT HOME, FOR GOD'S SAKE.
YES, AND THAT BABY NEEDS A FATHER WHO IS STRONG AND RESOLUTE, NOT A SUCKLE-CHILD SLURPING AT THE TEAT OF SUBMISSION.
GOD, YOU'RE RIDICULOUS. DON'T YOU EVEN LISTEN TO YOURSELF?
I SEE THE DIALOGUE BUBBLES BUT ACTUALLY I CAN'T READ, SO NO.
BLARBEDLY BLARBEDLY GOOK.
SEE, I DON'T KNOW HOW THAT LOOKS SPELLED OUT.
WE'RE GOING TO GET SOME SLEEP AND HEAD BACK HOME IN THE MORNING.
NO MORE WEIRDNESS TONIGHT, PLEASE.

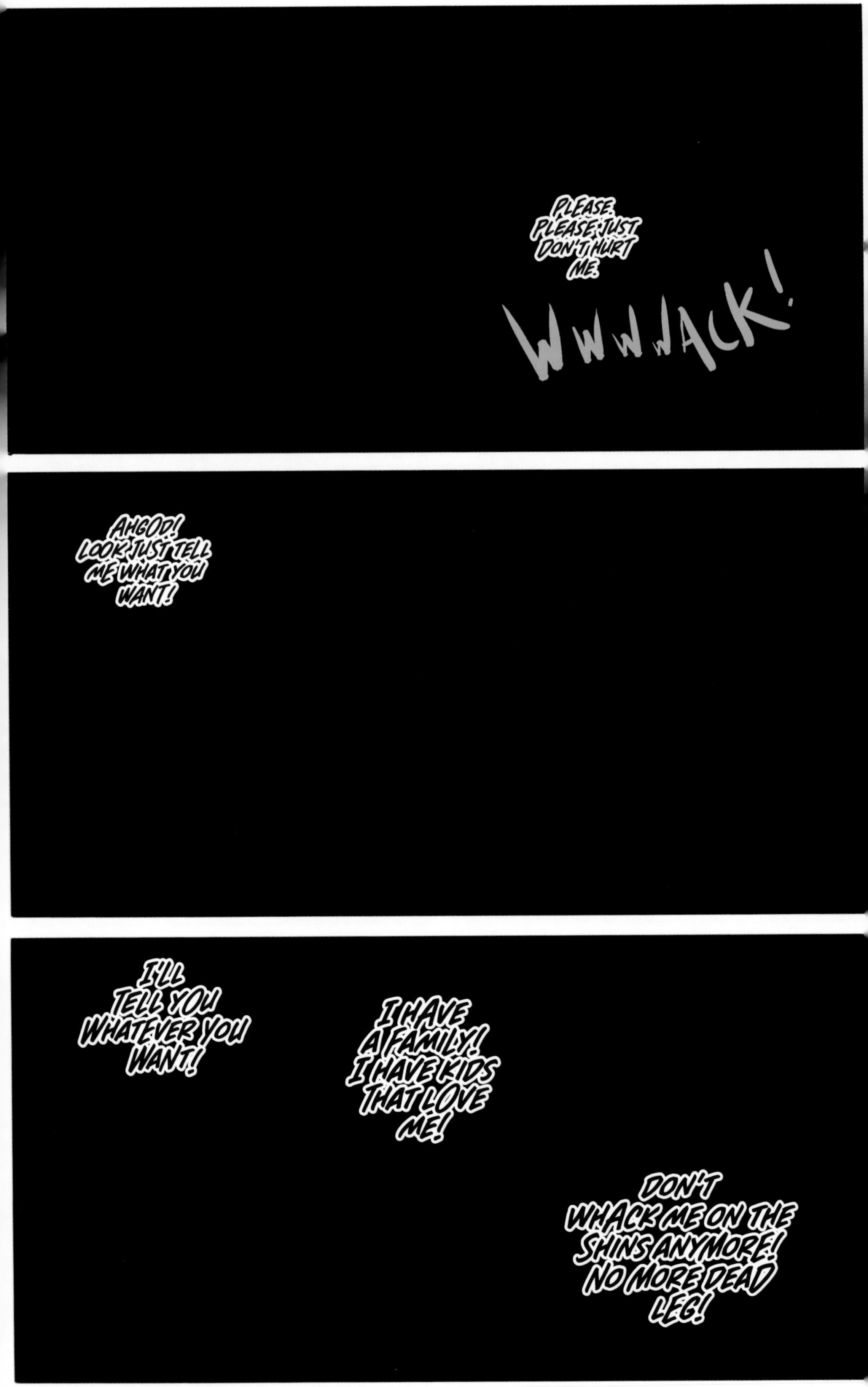
PLEASE. PLEASE JUST DON'T HURT ME.
WWWWACK!
AHGOD! LOOK JUST TELL ME WHAT YOU WANT!
I'LL TELL YOU WHATEVER YOU WANT!
I HAVE A FAMILY! I HAVE KIDS THAT LOVE ME!
DON'T WHACK ME ON THE SHINS ANYMORE! NO MORE DEAD LEG!

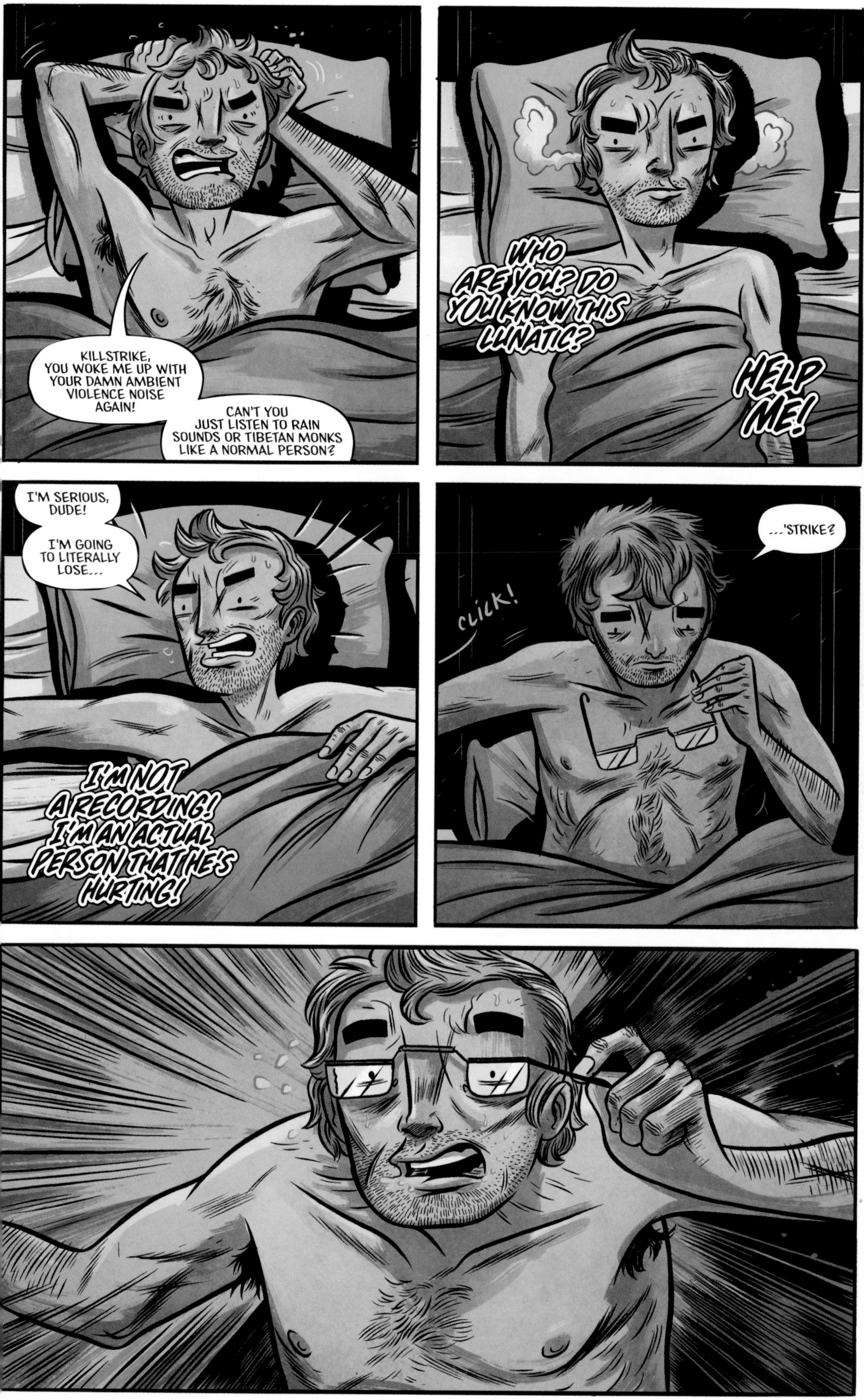
KILLSTRIKE, YOU WOKE ME UP WITH YOUR DAMN AMBIENT VIOLENCE NOISE AGAIN!
CAN'T YOU JUST LISTEN TO RAIN SOUNDS OR TIBETAN MONKS LIKE A NORMAL PERSON?
WHO ARE YOU? DO YOU KNOW THIS LUNATIC?
HELP ME!
I'M SERIOUS, DUDE!
I'M GOING TO LITERALLY LOSE...
I'M NOT A RECORDING! I'M AN ACTUAL PERSON THAT HE'S HURTING!
CLICK!
...'STRIKE?

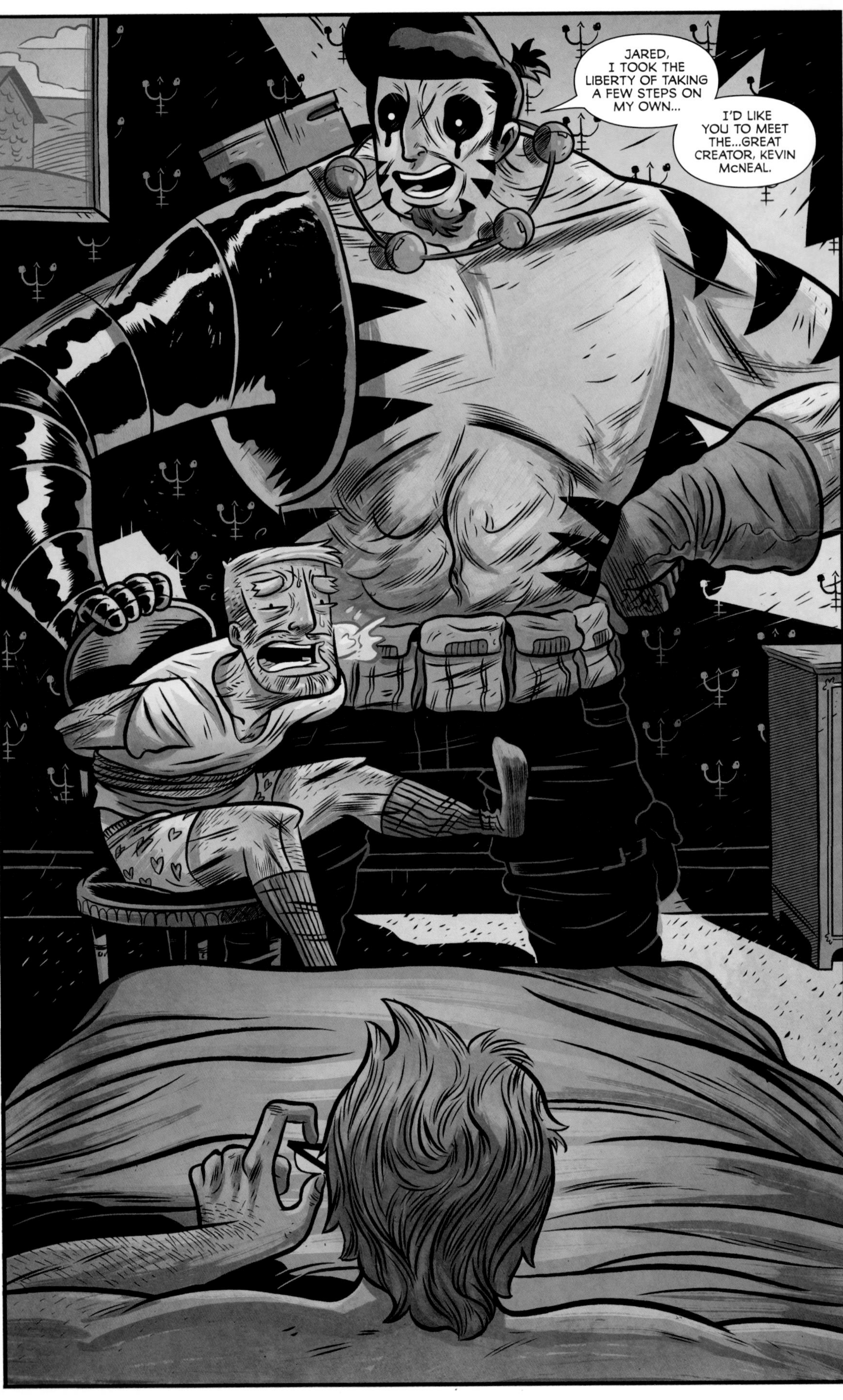
JARED, I TOOK THE LIBERTY OF TAKING A FEW STEPS ON MY OWN...
I'D LIKE YOU TO MEET THE...GREAT CREATOR, KEVIN McNEAL.

SQUISHQUISH

chapter
THREE

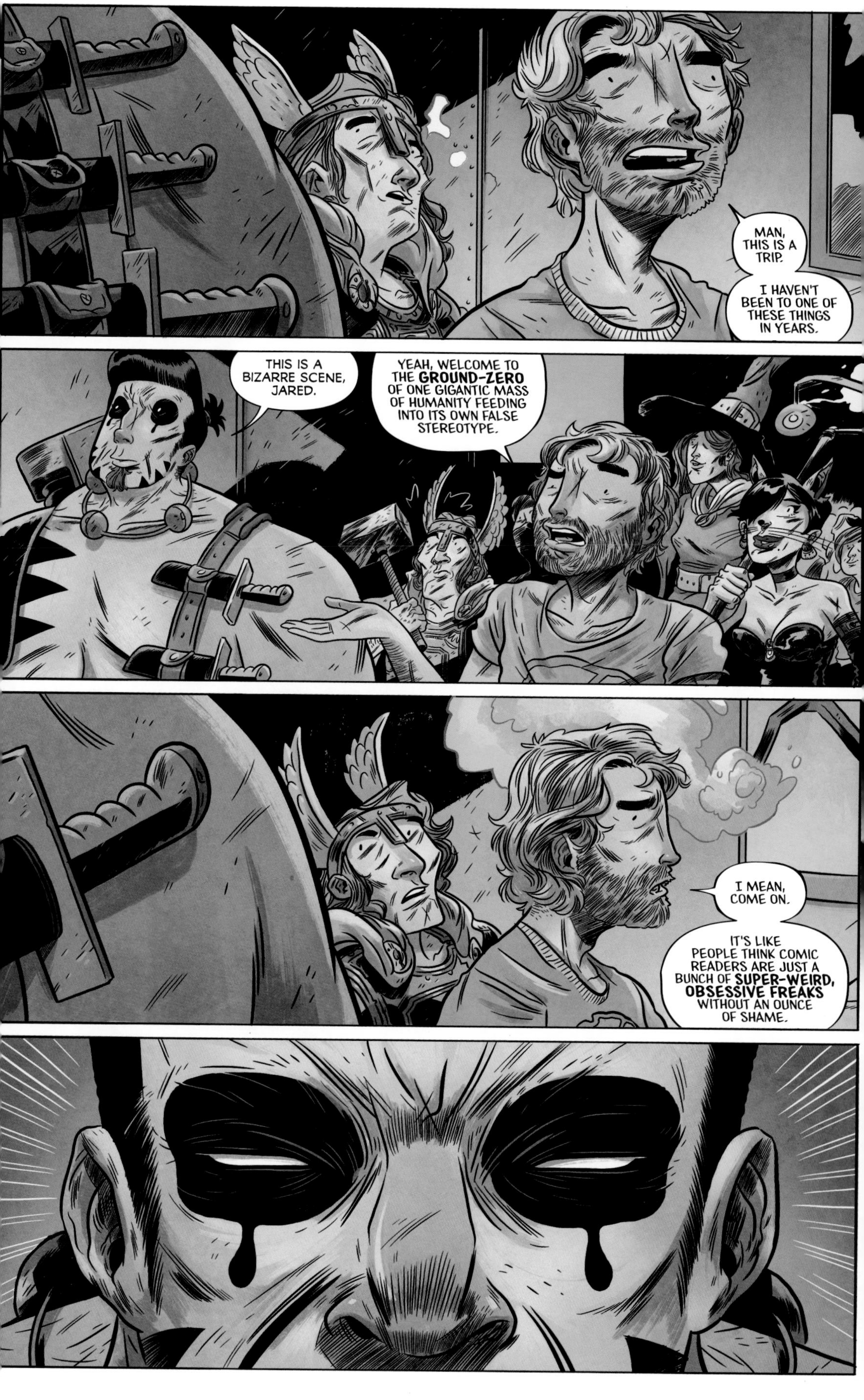
MAN, THIS IS A TRIP.
I HAVEN'T BEEN TO ONE OF THESE THINGS IN YEARS.
THIS IS A BIZARRE SCENE, JARED.
YEAH, WELCOME TO THE **GROUND-ZERO** OF ONE GIGANTIC MASS OF HUMANITY FEEDING INTO ITS OWN FALSE STEREOTYPE.
I MEAN, COME ON.
IT'S LIKE PEOPLE THINK COMIC READERS ARE JUST A BUNCH OF **SUPER-WEIRD, OBSESSIVE FREAKS** WITHOUT AN OUNCE OF SHAME.

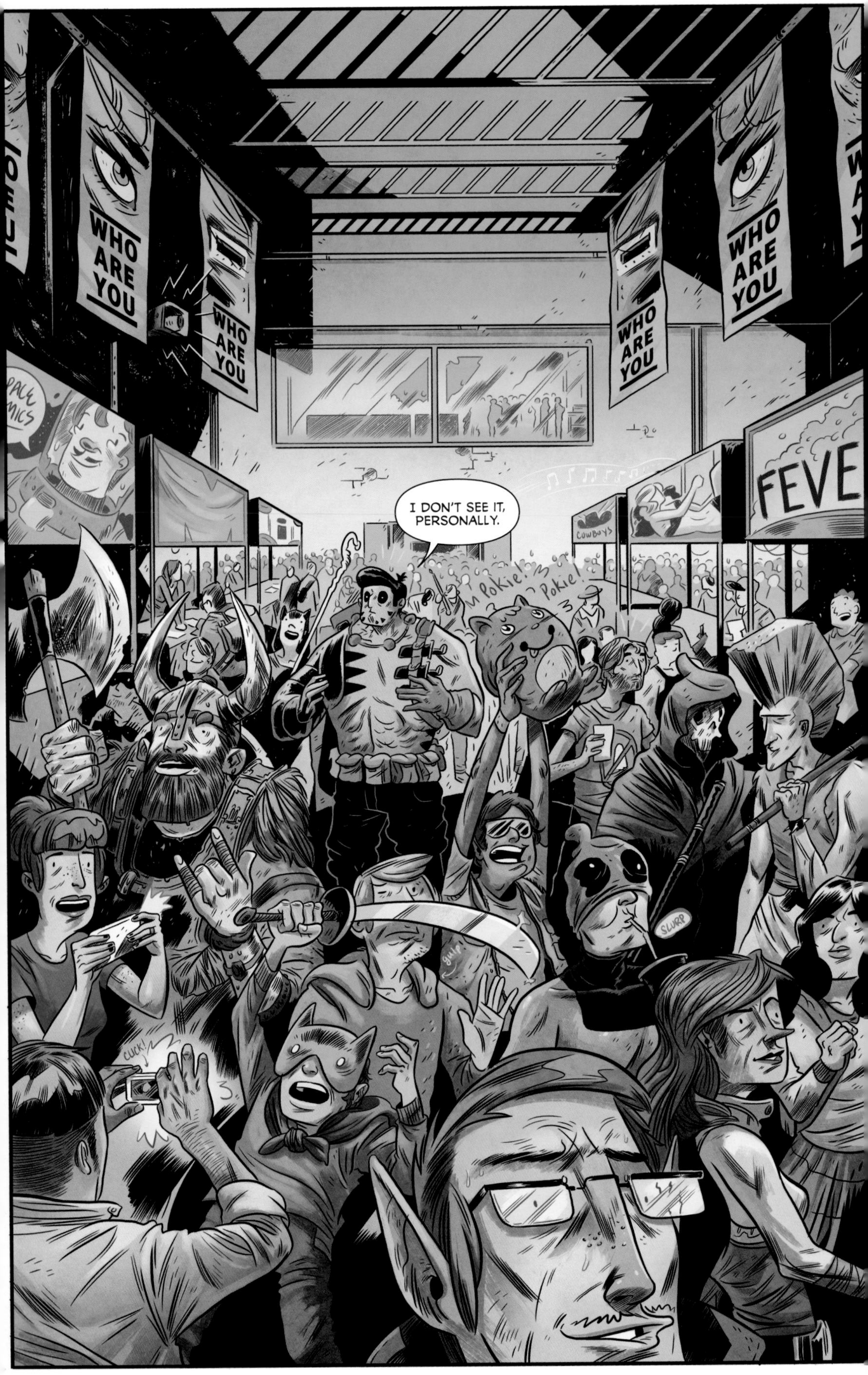
WHO ARE YOU
WHO ARE YOU
WHO ARE YOU
WHO ARE YOU
I DON'T SEE IT, PERSONALLY.
Pokie! Pokie!
COWBOYS
FEVE
SLURP
gulp
CLICK!

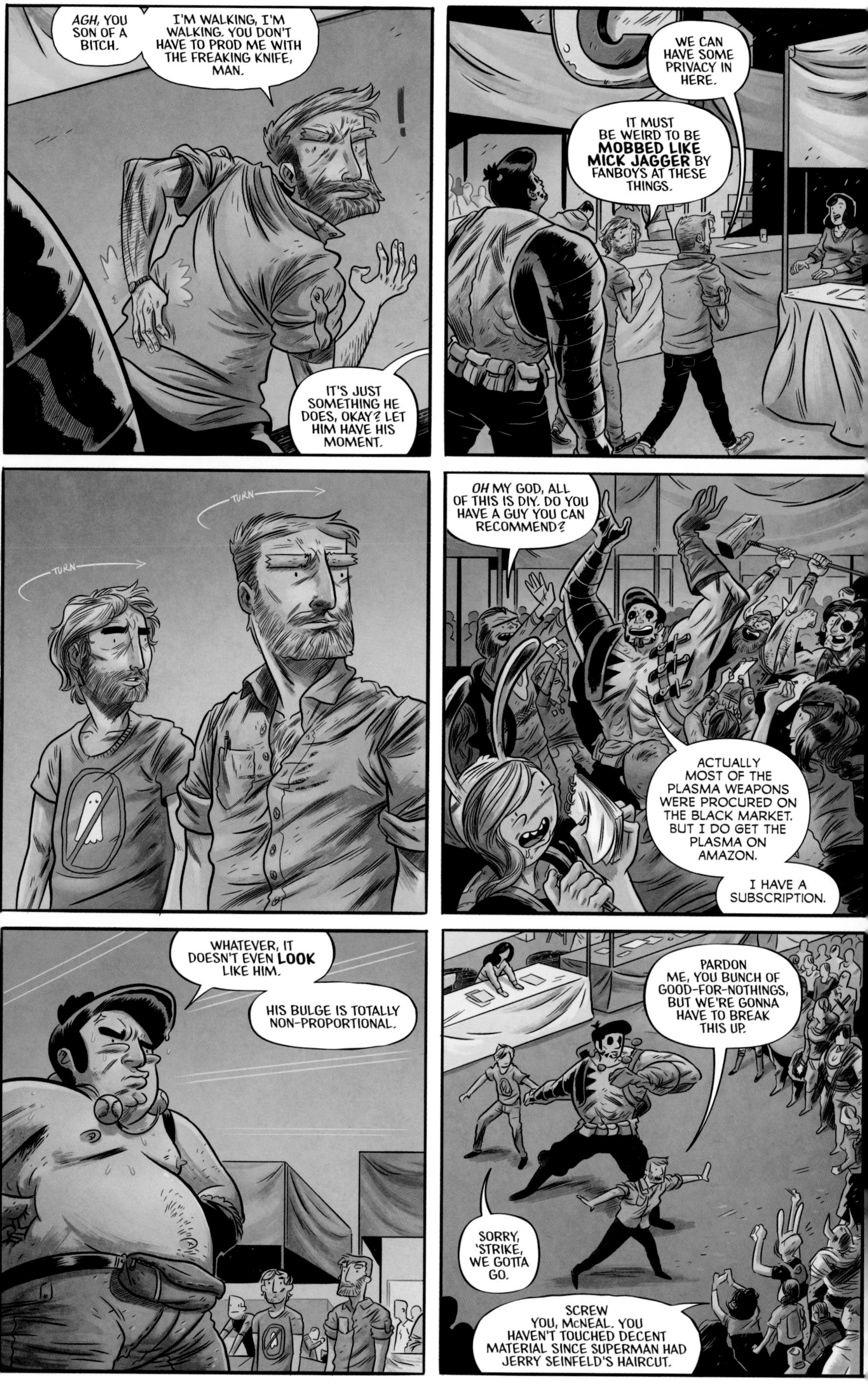
AGH, YOU SON OF A BITCH.
I'M WALKING, I'M WALKING. YOU DON'T HAVE TO PROD ME WITH THE FREAKING KNIFE, MAN.
!
IT'S JUST SOMETHING HE DOES, OKAY? LET HIM HAVE HIS MOMENT.
WE CAN HAVE SOME PRIVACY IN HERE.
IT MUST BE WEIRD TO BE MOBBED LIKE MICK JAGGER BY FANBOYS AT THESE THINGS.
TURN
TURN
OH MY GOD, ALL OF THIS IS DIY. DO YOU HAVE A GUY YOU CAN RECOMMEND?
ACTUALLY MOST OF THE PLASMA WEAPONS WERE PROCURED ON THE BLACK MARKET. BUT I DO GET THE PLASMA ON AMAZON.
I HAVE A SUBSCRIPTION.
WHATEVER, IT DOESN'T EVEN LOOK LIKE HIM.
HIS BULGE IS TOTALLY NON-PROPORTIONAL.
PARDON ME, YOU BUNCH OF GOOD-FOR-NOTHINGS, BUT WE'RE GONNA HAVE TO BREAK THIS UP.
SORRY, 'STRIKE, WE GOTTA GO.
SCREW YOU, McNEAL. YOU HAVEN'T TOUCHED DECENT MATERIAL SINCE SUPERMAN HAD JERRY SEINFELD'S HAIRCUT.

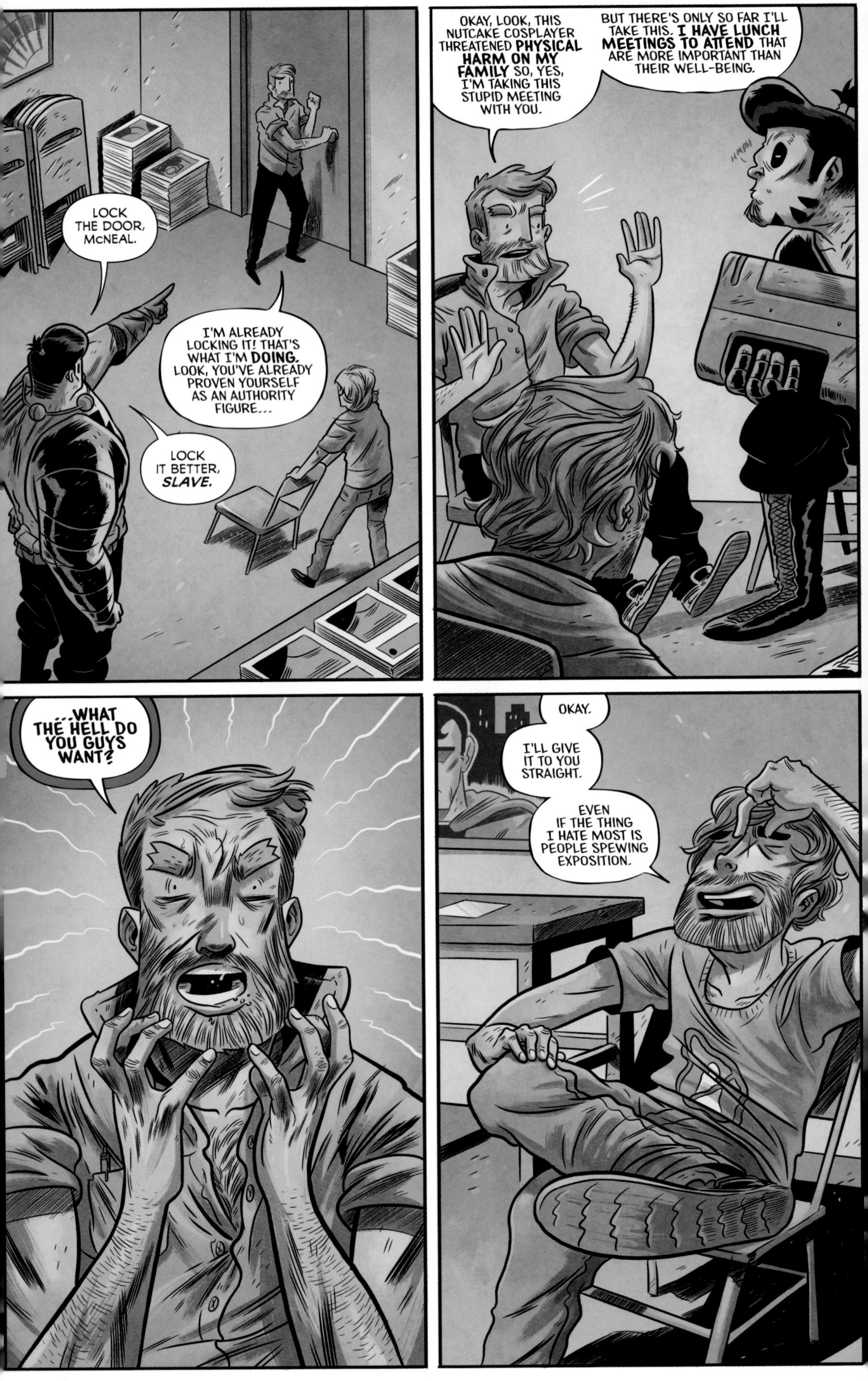
LOCK THE DOOR, McNEAL.
I'M ALREADY LOCKING IT! THAT'S WHAT I'M **DOING.** LOOK, YOU'VE ALREADY PROVEN YOURSELF AS AN AUTHORITY FIGURE...
LOCK IT BETTER, ***SLAVE.***
OKAY, LOOK, THIS NUTCAKE COSPLAYER THREATENED **PHYSICAL HARM ON MY FAMILY** SO, YES, I'M TAKING THIS STUPID MEETING WITH YOU.
BUT THERE'S ONLY SO FAR I'LL TAKE THIS. **I HAVE LUNCH MEETINGS TO ATTEND** THAT ARE MORE IMPORTANT THAN THEIR WELL-BEING.
HMPH
...WHAT THE HELL DO YOU GUYS WANT?
OKAY.
I'LL GIVE IT TO YOU STRAIGHT.
EVEN IF THE THING I HATE MOST IS PEOPLE SPEWING EXPOSITION.

AT LEAST FIVE PANELS OF DIALOGUE LATER (COMPLETELY USELESS TO ANYONE WHO'S READ THE FIRST TWO ISSUES, AND, REALLY, *WHO THE HELL JUMPS IN ON ISSUE THREE OF A FOUR ISSUE BOOK?*)...

HOLY HELL. YOU REALLY ARE HIM. PHIL'S BOY.

JUST...PLEASE ONLY REFER TO HIM AS PHILLIP. *IT KILLS ME.*

NOBODY NAMED PHIL WOULD HAVE CREATED A GRAPHIC NOVEL CALLED *"THE PAUCILOQUENTS"*.

AND AS HARD TO BELIEVE AS IT IS, THIS GUY REALLY DOES LOOK LIKE THE ORIGINAL KILLSTRIKE CHARACTER DESIGN...*TO A T.*

I SPENT LIKE, *FIVE HOURS* ON THESE POUCHES.

JARED, THE MAN IS STROKING ME...

LOOK, IF YOU *"DESIGNED"* ME, YOU KNOW THE SIZE OF HOLE THIS THING CAN PUT IN A MAN'S CRANIUM.

ALRIGHT, ALRIGHT...

LOOK, YOUR FATHER AND I NEVER WERE BOSOM BUDDIES TO BEGIN WITH...

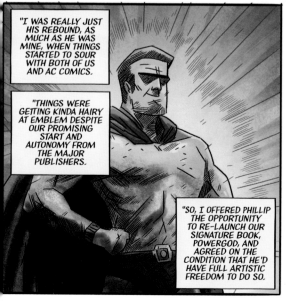

"I WAS REALLY JUST HIS REBOUND, AS MUCH AS HE WAS MINE, WHEN THINGS STARTED TO SOUR WITH BOTH OF US AND AC COMICS.

"THINGS WERE GETTING KINDA HAIRY AT EMBLEM DESPITE OUR PROMISING START AND AUTONOMY FROM THE MAJOR PUBLISHERS.

"SO, I OFFERED PHILLIP THE OPPORTUNITY TO RE-LAUNCH OUR SIGNATURE BOOK, POWERGOD, AND AGREED ON THE CONDITION THAT HE'D HAVE FULL ARTISTIC FREEDOM TO DO SO.

"SUFFICE TO SAY, HIS INTERPRETATION WASN'T A SUCCESS. AS USUAL, PHILLIP TRIED TO INCORPORATE HIS IDEAS ABOUT ANARCHISM, ANIMAL RIGHTS, AND METAPHYSICS INTO THE COMIC."

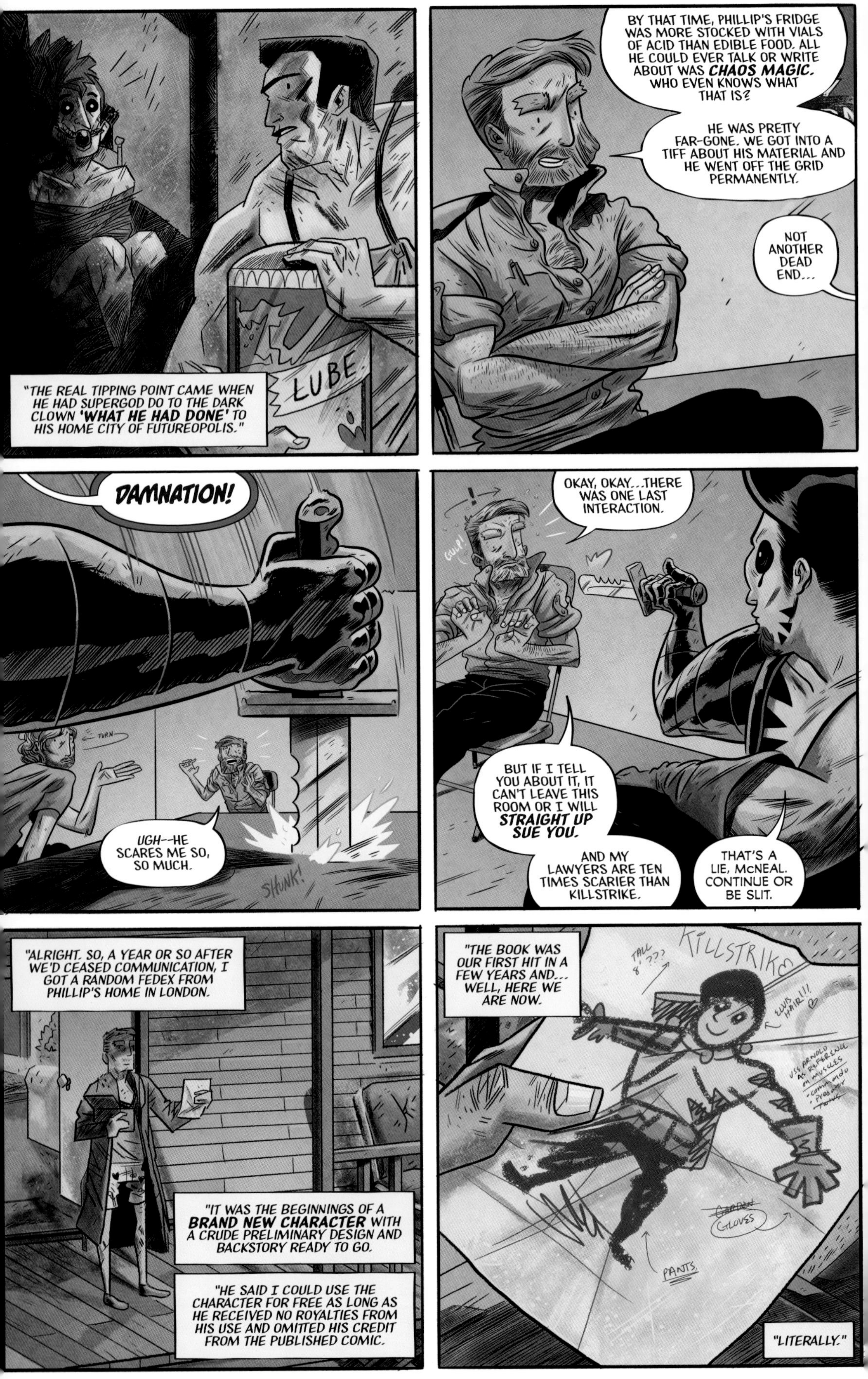

"THE REAL TIPPING POINT CAME WHEN HE HAD SUPERGOD DO TO THE DARK CLOWN **'WHAT HE HAD DONE'** TO HIS HOME CITY OF FUTUREOPOLIS."
LUBE
BY THAT TIME, PHILLIP'S FRIDGE WAS MORE STOCKED WITH VIALS OF ACID THAN EDIBLE FOOD. ALL HE COULD EVER TALK OR WRITE ABOUT WAS ***CHAOS MAGIC.*** WHO EVEN KNOWS WHAT THAT IS?
HE WAS PRETTY FAR-GONE. WE GOT INTO A TIFF ABOUT HIS MATERIAL AND HE WENT OFF THE GRID PERMANENTLY.
NOT ANOTHER DEAD END...
DAMNATION!
TURN
UGH--HE SCARES ME SO, SO MUCH.
SHUNK!
OKAY, OKAY...THERE WAS ONE LAST INTERACTION.
GULP!
BUT IF I TELL YOU ABOUT IT, IT CAN'T LEAVE THIS ROOM OR I WILL ***STRAIGHT UP SUE YOU.***
AND MY LAWYERS ARE TEN TIMES SCARIER THAN KILLSTRIKE.
THAT'S A LIE, McNEAL. CONTINUE OR BE SLIT.
"ALRIGHT. SO, A YEAR OR SO AFTER WE'D CEASED COMMUNICATION, I GOT A RANDOM FEDEX FROM PHILLIP'S HOME IN LONDON.
"IT WAS THE BEGINNINGS OF A **BRAND NEW CHARACTER** WITH A CRUDE PRELIMINARY DESIGN AND BACKSTORY READY TO GO.
"HE SAID I COULD USE THE CHARACTER FOR FREE AS LONG AS HE RECEIVED NO ROYALTIES FROM HIS USE AND OMITTED HIS CREDIT FROM THE PUBLISHED COMIC.
"THE BOOK WAS OUR FIRST HIT IN A FEW YEARS AND... WELL, HERE WE ARE NOW.
KILLSTRIKE
TALL 8'???
ELVIS HAIR!!!
GLOVES
PANTS.
"LITERALLY."

THIS IS IT, MY DELICATE AND INTREPID NEW FRIEND!

WE MUST MAKE OUR WAY TO YOUR FATHER'S HOME OURSELVES, AS IT SEEMS BOTH OF OUR ORIGINS STEM FROM THE SAME TREE!

OW. NO BRO-MASSAGE, NO BRO-MASSAGE.

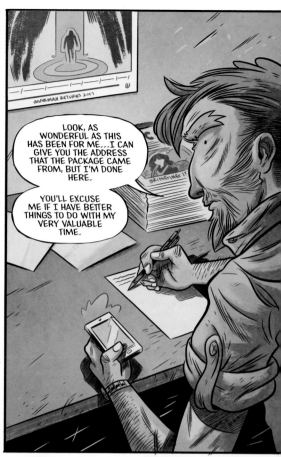

BANKMAN RETURNS 2017

LOOK, AS WONDERFUL AS THIS HAS BEEN FOR ME...I CAN GIVE YOU THE ADDRESS THAT THE PACKAGE CAME FROM, BUT I'M DONE HERE.

YOU'LL EXCUSE ME IF I HAVE BETTER THINGS TO DO WITH MY VERY VALUABLE TIME.

LOOK, BUDDY, YOU HAVE SOME NERVE LOOKING AT US AS LESSER THAN YOU JUST BECAUSE I'M JUST A COMIC FAN AND...HE'S SOME KIND OF GIANT MUTATED ABERRATION.

GIVEN WHAT YOU CREATED WITH EMBLEM IN THE '90s RUINED COMIC BOOKS FOR GOOD.

UNZIP

MAN, I'VE ALWAYS WANTED TO SAY THAT NOT ON A MESSAGE-BOARD.

JARED, I'VE MET YOUR KIND A THOUSAND TIMES BEFORE.

AND FRANKLY YOU HAVE NO IDEA WHAT YOU'RE TALKING ABOUT.

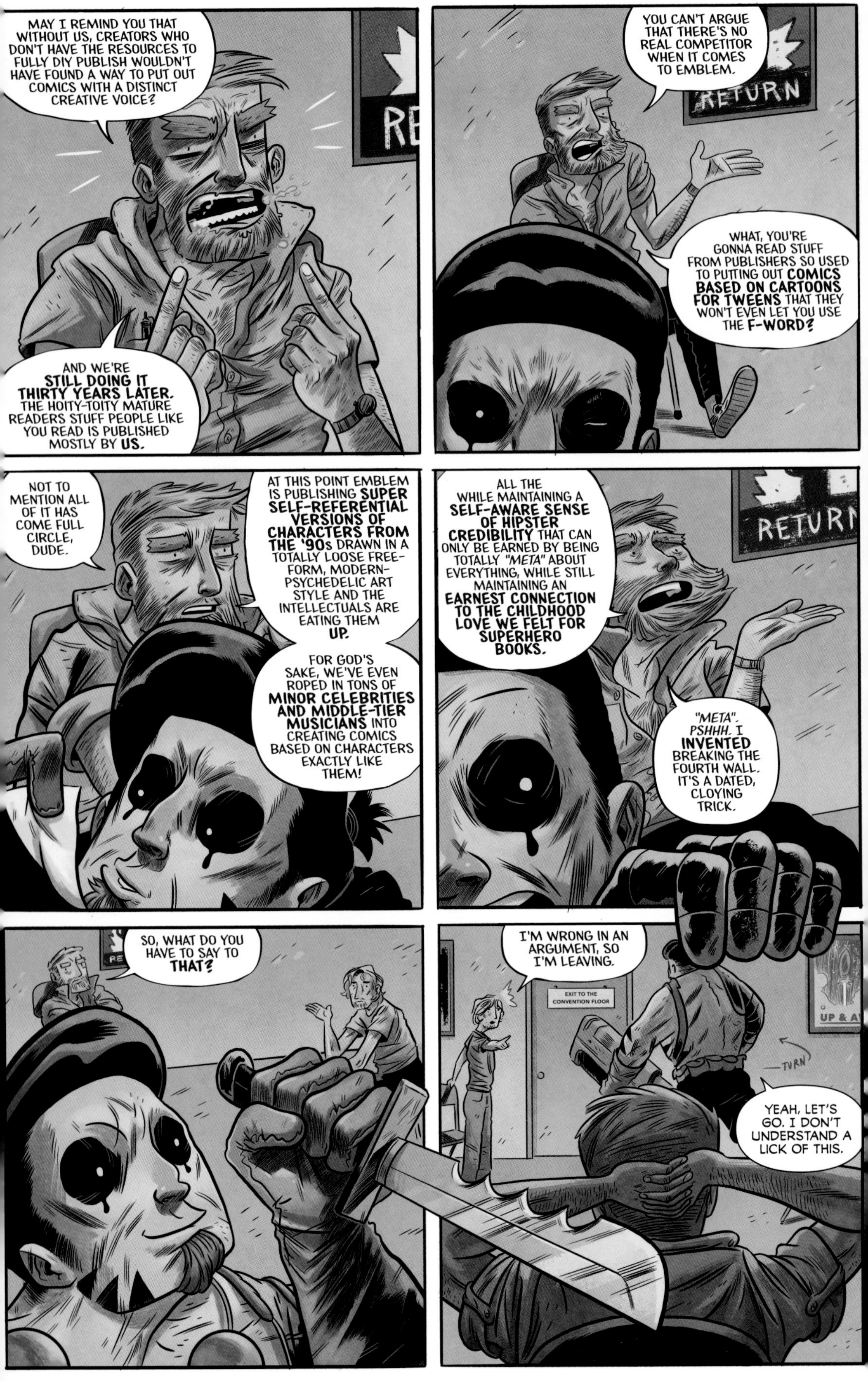
MAY I REMIND YOU THAT WITHOUT US, CREATORS WHO DON'T HAVE THE RESOURCES TO FULLY DIY PUBLISH WOULDN'T HAVE FOUND A WAY TO PUT OUT COMICS WITH A DISTINCT CREATIVE VOICE?
AND WE'RE STILL DOING IT THIRTY YEARS LATER. THE HOITY-TOITY MATURE READERS STUFF PEOPLE LIKE YOU READ IS PUBLISHED MOSTLY BY US.
RE
YOU CAN'T ARGUE THAT THERE'S NO REAL COMPETITOR WHEN IT COMES TO EMBLEM.
RETURN
WHAT, YOU'RE GONNA READ STUFF FROM PUBLISHERS SO USED TO PUTTING OUT COMICS BASED ON CARTOONS FOR TWEENS THAT THEY WON'T EVEN LET YOU USE THE F-WORD?
NOT TO MENTION ALL OF IT HAS COME FULL CIRCLE, DUDE.
AT THIS POINT EMBLEM IS PUBLISHING SUPER SELF-REFERENTIAL VERSIONS OF CHARACTERS FROM THE '90s DRAWN IN A TOTALLY LOOSE FREE-FORM, MODERN-PSYCHEDELIC ART STYLE AND THE INTELLECTUALS ARE EATING THEM UP.
FOR GOD'S SAKE, WE'VE EVEN ROPED IN TONS OF MINOR CELEBRITIES AND MIDDLE-TIER MUSICIANS INTO CREATING COMICS BASED ON CHARACTERS EXACTLY LIKE THEM!
ALL THE WHILE MAINTAINING A SELF-AWARE SENSE OF HIPSTER CREDIBILITY THAT CAN ONLY BE EARNED BY BEING TOTALLY "META" ABOUT EVERYTHING, WHILE STILL MAINTAINING AN EARNEST CONNECTION TO THE CHILDHOOD LOVE WE FELT FOR SUPERHERO BOOKS.
RETURN
"META". PSHHH. I INVENTED BREAKING THE FOURTH WALL. IT'S A DATED, CLOYING TRICK.
SO, WHAT DO YOU HAVE TO SAY TO THAT?
I'M WRONG IN AN ARGUMENT, SO I'M LEAVING.
EXIT TO THE CONVENTION FLOOR
UP & A
TURN
YEAH, LET'S GO. I DON'T UNDERSTAND A LICK OF THIS.

HOW MUCH IS THIS ONE?

KAT-POP

IT'S $250 DOLLARS. WE ONLY PRINTED ONE COPY OF IT BECAUSE WE'RE SO "ANTI". SO TECHNICALLY IT'S NOT EVEN A PRINTING, IT'S JUST A PHOTOCOPY.

WE CALL IT OUR "KINKOS VARIANT". HEHEHE.

I'LL TAKE IT.

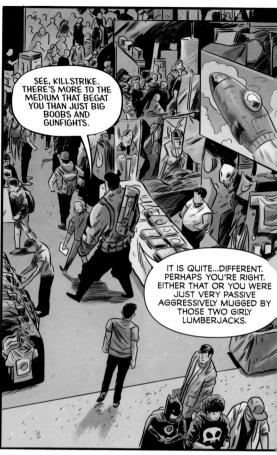

SEE, KILLSTRIKE. THERE'S MORE TO THE MEDIUM THAT BEGAT YOU THAN JUST BIG BOOBS AND GUNFIGHTS.

IT IS QUITE...DIFFERENT. PERHAPS YOU'RE RIGHT. EITHER THAT OR YOU WERE JUST VERY PASSIVE AGGRESSIVELY MUGGED BY THOSE TWO GIRLY LUMBERJACKS.

SO...WHAT ARE WE EVEN GONNA DO NOW?

GO TO LONDON? EVEN I'M NOT THAT CRAZY AND DESPERATE TO ESCAPE RESPONSIBILITY.

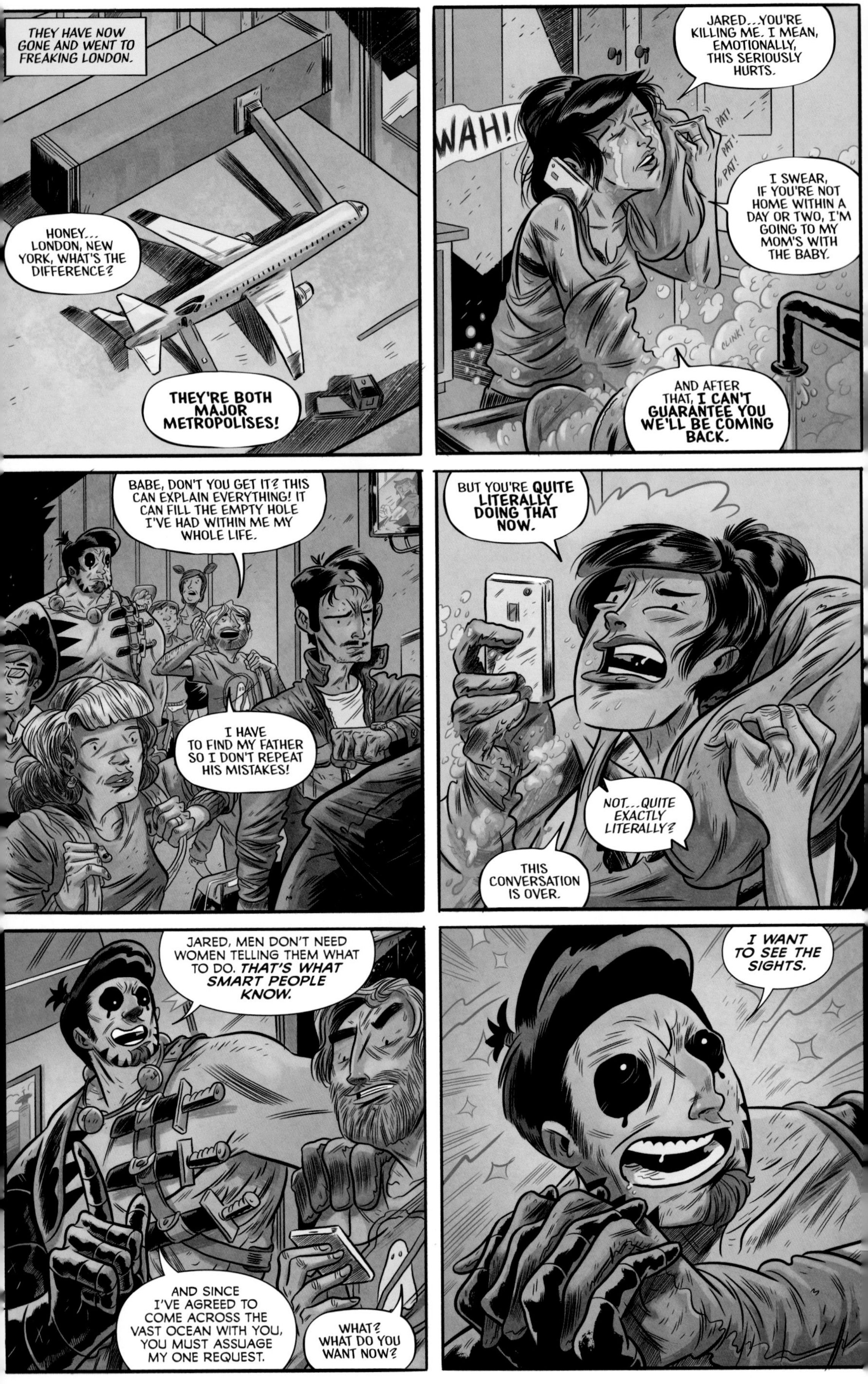
THEY HAVE NOW GONE AND WENT TO FREAKING LONDON.
HONEY... LONDON, NEW YORK, WHAT'S THE DIFFERENCE?
THEY'RE BOTH MAJOR METROPOLISES!
JARED...YOU'RE KILLING ME. I MEAN, EMOTIONALLY, THIS SERIOUSLY HURTS.
WAH!
PAT! PAT! PAT!
I SWEAR, IF YOU'RE NOT HOME WITHIN A DAY OR TWO, I'M GOING TO MY MOM'S WITH THE BABY.
CLINK!
AND AFTER THAT, I CAN'T GUARANTEE YOU WE'LL BE COMING BACK.
BABE, DON'T YOU GET IT? THIS CAN EXPLAIN EVERYTHING! IT CAN FILL THE EMPTY HOLE I'VE HAD WITHIN ME MY WHOLE LIFE.
I HAVE TO FIND MY FATHER SO I DON'T REPEAT HIS MISTAKES!
BUT YOU'RE QUITE LITERALLY DOING THAT NOW.
NOT...QUITE EXACTLY LITERALLY?
THIS CONVERSATION IS OVER.
JARED, MEN DON'T NEED WOMEN TELLING THEM WHAT TO DO. THAT'S WHAT SMART PEOPLE KNOW.
AND SINCE I'VE AGREED TO COME ACROSS THE VAST OCEAN WITH YOU, YOU MUST ASSUAGE MY ONE REQUEST.
WHAT? WHAT DO YOU WANT NOW?
I WANT TO SEE THE SIGHTS.

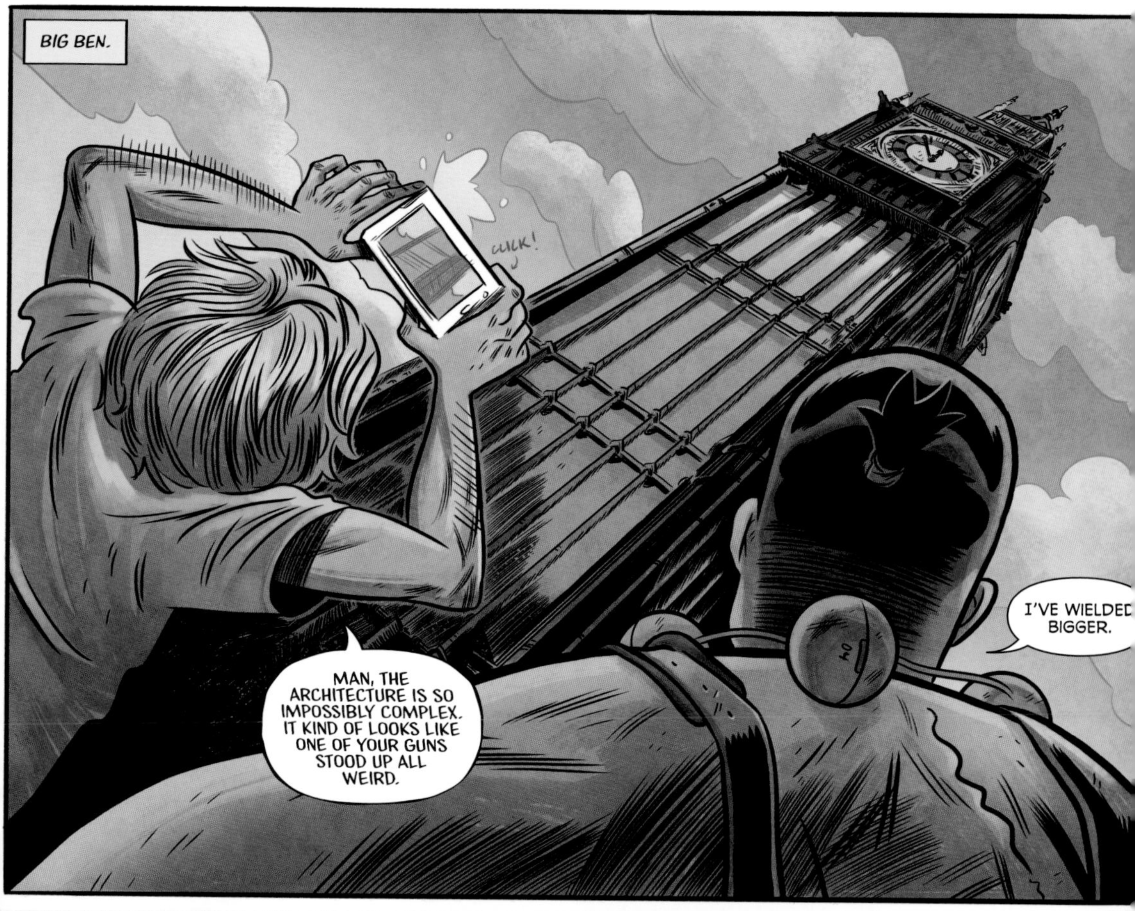
BIG BEN.
CLICK!
MAN, THE ARCHITECTURE IS SO IMPOSSIBLY COMPLEX. IT KIND OF LOOKS LIKE ONE OF YOUR GUNS STOOD UP ALL WEIRD.
I'VE WIELDED BIGGER.

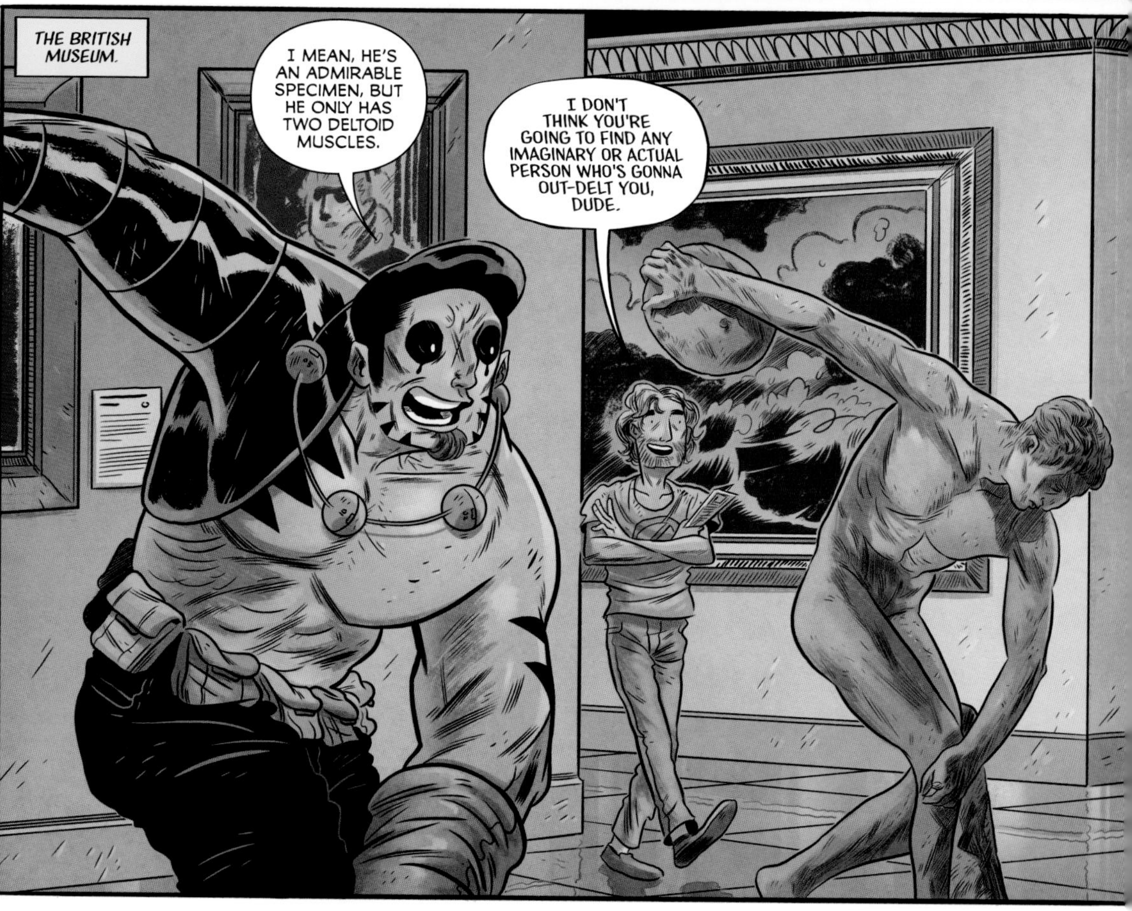
THE BRITISH MUSEUM.
I MEAN, HE'S AN ADMIRABLE SPECIMEN, BUT HE ONLY HAS TWO DELTOID MUSCLES.
I DON'T THINK YOU'RE GOING TO FIND ANY IMAGINARY OR ACTUAL PERSON WHO'S GONNA OUT-DELT YOU, DUDE.

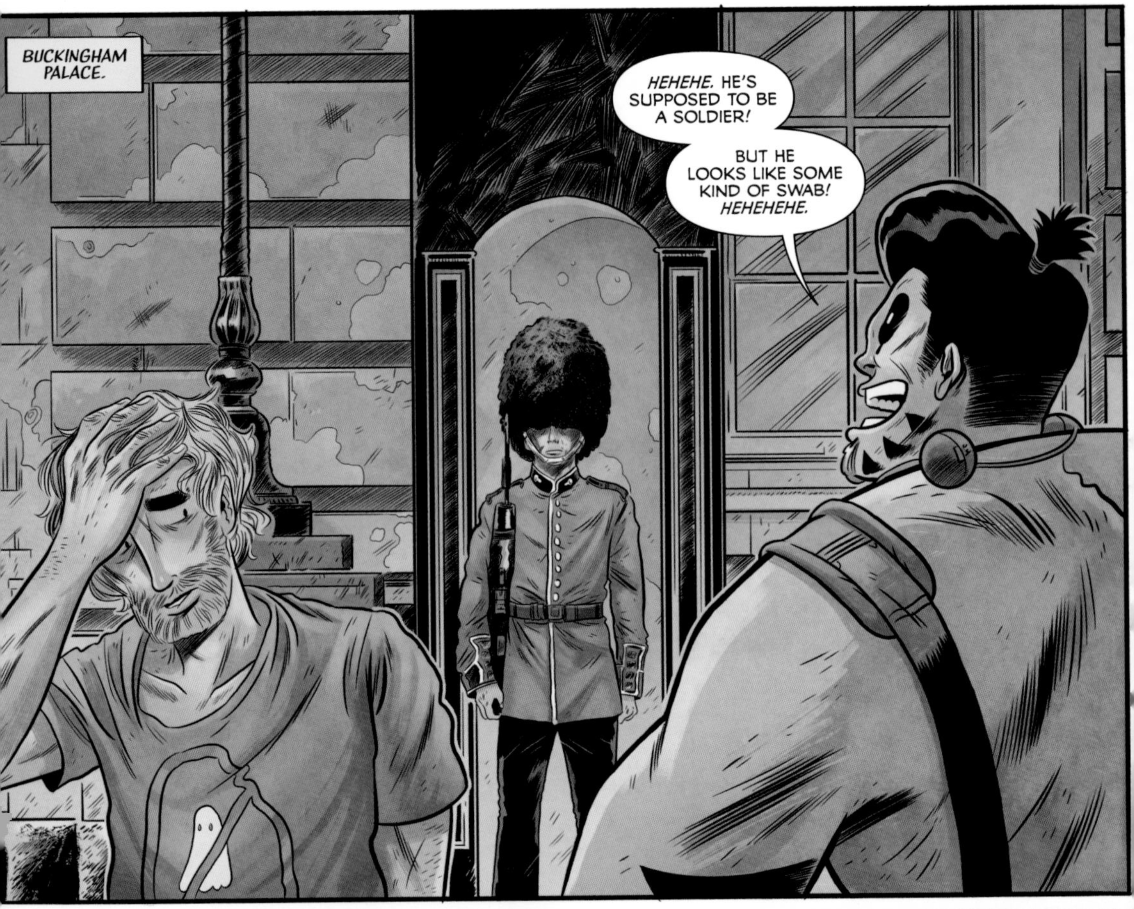
BUCKINGHAM PALACE.
HEHEHE. HE'S SUPPOSED TO BE A SOLDIER!
BUT HE LOOKS LIKE SOME KIND OF SWAB! HEHEHEHE.

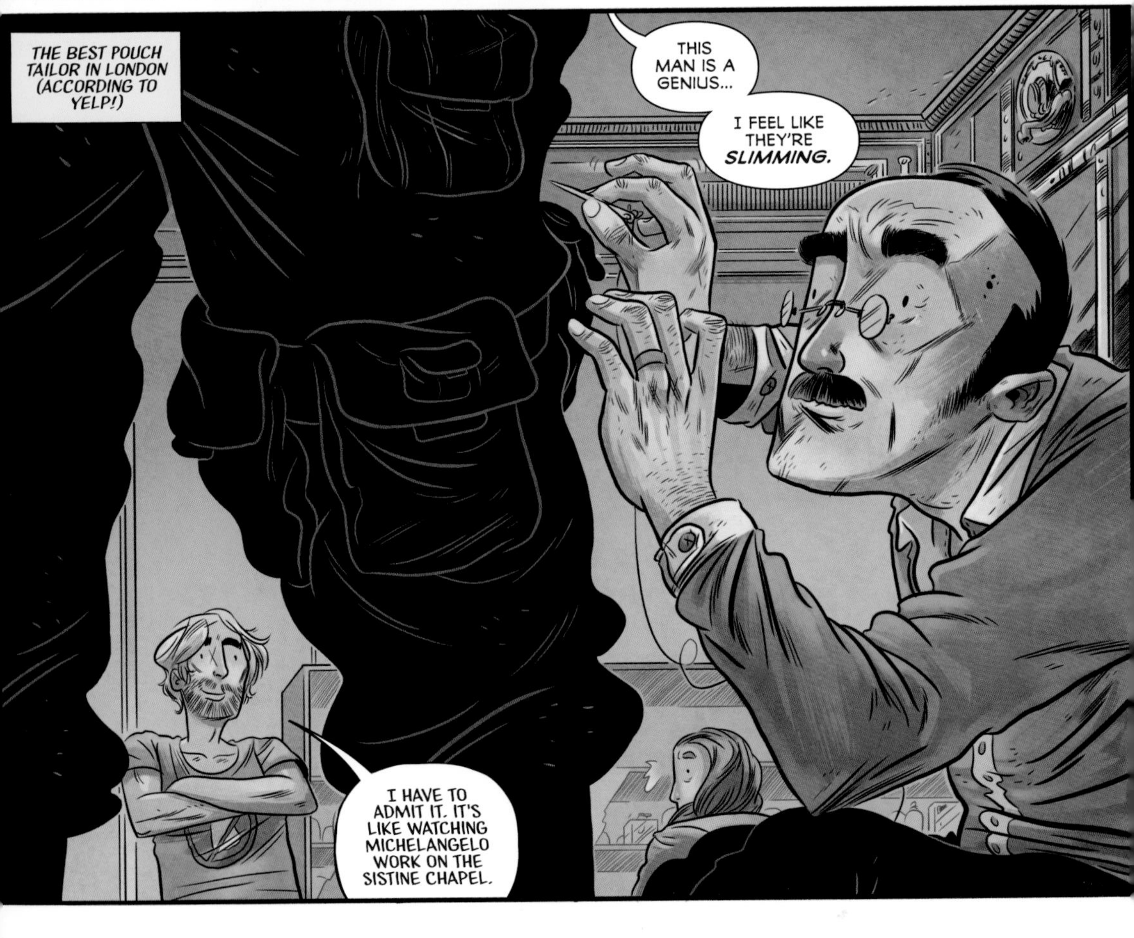
THE BEST POUCH TAILOR IN LONDON (ACCORDING TO YELP!)
THIS MAN IS A GENIUS...
I FEEL LIKE THEY'RE SLIMMING.
I HAVE TO ADMIT IT. IT'S LIKE WATCHING MICHELANGELO WORK ON THE SISTINE CHAPEL.

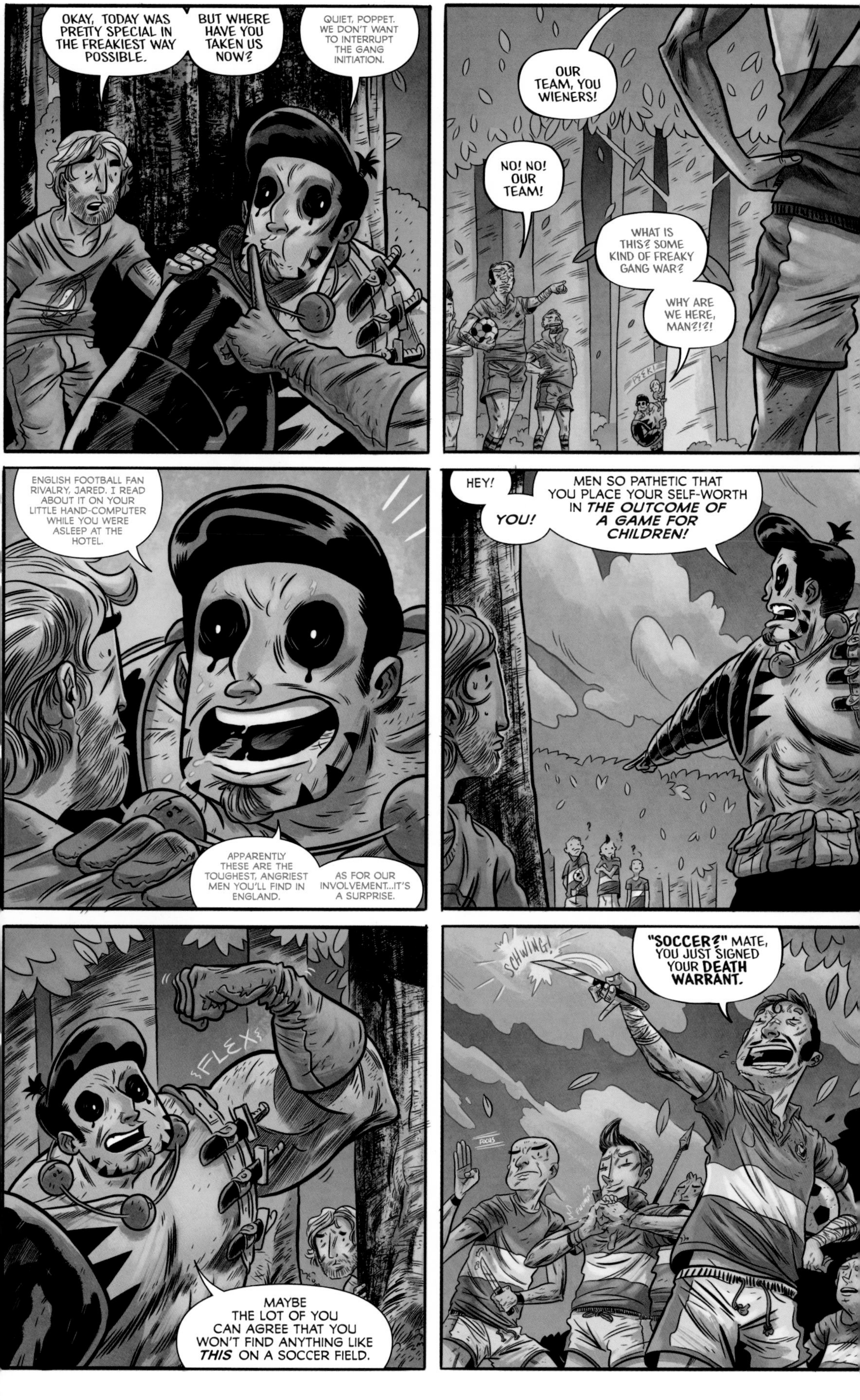

OKAY, TODAY WAS PRETTY SPECIAL IN THE FREAKIEST WAY POSSIBLE.
BUT WHERE HAVE YOU TAKEN US NOW?
QUIET, POPPET. WE DON'T WANT TO INTERRUPT THE GANG INITIATION.
OUR TEAM, YOU WIENERS!
NO! NO! OUR TEAM!
WHAT IS THIS? SOME KIND OF FREAKY GANG WAR?
WHY ARE WE HERE, MAN?!?!
ENGLISH FOOTBALL FAN RIVALRY, JARED. I READ ABOUT IT ON YOUR LITTLE HAND-COMPUTER WHILE YOU WERE ASLEEP AT THE HOTEL.
APPARENTLY THESE ARE THE TOUGHEST, ANGRIEST MEN YOU'LL FIND IN ENGLAND.
AS FOR OUR INVOLVEMENT...IT'S A SURPRISE.
HEY!
YOU!
MEN SO PATHETIC THAT YOU PLACE YOUR SELF-WORTH IN THE OUTCOME OF A GAME FOR CHILDREN!
FLEX
MAYBE THE LOT OF YOU CAN AGREE THAT YOU WON'T FIND ANYTHING LIKE THIS ON A SOCCER FIELD.
SCHWING!
"SOCCER?" MATE, YOU JUST SIGNED YOUR DEATH WARRANT.

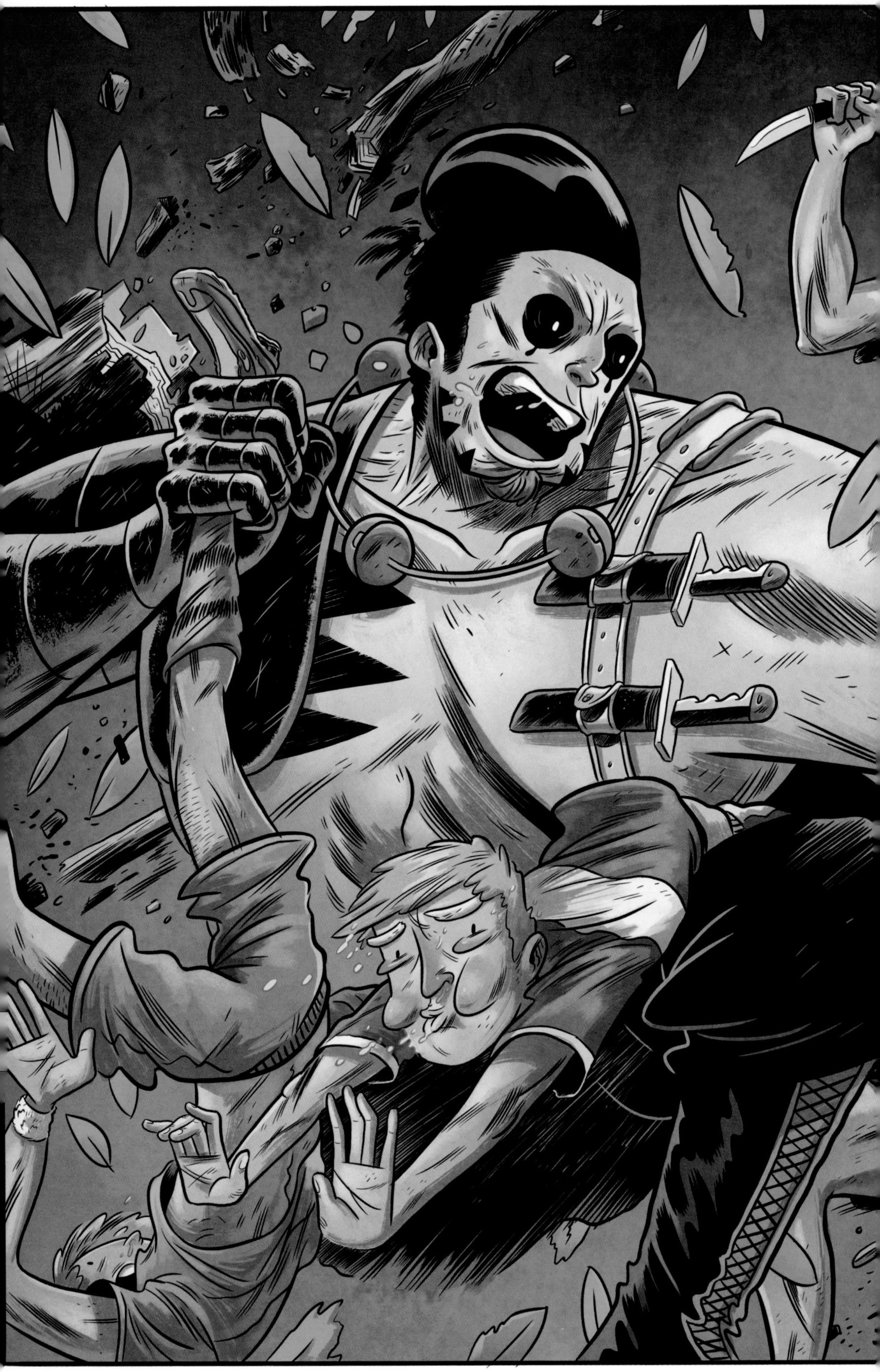

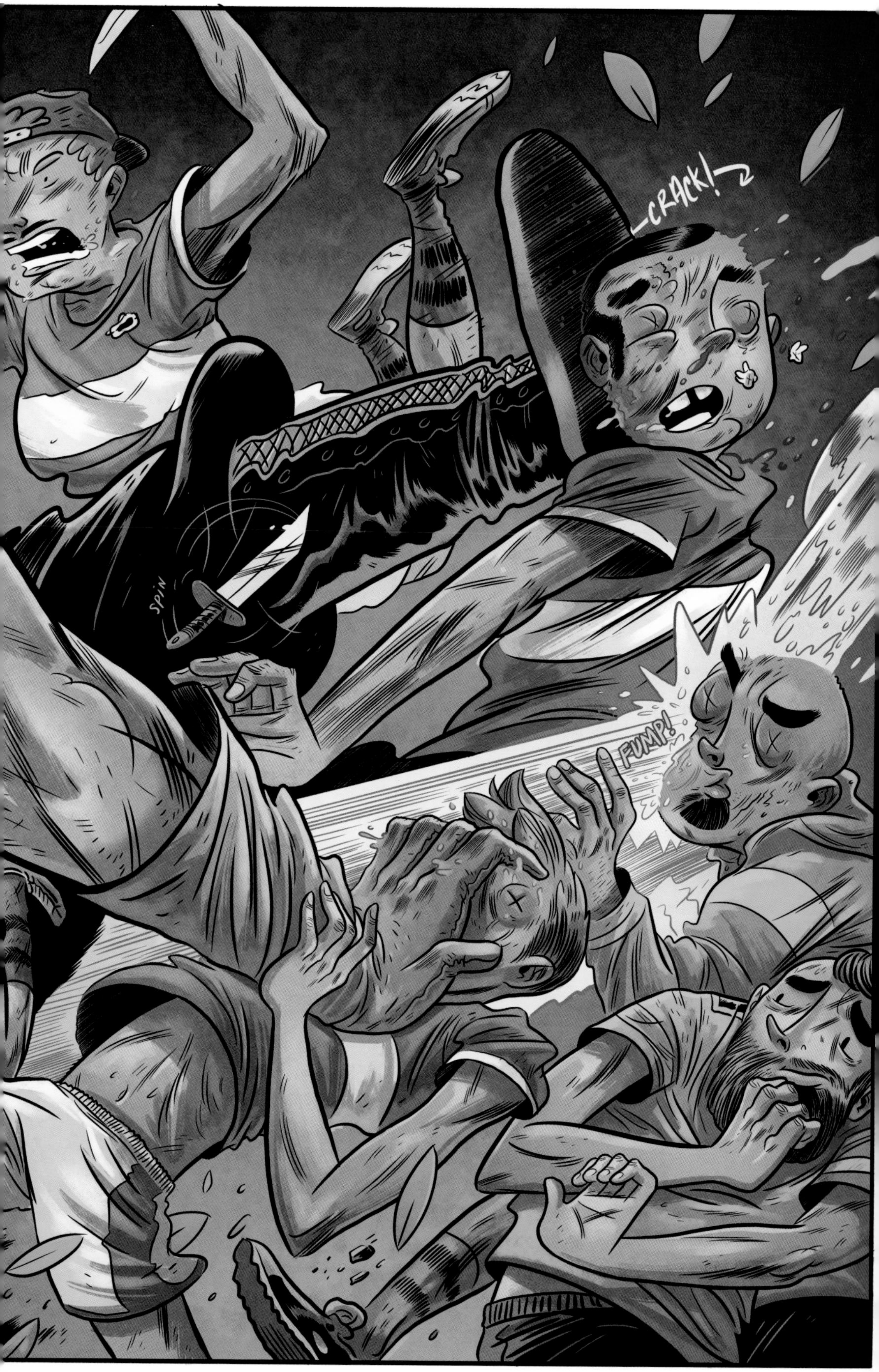
CRACK!
SPIN
FUMP!

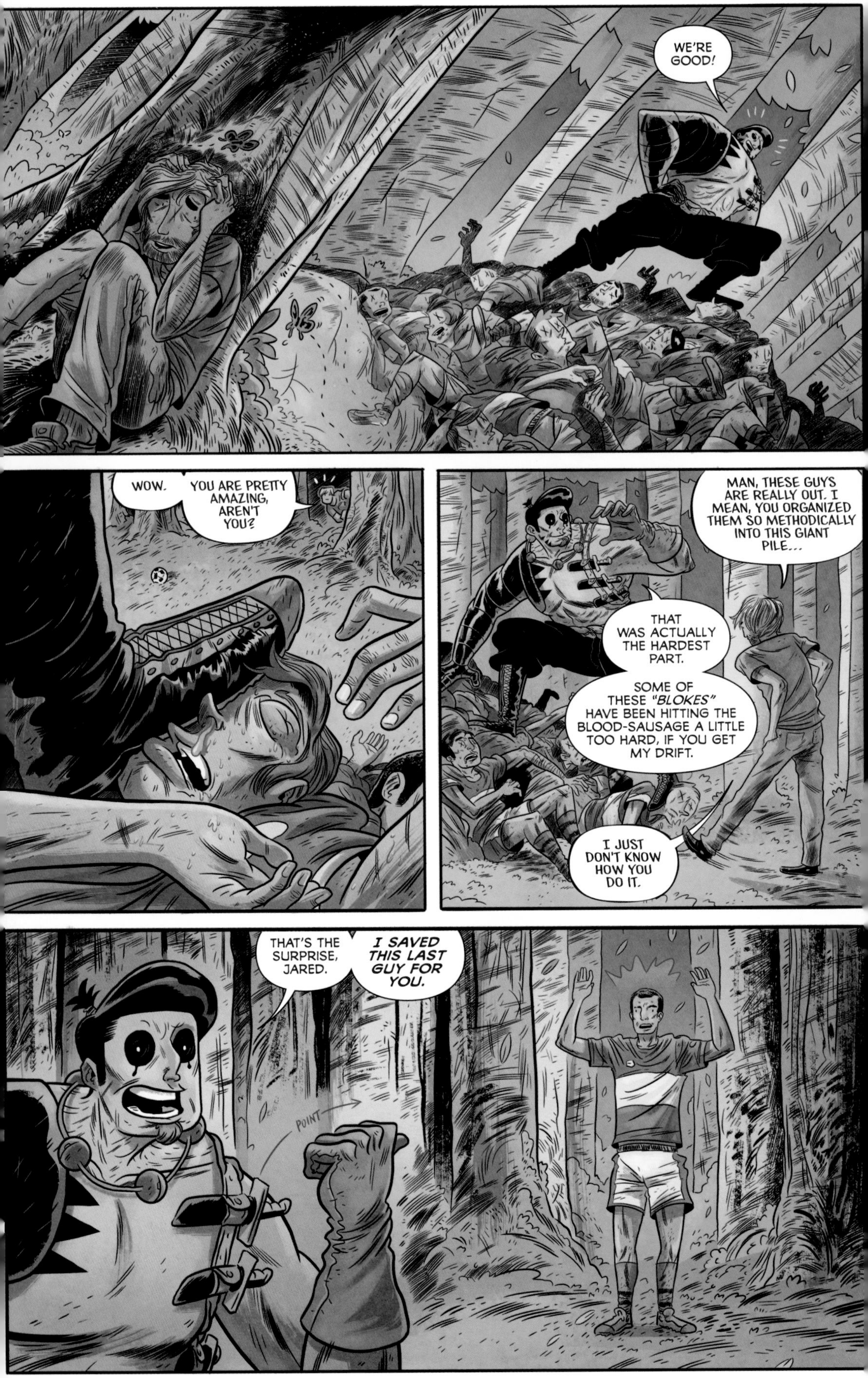
WE'RE GOOD!
WOW.
YOU ARE PRETTY AMAZING, AREN'T YOU?
MAN, THESE GUYS ARE REALLY OUT. I MEAN, YOU ORGANIZED THEM SO METHODICALLY INTO THIS GIANT PILE...
THAT WAS ACTUALLY THE HARDEST PART.
SOME OF THESE "BLOKES" HAVE BEEN HITTING THE BLOOD-SAUSAGE A LITTLE TOO HARD, IF YOU GET MY DRIFT.
I JUST DON'T KNOW HOW YOU DO IT.
THAT'S THE SURPRISE, JARED.
I SAVED THIS LAST GUY FOR YOU.
POINT

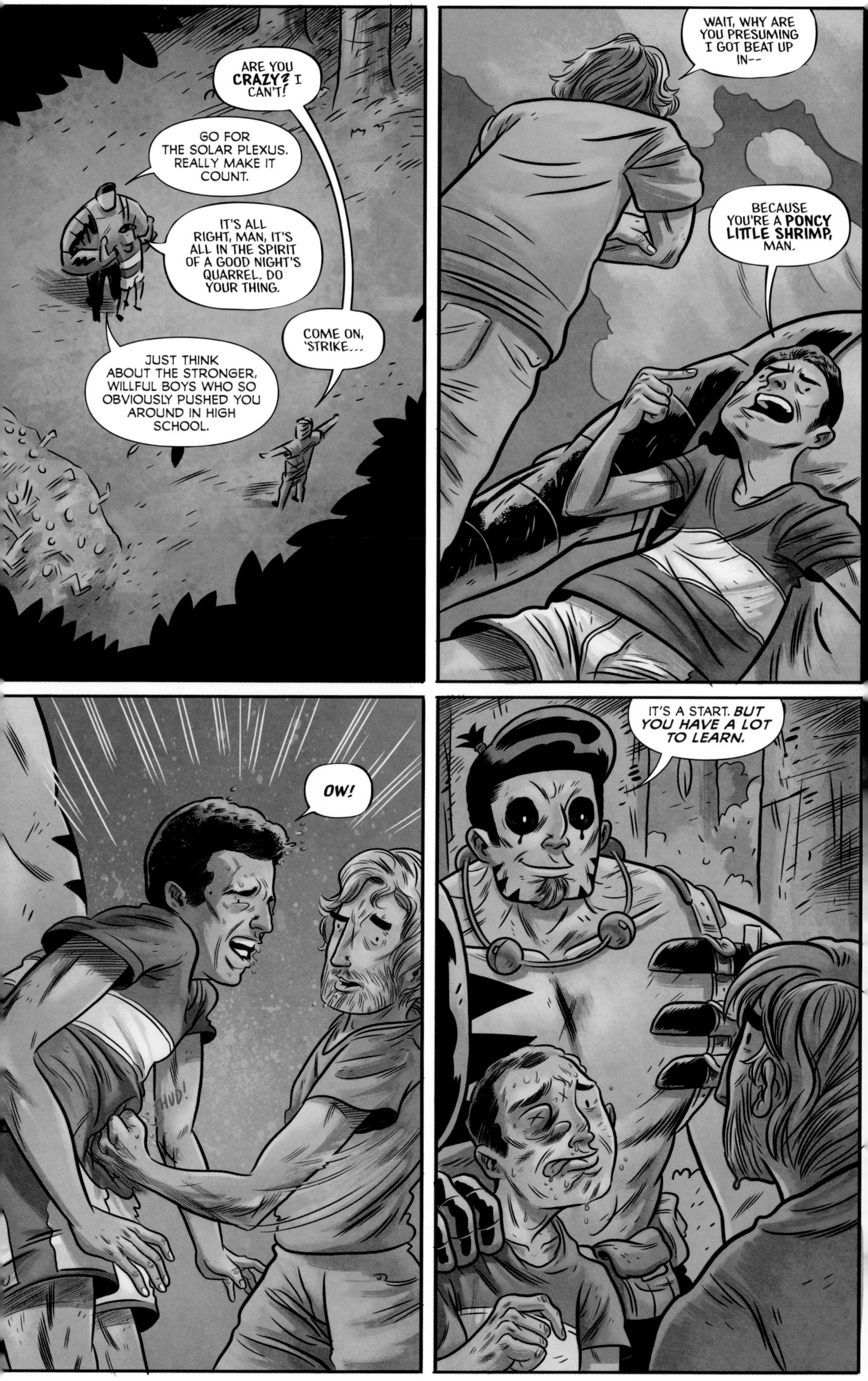
ARE YOU **CRAZY?** I CAN'T!
GO FOR THE SOLAR PLEXUS. REALLY MAKE IT COUNT.
IT'S ALL RIGHT, MAN, IT'S ALL IN THE SPIRIT OF A GOOD NIGHT'S QUARREL. DO YOUR THING.
JUST THINK ABOUT THE STRONGER, WILLFUL BOYS WHO SO OBVIOUSLY PUSHED YOU AROUND IN HIGH SCHOOL.
COME ON, 'STRIKE...
WAIT, WHY ARE YOU PRESUMING I GOT BEAT UP IN--
BECAUSE YOU'RE A **PONCY LITTLE SHRIMP,** MAN.
OW!
THUD!
IT'S A START. *BUT YOU HAVE A LOT TO LEARN.*

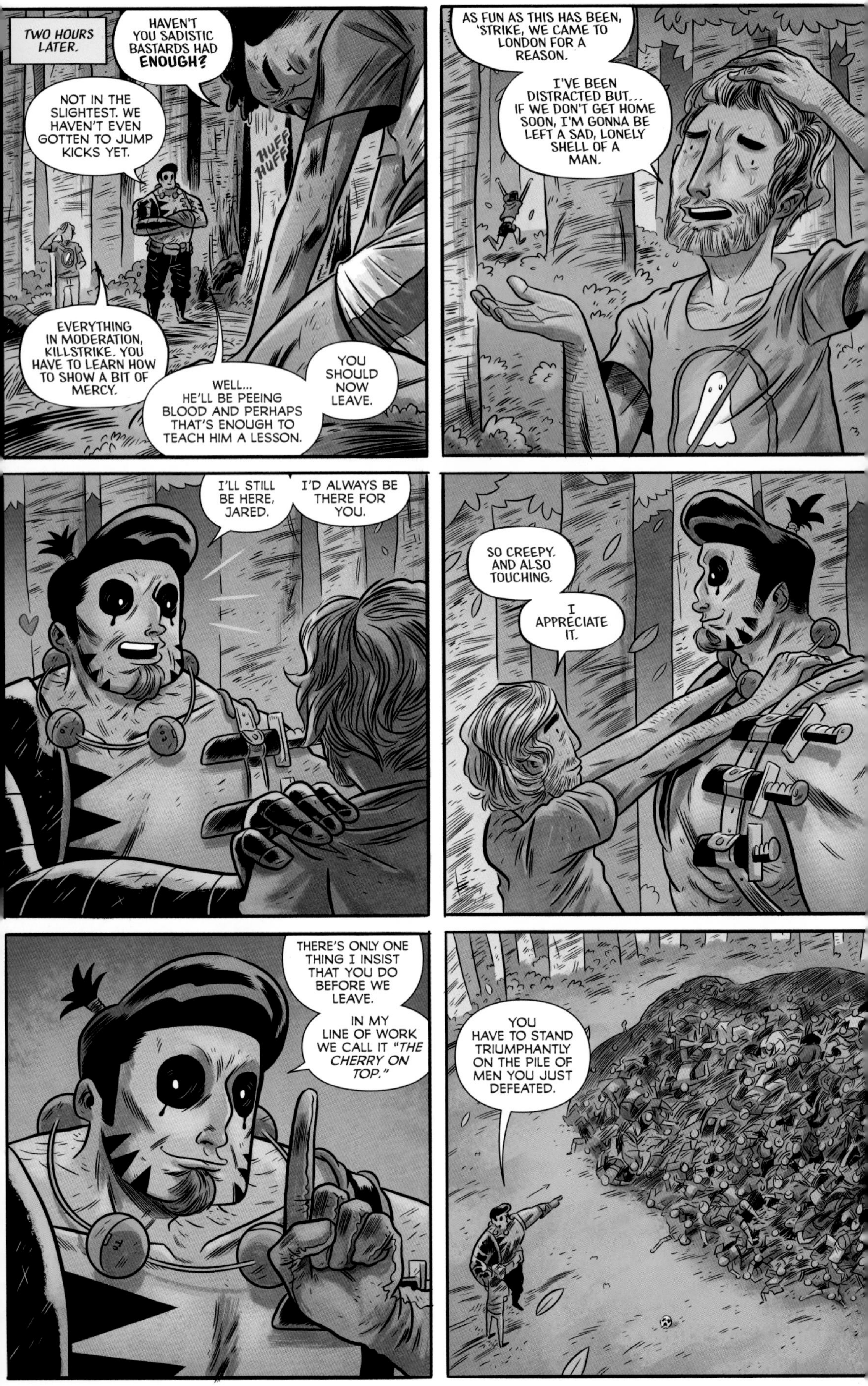
TWO HOURS LATER.
HAVEN'T YOU SADISTIC BASTARDS HAD **ENOUGH?**
NOT IN THE SLIGHTEST. WE HAVEN'T EVEN GOTTEN TO JUMP KICKS YET.
HUFF HUFF
EVERYTHING IN MODERATION, KILLSTRIKE. YOU HAVE TO LEARN HOW TO SHOW A BIT OF MERCY.
WELL... HE'LL BE PEEING BLOOD AND PERHAPS THAT'S ENOUGH TO TEACH HIM A LESSON.
YOU SHOULD NOW LEAVE.
AS FUN AS THIS HAS BEEN, 'STRIKE, WE CAME TO LONDON FOR A REASON.
I'VE BEEN DISTRACTED BUT... IF WE DON'T GET HOME SOON, I'M GONNA BE LEFT A SAD, LONELY SHELL OF A MAN.
I'LL STILL BE HERE, JARED.
I'D ALWAYS BE THERE FOR YOU.
SO CREEPY. AND ALSO TOUCHING.
I APPRECIATE IT.
THERE'S ONLY ONE THING I INSIST THAT YOU DO BEFORE WE LEAVE.
IN MY LINE OF WORK WE CALL IT *"THE CHERRY ON TOP."*
YOU HAVE TO STAND TRIUMPHANTLY ON THE PILE OF MEN YOU JUST DEFEATED.

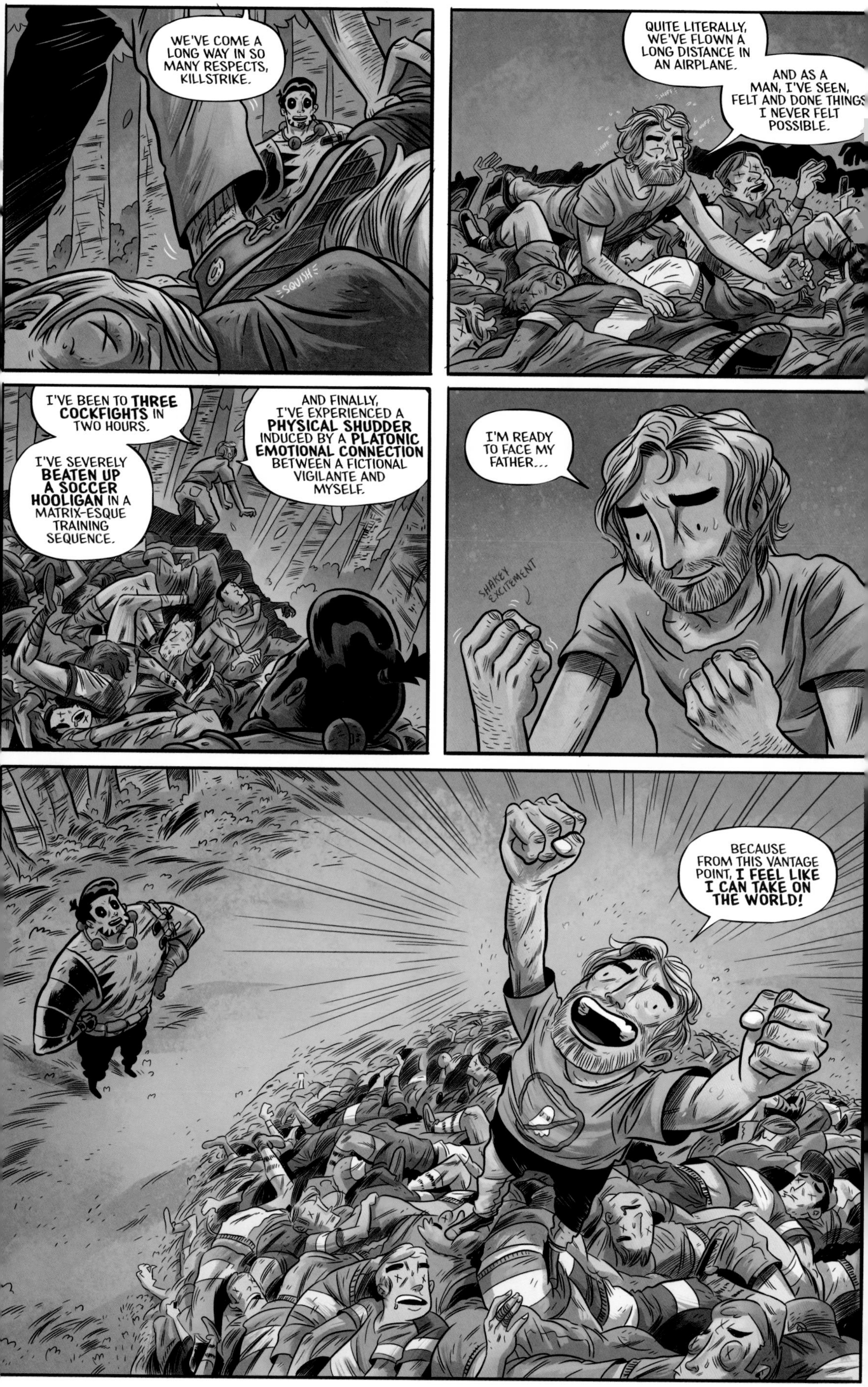
WE'VE COME A LONG WAY IN SO MANY RESPECTS, KILLSTRIKE.
SQUISH
QUITE LITERALLY, WE'VE FLOWN A LONG DISTANCE IN AN AIRPLANE.
AND AS A MAN, I'VE SEEN, FELT AND DONE THINGS I NEVER FELT POSSIBLE.
I'VE BEEN TO THREE COCKFIGHTS IN TWO HOURS.
I'VE SEVERELY BEATEN UP A SOCCER HOOLIGAN IN A MATRIX-ESQUE TRAINING SEQUENCE.
AND FINALLY, I'VE EXPERIENCED A PHYSICAL SHUDDER INDUCED BY A PLATONIC EMOTIONAL CONNECTION BETWEEN A FICTIONAL VIGILANTE AND MYSELF.
I'M READY TO FACE MY FATHER...
SHAKEY EXCITEMENT
BECAUSE FROM THIS VANTAGE POINT, I FEEL LIKE I CAN TAKE ON THE WORLD!

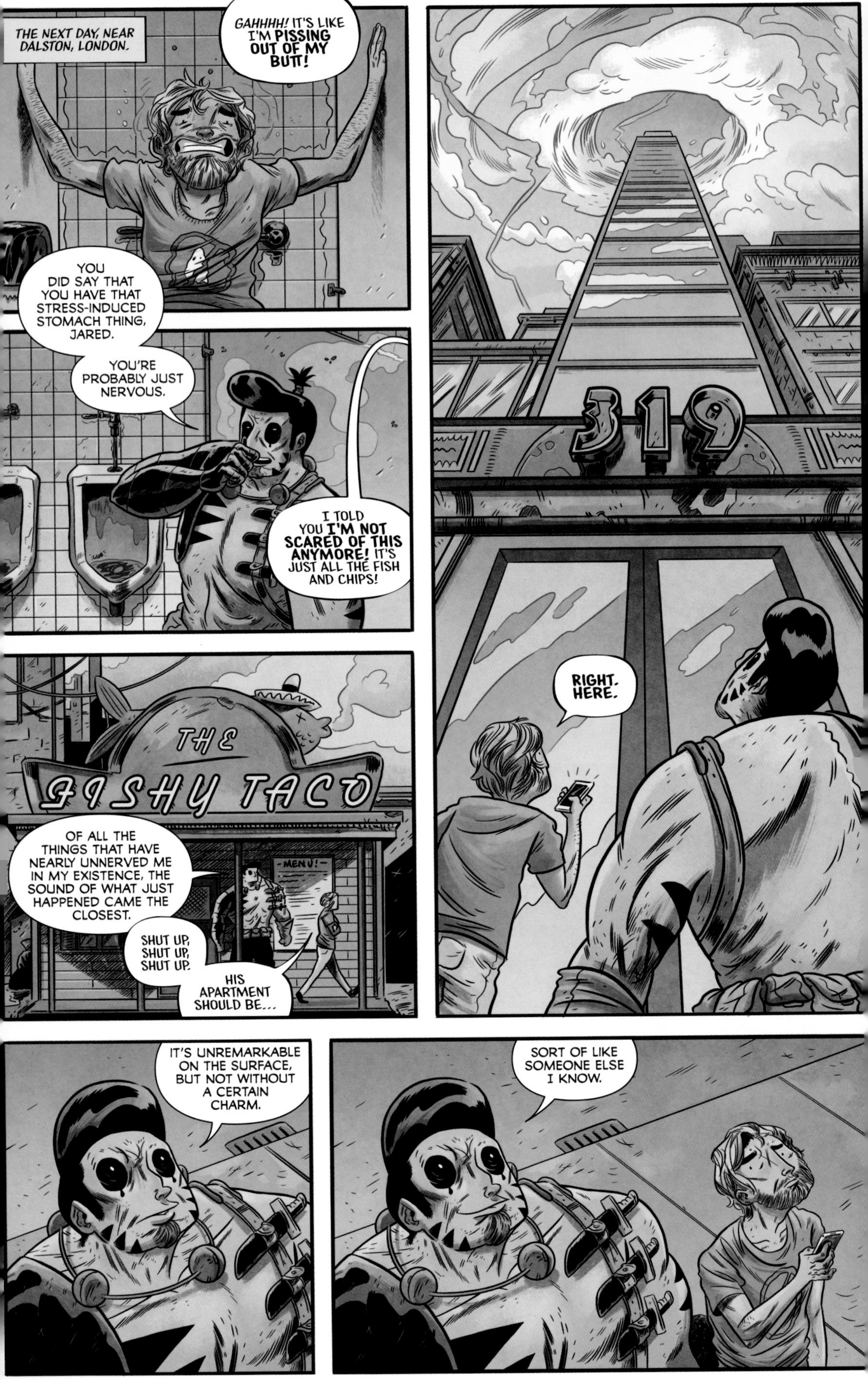
THE NEXT DAY, NEAR DALSTON, LONDON.
GAHHHH! IT'S LIKE I'M PISSING OUT OF MY BUTT!
YOU DID SAY THAT YOU HAVE THAT STRESS-INDUCED STOMACH THING, JARED.
YOU'RE PROBABLY JUST NERVOUS.
I TOLD YOU I'M NOT SCARED OF THIS ANYMORE! IT'S JUST ALL THE FISH AND CHIPS!
THE FISHY TACO
-MENU!-
OF ALL THE THINGS THAT HAVE NEARLY UNNERVED ME IN MY EXISTENCE, THE SOUND OF WHAT JUST HAPPENED CAME THE CLOSEST.
SHUT UP, SHUT UP, SHUT UP.
HIS APARTMENT SHOULD BE...
319
RIGHT. HERE.
IT'S UNREMARKABLE ON THE SURFACE, BUT NOT WITHOUT A CERTAIN CHARM.
SORT OF LIKE SOMEONE ELSE I KNOW.

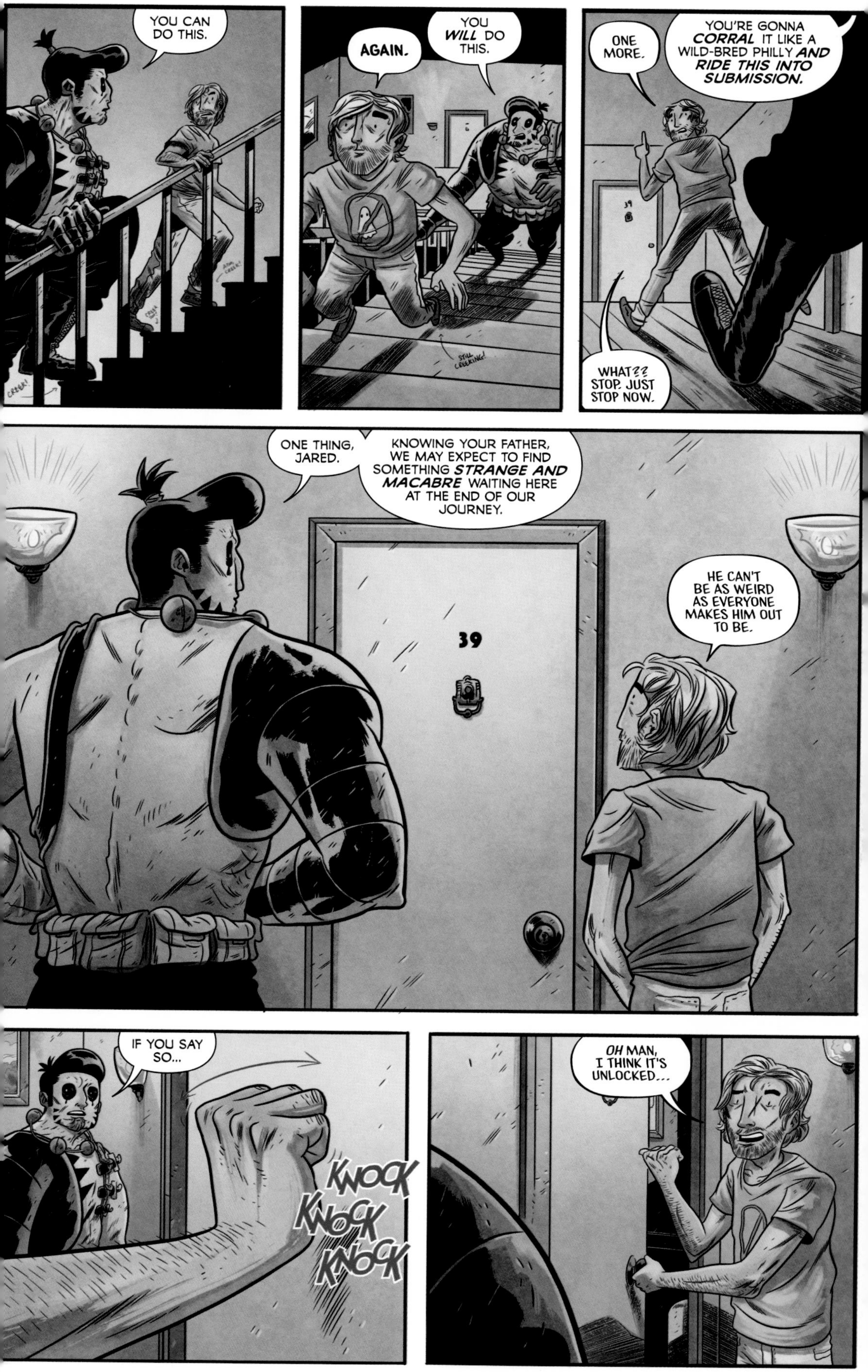
YOU CAN DO THIS.
AND CREEK!
CREEK!
AGAIN.
YOU WILL DO THIS.
STILL CREEKING!
ONE MORE.
YOU'RE GONNA CORRAL IT LIKE A WILD-BRED PHILLY AND RIDE THIS INTO SUBMISSION.
WHAT?? STOP. JUST STOP NOW.
ONE THING, JARED.
KNOWING YOUR FATHER, WE MAY EXPECT TO FIND SOMETHING STRANGE AND MACABRE WAITING HERE AT THE END OF OUR JOURNEY.
39
HE CAN'T BE AS WEIRD AS EVERYONE MAKES HIM OUT TO BE.
IF YOU SAY SO...
KNOCK KNOCK KNOCK
OH MAN, I THINK IT'S UNLOCKED...

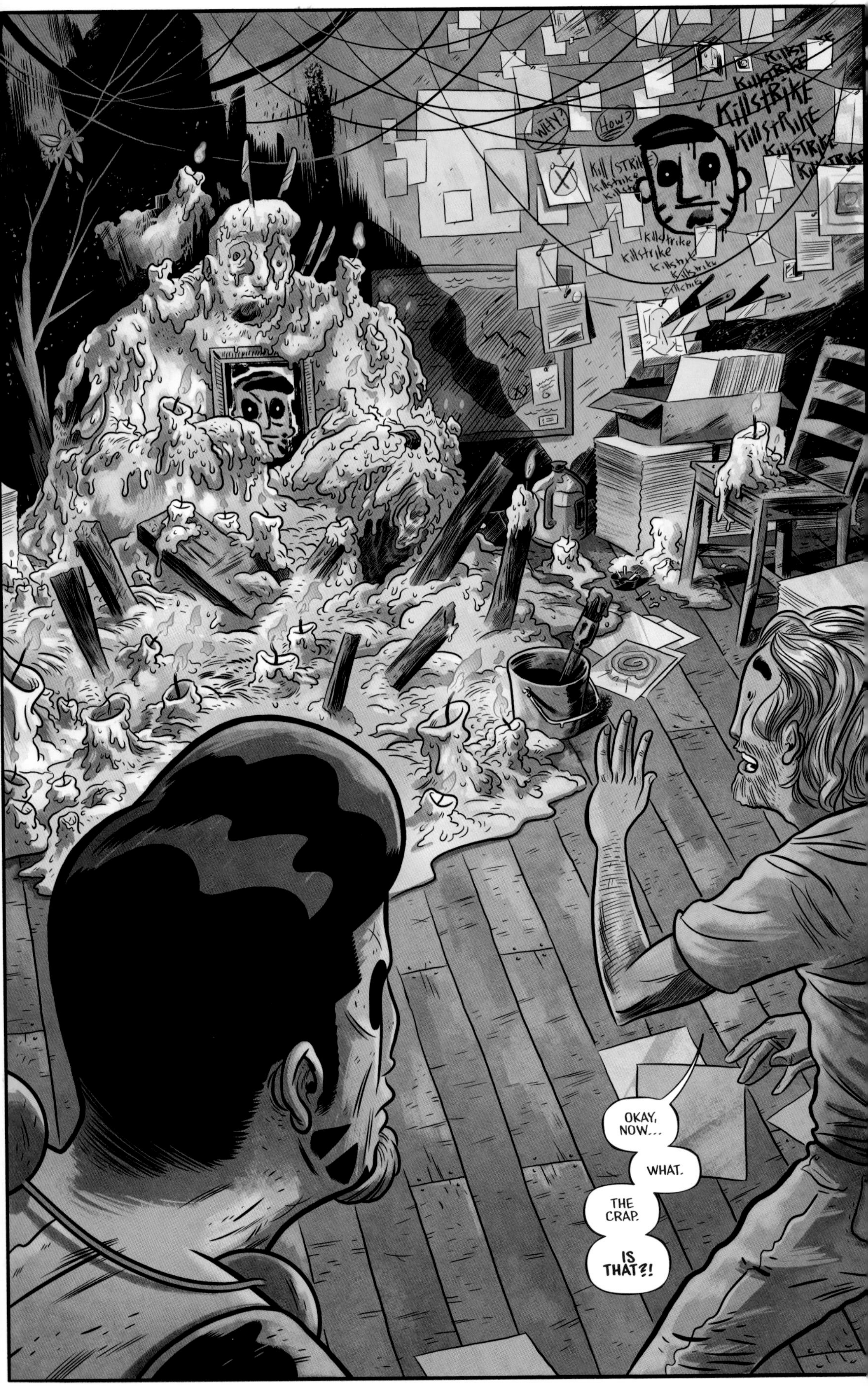

WHY?
How?
KillSTRIKE
KillSTRIKE
KillSTRIKE
Killstrike
Killstrike
OKAY, NOW...
WHAT.
THE CRAP.
IS THAT?!

BLAM

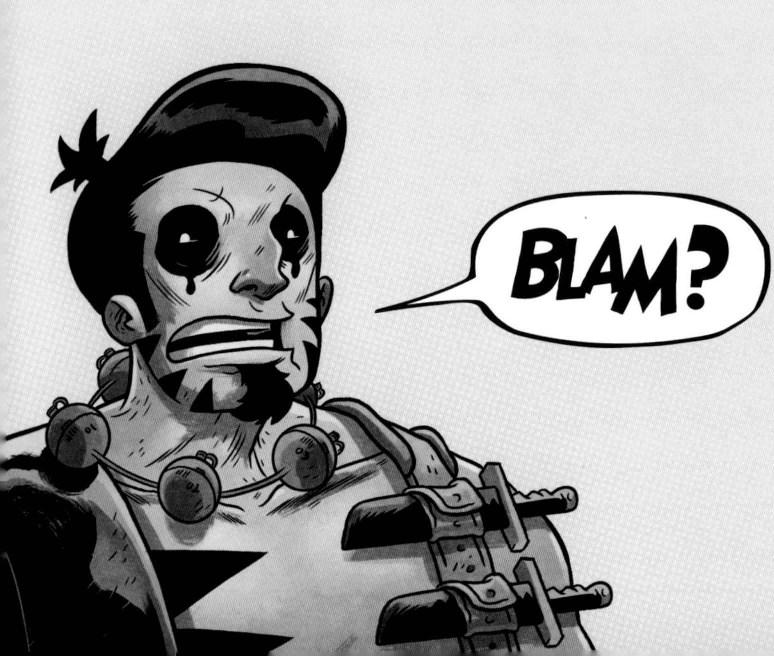
BLAM?

chapter
FOUR

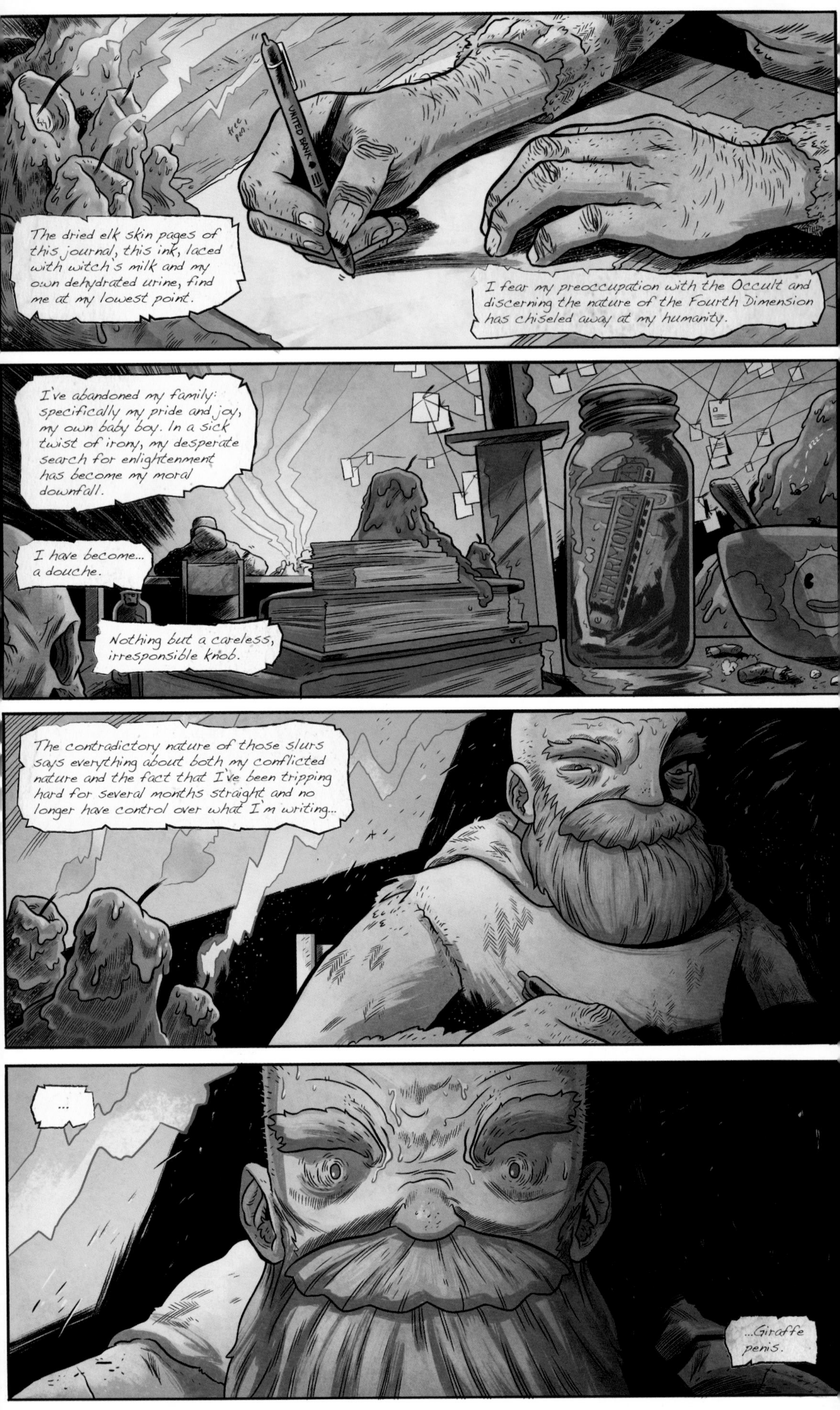

free pen!
UNITED BANK
The dried elk skin pages of this journal, this ink, laced with witch's milk and my own dehydrated urine, find me at my lowest point.
I fear my preoccupation with the Occult and discerning the nature of the Fourth Dimension has chiseled away at my humanity.
I've abandoned my family: specifically my pride and joy, my own baby boy. In a sick twist of irony, my desperate search for enlightenment has become my moral downfall.
HARMONICA
I have become... a douche.
Nothing but a careless, irresponsible knob.
The contradictory nature of those slurs says everything about both my conflicted nature and the fact that I've been tripping hard for several months straight and no longer have control over what I'm writing...
...
...Giraffe penis.

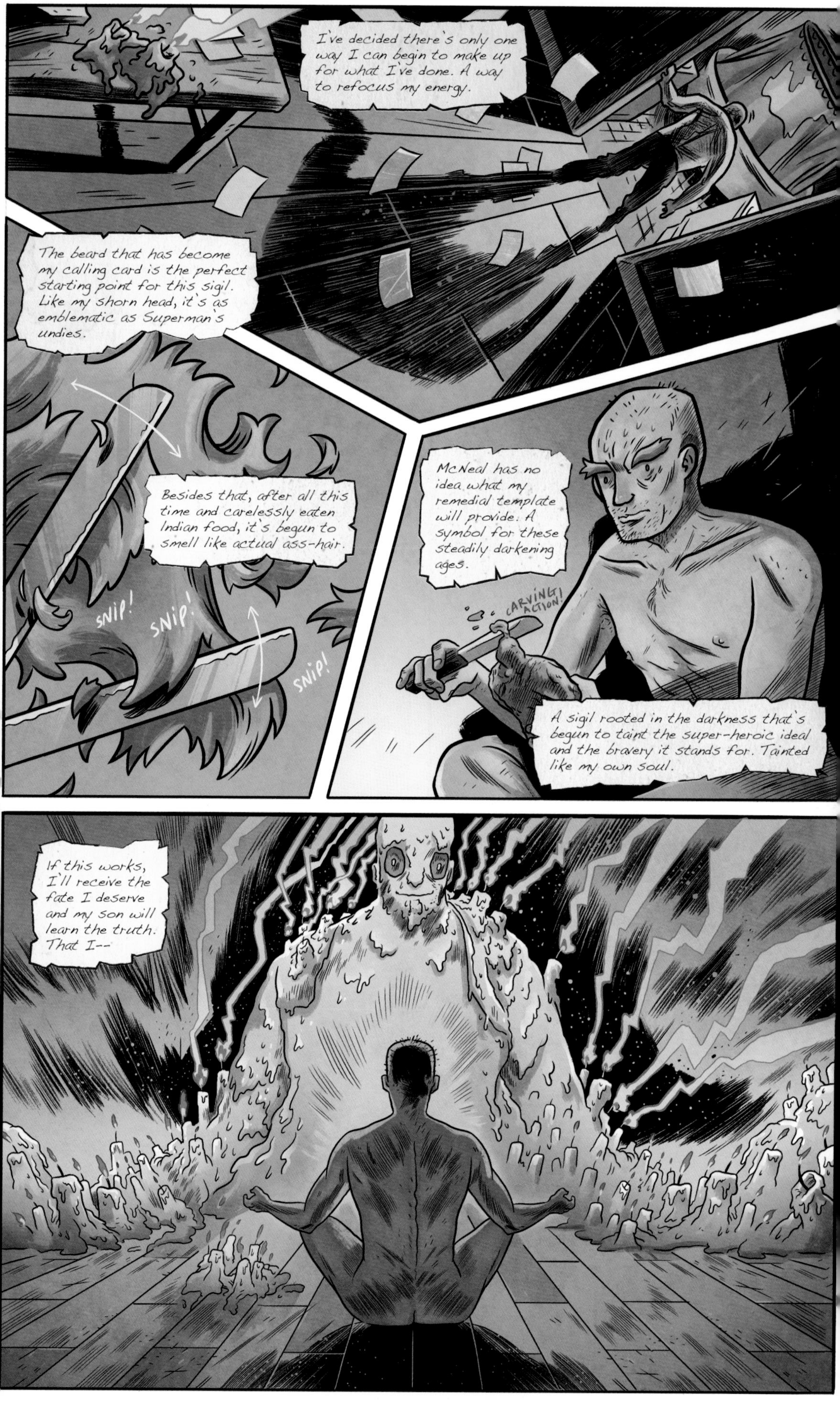
I've decided there's only one way I can begin to make up for what I've done. A way to refocus my energy.
The beard that has become my calling card is the perfect starting point for this sigil. Like my shorn head, it's as emblematic as Superman's undies.
Besides that, after all this time and carelessly eaten Indian food, it's begun to smell like actual ass-hair.
SNIP!
SNIP!
SNIP!
McNeal has no idea what my remedial template will provide. A symbol for these steadily darkening ages.
CARVING ACTION!
A sigil rooted in the darkness that's begun to taint the super-heroic ideal and the bravery it stands for. Tainted like my own soul.
If this works, I'll receive the fate I deserve and my son will learn the truth. That I--

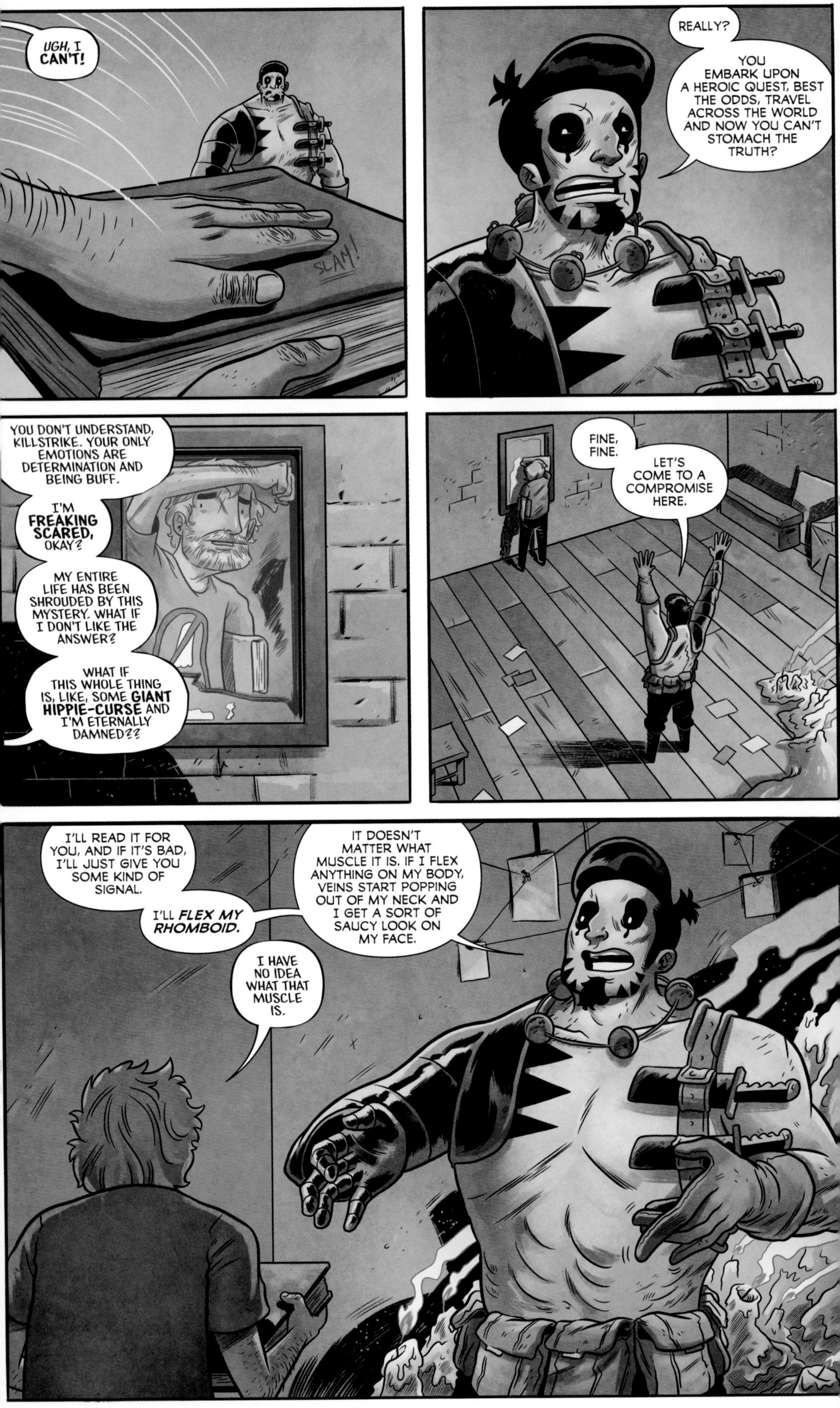
UGH, I **CAN'T!**
SLAM!
REALLY?
YOU EMBARK UPON A HEROIC QUEST, BEST THE ODDS, TRAVEL ACROSS THE WORLD AND NOW YOU CAN'T STOMACH THE TRUTH?
YOU DON'T UNDERSTAND, KILLSTRIKE. YOUR ONLY EMOTIONS ARE DETERMINATION AND BEING BUFF.
I'M **FREAKING SCARED,** OKAY?
MY ENTIRE LIFE HAS BEEN SHROUDED BY THIS MYSTERY. WHAT IF I DON'T LIKE THE ANSWER?
WHAT IF THIS WHOLE THING IS, LIKE, SOME **GIANT HIPPIE-CURSE** AND I'M ETERNALLY DAMNED??
FINE, FINE.
LET'S COME TO A COMPROMISE HERE.
I'LL READ IT FOR YOU, AND IF IT'S BAD, I'LL JUST GIVE YOU SOME KIND OF SIGNAL.
I'LL ***FLEX MY RHOMBOID.***
IT DOESN'T MATTER WHAT MUSCLE IT IS. IF I FLEX ANYTHING ON MY BODY, VEINS START POPPING OUT OF MY NECK AND I GET A SORT OF SAUCY LOOK ON MY FACE.
I HAVE NO IDEA WHAT THAT MUSCLE IS.

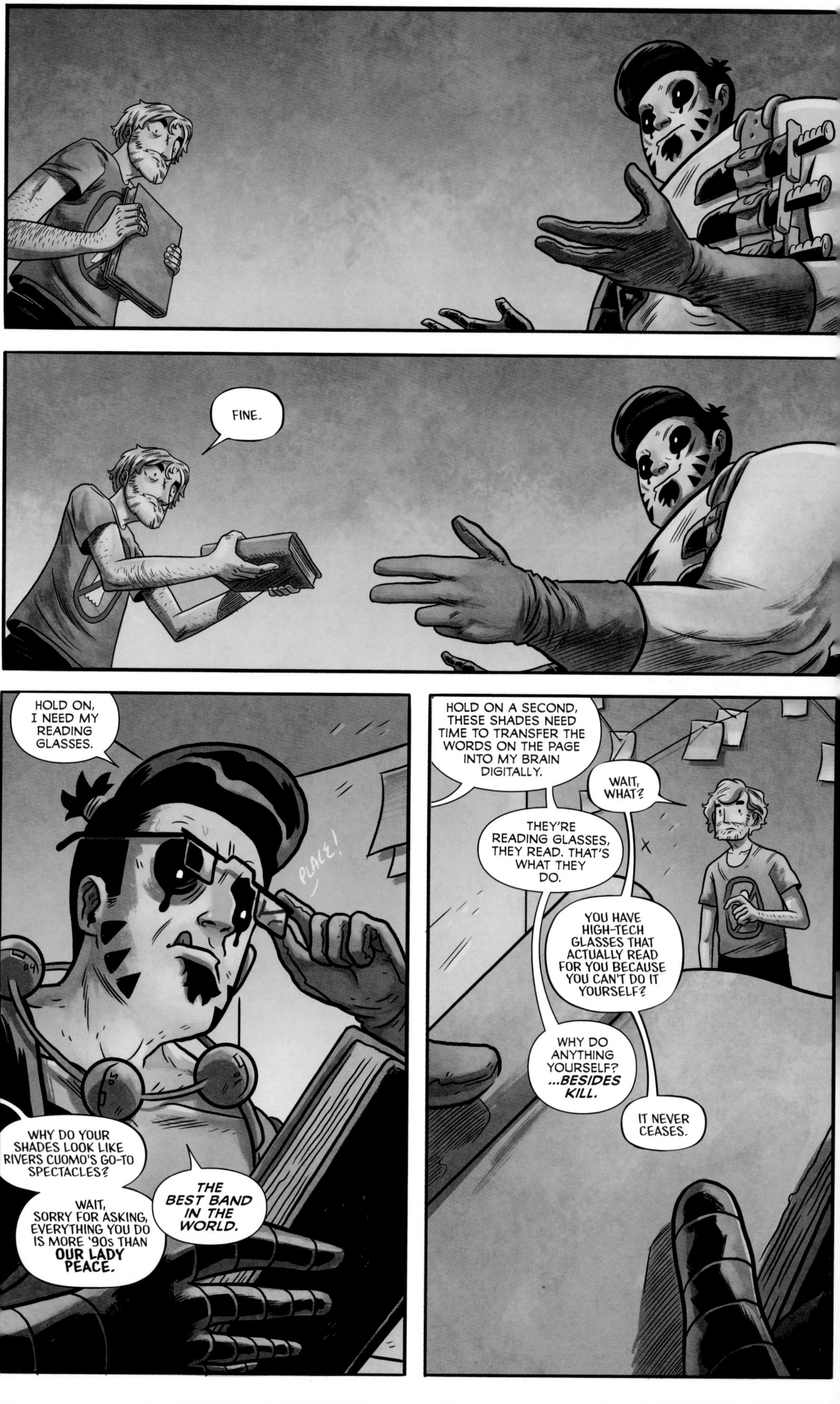
FINE.
HOLD ON, I NEED MY READING GLASSES.
PLACE!
WHY DO YOUR SHADES LOOK LIKE RIVERS CUOMO'S GO-TO SPECTACLES?
WAIT, SORRY FOR ASKING, EVERYTHING YOU DO IS MORE '90s THAN **OUR LADY PEACE.**
THE BEST BAND IN THE WORLD.
HOLD ON A SECOND, THESE SHADES NEED TIME TO TRANSFER THE WORDS ON THE PAGE INTO MY BRAIN DIGITALLY.
WAIT, WHAT?
THEY'RE READING GLASSES, THEY READ. THAT'S WHAT THEY DO.
YOU HAVE HIGH-TECH GLASSES THAT ACTUALLY READ FOR YOU BECAUSE YOU CAN'T DO IT YOURSELF?
WHY DO ANYTHING YOURSELF? ***...BESIDES KILL.***
IT NEVER CEASES.

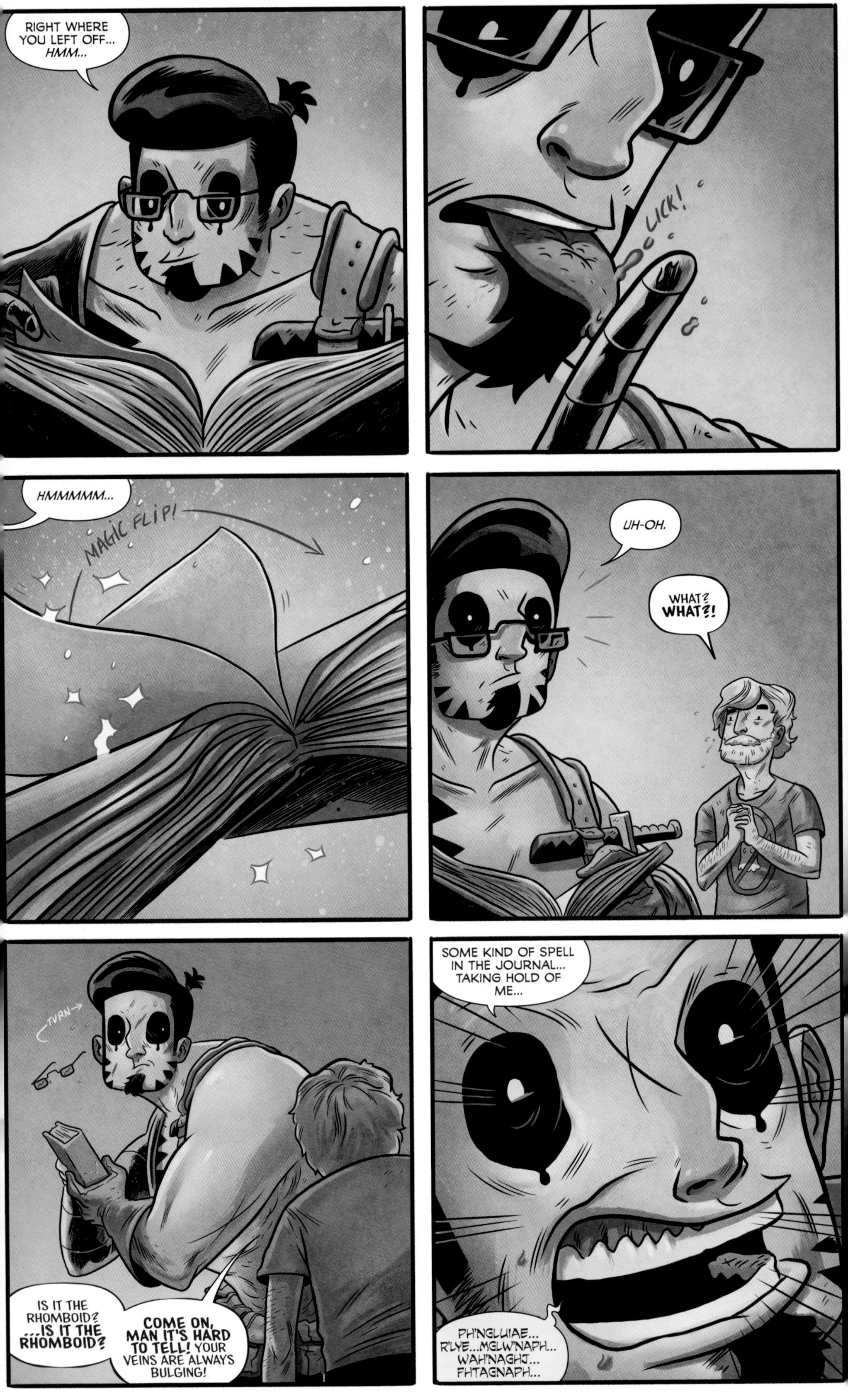

RIGHT WHERE YOU LEFT OFF... *HMM...*
LICK!
HMMMMM...
MAGIC FLIP!
UH-OH.
WHAT? **WHAT?!**
TURN
IS IT THE RHOMBOID? **...IS IT THE RHOMBOID?**
COME ON, MAN IT'S HARD TO TELL! YOUR VEINS ARE ALWAYS BULGING!
SOME KIND OF SPELL IN THE JOURNAL... TAKING HOLD OF ME...
PH'NGLUIAE... R'LYE...MGLW'NAPH... WAH'NAGHJ... FHTAGNAPH...

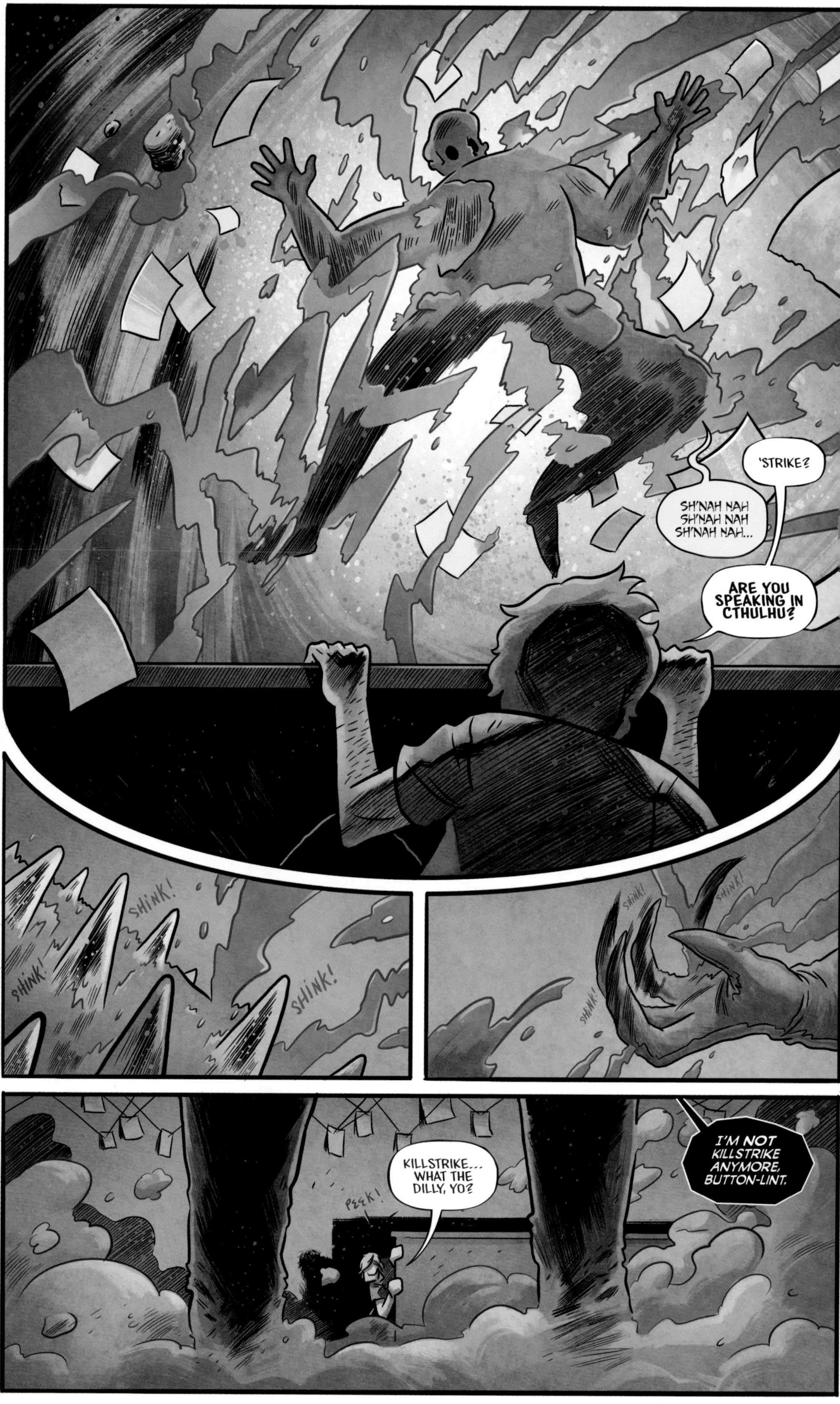
SH'NAH NAH
SH'NAH NAH
SH'NAH NAH...
'STRIKE?
ARE YOU SPEAKING IN CTHULHU?
SHINK!
SHINK!
SHINK!
SHINK!
SHINK!
SHINK!
PEEK!
KILLSTRIKE... WHAT THE DILLY, YO?
I'M NOT KILLSTRIKE ANYMORE, BUTTON-LINT.

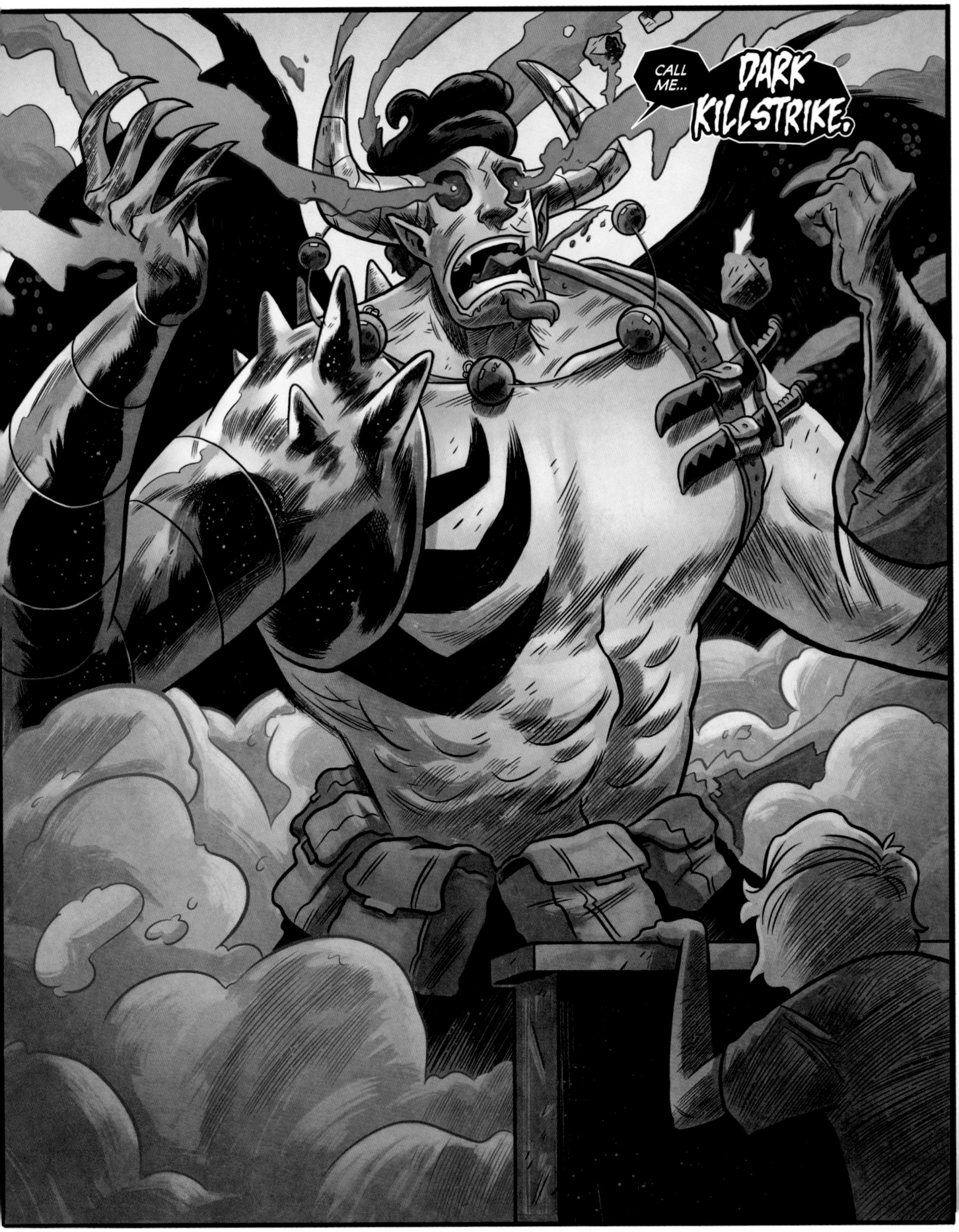
CALL ME...
DARK KILLSTRIKE.

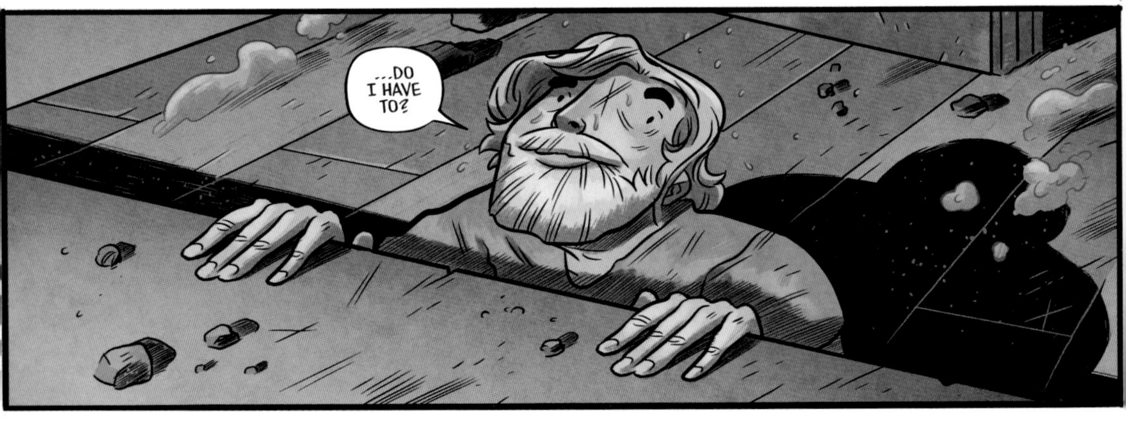
...DO I HAVE TO?

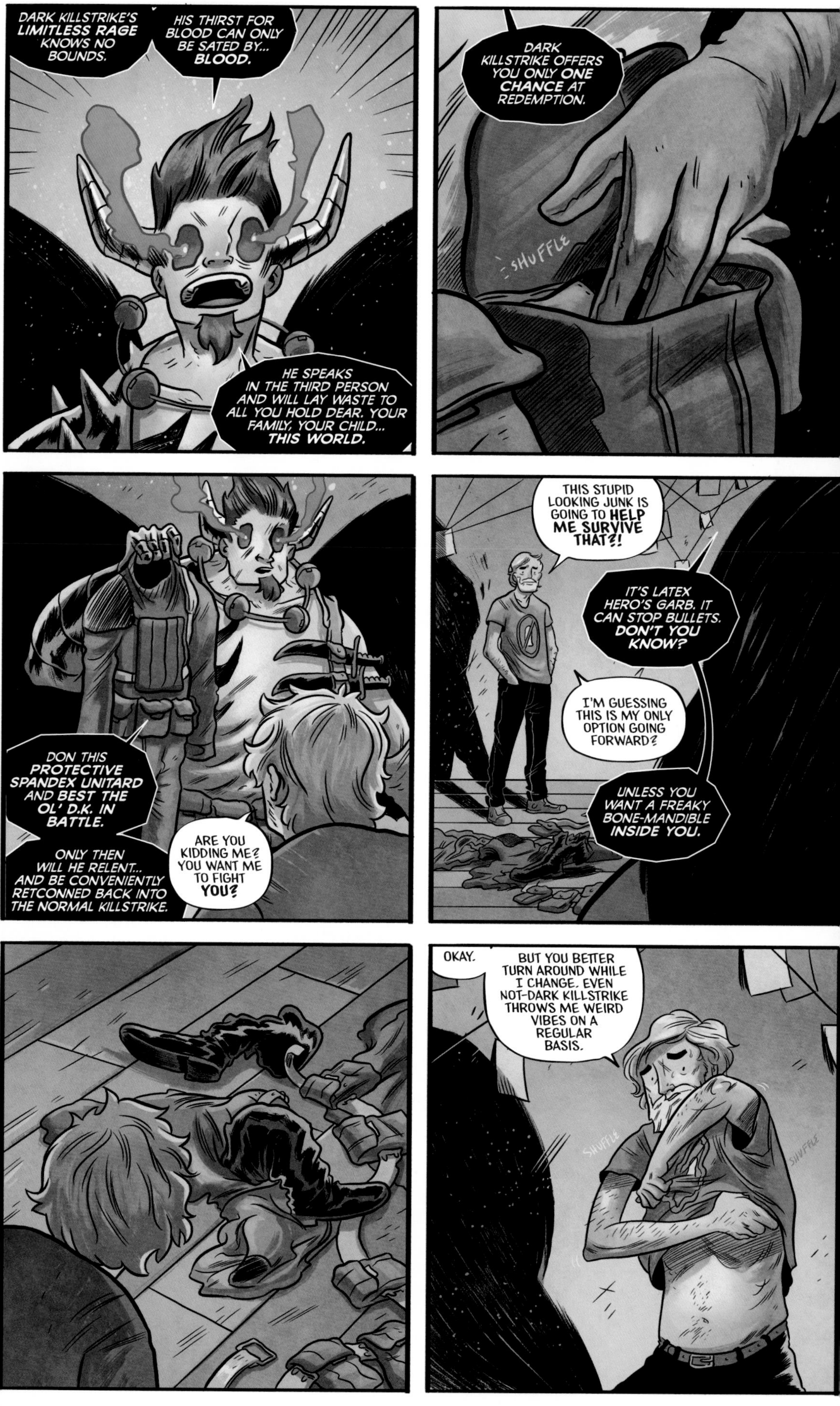
DARK KILLSTRIKE'S LIMITLESS RAGE KNOWS NO BOUNDS.
HIS THIRST FOR BLOOD CAN ONLY BE SATED BY... BLOOD.
HE SPEAKS IN THE THIRD PERSON AND WILL LAY WASTE TO ALL YOU HOLD DEAR. YOUR FAMILY, YOUR CHILD... THIS WORLD.
DARK KILLSTRIKE OFFERS YOU ONLY ONE CHANCE AT REDEMPTION.
SHUFFLE
DON THIS PROTECTIVE SPANDEX UNITARD AND BEST THE OL' D.K. IN BATTLE.
ONLY THEN WILL HE RELENT... AND BE CONVENIENTLY RETCONNED BACK INTO THE NORMAL KILLSTRIKE.
ARE YOU KIDDING ME? YOU WANT ME TO FIGHT YOU?
THIS STUPID LOOKING JUNK IS GOING TO HELP ME SURVIVE THAT?!
IT'S LATEX HERO'S GARB. IT CAN STOP BULLETS. DON'T YOU KNOW?
I'M GUESSING THIS IS MY ONLY OPTION GOING FORWARD?
UNLESS YOU WANT A FREAKY BONE-MANDIBLE INSIDE YOU.
OKAY.
BUT YOU BETTER TURN AROUND WHILE I CHANGE. EVEN NOT-DARK KILLSTRIKE THROWS ME WEIRD VIBES ON A REGULAR BASIS.
SHUFFLE
SHUFFLE

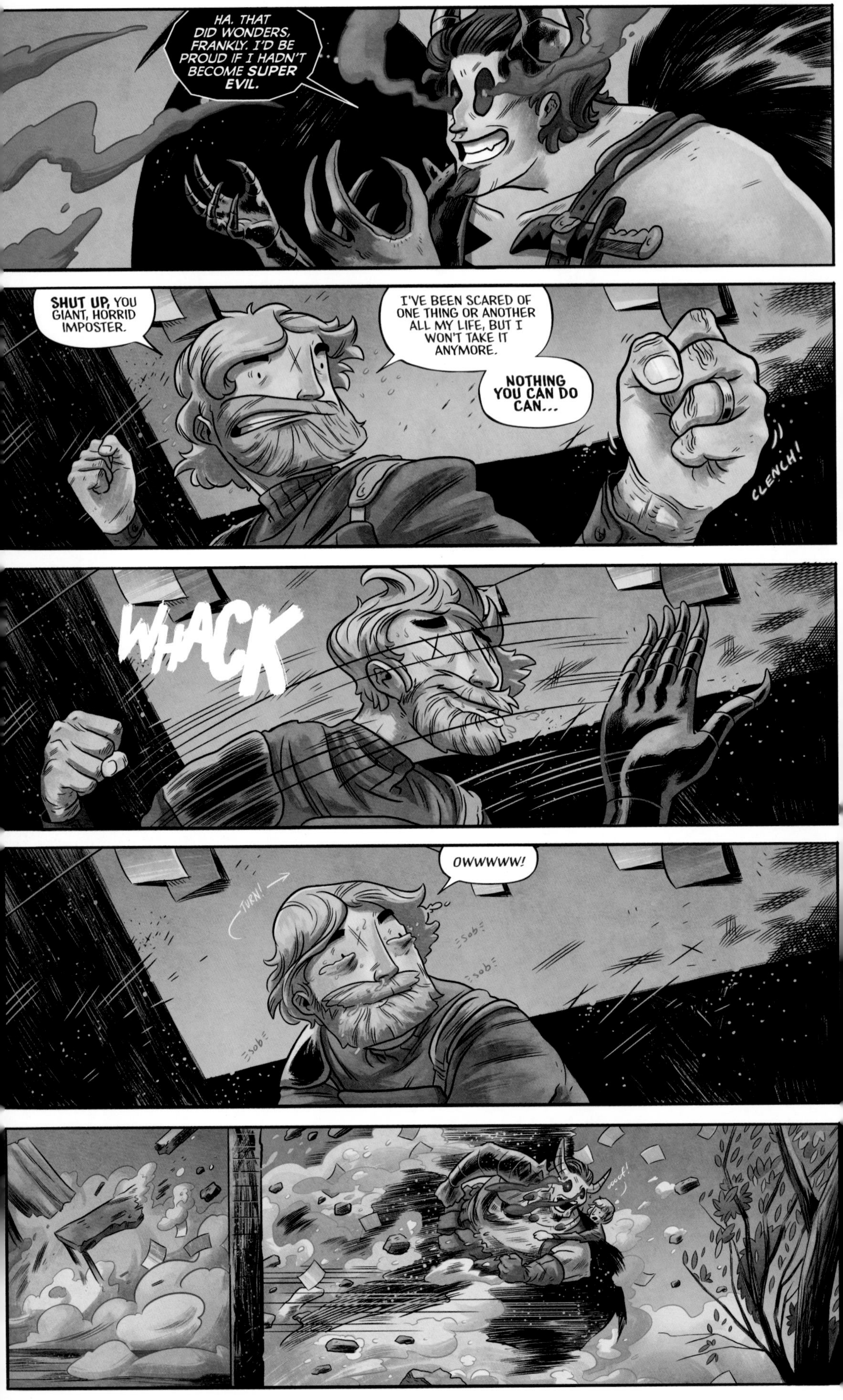
HA. THAT DID WONDERS, FRANKLY. I'D BE PROUD IF I HADN'T BECOME SUPER EVIL.
SHUT UP, YOU GIANT, HORRID IMPOSTER.
I'VE BEEN SCARED OF ONE THING OR ANOTHER ALL MY LIFE, BUT I WON'T TAKE IT ANYMORE.
NOTHING YOU CAN DO CAN...
CLENCH!
WHACK
TURN!
OWWWWW!
sob
sob
sob
oooof!

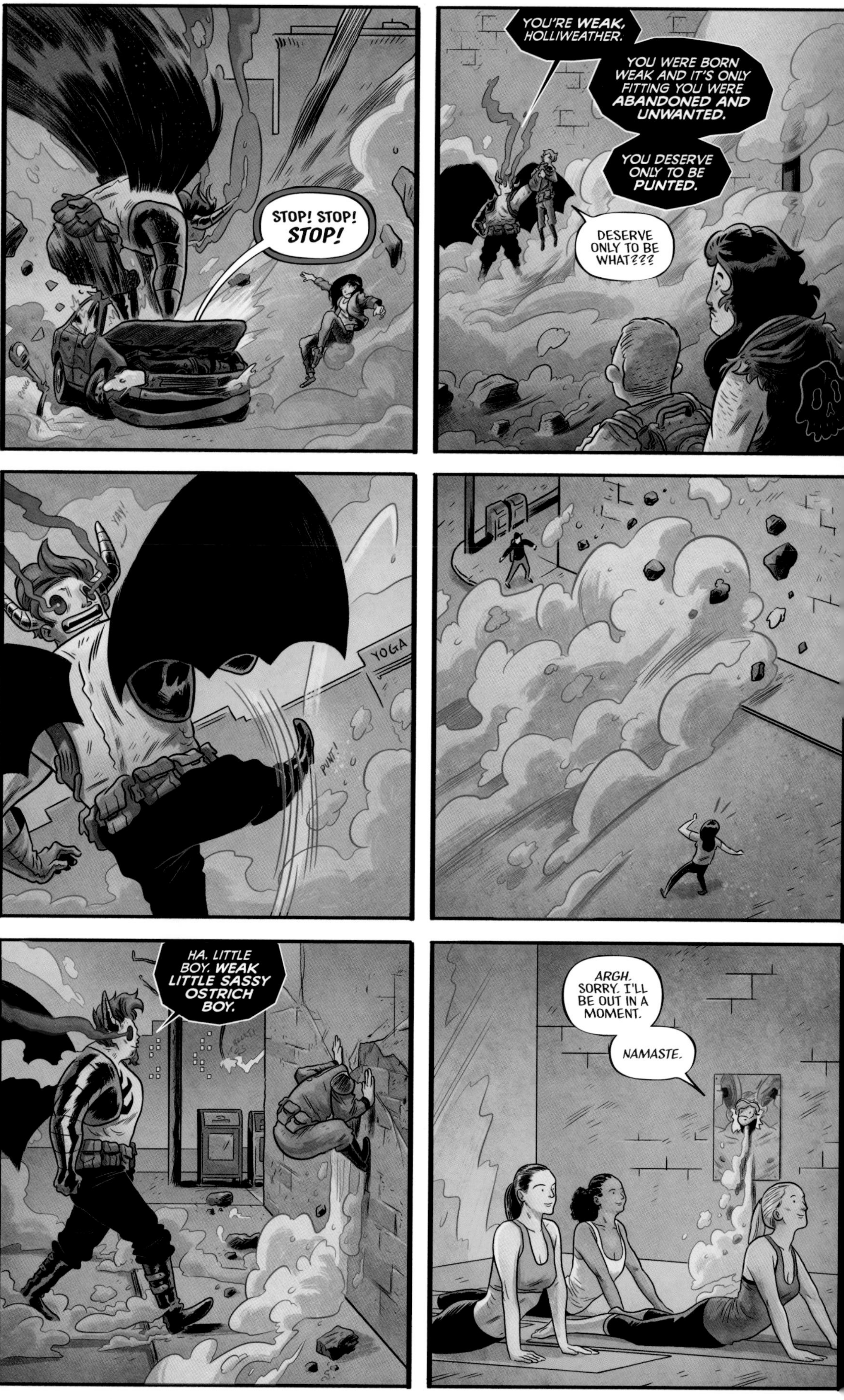

STOP! STOP! STOP!
YOU'RE WEAK, HOLLIWEATHER.
YOU WERE BORN WEAK AND IT'S ONLY FITTING YOU WERE ABANDONED AND UNWANTED.
YOU DESERVE ONLY TO BE PUNTED.
DESERVE ONLY TO BE WHAT???
YAY!
YOGA
PUNT!
HA. LITTLE BOY. WEAK LITTLE SASSY OSTRICH BOY.
ARGH. SORRY. I'LL BE OUT IN A MOMENT.
NAMASTE.

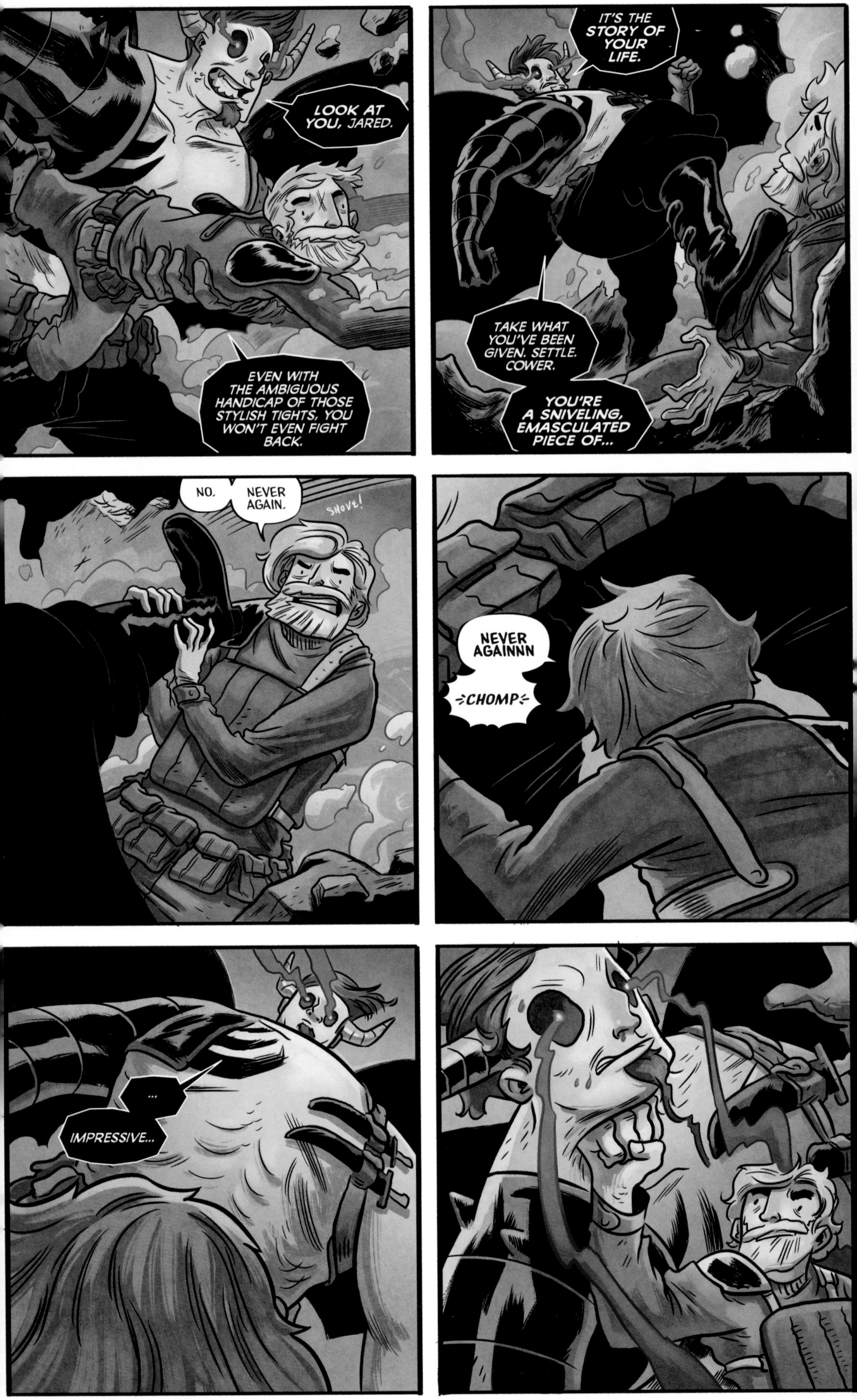

LOOK AT YOU, JARED.
EVEN WITH THE AMBIGUOUS HANDICAP OF THOSE STYLISH TIGHTS, YOU WON'T EVEN FIGHT BACK.
IT'S THE STORY OF YOUR LIFE.
TAKE WHAT YOU'VE BEEN GIVEN. SETTLE. COWER.
YOU'RE A SNIVELING, EMASCULATED PIECE OF...
NO.
NEVER AGAIN.
SHOVE!
NEVER AGAINNN
CHOMP
...
IMPRESSIVE...

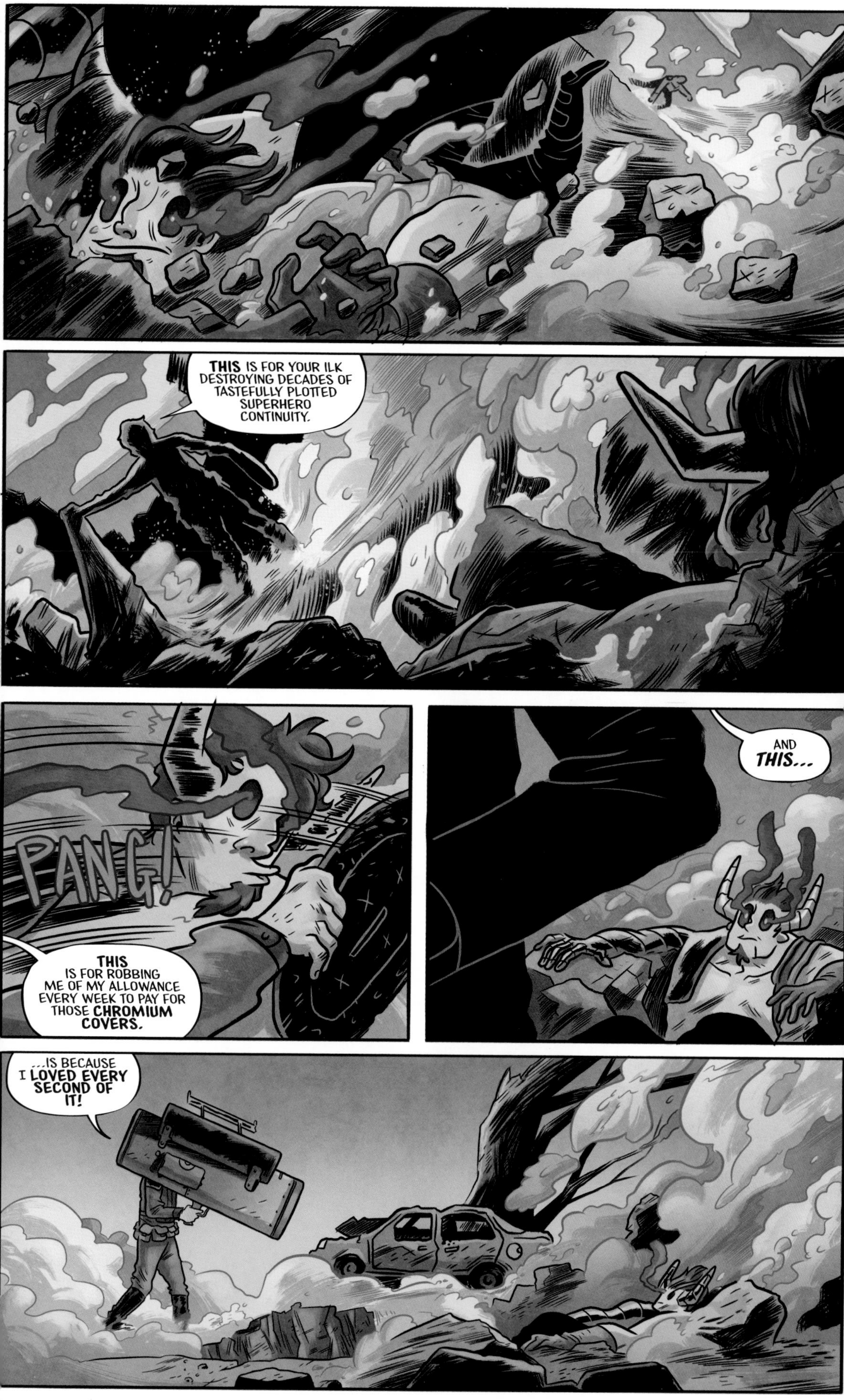

THIS IS FOR YOUR ILK DESTROYING DECADES OF TASTEFULLY PLOTTED SUPERHERO CONTINUITY.
PANG!
THIS IS FOR ROBBING ME OF MY ALLOWANCE EVERY WEEK TO PAY FOR THOSE CHROMIUM COVERS.
AND THIS...
...IS BECAUSE I LOVED EVERY SECOND OF IT!

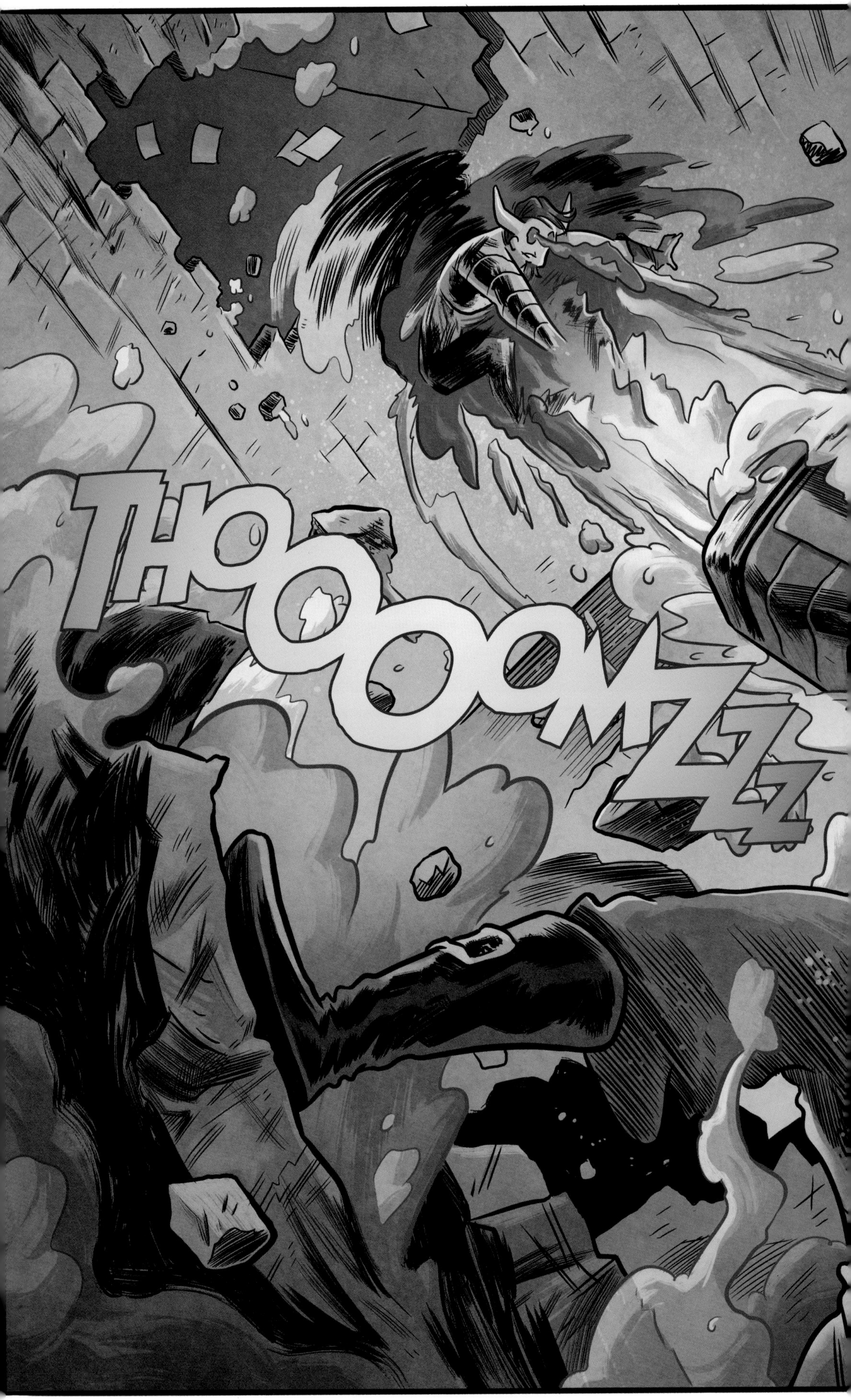
THOOOOMZZ

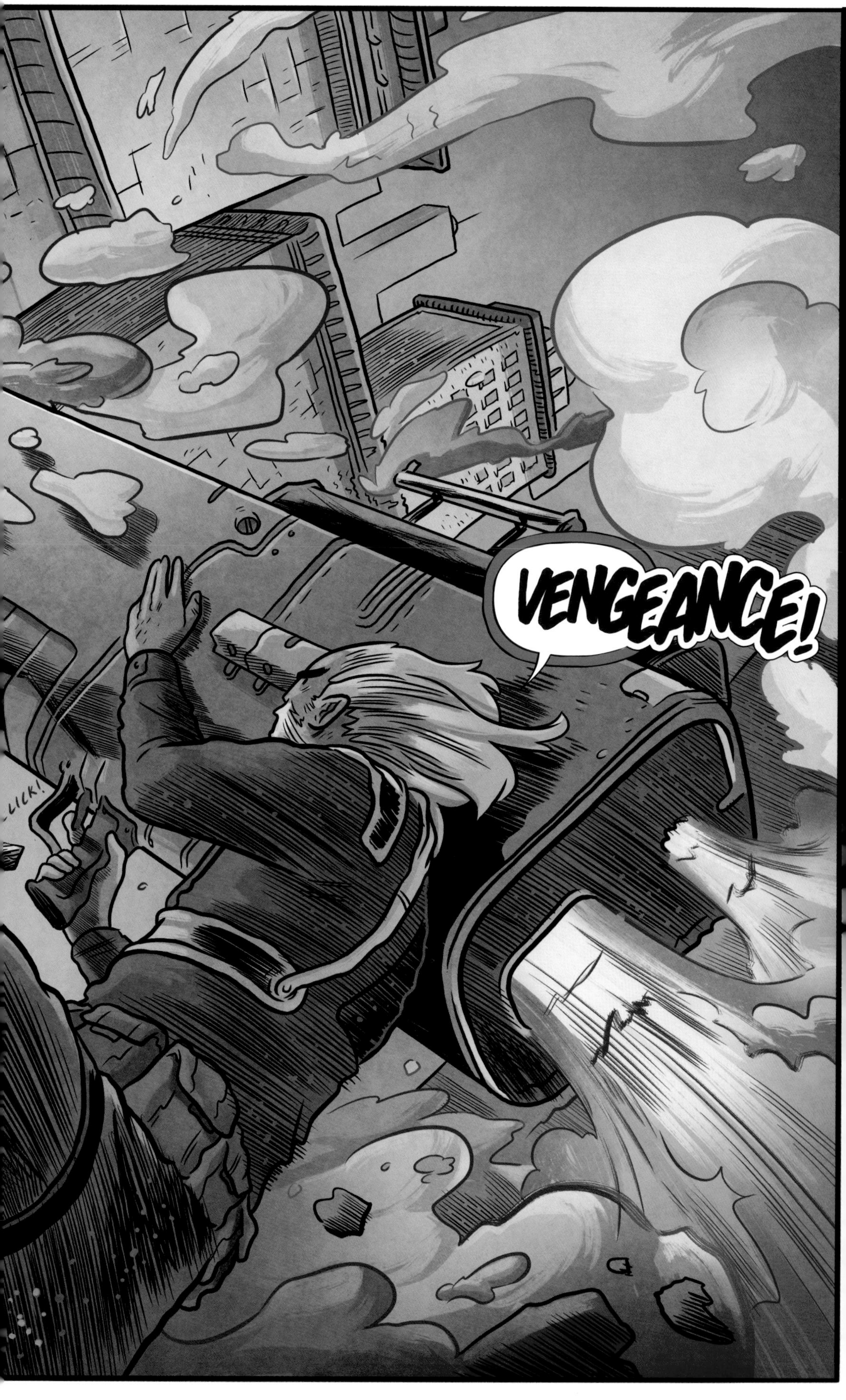
VENGEANCE!

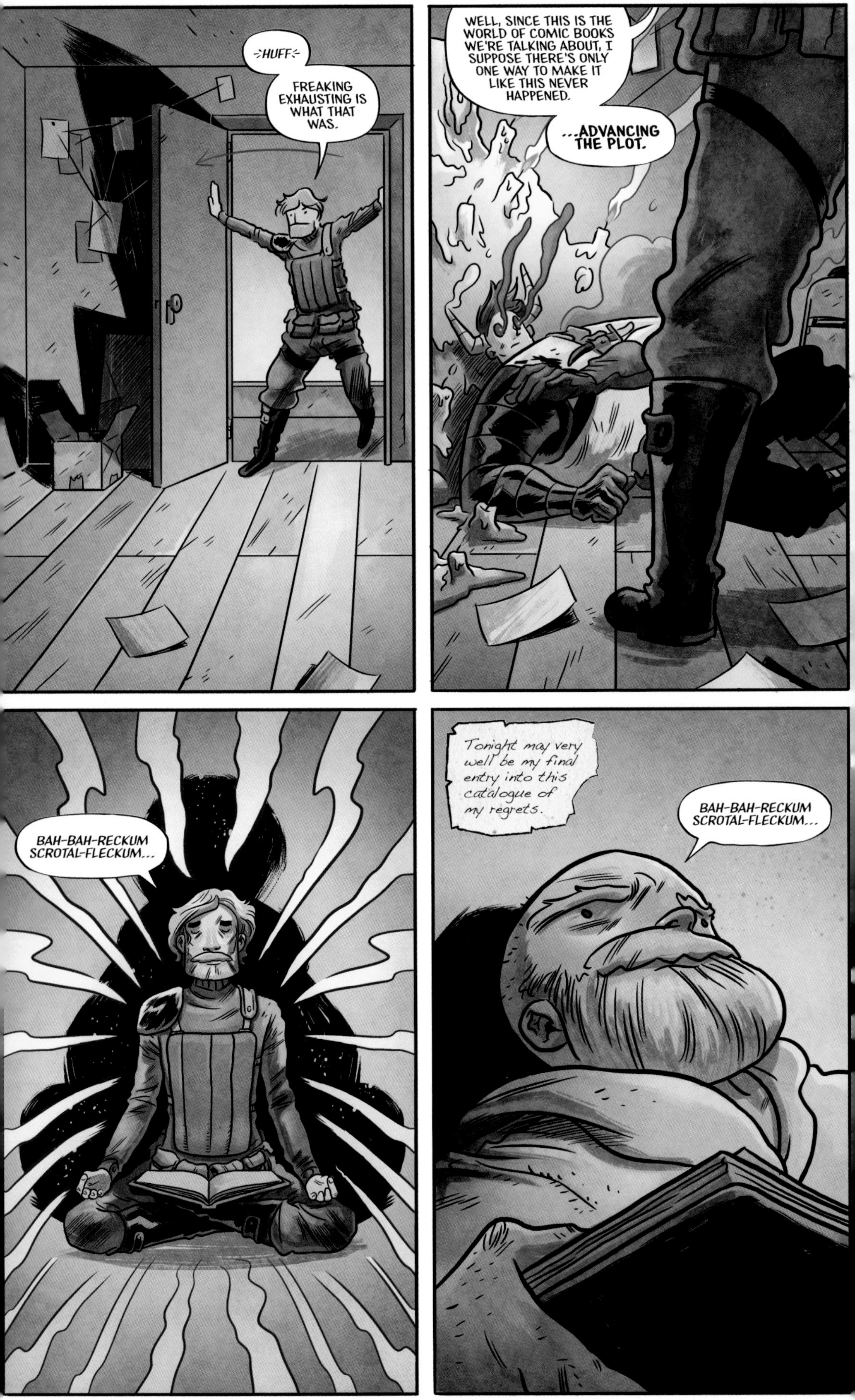
HUFF
FREAKING EXHAUSTING IS WHAT THAT WAS.
WELL, SINCE THIS IS THE WORLD OF COMIC BOOKS WE'RE TALKING ABOUT, I SUPPOSE THERE'S ONLY ONE WAY TO MAKE IT LIKE THIS NEVER HAPPENED.
...ADVANCING THE PLOT.
BAH-BAH-RECKUM SCROTAL-FLECKUM...
Tonight may very well be my final entry into this catalogue of my regrets.
BAH-BAH-RECKUM SCROTAL-FLECKUM...

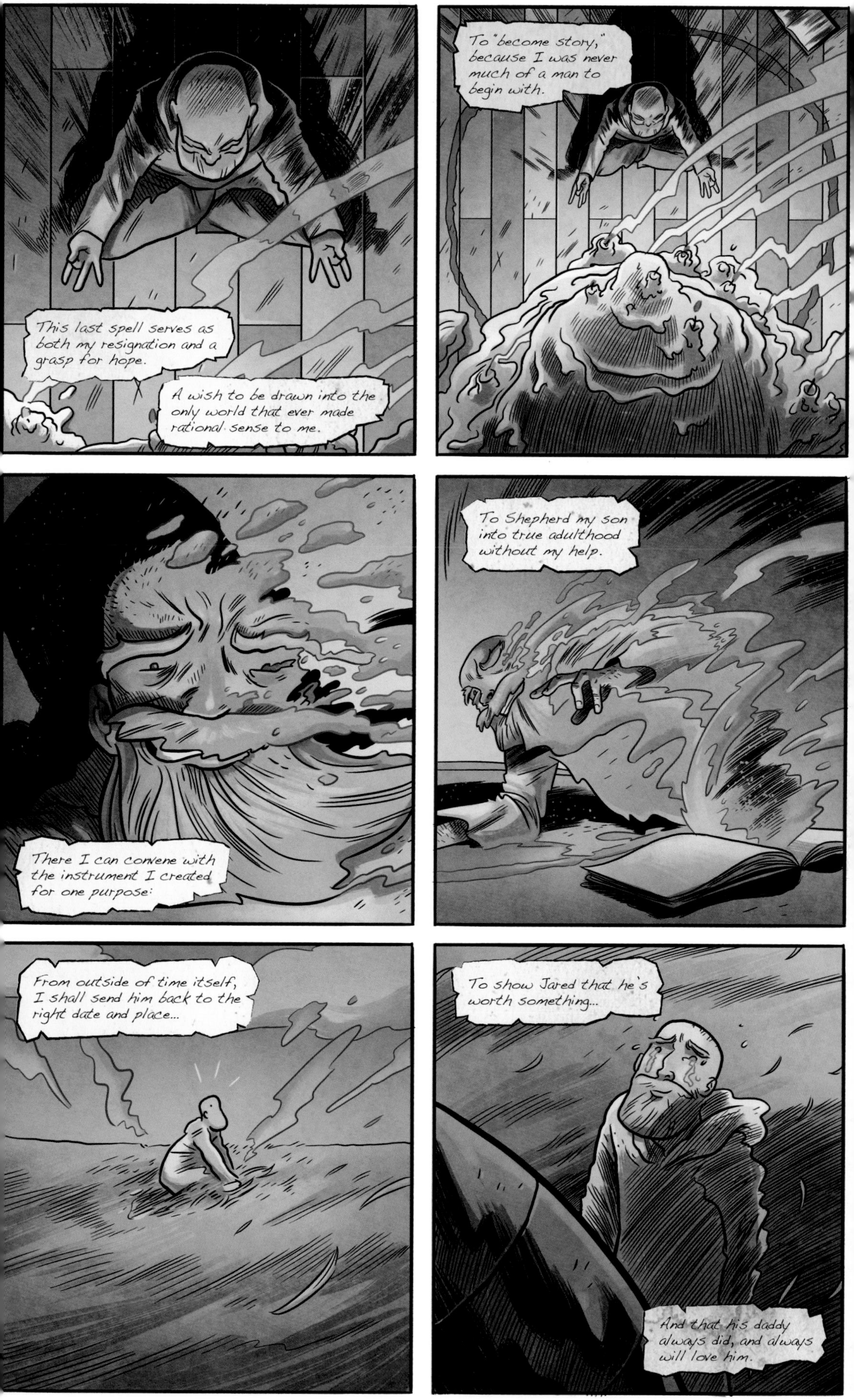
This last spell serves as both my resignation and a grasp for hope.
A wish to be drawn into the only world that ever made rational sense to me.
To "become story," because I was never much of a man to begin with.
There I can convene with the instrument I created for one purpose:
To Shepherd my son into true adulthood without my help.
From outside of time itself, I shall send him back to the right date and place...
To show Jared that he's worth something...
And that his daddy always did, and always will love him.

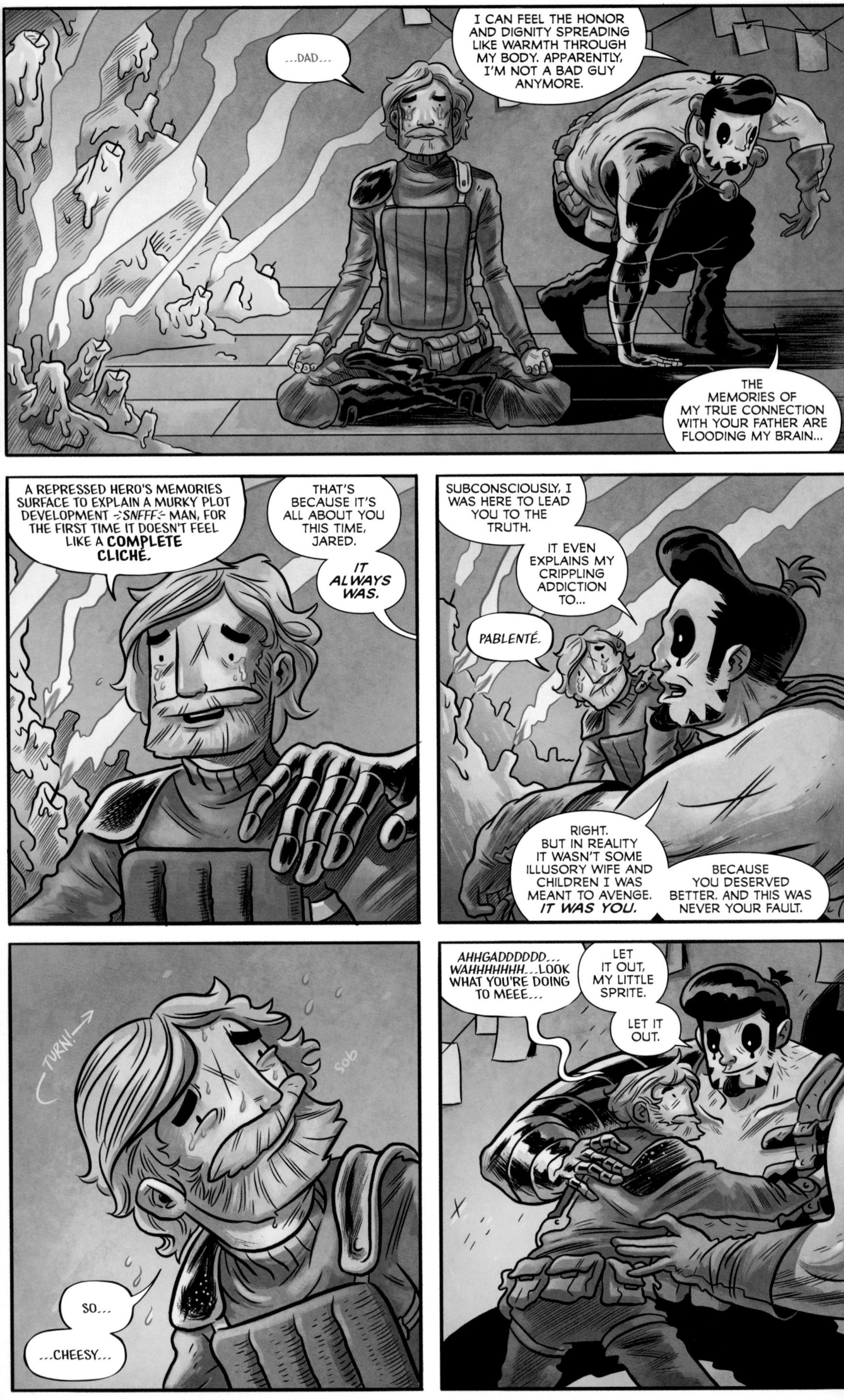

...DAD...
I CAN FEEL THE HONOR AND DIGNITY SPREADING LIKE WARMTH THROUGH MY BODY. APPARENTLY, I'M NOT A BAD GUY ANYMORE.
THE MEMORIES OF MY TRUE CONNECTION WITH YOUR FATHER ARE FLOODING MY BRAIN...
A REPRESSED HERO'S MEMORIES SURFACE TO EXPLAIN A MURKY PLOT DEVELOPMENT -SNFFF- MAN, FOR THE FIRST TIME IT DOESN'T FEEL LIKE A **COMPLETE CLICHÉ.**
THAT'S BECAUSE IT'S ALL ABOUT YOU THIS TIME, JARED.
IT ALWAYS WAS.
SUBCONSCIOUSLY, I WAS HERE TO LEAD YOU TO THE TRUTH.
IT EVEN EXPLAINS MY CRIPPLING ADDICTION TO...
PABLENTÉ.
RIGHT. BUT IN REALITY IT WASN'T SOME ILLUSORY WIFE AND CHILDREN I WAS MEANT TO AVENGE. *IT WAS YOU.*
BECAUSE YOU DESERVED BETTER. AND THIS WAS NEVER YOUR FAULT.
TURN!
SOB
SO...
...CHEESY...
AHHGADDDDDD... WAHHHHHHH...LOOK WHAT YOU'RE DOING TO MEEE...
LET IT OUT, MY LITTLE SPRITE.
LET IT OUT.

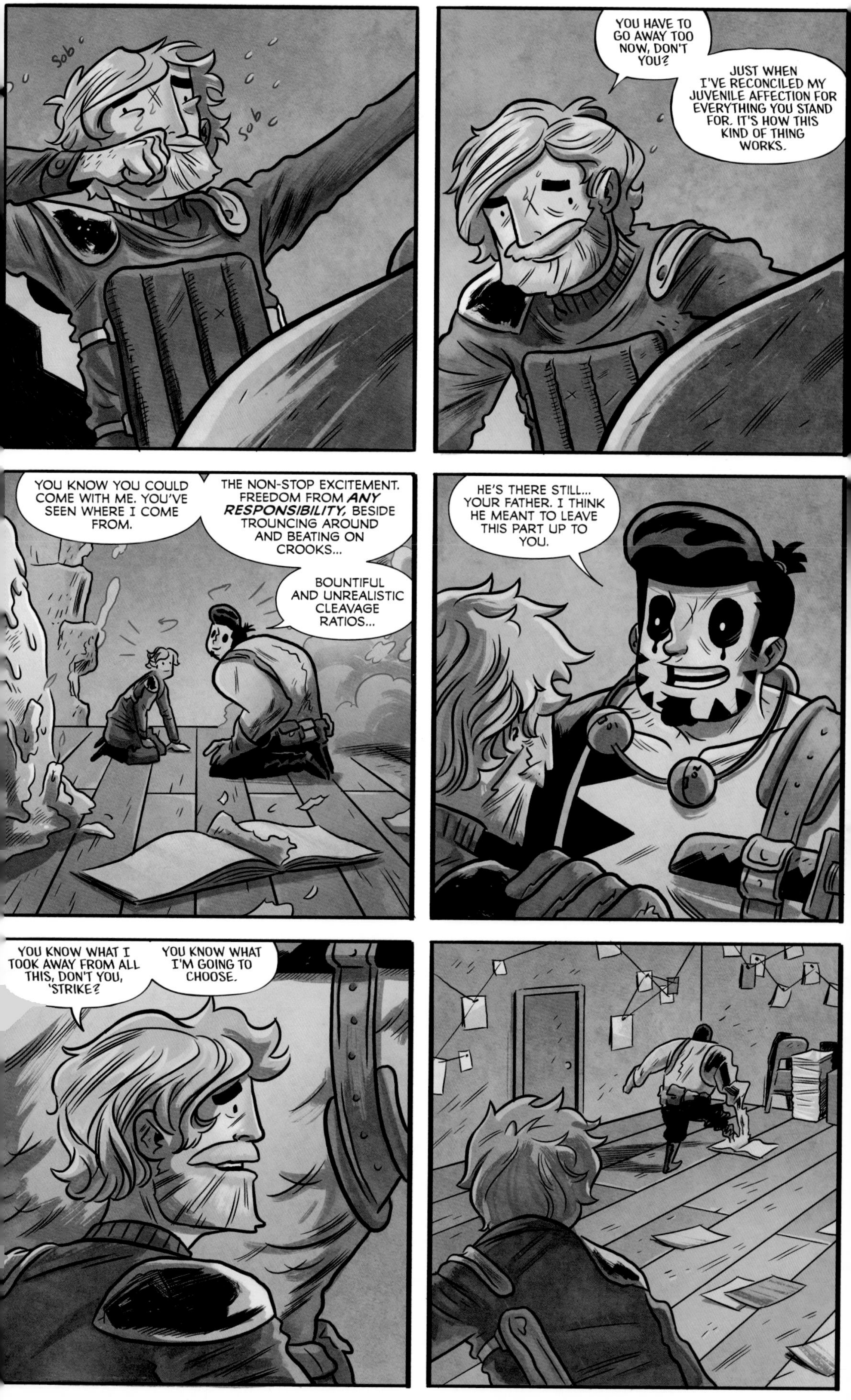
SOB
SOB
YOU HAVE TO GO AWAY TOO NOW, DON'T YOU?
JUST WHEN I'VE RECONCILED MY JUVENILE AFFECTION FOR EVERYTHING YOU STAND FOR. IT'S HOW THIS KIND OF THING WORKS.
YOU KNOW YOU COULD COME WITH ME. YOU'VE SEEN WHERE I COME FROM.
THE NON-STOP EXCITEMENT. FREEDOM FROM ANY RESPONSIBILITY, BESIDE TROUNCING AROUND AND BEATING ON CROOKS...
BOUNTIFUL AND UNREALISTIC CLEAVAGE RATIOS...
HE'S THERE STILL... YOUR FATHER. I THINK HE MEANT TO LEAVE THIS PART UP TO YOU.
YOU KNOW WHAT I TOOK AWAY FROM ALL THIS, DON'T YOU, 'STRIKE?
YOU KNOW WHAT I'M GOING TO CHOOSE.

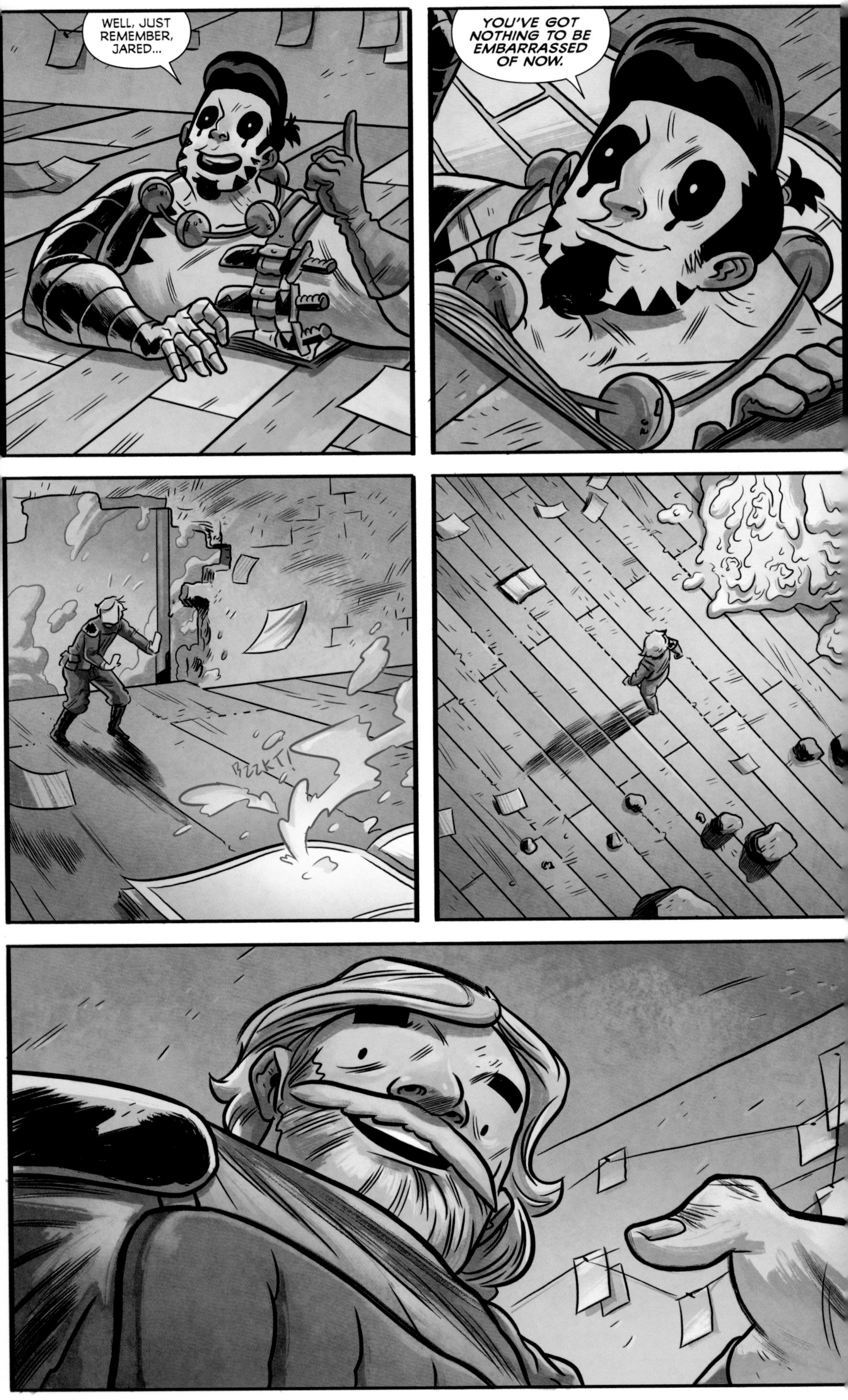

WELL, JUST REMEMBER, JARED...
YOU'VE GOT NOTHING TO BE EMBARRASSED OF NOW.
BZZKT!

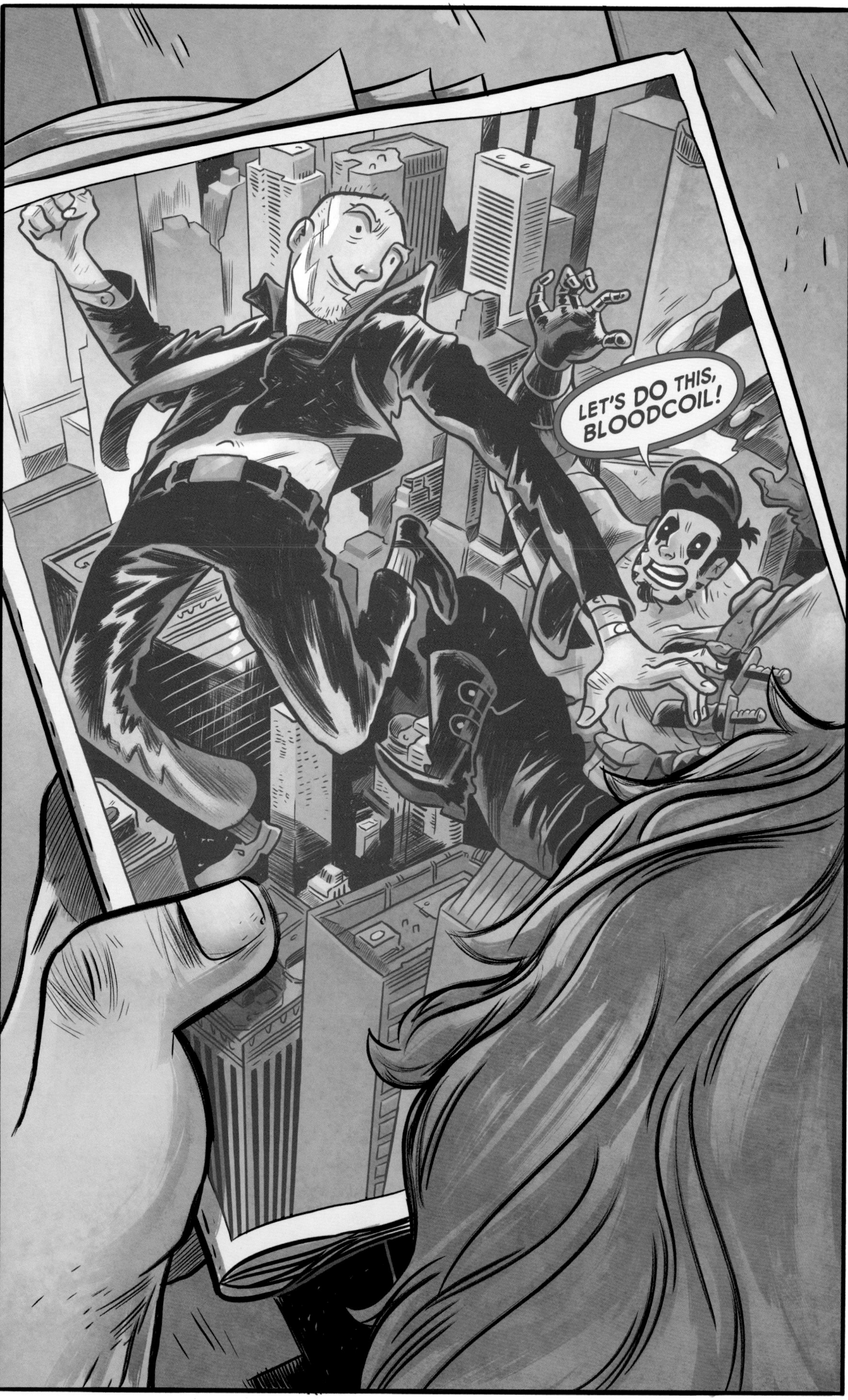

LET'S DO THIS, BLOODCOIL!

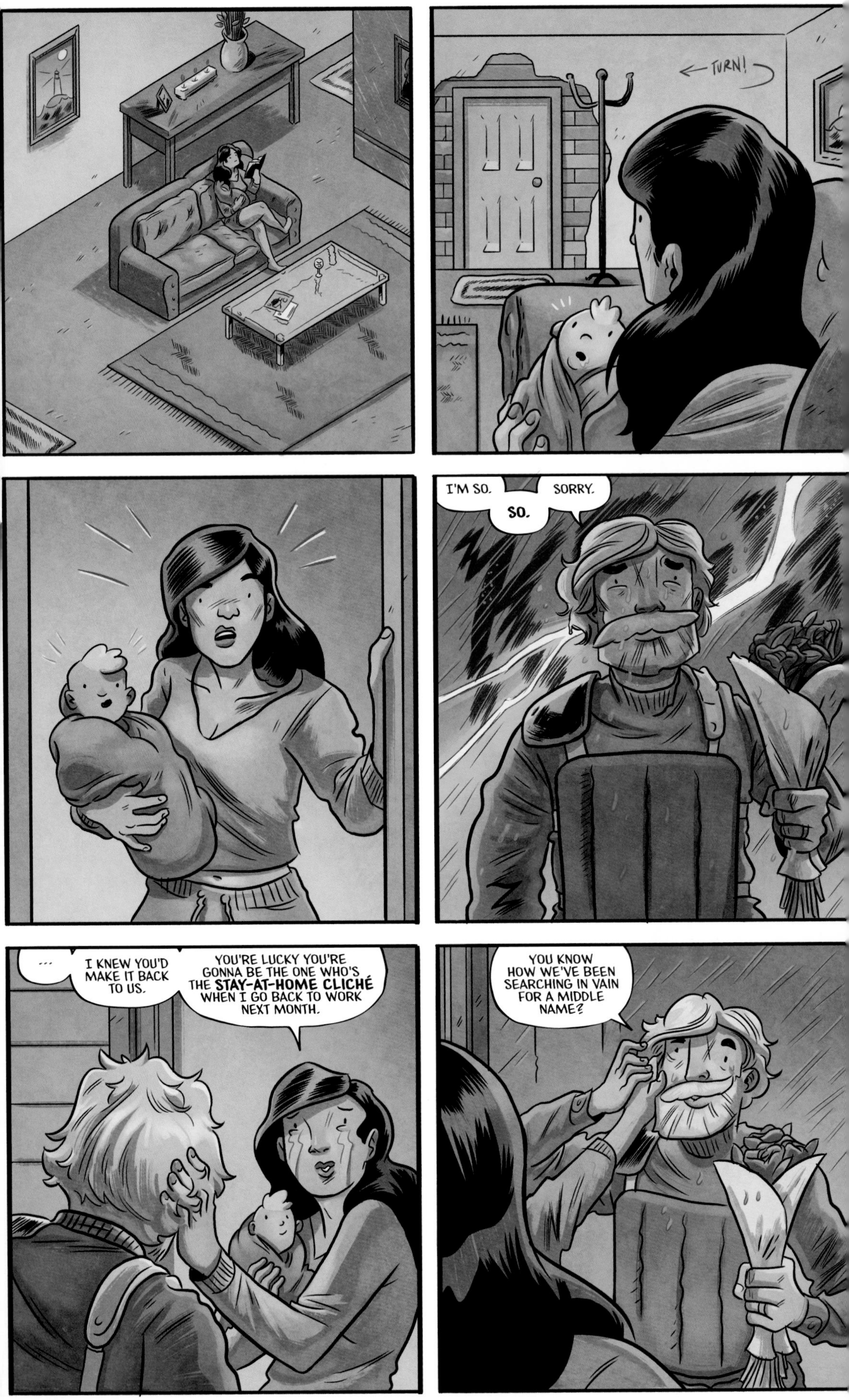

← TURN! →
I'M SO.
SO.
SORRY.
...
I KNEW YOU'D MAKE IT BACK TO US.
YOU'RE LUCKY YOU'RE GONNA BE THE ONE WHO'S THE **STAY-AT-HOME CLICHÉ** WHEN I GO BACK TO WORK NEXT MONTH.
YOU KNOW HOW WE'VE BEEN SEARCHING IN VAIN FOR A MIDDLE NAME?

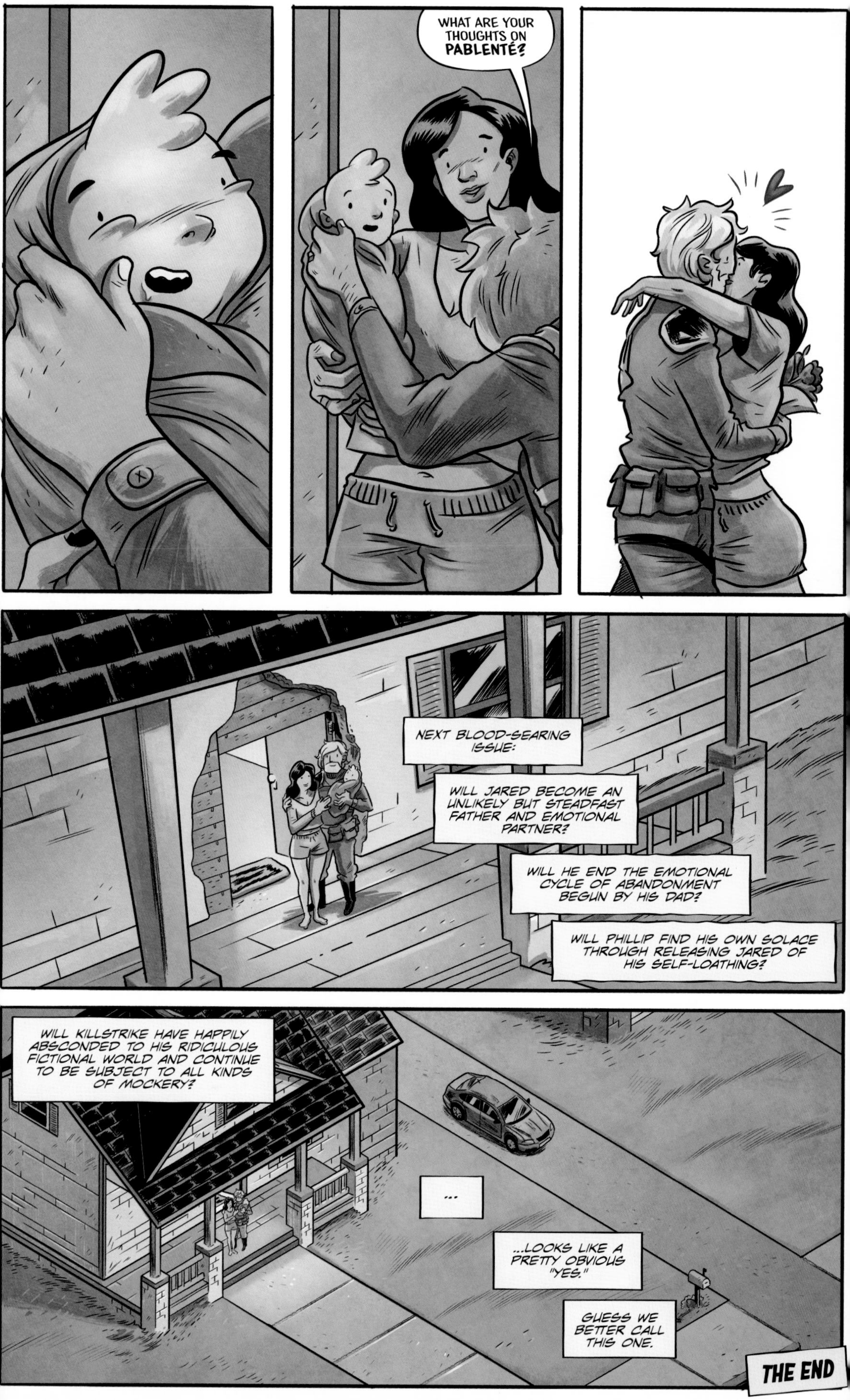

WHAT ARE YOUR THOUGHTS ON PABLENTÉ?
NEXT BLOOD-SEARING ISSUE:
WILL JARED BECOME AN UNLIKELY BUT STEADFAST FATHER AND EMOTIONAL PARTNER?
WILL HE END THE EMOTIONAL CYCLE OF ABANDONMENT BEGUN BY HIS DAD?
WILL PHILLIP FIND HIS OWN SOLACE THROUGH RELEASING JARED OF HIS SELF-LOATHING?
WILL KILLSTRIKE HAVE HAPPILY ABSCONDED TO HIS RIDICULOUS FICTIONAL WORLD AND CONTINUE TO BE SUBJECT TO ALL KINDS OF MOCKERY?
...
...LOOKS LIKE A PRETTY OBVIOUS "YES."
GUESS WE BETTER CALL THIS ONE.
THE END

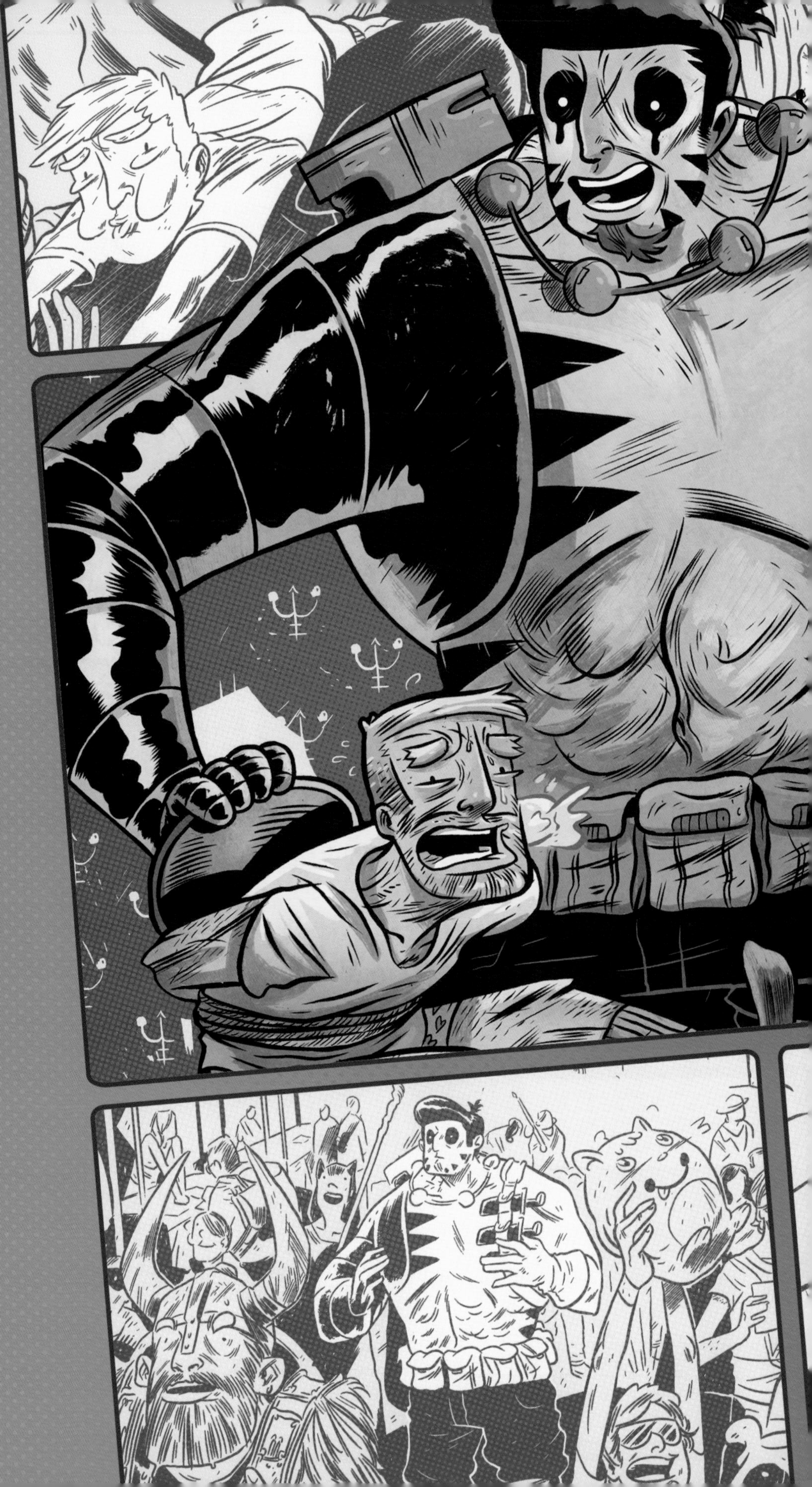

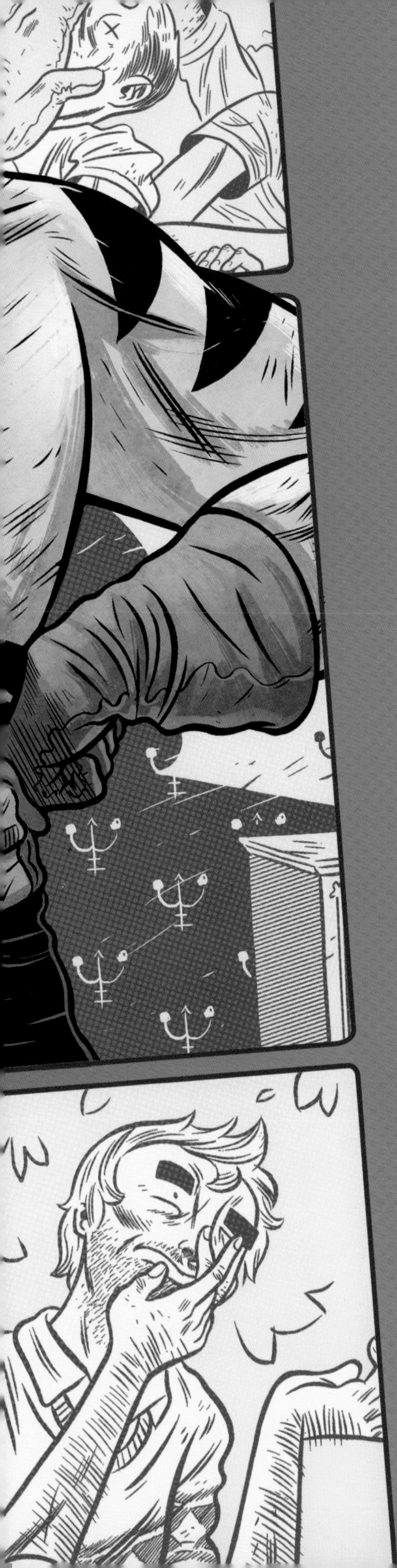

cover
GALLERY

SSUE ONE COVER
LOGAN FAERBER

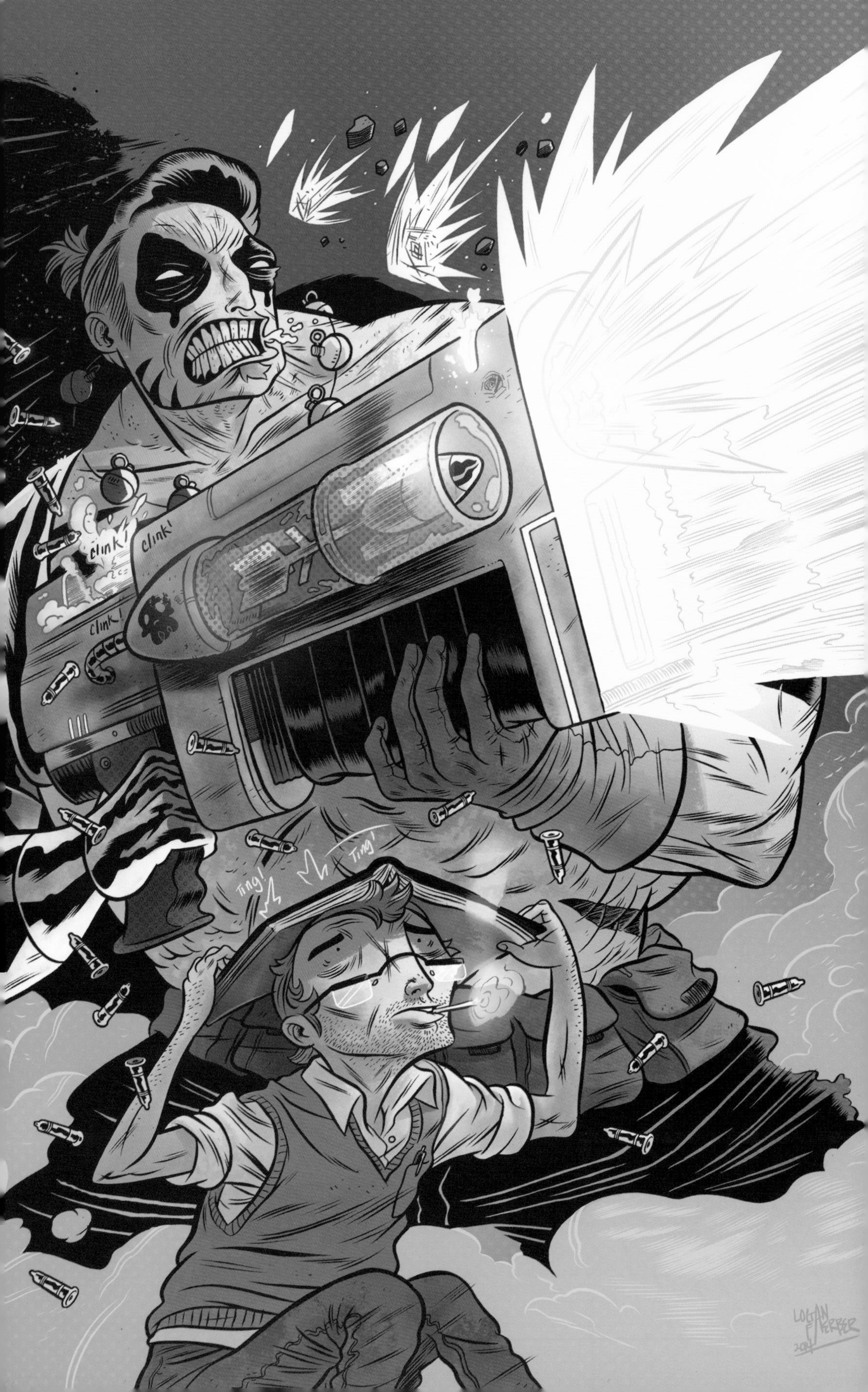
clink!
clink!
clink!
Ting!
Ting!
LOGAN FAERBER
2014

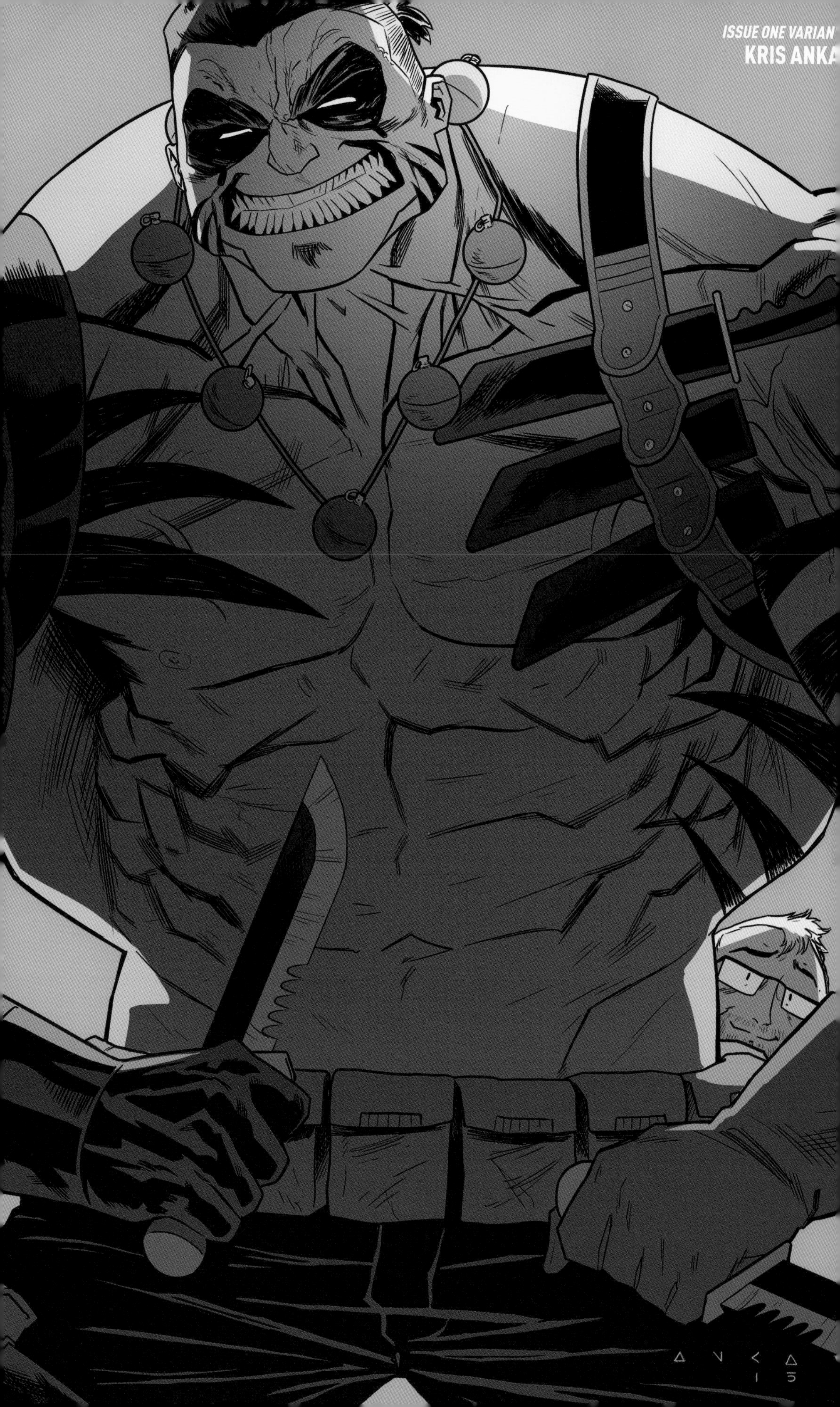

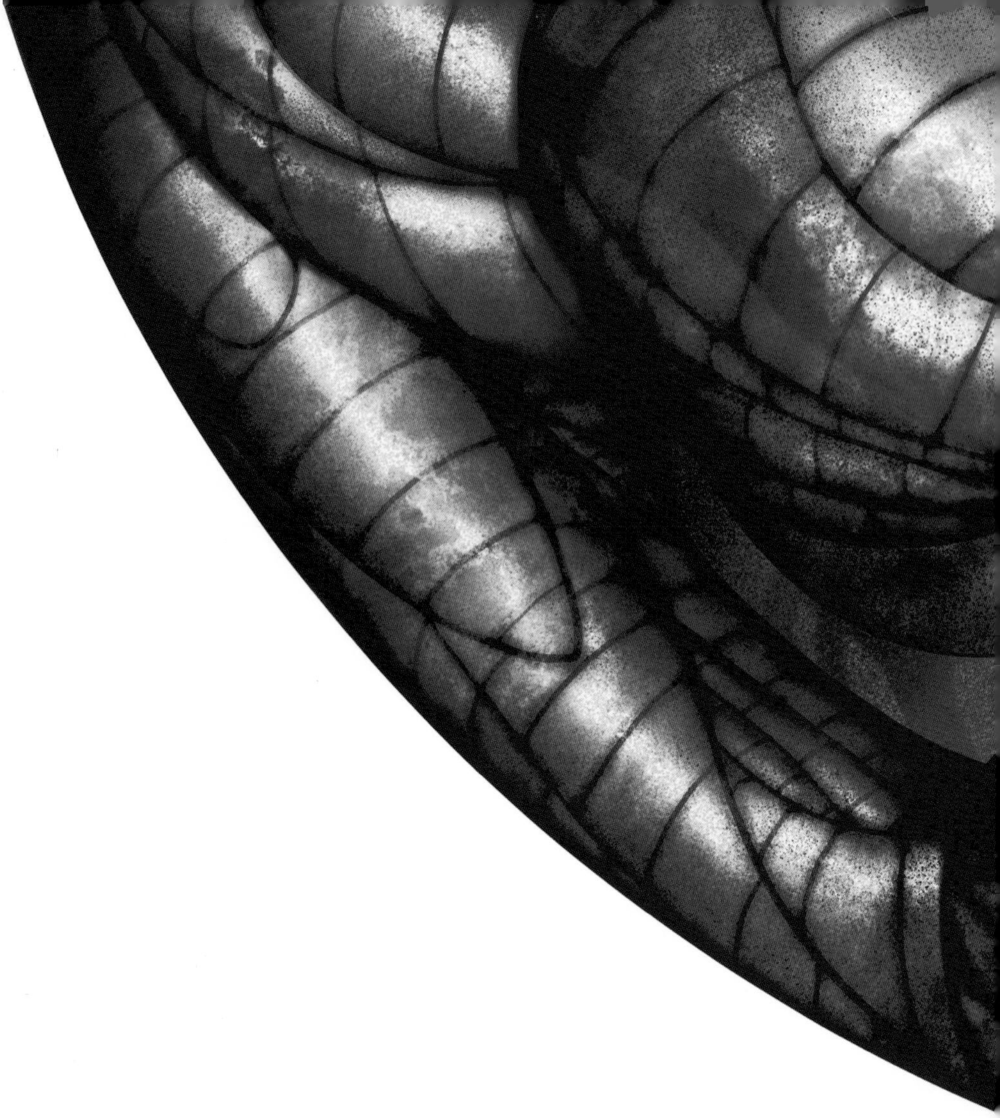

ISSUE ONE BOOM! TEN YEARS VARIANT
FRAZER IRVING

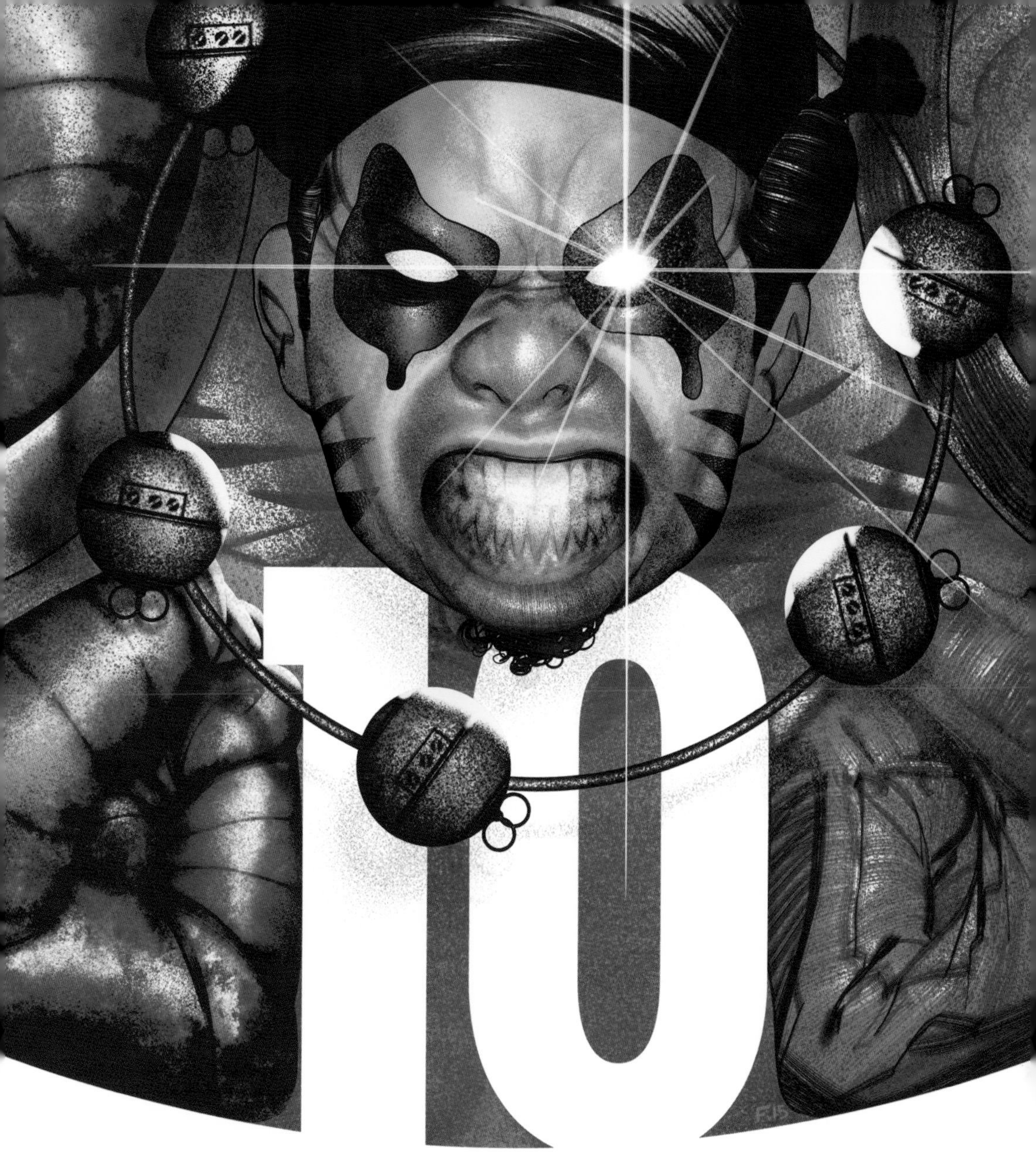
10

SSUE ONE UNLOCKED RETAILER VARIANT
DAVID LAFUENTE

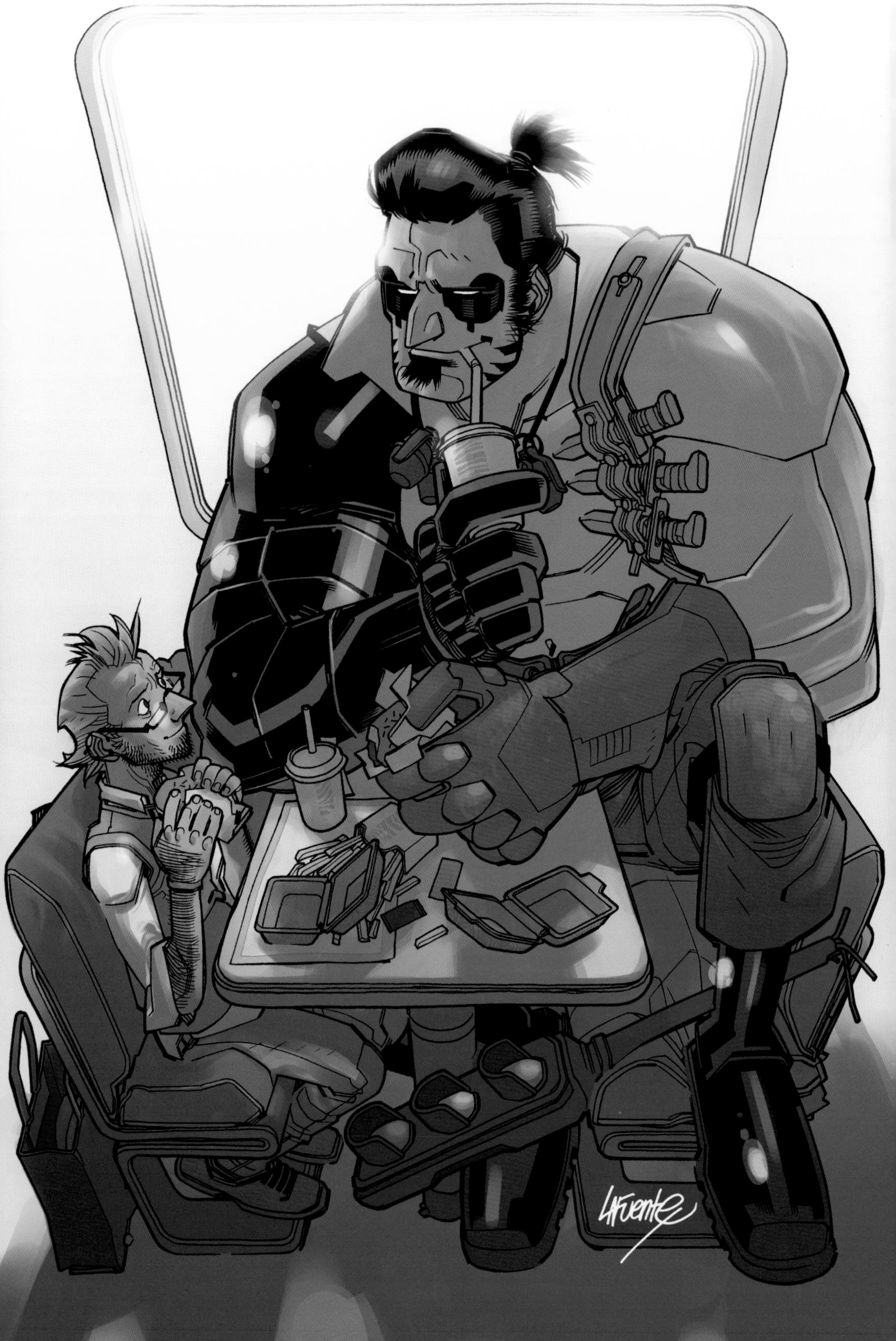
LAFUENTE

ISSUE TWO COVE
LOGAN FAERBER

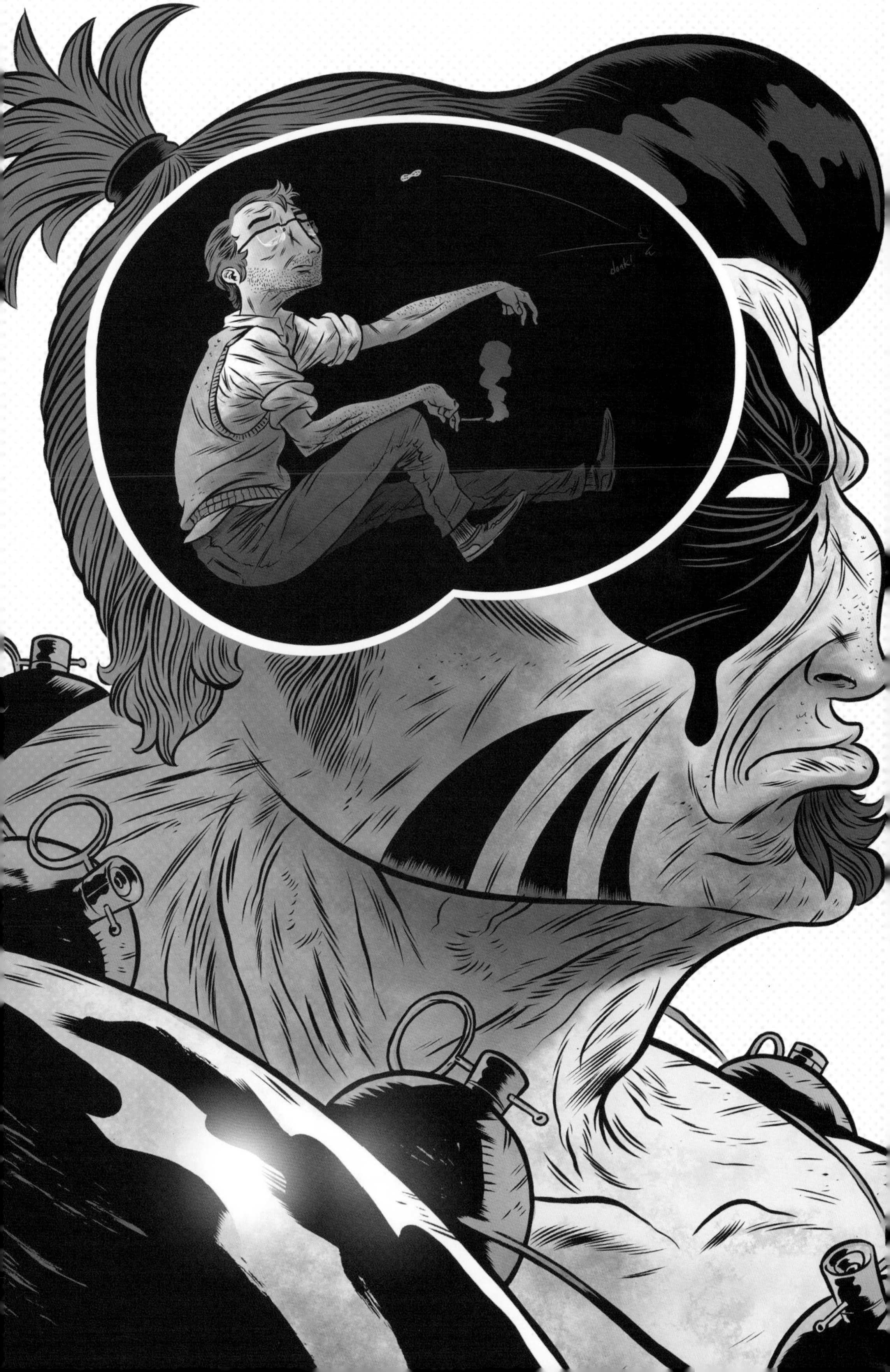
donk!

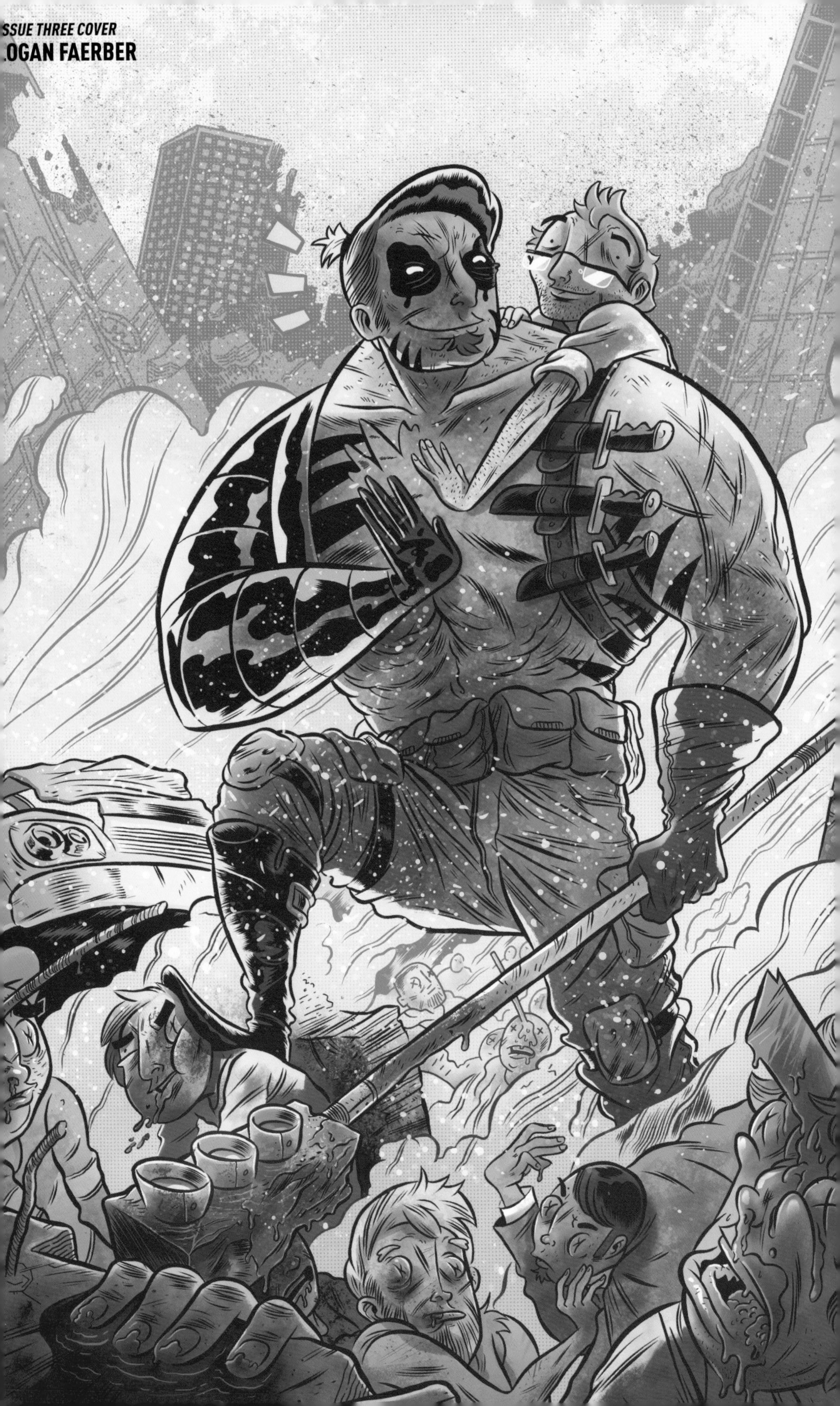

ISSUE THREE COVER
LOGAN FAERBER

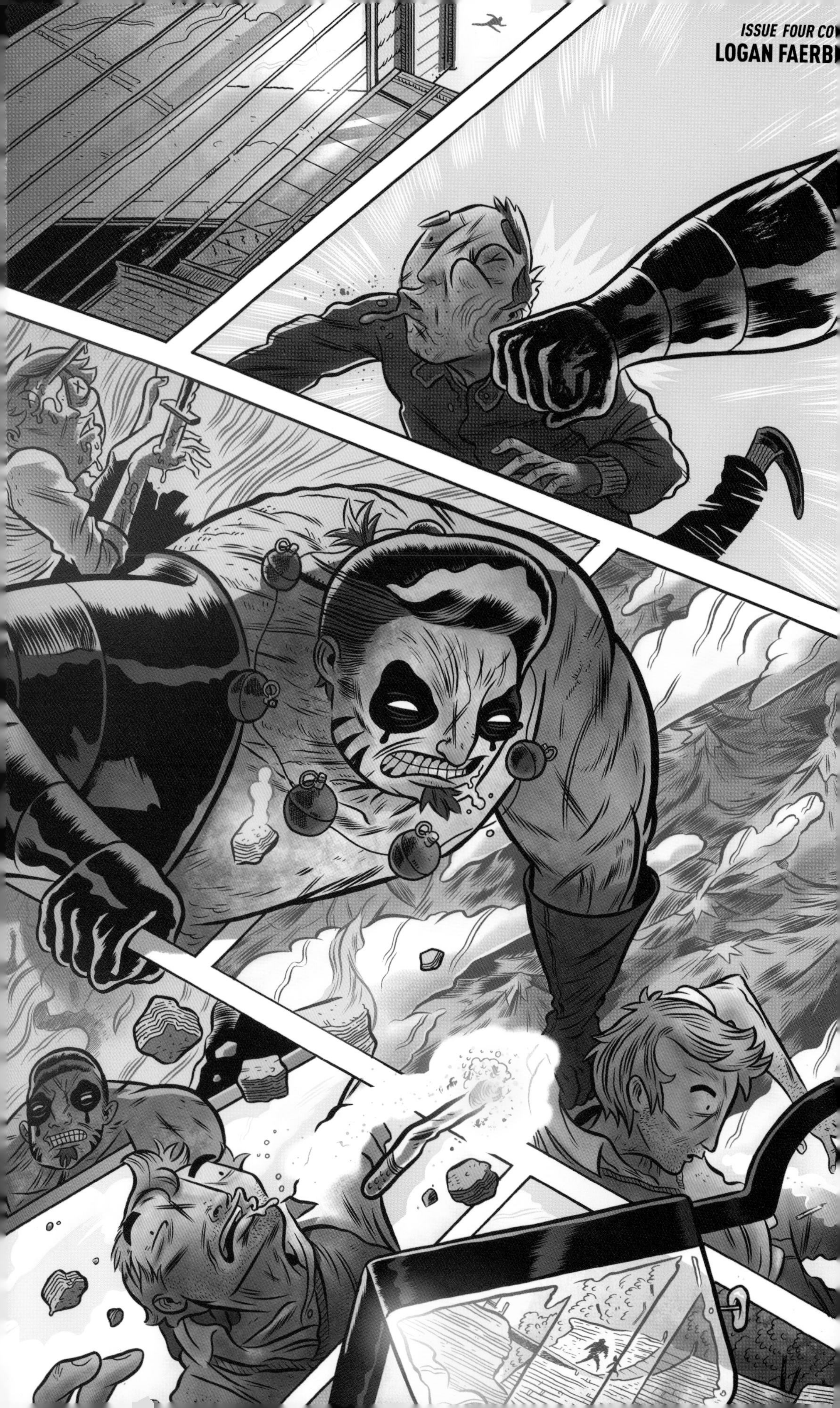

ISSUE FOUR CO
LOGAN FAERB

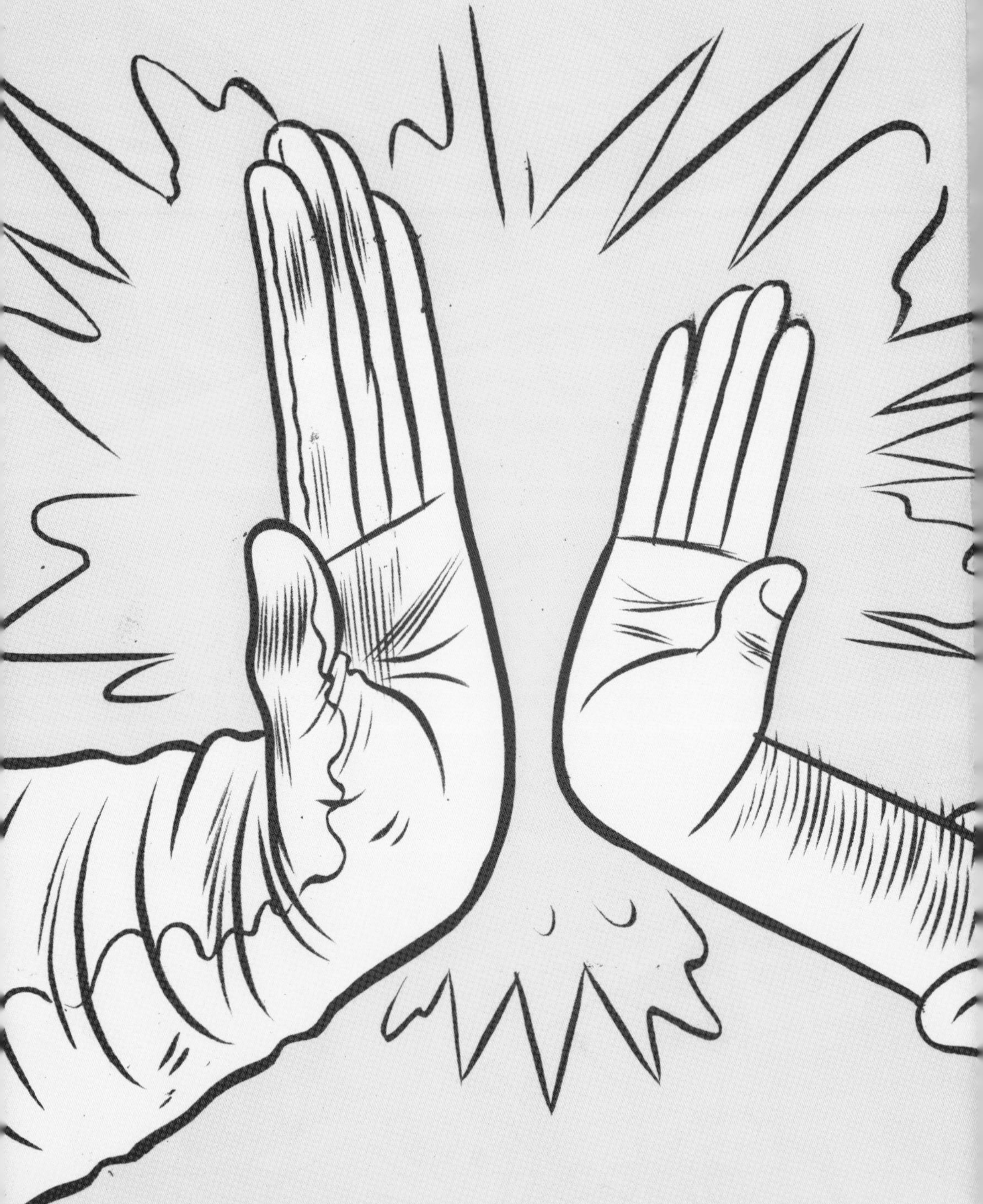